Mercy Sky

Mercy Sky

Dawn Dyson

iUniverse, Inc.
New York Lincoln Shanghai

Mercy Sky

iUniverse books may be ordered through booksellers or by contacting:

iUniverse
2021 Pine Lake Road, Suite 100
Lincoln, NE 68512
www.iuniverse.com
1-800-Authors (1-800-288-4677)

ISBN: 0-595-34515-8

Printed in the United States of America

For Carter, Bruce and Riley.
And for my best friend Bummer.
Angels walk the commonest places on earth....

There are stories of our young American heritage held silent in the graves, in the dust. Stories only the winds of time whisper around the crumbling resting places of the true characters—victim and villain and standers-by. Stories that fall indecipherable to those who live now.

But there is a house.

It holds its story in bondage, secrets branded beneath sealed skin of stone.
And in this house, the only thing to see is darkness.
The only sound is a forgotten scream…, it seems to echo silence.
The only taste is the tongue's own blood…, you did not realize you were biting down….
And the only touch is none.

There is an odor of pleasantry there…, it rises from the parcel of living land which it covers. Land that bears its weight of century, of pain. Holds its structure up, steady, secure, like an unfurled, bloody banner waving warning throughout the years. The scent rises through the dankness of age to bring memory. Breathe in the recollection of fresh springtime sky shows rolling out thunderous blankets of threat and wonder, summer hills lit with sun's love dancing to the pure melody carried on the breeze, unmolested dew on a glorious-colored carpet of leaves fallen unseen, and the soft and subtle fragrance floating in the diamond-shaped spaces of the first crystal snowflake of winter. Release your breath and realize that the aromas summoned and stifled with each passing dawn and dusk drift over the river banks in remembrance of the peaceful ways once found there—of the freedom once laced through that land like a precious gift—in those days, in those moments, before it all began.

There is a house….

It stands there still, least we should ever forget.

.   .   .

John Hart Crenshaw (1797–1871) was known as the "Salt King of Southern Illinois" and conductor of a Reverse Underground Railroad for many years. Lewis Kuykendall was a slave trader in association with Crenshaw. There is a wealth of historically correct information about these individuals provided by notable historian Jon Musgrave of Springhouse Magazine at www.illinoishistory.com. A preservation project involving Crenshaw's Hickory Hill Plantation (Old Slave House) is currently underway.

My sincere gratitude to Jon Musgrave for making this piece of history known as well as for his bringing forth the lost section of the Trail of Tears— nearly 9,000 Cherokee passing through Southern Illinois between November of 1838 and January, 1839…, this book is dedicated to the memory of these….

…I couldn't see it coming, but I could feel it. In my bones. I remember telling you, my precious girl. I told beautiful Ammie. I told warmhearted Colton and he wanted to fight it. But I told them a storm was blowing in. And I told them I'd have to ride it out. It was time.

I put these letters to you, Mercy, in my mother's box, as many as it could hold, and I bundled the rest with a silk ribbon. I stuck a dried flower—one your own tiny hands had picked—in the bow.

On that morning the wind changed. I walked out toward the dream circle and I waited on a fallen oak log. I waited all morning, chilled to the bone, just staring at a naked seedling bending under the cruel gusts. I thought of you….

You would want to know why….

You see, I was saved. He was not. The River, it was calling me. And I would not kill—not ever again.

It happened quickly, the cut was deep this time. He got his revenge, but his pain had only been planted—sin to sprout in another season. He was without purpose and, now, without himself. Without God. Without hope.

Since I knew he was coming, I wrote him a letter, too. My heart was in that letter…my hope for the living. It blew out of my stiffening hand like a seed to the winter wind. He didn't read it, but I saw him take it with him…. I saw him take it with him, my lovely child.

It is written.

It said I forgave him.

Among other things….

Contents

Letter One

The Great Mystery

Chapter One

The year of 1857 had a menacing feel. Time had everyone trapped in a thick soot of rancorous sin that piggybacked the Illinois gusts making it difficult to separate the air from dust. Or maybe it was the spirit of the land that was seeking vengeance, stolen like it was…right there in its place. Lying there under a blanket of borrowed shame for sky as its breast became oddly dotted with unnatural and rather unattractive things labeled "progress." (Imagine. Think for just a moment on the name—Shawnee**town**.)

Either way—time, land, spirit or man—it was hard not to breathe the evil in. And it was harder still for Lemn. He sensed things…, spiritual things, and it was nearly impossible for him to keep the imprinting grains of evil's sand out of his innocent, wide eyes as they were searching. Learning. Craving the future like only the blind hunger of youth can do.

.   .   .

This widespread hope of the young, this energy source they all spring forth…. Perhaps it exists because they have yet to learn of the past. They have yet to grimace, yet to judge, yet to witness the foreboding images, beyond the reflection in the mirror, that chain them to a heritage. They have yet to question the mystical forces from which they have arrived.

Seeds of Chance….
They brought them here to stand new and shining amidst the colliding winds that blow. Gave them a fighting spirit and strong legs to run over this glorious, peaceful prairie that is older than the days. This prairie rooted with eyes of sorrow

that are still watching, sowing each seed of chance with the same tender hope it
might one day bring....

And they have yet to make a mistake of their own.

> .   .   .

Lemn soon found that nearly everything had a downward slant to it. A sharp, invisible tilt toward hell. He felt himself beginning to slide that year. Everything began to unsettle him, every*one*, but Drake. And even he wondered from time to time, *How can that be?*

For Drake had nothing less than *stature* slung across his shoulders. Like a cape of iron, it did not move. Wherever the man stood, he just rolled there like a thunderstorm of dark silence—night or day didn't matter, his nature was untouchable. He carried strength and legend right there in his belly. Whenever one laid eyes upon him, the brain replied, "Colossal...," as much as any word. And, every so often, from somewhere deep inside him, shards from a collision would rise, an explosion might very well erupt at surface..., it would flash across the smoke or sky and leave a quick and direct kill—so quiet, it was almost polite. So fast it immediately bred doubt. But the slow death settling in testified. And what followed lacked remorse. The only expression changed would be the lifeless one.

But still, Lemn found himself stricken unafraid of this man.

And Drake's eyes.... Those electrifying blue eyes of his when flashed, almost sorrowfully, toward another, left their lungs empty and still in that frozen moment between heartbeats. They were eyes that defied an icy stare, themselves holding an inhuman aura, empty but alive..., striking up raw shock in those left standing on the other side of them. He was so cold.... And those eyes..., nothing short of cruel. Piercing.... The thinnest of lines drawn of a mythical color, a liquid wall built between breathtaking and beautiful, shy and terrified..., maybe they were a curse of his to carry. The reason why he stood alone and apart. Always.

Everybody knew of the Gambler, the dealer of men and their money..., knew of the legend gracing their dry part of the world and going—currently— by the name of Drake. Everyone held on to a piece of this man, the fallen crumbs, unraveling threads, butted cigarettes, the fading images trailing him in the shadows of midnight streets, they anticipated his return in the hint rising off the morning, bloodied pools of mud drying where he had no sooner walked, and another had not..., and these assumptions were considered to be credible enough to incriminate, to freely spread the flurry.... But still, he was a step beyond them. The freest of men, so it seemed.

But tonight, something started to change all that....

And, on this first night out, Lemn awkwardly crept a mismatched step behind. With the wide eyes of a curious boy, he noticed things from the depths of that shadow..., like the path that seemed to spread before them, crowds of people parting like drops of the Red Sea. They dodged Drake as lepers would—weary eyes hidden under brims, cast down and to the side. Lemn wanted to reach out to some..., they were just humble, common people who didn't want any trouble. And it was plain for Lemn to see they'd had enough of that.

But then, there were always the other sort of men..., plenty, actually. Men who wanted trouble, needed a good dose of it to tuck themselves in at night. And when Drake went to sit down in the company of men like these—duster gliding over the high chairback, purring through the air, sliver pistols shined to pristine, gleaming out a smug-smile warning against the scowling black backdrop of him—a different kind of air would settle. A shiver might spring out on prairie-toughened skin, a sign the temperature must have dropped like a Dakota rain. It was then Lemn realized that *there are some people in this world who, God bless 'em, can't sense a thing.... People who*, he imagined, *while finding themselves face to face with a ton of raw muscle hanging on a red-eyed bull, will just stand there. Staring. Or even worse. They'll antagonize. Ignorantly mimic, paw the ground like cockamamie fools—a good start on their own graves....* He figured this because he'd seen as much..., on this, their first night out.

Lemn found himself sitting behind Drake who was sitting amongst a table of these. When they opened their mouths to talk, Drake's jaw muscles would quiver and ripple, tighten and flex—silent words spoken of undermined curse, indicating he was downright agitated. Lemn noticed it—right away. He also noticed nobody else did. And those muscles continued to dance on..., some kind of sporadic Irish clog in the wee and shameless hours..., they danced on under an intrusive line of incendiary questioning regarding Lemn. Statements of stupidity falling increasingly thicker and heavier from the collective insecurity flanking the poker table....

"Who's this, Drake? Long lost son of yours?"

And...

"You sure he ain't here to learn how to cheat, Drake...? He'd be learnin' from the best...."

At the challenge of these remarks, the slow, warm breath of a silent sigh roused the edge of Drake's moustache—tiny bristles alerted like an archery line, though he did not fire. He calmed his mind for the boy's sake. Shook it off. Then spoke his words with regret for the wasted effort they required, "You gonna play or not?" His low, monotone voice drew immediate and mandatory attention like a classroom ruler tapping out warning against a tired spinster's hand. His gaze remained fixated on his own hand as he strategically situated his cards. Most of his fellow players took quick heed, their jeering long since fallen into a flat and worthless memory.

But for one.... The most avid, or the most dim-witted..., this man sighed loudly and cussed. Plunked his elbows down heavily, hanging on the far edge of the table like a sulking child forbidden his supper. His sweating brow and shifting eyes marked him unfocused. His expression carried a hint of annoyance that fed into a rapidly burning edge of anger, declaring him a premature loser.

Lemn caught Drake smirking, chuckling under his breath. The reason why being that he never had to work very hard to convince the players to hand over their money. Their own mindless addictions did that.

Moods soon settled into a fraudulent form of camaraderie..., enough to get on with it. *And it*, Lemn thought, *is in my blood.* Love at first sight ringing true for him here, though not in the rivers of money, in the secrets of men, nor was it in the frilly packages wrapping used saloon girls or in a fanciful dream held of the high ceiling, lost to a sky of smoke billowing up from the onlookers..., but, for him, it was in the cards. He sat there, peering past Drake's shoulder, predicting them, recognizing their faces, their rhythm and flow, and he was dead on. It struck him strange after an uninterrupted streak. Started to scare him after three-quarters of a game. He sat as stiff and unnoticeable as the hardwood chair he was perched upon. He tried to change focus, tried to study the men's faces, eyes, gestures, their degrees of steadiness intently, just as he was instructed, but he was drawn back.... For him, the game was in the cards—all of it. And the cards were in his mind, clear as yesterday's memories to be lived out tomorrow. He didn't move a muscle, didn't say a word about what was happening to him—God forbid he should have to use the latrine.... He pinned his sweaty palms under his thighs to resist any nervous fidgeting. He felt like the man on the far side looked. Strung out, insecure, agitated..., owner of a perpetual headache.

Lemn studied this man, squirming in his blatant discomfort. He considered the cause..., found himself thinking about addictions as the chips rolled, about the habits and avoidances that must lead to them, about what it would be like to be a grown man and feel progressively more vacant as each entertained distraction fades. He watched that man…, listened to him talk, useless were the words he used. Empty. It was an easy decision for him to make. He wasn't sure why he was making it but, nonetheless, there he was. It seemed he learned something that first game…, he learned what kind of man he didn't want to become.

At thirteen, he made that decision, while the cards steadily eluded the man. Paraded past him, dragging his bankroll away, dressed up in illusion, in shredded and mirrored ribbons of luck.

.   .   .

Drake sensed it, immediately. Like one habitually predicts the day's weather from the first glance of morning sky. It was the way the kid handled the cards for the first time…, he was more comfortable with them than most seasoned gamblers. They didn't slip from him nor did they stick. There wasn't one awkward fumble in the shuffle nor wayward pitch across the table. When dealt and gathered, they rested evenly against the kid's curved hand…, he barely had to space them—they just *flowed*. Almost *through* him. His motions were fluid— quick and graceful, almost mesmerizing…, the cards purred like kittens beneath them so that even Drake, preposterously, found himself questioning trickery. Just this, this talent of his, would be enough to gain an edge. It would set him apart. It would bend concentration. It would intimidate. Immediately.

And then he played….

And it was soon discovered that not only was his touch masterful, Lemn had an instinct for the game—all facets of it. Rules fell dead and away, void of expected description…, Drake hardly had to explain anything at all. And that got Drake thinking…, thinking on how Lemn's personality could compliment his obvious skill. Drake had known Lemn for a lot of years and ever since that boy could stand on his own, he kept his mouth shut and his ears open. He picked up on things. And when he was pushed, he listened to his gut for guidance—he didn't look to anybody else. And those large vulnerable eyes of his threw people off guard. Softened them, somehow. They were a warm, kind, chestnut brown and his childish grin made them sparkle with life. He had a shy way about him, always had…. He was too quiet to appear interesting, too considerate to be a leader, but this was good. This would work to his advantage. Because no one would suspect that he had more years of concealed wisdom than men three times his age.

It was time. They both knew it....
It was time for Lemn to play..., out in the open.

And Drake did his best. He gathered up a casual game of frequent locals—a small, easygoing circle bound with a common understanding—but, just like a southward turn in luck, it all started to unravel and present itself like a bad dream, one of those nightmares that grips the hostage's brain and forces it to record the horror in its entirety. And while it was happening, the only motion leaking out through Drake's shock was the silent sweat of shame and, underneath, the punishing heartbeat of a private panic. He watched on as the uninvited pushed through the protective bubble he'd tried to hold so delicately in his hands, but that was the problem—it seemed to burst with his own cursedluck touch. It stripped his own unknown vulnerabilities down—that boy was as good as his own. If he had only considered, looked down the road a ways.... It was so obvious now that it never should have started. Any of it. But it was too late. The kid did it—*he won.*

"Why you little punk! What the hell, Drake? You *did* teach 'im ta cheat, an' don't ya dare sit there 'an deny it!" the drunken man belched out in a stream of accusation. It was the same sorry shell of a man Lemn had based his life decision on just weeks prior. He was tall, lord.... And slender like the razor he should have used. And he was fuming with rage. And when his chair tipped over as he jumped up, it struck the planked floor and broke the silence with a deafening exclamation. The crash seemed to accent his growing hatred of the pair mocking him with wordless age and skill comparisons.

"He won fair and square. Boy's good for his age, that's all," Drake explained, atypically aloof, trying to wilt the tension he felt sprouting all around him like an unwanted weed. But it was no use. He glanced at Lemn, gave a slight wink as cue and both the money and Lemn were soon gone....
But the drunk had help. The two sidekicks were leery of Drake's reputation, tried to take him down fast and hard.... The deathly thin, wiry man grabbed a hold of the back of Lemn's shirt collar, by the belt around his waist, giving the boy a heave into the massive mirror lined with shot glasses and whiskey bottles. Lemn's arms flung out in front of him to defend his face, but the shattering glass threw greedy razors at his tender, young flesh—they ravenously flew toward his descending body as if it had magnetic attraction. The hard floor cruelly signaled his landing. More glass followed to cover him like a blanket of thistles. Finally, a flash of relief renewed him as he became aware that nothing was knifing his gut—he'd survived. So far. He dared to peer out from behind

his thin, ill-shielding arms, a move that met with the attacker's fist, presented in full view and aimed to concave his face....

But it didn't get the chance.

Drake's hand, though bloodied and bruised, gripped the man's shoulder with the intrusive force of steel talons. Lemn watched the drunkard's blood-shot eyes widen with surprise, then wince with fear..., his frail body seeming to prepare for the pain by folding tightly against itself. And then, the last thing Lemn could remember—a gunshot blast. It rose deafening and absolute through the saloon, stilling his heart and stealing his breath.

A morbid silence followed....

The question of death delicately lighted upon the flesh of everyone like butterfly to flower, as if testing, choosing and, at that, taking its dear, sweet time.... Feeling himself being propelled off the floor rather harshly, then on into the air, Lemn began to breathe—body relaxing half-lived moments before his mind realized that he was being carried out. By Drake.

The bar held a silence unparalleled. Drake didn't acknowledge a soul. People watched—some mouths gaping, some eyes smiling, some minds judging—as he carried the boy effortlessly over his shoulder, a warm gun in one hand, and the boy's money—all his money—in the other. Loose, cold bills stacked across the boy's back seeming to wave a good-bye with each marked step toward the swinging doors.

What they left behind slowly awakened in their absence—it was a room full of feverish recounting surrounding two men—stiff and slow, the third—silent and still, all sprawled out on the floor amidst broken glass and shattered egos.

But what neither Drake nor Lemn knew was this.... Had the hollow man been absent his addiction to whiskey, had the shakes held off, had he been able to resist the effects of his slow poisoning just a little while longer..., it would have meant a different man down.

With more shattered than ego.

For Lemn was destined to gamble. And, sometimes, even Destiny herself needs an earthly guide.

.   .   .

Lemn could recall being carried once before..., when he was thrown from his horse as a small boy. Though the circumstances were nothing alike, almost shameful in comparison, the sentiment seemed carbon made. His father's strong arms had gathered him up, tears and dust, and held him securely.

There's no place in the world quite that close. He smiled now, remembering how he was wailing a little too theatrically, but his father didn't mind a bit. And he remembered what it felt like…crying out in fear while, at the same time, knowing he'd already been rescued.

About two mute miles after they left the saloon, Lemn got the courage to ask Drake if he'd shot anybody.

"Didn't need to," and he lit a cigarette he had finished rolling.

That first drift of smoke smelled good as it warmed a strand of crisp, night-time air. Lemn noticed his own hand was throwing a shaking fit, annoying his good-natured horse through the vibrations rattling the bit at the end of the quivering reins. He decidedly draped the soft strips of leather freely over the horse's neck and then sat on his left hand to force it steady while his other hand minimized the gush of his own blood. *Drake must 'a shot a hole through the ceiling. He stopped 'em—without saying a word.*

After a while, Lemn's arm grew numb from holding the handkerchief to his head, the flow of blood now thick and tired. He lowered it and covertly studied Drake's hands as much as he could in the wavering moonlight. He was in awe—*how could they be so steady and calm?* Those same hands that flew like lightning at the charge of a gun, like that's exactly what they were designed for. The reflex was intense, deadly. Those strong hands reacted without hesitation or fumble when ignited to action through something in that mysterious mind—*what flips that invisible switch…?* Lemn shuddered to think of how many men died at the end of those fingertips, the same ones that ruffled his hair when he was younger and followed the lines of a children's fairytale by firelight—that same old, tattered book read differently every single time. His gaze traveled the lines of Drake's hands—the slowing trickles of drying blood looked like ink in the dark, but had no story to reveal—and back up the strong forearms and solid biceps to the edge of his sturdy jaw partially covered by a long mustache and a faint shadow of beard with jets of scars trying to escape from under the dark whiskers. The brim of Drake's black hat tipped down to mask the wrinkled, leathery skin encasing those lightning-blue eyes. Eyes that burned into the memory of anyone who saw them once—few dared to look directly into them again. Those eyes could see through the tunnels of hell and find the face of God Himself at the end and Lemn doubted he'd turn away from what he saw. Doubted he'd even blink or wait for the reasons why—almost like he'd seen it all before. Everything…. Lemn shivered. His shoulders became noticeably tense as he wondered who this man really was.

He smiled at the answer that finally came.

He's family....

. . .

This first run confused the boy. *Had to,* Drake thought, as his mind wound back through the past like a dried river bed, life source all dammed up. His feelings snagged on something deep inside—it was a memory and he found it lying there, hollowed out, cracked and chalky like his throat. He coughed up the stubborn, dry smoke clinging to the lining of his charred and blackened lungs. The reason why he was the one still breathing was beyond him.... Here he was, still standing like the wooden pillars holding up hell, raising Devon's kid in a way only fathomed in the man's vilest nightmares. But there was no other trade he could teach the boy. Drake was no farmer, he was a loner and a drifter. And the game—with all its sweetness and horror—the Game, she let him live like this. He had no publicly evident attachments except to his dead friend and this kid, now, who was growing on him a little.

Drake grew up in the streets because he was the son of a prostitute. He didn't know his father from one regular customer to the next and he didn't belong to anybody but himself. He knew he was doing the wrong thing with Lemn, the fight tonight proved it, but he was doing the only thing he knew how. And he had to do something. He couldn't leave the kid in a world like this without some kind of father....

He tasted a fear like none other, it was salty and it flooded his mouth. It dripped down from inside his brain to his cold, silent guns and then it lost connection. It shook him—the fear of helplessness. For the first time, he realized what it felt like to be a dad. He couldn't protect the boy from anything, not out here, not for long—this southern part of Illinois where fairness was a falsehood and Lemn was smack in the middle of its lie. No matter what Indian name they placed on the territory with scarcely an Indian allowed on it, everything ran together with a backward, chaotic hatred that kept people looking over their shoulders. Constantly. Lemn would have to learn to fight. He'd have to. And waiting it out wouldn't make him strong, it would make him soft and soft died in this territory—*God rest his Irish soul.*

Drake glanced at Lemn's blood splattered forehead. It was bad. He'd have at least a two-inch scar to show for his first game. But he'd always remember he won....

When they finally arrived at the cabin, Drake followed Lemn up those same log steps that he forged with Devon a decade before. He ran his thumb along the palm of his hand where the blisters once formed painful craters in his skin, longing that those blisters and callouses would be there still. That he'd be back to the time when he could see so much hope in a man's eyes that it felt like home. He pressed a hand to the boards that constructed the creaking, front door—*from a fallen oak drug up from the river*. He strained his smoke-stained eyes to peer into the darkness. He made out Lemn's shadow as it crept silently across the room searching for a cloth to clean up the blood. Both of them were trying with all their might to go unnoticed, prolonging the long awaited confrontation that may as well happen because the suspense was like a festering sore about to erupt and ooze.

Neither knew they were being watched. A small, desolate voice quietly cracked, "Drake, tell me, are you tryin' ta kill me, too?"

The desperation in the tiny voice calmed and saddened, rather than startled them because it was the voice of the fallen. Once self-assured, once determined like the spirit of the woman who sang it, it now had the whining tone of a defeated, locked away prisoner in an imaginary cell. Oh, she'd gone through hell alright. Who hadn't.

They stood still for an eternity in the second of darkness that evaporated when she lit a single candle, exposing every weakness in the room.

"I do apologize, ma'am," rolled Drake. He considered stammering out an explanation but thought better of it as he took his hat off and sat down studying the object's blankness. He ran his hands nervously around the brim, suddenly intent on reinforcing its shape. He was unable to lift his eyes to the metamorphosed woman perched across the rickety table from him—butterfly gone backwards. He couldn't bear to witness the look of oppression that had settled into her dull eyes. She lost her husband, only one year ago, and now he was pouring salt on her wounds, influencing their only boy to stray from Devon's values. But it would be impossible for Lemn to salvage their farm just by working the land—he'd either die doing all the grueling work or the landlord would kill them both off and reclaim it.

"Apologize for…" Then she saw him, her blood-soaked child, through her blurred, teary eyes.

"Dra-a-ake?"

She screeched Drake's name out in three, extended, accusatory syllables before she sprung across the table toward Lemn in a state of angry panic.

Lemn's eyes grew big. He drew back from her reaction. She had barely taken notice of him over the entire past year and now all her attention was raining down at once. His high-pitched, uncertain tone contradicted his words, "I'm *okay*, Ma."

"Like *HELL* y' are!!!"

She had done it so quickly, no one had time to process the possibility. Lemn's throbbing face held the mark of her white handprint contrasted against a frame of red, burning skin. It was a mark that served a poor model of the magnitude of pain she had instantly and permanently inflicted on the inside of him. Lemn's eyes quickly searched for, then looked into Drake's. And in the deep and stormy blue of them, he read things. Things that said this man remembered. And understood. Understood the kind of helpless pain that only a son or daughter has to endure at the hands God trusted to nurture life.

Her screaming language seemed so foreign in the background as she raged on about what Devon would think, what Devon would do—her own behavior obviously void, for Devon would never stand for it. Lemn had given them nothing but joy…, for all of his years…. Nonetheless, the morbid sound of anger and defeat singed the air, sadistic sounds coming from a woman who never missed church meeting, never cursed or took the Lord's name in vain. In her lifetime, she had dealt with adversity. She had traveled hundreds of miles with a small child into volatile territory, stood up to disaster, helped her neighbors, took in a lowlife gambler for dinner. Now the woman behind this voice couldn't make sense of waking up in the morning, couldn't stand the thought of having to endure another day.

Drake wanted to pick the boy up and carry him out of all this. Carry him someplace safe, but he hadn't found that place himself. So rather, he sat deathly still and thought of all the people he had encountered with torn and broken dreams—pretty much everyone, if they were old enough…. Some rise above, some just go on, numb like walking dead, some never get up again. The thing that made him unknowingly wince then, was the memory of his mother. *She could have done so much more….* Her wasted life's memory so harassed Drake's own life, that he forced himself *not* to care—about anyone. Not get close enough to feel the effects should they crumble right beside him. Again. And yes, he made some mistakes. He failed and got too close. And with each passing failure, he found that another piece of his soul had been chipped away. It's why he was almost relieved when Devon was killed—one less of the very few he cared about, one less to worry about. He felt guilty for the thought, but he knew a man who carried an unloaded gun was not aware enough to survive. Although he tried to tell him, Devon refused to accept the notion that this "freedom country" could be that volatile. But Drake knew better…, and it was like watching the man play a solitary game of Russian roulette. In a way, Drake was almost lucky—he was born into the evil of the world. Was swaddled in it. It almost felt comfortable. And it was this ill form of comfort that enabled him to appear protected and calm during a gunfight, his acceptance of it that allowed him to witness an unjust hanging without protest. His icy, cold stare— a direct reflection of the pain drilled into his innocent eyes with the sharpness of ten thousand knives when he witnessed his mother being strangled to death by a customer through a crack in the closet door that served as his room. Somehow he survived. He guessed he was *lucky* to be alive.

But, to this day, he could not forget that shade of blue, could not erase the distinct color of that man's eyes….

Lucky…. That blasted word burned white light into his conscience like a brand and its singeing stench turned his stomach. If he could just get his hands on that bastard Fate at the end of the iron…but he couldn't grasp it. That chain of events that led to his endless torture—the guilt, shame and regret—just whipped wildly about the air above him, an accident always waiting to happen…, landing and hitting hard was his memory, yet, somehow, the threat was never-ending….

He had invented an idol over the years. A boy. This kid was hidden in the closet with him that day but, unlike him, this boy had guts. He strained every muscle and fiber in his small body to rage out of the closet while Drake held his breath…, waiting…, inside…, in the dark. The boy lunged into that man who represented everything Evil in the World. That man's icy eyes sparked with unfair power as he smiled and wrapped his arm around the small, strung body. Without a thought, he threw him across that dirty room and then, the boy's skull…, it shattered. Into a million pieces. A dark, brass wall lantern had jutted into his unprotected brain. Blood had been splattered. On Drake's mother…, on her placid face…, and, just like that, all of them wilted in Evil's hands….

…Drake snapped out of it with a lurch and his heart skipped a beat then fluttered back into rhythm. He died that day. He wondered why no one had told that to his stubborn heart. His brain swam with waves of warm, throbbing blood as he realized where he was—same old misery, new boy. He absent-mindedly traced the series of scars concealed carefully under a shield of whiskers…, a shield guarding him from questions best left unanswered. He didn't feel "lucky" to be alive. He felt like a forgotten joke—a prank or a fluke still wandering the earth by mistake. He remembered that filthy closet…, and still to this day, in the middle of the night, he'd wake up surrounded by its smell. He'd spend the rest of the sleepless night reveling at how it sucked down light and time like candy. But on the day his mother died, it was different somehow. More like a cocoon. It felt like a second skin that made him invisible to the whole world. And that day, while he was hiding in it, it told him things. While she was dying, it said there was something better to hang on for. It wrapped around him and wouldn't let him out. Its voice was louder than his mother's screams, softer than her final silence. It ripped his ability to breathe and move away from him and chained him to his life.

But he knew now, that at that young age, that damn voice lied. And that lie lasted for a lifetime. It kept him cold. Kept him angry—a slow, festering anger that had become the fuel that he burned in each breath.

And, lord, how it flamed up with each new chunk of hurt tossed on the cinders.

He glanced over toward her—Anne. He was repulsed by her…. She had cooled off and become a softer version of herself. She was attempting to doctor the cut, fumbling awkwardly in her own shame and self-loathing. While he watched her, he had more time to think….

What am I still doin' here? I have an attachment to that boy that I can't under-stand. Why can't I just leave them alone? I'm killing her. But that boy has some-thing….

He no longer had the energy to fight it off. His subconscious engulfed him like thirsty waves in an unfamiliar ocean. It pulled him underneath, showing him the separate life hidden there.

Sickness overtook him. He was queasy, breathless. And what he saw was his idol, his boy. Lying there crumpled on the dirty bedroom floor in a bloody mess, still breathing—he'd been waiting all these years. Drake had never caught a glimpse of his face before, never had the chance to look into those soft, brown eyes. They were looking right through Drake's soul with an intense, pleading gaze. Looking right through him, staring straight into Lemn's eyes.

He is still alive....

Drake's vision clouded and the blood rushed past his inner ear, veins throbbing as the warm liquid drained from his brain. His hat rolled out of his limp hands and fell to the floor as his body lurched forward. He was about to pass out, but he opened his eyes in one last desperate attempt to stay focused. Lemn was staring through him with those eyes. The same eyes that had seen everything.

It's always been Lemn....

Sweat ran down Drake's forehead and he felt a fever lapping over his skin like flames.

"You've done enough here," she slashed with a razor-tonged hiss that sliced through the moment like ice water.

"Yes, ma'am." he heard himself choke out. He slowly reached for his hat and heaved himself off his chair with all the strength he had left. His slumped shoulders and limp, wasted body sauntered unsteadily through the door. The cool air felt clean and fresh as it splashed against his face. He searched deeper into the strange, black night for a sense of security. It whispered back only question. As he gripped the railing, he felt Devon's hand. He tried to force his mind to stop turning, stop pushing him toward insanity as his stomach suddenly revolted, changing his focus. As he recovered slowly, he couldn't help but wonder if God would grant him the grace of a decent tomorrow. He just didn't know how to shed his skin of confusion and anger—it'd been too many years.... The world, it felt different to him somehow...like he wasn't really a part of it anymore. It was almost saying that he never had been....

...Lemn's eyes followed Drake's soul into the darkness. As far as they could.

Chapter Two

If she would just say something, it'd help. Say anything…. But silence. Still as death. The very instant Drake's image had faded, her role as a mother evaporated into the thin night air that rippled out from his wake of darkness, leaving nothing behind but chills racing along Lemn's spine, his split forehead sweating and throbbing as if trying to gurgle out words of warning through its tongueless gap. It felt like an All Hallow's Eve had swooped down and covered their isolated patch of prairie with hideous cackles—a sinister prank conducted just one shaky breath beyond the natural. Bloodcurdling moans of despair loosed upon the heart—distinctly *felt* rather than heard. There was a raven in the midst of the white-flamed circle that had dropped. Its incarnate eye gazing upon the boy as the spirit of his mother lifted, her body refilled with the eerie strangeness of another. Lemn looked to her face—a placid disguise. He could see it in her waxen eyes…that it was no longer Anne lurking behind them.

The wind. It changed direction. A *stronger* wind…. It came calling, howling, circling, just as suddenly. The face of this wind was half-painted. The soul of this wind burned, leapt like fire. It danced. Lemn could hear its voices swirling beyond the closed door, the wise and warm voices breathed of the prairie, in a language he was never taught.

Memory Cries….
…It is a language born of the land—land of plain, river and of buffalo, a sacred Eden ruled only by the silent eye of an Eagle. It is a language born of freedom. Memory Cries flowed through after the blood spilled and the spirit waves were stifled. No man can carry that sound here with him. And no man can ever tear it apart from these echoing hills….

The Voices, they knew things. They saw things. But were unable to tell these things, stripped so harshly of the familiar avenues they used to reach the human world, the stories once so easily laid upon a human heart. Now they only blew amidst the winds of chance. Blew across the prairie on snow, wind and rain left unheeded, wordless chapters forgotten with the passing of seasons. But sometimes—a strain of blood trickled down through generations—there's born a gifted one, a lonely dreamer who hopes, a lost wanderer who searches. And upon this one the gentle breeze of wisdom settles like a blanket to bless. Such was the spirit of Lemn and he could sense it all from the inside, from the whisper of the blood stories that flowed through him like the river. And what the voices had to say, he could feel with his heart. And what he felt told him it wouldn't be long. For him…, his journey…, he would not run far.

Bravery filled his lungs as he listened to his-story. He looked to her again—the vacancy of his mother. The raven had taken flight.

And his own journey was born of that night.

Chapter Three

As he lay there in bed, his rambunctious mind rose, splintered from body and evolved into an unwelcome and noncompliant source of company. So filled with energy, it had almost formed its own entity. It insisted upon reliving the day his father never returned from town…, the very same day his mother was stripped of the will to live….

…At the strike of that single and final sound ripping through the unsuspecting air, Lemn watched her body snap like an invisible whip had cracked across the small of her back—it nearly severed her in two. The wicker basket fell from her limp arms, newly folded sheets tumbled to the sand, unfurled and escaped slowly with the wind. She fell to her knees, to the ground, feebly clawing after them. She clutched fistfuls of sandy soil that drizzled from her grasp like liquid future.

How could we possibly have known? He wondered as he lie deathly still now…, *How did we decipher the malicious intention behind that shot from that of a hungry hunter's?*

Her glassy green eyes clashed still against the continuance of blue sky like tethered buoys half-drowned in splashing sea. Was it she spinning or the world…? She no longer cared to know, he could see…. He watched as her soul stopped dead in the middle of all motion, her reason for living still drifting, drifting…. She looked up into his eyes just then, asking him why—almost blaming him with that one, wordless stare. He would never forget it. And he would never forget that he had no answer to follow that sound of question. Nor apology. His feet obstinately disobeyed his command to retrieve the scattered laundry for his mother. But neither could he rip his body away from its frozen stupor to greet what was left of his father. So he stood there, locked between his choices, divided, motionless and numb. Unable to offer comfort. And with no comfort offered him.

As he coveted that first shadowed glimpse of his father's silhouette rising upon the hill, the trail, his eyes remained fixated on that daunting, blank horizon..., body postured as if cast in bronze, mindless that in his inert stance, upon his youthful face was being chiseled the same anxious expression such that he was taught.

Nobody came....

That one shot in the distance was all they ever heard of his good-bye.

.   .   .

Why should we go west. Why.... Bitter questions were these, so much so, they had dropped the courtesy of inflection years ago. They still rattled on in her head—endlessly, it seemed, still spoken with her younger voice. And still, they found no reply other than silence..., silence with an edge. Devon had been so stubborn with this, but how could she complain..., logically? It had been his one, his only, demand. But, even back then, she knew..., as women usually do. Impossible to and without proof of.... But yet she knew it was a tainted notion, cursed would be their travels and, should they make it to the end of their road, they'd find that it had led them straight into hell. She'd dreamed it..., nights thrashing, swimming in sweat. She dreamed vivid, bloody dreams..., dreams of fire and of death, dreams departing from her cruelly, leaving her baby in the midst of the ashes, crying and alone....
But he wouldn't listen. They were just dreams, after all....

And bitterness had made for a twisted little companion..., weaving its cage around her over the years. Heavy-laden, now, was she. And trapped. In nothing but memories..., an abyss of reminiscence for the things she should have done....
She'd always been outspoken, bossy, relentlessly demanding of him. And yet, her regrets had come unraveled thus,...*perhaps not nearly enough.*

Her Devon, with her demands, became increasingly introverted over the dusty miles they tread. She wanted only to know him, he wanted only to keep the atrocity from her....
These Americans he did not understand.
He'd be damned. Strong word, but for an adequate measure of feeling. He didn't say what he didn't mean, so yes. He would be damned if he'd allow himself to be dictated by another form of law—he'd seen civilization at work. And Boston. And New York. Civilization on the verge, if not already gone horribly

awry. Ireland…, he missed her sweet days. Never so much as the day he set foot on this chaotic soil.

He wanted nothing more than to get away from civilization. Nothing more. Nor less.

He'd heard of freedom in this country—out west. And if he couldn't find it, he'd live the dream of it. 'Til it came calling for him.

But of these things, of these freedom dreams of his, he grew weary of speaking—way back, when he was but a wee lad.

As Lemn quickly grew, the waiting, the constant anticipation, had slowly worn Devon down. Lemn could see it for what it was, boy or not. He watched the uneasiness taking over his father like a deadly ailment. Heard the man's beautiful voice waver after another trip into town—predictably, his accent became thicker with defiance for an evening, then dropped off somewhere in the night. The next morning, his bones would crack and pop. He'd rub at the tenseness pooled at the base of his neck, to no avail. His aging eyes would toss weary glances to the horizon constantly, with or without the hint of approach. And they grew dull, those eyes. The word "old" settled in amongst the indistinguishable color of them. And evident in the dryness of them was a severed river of homesickness, a longing for a more peaceful stream to carry him back to something…, to his dream that was quickly fading. With his life. It was as if he had to work to remember it anymore…, perhaps he could no longer find it at all. And, right before his boy, his spirit slowly drifted deeper into stone.

And Anne…, she grew cold.

Time's Masterpiece….

Losing hold, the pieces of a woman's shattered family, is a mirrored curse. Somewhere amidst the skilled hands of time, she finds her spirit has been forged a dusty shelf, her soul, trapped, a stagnant source of glue…, should she want to become these or not…, there is no matter. Lost to the silence of infantile servitude, the old adage rings in her ear, that to step on a crack would break a mother's back, and she professes that indeed it must be true. But it is her failure, only, in shouldering the responsibility of perfection. For without splinters or childish flaw, without the scattered disarray of man and his choice, there is no avenue to see the Light shining through…. And what does He use of time's masterpiece, but weathered jars of clay….

So at this, would it not be time then, she should put herself upon the wheel?

Lemn spent his childhood zest quickly, freely, continuously burning the wick nestled in his deepest spirit. With it, he was trying to rekindle his father's.

It was little use, but Lemn had a cause for which to fight. He was determined. And therefore, he attended every day of school, often drifting in and out of sleep mid-lesson. When dismissed, he did not linger with the others but rather, walked through the uninviting town alone, posture stretched taller, shoulders spread to more manly poise as the rowdier, late afternoon crowds started coming to life. He jogged the four miles of dirt road to get home to work in the fields or tend the livestock until lack of daylight forced him inside. He was trying to prove it to his father. Trying to prove, that with the three of them, they could make the farmstead sustain. Not for his own sake, or for the love of farming, but rather, to keep his father's will uplifted.

But things are missed when there happens a murder.... Irretrievable things now fallen between the cracks that the beloved vacant would have caught, held up, stopped or saved....

Lemn was old enough at his father's passing to take on the unspoken expectation that he abruptly finish his schooling to work. And work he did, 'til his fingers and heels bled through the blisters. But it was a constant battle, one his mother was backing out of a little more each overwhelming day. The steep land payment came due and passed on unpaid for the second consecutive year. Anne knew more of its consequence than she was letting on, but Lemn could see how the fear solidified her defeated desire to escape while standing still, disappear inside her own flesh. He tried to talk it out of her, but she just stared through the window or changed the conversation with an order for Lemn to go do something else. She was dying inside, losing her farm and her son, and she wasn't fighting herself to get either of them back. She was going like his father had. And Lemn couldn't witness it all over again.

Thank God there was Drake. And the game of poker. And a whole other life.

.   .   .

The sleepless night took its sweet time, but eventually folded itself under and the sun peeked over the horizon, assuming it safe to venture out once again. Lemn rose easily before his mother who, anymore, preferred to see only the hours brought of the lazy, afternoon wind. Lately it seemed he couldn't breathe fully in the space they shared. He needed to move out from under the desolate air—it hovered over their home like a smothering blanket of soot. So he fed the livestock, then saddled his sorrel gelding and loped to Drake's shanty where he stayed when he was in the area. The smooth morning breeze lapped across his sliced and bruised skin, each powerful stride handing him cool freedom.

Thank God for horses, thank God for horses, thank God for horses....

When Lemn arrived, he wasn't surprised but, still, his heart sank as he realized Drake's horse, bed roll and supplies were gone. It would be impossible to track Drake and Lemn knew of no one he trusted to ask where he might have gone. But Drake had to come back sooner or later, so Lemn decided to check the shanty every day until he returned. Lemn hoped Drake was not upset with him for winning the game—they hadn't really discussed it and he wasn't sure what had happened with everyone's mood swings flying around him like rings of fire. The whole thing turned into a bloody circus. He imagined the things Drake might be thinking about—what kind of a burden a kid was, Anne's obvious disapproval....

Just as Lemn turned to leave, he saw a young lady walking toward him from the crest of the protective hill surrounding the shanty. She was carrying something in her arms. *Maybe she knows where he went....* He jogged enthusiastically up the hill to meet her.

"Mornin' ma'am."

"Well, hello! Didn't know Spence had a boy holed up here."

"This is Drake's place, ma'am, don't know of any *Spence*."

"You ain't from these parts are ya—your talk is real becomin, boy," she flowed as she looked down at him, shading her eyes from the sun.

"Well, I am from here, schooled in Shawneetown, but m' folks are from Ireland."

"Thought so, it's nice to see somethin' a little different in a man for a change. Spence is my name for Drake..., he goes by both.... I'm his sister."

She held out her hand to shake his and politely chuckled at the apparent confusion in the boy's face—he was attempting to mask it rather unsuccessfully.

"Not his blood sister..., but I'm his fam'ly if he wants one er not. Came to give 'im some cin'mon rolls, since I know he cain't cook, let alone bake. An' I can see he ain't here—ya jus' never know 'bout him. But I'm glad ta see my trip wasn't a wasted one."

Lemn watched as her smile lit up her face—the whitest, most pure and radiant smile he had ever seen. Her skin was the color of the prettiest red oak leaf in the fall when the morning sun hits it just right so that it takes a breath away…, one has no choice with certain trees of fall, with their ephemeral elucidations that so covet artists' hearts…, no choice at all but to stand still and stare and marvel at the impossible brilliance there…. A golden glow graced her bronze skin, it was a light born of something inside…, it couldn't help but shine out.

It wouldn't matter what she said next, he knew it would sound like a song from heaven's angels.

"My lan's! What happened to y' face, boy?"

Lemn looked down, ashamed of his appearance, "Got in a fight."

"Don't tell me that a boy like you has to stoop to fightin.' I know just by talkin' to you that you got more in ya than that." She leaned over to touch his chin and she gently tilted his face to get a better look.

She felt like an angel.

"An' Spence wouldn't have anythin' to do with that fight?"

By the direct look in her eyes and tone in her voice, Lemn knew her question was more of an accusation.

"Uh…, no ma'am," Lemn's gaze darted back to the ground as he spoke.

"Lyin' ain't in ya either, boy."

The small shock of being so easily discovered and directly called on it took his shallow breath even further away and he was embarrassed but, at the same time, he felt safer with her. As he looked back up at her, she wasn't scornful, she was smiling, and that was different.

They went to the shanty. Lemn fetched some water and they ate sweet rolls and drank from one old tin cup. It was all they could find.

He knew he should keep his mouth shut about the fight, and what Drake had to do with it, but he heard himself answer each question truthfully and in more detail than necessary. He couldn't seem to break away from her. She learned his name and he learned hers—Avi.

Avi was different from most anyone he'd ever met—*special*. It seemed a dream that she was with him, in this land, still seemingly untouched as a flawless rose after a hail storm. She wasn't like most adults. She talked about herself as if it were important that he know just as much about her as she was discovering about him. She was interested in Lemn, seemed to automatically attach to him, like he was someone she should know but couldn't quite remember. And he felt secure with her, like this was his real life and everything before it was a hollowed out nightmare. He never wanted to go back to sleep again.... At this table with Avi, he wasn't in debt to a rich slave owner, he didn't loose his father, he never saw evil—it just didn't exist anymore.

Five minutes elapsed in the course of about two hours. Avi stood up, arched her beautiful back that even too much material over an unforgiving corset could not mask, and smiled that angelic smile down at him. She said she had to get back to town or her mama would worry. She said her mama liked to keep her in sight most of the time even though she was a grown woman, but she didn't like to leave her mama alone for very long either.

"Do you have a mama, boy?"

"Yes'm."

"Well, ya best not worry her none, either."

Lemn walked her up the hill and said good-bye. He knew he would see her again even though it went unspoken. If he didn't he would starve. She had something he needed and he didn't know how he had ever lived without it. He was already feeling it drain from his soul with every step she took away from him. She had been so kind. And she noticed him, looked right at him, like no one had bothered to before.

He sat cross-legged on the crest of the hill, practicing his whistling across a perfect blade of prairie grass. She turned and waved at him once, then he watched her until he couldn't see her any longer. He thought about catching up, following her into town to make sure she would remain unchanged and safe, but he had to avoid town for a while in order to survive. He couldn't imagine how she could live in the middle of all that darkness and still shine, especially since she was...

Thundering hooves straining his senses and tightening his muscles ripped him back to his nightmare and he knew before his eyes met them that their direction was not aimed past him, but for him. He was quickly relieved they weren't after Avi and he hoped she was far enough away not to hear. As he thought this, he felt his body propel itself upward with more speed and strength than he normally possessed. His horse was closer than they, and his only avenue of survival. He knew who the leader was. The whoops of excited hunting calls mixed with laughter were already slashing his flesh to the bone. His face felt more bruises that were not yet impacted and he nearly collapsed as his shaky hands reached for the tangled reins. He heaved himself into the saddle while kicking his horse forward, nearly sliding off at the powerful response. His horse sensed it, too.… The strong arms wrapped around him and, instantly, the stiff earth rushed up to slam into him, jarring pain through his shoulder and into his chest.

…His mind was not afraid, it was tired. He was exhausted and in agreement with a life span of thirteen years as he waited for the first strike of a fist three times the size of his to end it all.

"Where's your hero now, ya little punk? Well, I guess he jus' took tail out of town—don't ya know he always does?"
    …*White lights.*

"Did ya think we wou'nt finish ye?"
    …*Choking on dirt and blood.* (*There are too many, God.*)

"You better think of a new trade if Slim don't kill ye, damn pup."
…*Can't breathe,* (Bye, ma.)

"That's **enough**, Jed! He's just a boy!!"
    …*Feel warm, no more hurt*—"Where's Pa?"

"Here that, Slim? Baby wants ta know where his Pa is."

"Wake up, boy. You wake up good'n hear what I'm sayin'!"
    …*Shaking hard.* (No, I don't wanna come back. No….)

"You're Alive, dammit—WAKE UP!! We're gonna leave yer ass here on Drake's door step so maybe he'll think twice 'bout usin' a kid ta cheat with. Ya best think 'bout what the hell yer doin.' Ya ain't got the guts to survive here…. How long did yer pa stay alive around these parts, anyway? What was it kilt'em, Jed?

"Hell, Slim—I bet ya it wan't much lookin' at 'is Pride-and-Joy, here—over a sack a' gal-damn flour. Fumblin' 'roun' with that gun thit weren't even loaded…, or so I heard."

"See, boy—survivin' ain't even in ya. Ya lil' Irish punk."

The ground sprang up one last time to contact Lemn's skull and, after their trail of dust and victory cries evaporated, he saw that they were gone. He then curled up with his pain, felt a dull disappointment at the ability to draw in dry, dirty air. For it would have been easier for him to die. Dying felt right.

.   .   .

Sounds were knocking at Lemn's ears for a while before his mind connected the underwater noise to life as he knew it, "Com' on, boy. You gonna be a man. Come back to me, ya hear? You gonna be a GOOD Man, but ya gots ta come back. Come BACK!"

Angel talk.

Lemn waited to open his eyes long after he could have. He hoped all of his struggles had ended, that he was dead, but he knew the angel rocking beside him was crying, and that only happened on earth. A thin trace of light came through as he forced his swollen eye lid to open slightly. He took on the pain in order to show her that he was still with her, still in his life.

"Thank God All Mighty, boy! Thank You, Sweet Jesus! Boy, you're gonna be okay, you're gonna be okay, boy." She rocked back and forth nervously, though gently, as she held his hand to her soft face.

And there it was—that smile. It's peaceful beauty returned, changing the route of her tears, making it alright for him to venture back into the real dream, pain and all. If Lemn could have spoken he would have tried to make her laugh, somehow. Because in his mind, he saw GOOD MAN written across his heart, shining letters of light, and now he knew exactly what those words meant.

Chapter Four

Avi ran for water, brought it in the same tin cup they were both contentedly drinking from a half-hour before. Beyond the blood and dust, Lemn could smell the faintness of sweet rolls, could remember the laughter they shared. The recent memory triggered tears that leaked out of his swollen eyes as he found it hard to make sense of the punishments placed so unfairly upon him. As quickly as they came, he forced his thoughts to stop. He buried them deep in his heavy heart. He didn't want to upset Avi further with his tears. She was now busily intent on making him comfortable. He couldn't tell her it was an impossible task. He couldn't tell her that the price tag hanging on each breath was a shot in his side, inescapable pain that shook his entire being.

"It's gettin' warm out, boy…. Ya need ta try 'n drink dis, com' on, Lemn."
He did his best to take a couple sips through swollen, split lips without spilling, then Avi examined his side, his tattered shirt soaked with a rapidly spreading circle of fresh blood. As she looked closer, she gasped at the sight of a jagged piece of blood-stained bone jutting through his flesh. It was a good hour's walk to the town doctor. And with the amount of lost blood, well…, she feared it would be too late. But she could think of no other option…. She took off her white cotton underskirt and placed it over his wound.

"Keep yer arm up 'gainst here. Keep it tight…, I know it hurts. I'll be back with Doc as soon as I can. They ain't comin' back?"

Lemn tried to shake his head, *No.*

With that, Avi took off running for town. Lemn felt exposed without her presence. Between mind-numbing juts of pain, he moaned in discomfort and disbelief, thinking that there must be some place on earth he belonged. Some place without so much unfairness and pain. He kept searching for this place in his mind, never reaching it in consciousness.

.   .   .

Waves of sound brushed against his eardrums again…. The simultaneously dull and piercing stabs of pain slapped him to awareness and assaulted the air in an autonomous scream of agony and anger. Unsteady hands lifted his swollen, darkening body into the back of a wagon padded feebly with quilts. The doctor examined the rib and decided the loss of blood, the overall ghastly condition…, warranted travel to his office in town. Travel upon rutted trails of twisted erosion. As their slow progression began to pitch his limp body against the unyielding wagon bed—cruelly pressing unbearable pain from his tender bruises—mercifully, his eyes fluttered and rolled back, signaling him unaware.

Hours later, he awoke. Fully this time, enough to be aware of the comfortable bed cradling him. He inhaled the unfamiliar scent of whiskey, realized it was wafting off his own breath. The slight burn in his hollow stomach, the numbness solid on his sluggish mind…, he preferred it over the complete agony he knew was jealously crouched on the other side. At every breath, at every slight movement, he was reminded that peace was not his. Yet he felt safe…, as safe as possible in Avi's house with Doc, Avi and Avi's mother constantly checking on him—they were the buffers standing between he and his jagged world. He had heard them, heard their quiet voices passing through his dreams like silk ribbons on a slow wind….

"What did the boy do to git in all dis trouble?"

"Don' he have no fam'ly?"

"He a lucky one—ain't no 'fection settin' in."

"He'll make it, this time anyway. Don't know if they'll come back, though. You ladies know where to find me. If I have to go on a call, I'll make sure the sheriff sends someone to guard the doors."

.   .   .

Four days, or nearly…, had passed. But Lemn did not count them, did not stack them as measure against his healing. Instead, he used his stronger eye to study details—the oak-trimmed windows, the framed pictures—hand painted oils, the red and gold papered walls, the expensive lamps (*American or import? He assumed the latter.*), the chairs covered with crimson shades of velvet material. He studied the craftsmanship evident in the bed posts, the dressing stand with a beveled mirror and marble top, the brass door handles—polished. And he was awed by them all. *How,* he wondered, *could elegance of this magnitude exist in Shawneetown? Without being ransacked or burned to the ground out of bigotry or jealousy? It stands out like they...,* he mused, *something like a solid bar of gold in a den full of blind robbers.*

He drifted in and out of sleep, soft and unencumbered as a cloud's trip across a level sky. His dreams revolved, streams of busy and overlapping circles, bringing images of his mother up through their fog—sometimes she'd be seething with rage toward him, and other times, only sad, robed in the melancholy assumption that he had abandoned her according to her own expectations, just like everyone else in her life. He'd wake to these..., guilt-stricken, though he'd done nothing all that *wrong....* He'd only grown up, matured, began to separate as his own. And through all this, it had never been his intention to leave her, but she would not see it that way, not through the dizzying pattern her defeated thoughts stamped across her reason. She didn't really know him..., and how odd, isolated as they were from the rest of the world, living together. But alone. She didn't care to know him..., and how sad, for he thought he was someone worth knowing. He was her son. But the oddity, the sadness of rejection notwithstanding..., he found he didn't love her any less. He'd like, one day, to be able to talk to her—to really talk to her. He'd like that very much. But he knew there would be nothing he could say.

.   .   .

Weeks passed....

The recovery of his beating became a sabbatical from his life granted by God. He did not realize how exhausted he was. Of the mundane. Of living youth under the heavy loss dropped down by death, solidified hollow by surrounding depression.... Tears flowed from him like a river, but they could not carry him away. The tensions, the injustices placed upon him sank in the midst, movement forbidden. But their sinking had synchronously forced him to rise up from underneath them, should he want to breathe again..., should he want to move on his own ever again.... It was this process that was making him a man. And a stronger man than his assailants could ever hope to be. It was through this, he decided. He decided he would take all the punishments of life, and if that meant a shorter life, so be it. He'd do this openly in return for the increased awareness and strength such things place inside a heart. This was all the answer he needed…, tears flowed into a sweet smile. His restoration seemed nearly complete. He nodded equivalency in understanding toward God with his soul and allowed himself to drift…another day or so. He was in no hurry for the things that lie ahead.

Drake stood over him. Silent and unmoving. Like a hovering storm balled around its own caged lightning. He was watching over the boy with the concern of a natural father—and it was an unsafe place for him to be. Not more than a month ago, he would have walked out of the room, out of Lemn's life, for good. Not only that, he wouldn't have bothered to look back, wouldn't have given it another thought…, but something was changing. On the inside of him, something was definitely changing. He could literally feel it. In places he'd long since had any feeling at all…. He felt the pressures in his chest being unlocked with a hexed key and flying away…, only to be replaced with an in-streaming compassion, empathy, for the young life lying in front of him, half-dead already. He was letting his guard down, growing soft like that Irish soul he repeatedly tried to warn. This was going to make him vulnerable, put those he cared for even more so in the light of danger, but he felt powerless to stop it, the transformation rolling like a freight train inside of him. He was a prisoner on it, a passenger of random destination…. The guilt nearly dropped him to his knees when he allowed himself to experience it, when he imagined the pain chained on this boy, as if he threw the grotesque punches himself.
Perhaps, in a way, he did.
This boy…. He was in his family's home. And rather than being prideful, he felt helpless because of it. He realized he was getting old—he was aging exponentially under the weight of his conscience. Lost years…, he should have been a little softer, a bit more human, *whatever that is*…. He admitted it—he would die empty. *It's how it should be*…. He'd set it up that way. He remembered the very day. It was the day Emma left. The world. Since then he'd carried it on his shoulders, paraded it around, showing anyone who'd look how senseless, how evil it could be. But here, in this room, with this boy…. He couldn't hold it up anymore, he was getting crushed. Unfamiliar as a snow shower in summer, tears came from the corners of his eyes. At first he thought them sweat, a leak in the roof on a rainless day…. Upon knowing, he did not attempt concealment. He did not block them. Instead, they splashed delicately onto his weathered hands, flowing down creased trenches chiseled into his skin by time. He studied their route, imaging a miniature river that could wash it all away.

Avi breezed through the doorway intent on chore, then halted, surprised. Her skirts swirled about her ankles with momentum—from pendulum evenness, slowly back down to still. She hadn't known Drake was back, let alone in the house. She realized, by the sallow shadows about his eyes and pursed lips, that she had interrupted. Apologetically, she diverted her glance to Lemn's huddled mass, hoping in the moment that she had kept her brother from becoming embarrassed and evasive. She walked around to his side of the bed and slid her hand up around his hunched shoulders in a partial embrace. She rested her cheek against his unyielding arm..., closed her eyes. Through his leather coat, worn and beaten to a perfect texture of baby-like softness, she could feel his strong body draw in air and hold it, long enough for it to be released in silence, masking the host's forbidden sobs.

"He seems to be your boy, now. Ain't he, Spence...." She whispered her words in more of a sentence than question.

"I guess so, Avi. But I have no idea how to care for a boy," Drake's voice quivered.

Avi let go. Tracing the frailty of his words in her mind. She eased her body into a sitting position on the floor, contemplating what to say. *Does anyone know how to care for a boy?* She doubted so, but these words did not seem right. She did not speak of them. She looked at the sleeping boy beside her, then back up to her troubled brother. She kept her voice very quiet, very low, hoping that her words, as they tended to during times like these, would not come out masked in misunderstanding.

"You've got ta learn that you aren't alone anymore, Spence. You ain't been alone since me an' Mama picked ya up off the street. You got fam'ly. I know it ain't how you planned it, but that don't make it any less. This boy needs you. He's the one needin' a fam'ly now.... We can all help."

"I know, Avi, I know...." Drake swallowed, took a deep breath. "You are my family, you and Mama. I don't deny that. But you know it just as well as I..., once the gamblers find out I got attachments, they'll come here causin' trouble for you. The only way I have to protect you is to act like I don't give a damn about ya. Sneak around all the time. But just look at what they did ta Devon's boy, Avi. Just for bein' around me.... No way in hell they're gonna think twice 'bout usin' a couple of colored ladies to get to me, even if you are well kept. In fact, they'd take joy in it—it shakes me to think what they could do to you....

Some of these gamblers just don't give a damn about the way things work 'round here."

Avi reached up, took her brother's rough hand in hers and guided him to take a seat in a nearby chair. She put her head against his leg and sighed as her eyes followed the faded bruises and shrinking welts oddly placed on the young, smooth skin of the boy lying next to them. They read like the manic sheet music of hell's anthem.

"I'm gettin' so tired of all the trouble, Spence. And this ain't the end of it, neither. We don't have any choice with this boy. We need to do right by him. They're on to 'im now…, they're such a wretched lot…. They want a response from you, Spence. And if they don' git it, they'll hunt him just for sport even if he does quit the game."

"How did you know he was playin'? I thought he hadn't spoke yet."

"I was with him jus' 'fore it happened. We visited for a time. He's a good boy, Spence. Easy talker, has a real heart. That's hard to find 'round here. He didn't want to tell me some things, but somewhere 'long the line he learned not ta fib to a lady."

Drake smiled inside, in spite of everything, thinking Devon's values must have rubbed off on the kid, but it was a positive short-lived.

"I feel out of control, Avi. I don't like it. I feel trapped, backed into a corner. And I led him right into it with me."

His eyes turned dark. The wrinkles flanking them creased, spreading out like rays from a midnight sun. She wanted so to help him….

"You did what ya thought best at the time, Spence."
…But he sank even lower….

"Damn, Avi! I'm bound to hurt the people I—I guess that I love. Ever since Emma…I can't take it. I can't take anymore…."

The depth of pain in his eyes, the restriction of his throat as he tried to speak—they were things that wrenched severely at her own heart. She remembered Emma. Or rather, Emma through his eyes—the way they could take in nothing else in a room but her. Just as soon as that girl entered it, they'd shine…, they'd follow her every move…, they'd smile at her slightest attempt at humor, at her most finite subtleties of which only he was aware. They held a timeless hue of enlightened joy when his mind was filled with the mere thought of her—a look that had been unduplicated since her end. She looked now, finding not one ounce of recognition for the way he was back then.

Avi mustered up enough calming, direct strength in her voice for both of them.

"You gotta follow your heart, Spence. That's all ya can do."

"I don't think I have one anymore, Avi…."

And she almost caught herself silently agreeing.

"But about you…, you be careful, ya hear? Use your head. Don't get lax about nothin', like the back door…, it was unlocked again, Avi…. I have a feelin', well I don't know…maybe I'm just uneasy about the boy here, but I have a feelin' things might git out 'a hand—for us all. It's been too long…. Luck can't stay on our side forever. And if you ever feel worried, if you ever feel things ain't right and I'm not around, you let Doc know what's goin' on. If it comes to the point they think they need to move you someplace, you go. Understand…? I'll never forgive myself. For Lemn here…. And should anything ever happen to you or Mama…."

Avi reached over to squeeze his hand, knowing he could not go on. She found herself wondering, yet again, who *they* were exactly…….*If they think they need to move you….* She'd like to come face to face with this ghost of *They*—the one she could feel tugging at the reins strapped to her runaway life.

Her thoughts blended into the icy glare ahead, beyond the blinding white of Drake's victimized and perpetually hostile eyes as they stared straight through her. Glimpses of a shadow started to bleed out from behind them—the watercolor shadows forming a different man. And she hoped it was not as it seemed…. But how could she know for sure?

Avi's safety, more so than her mother's, had weighed on him over the years. Constantly. But he had always kept his fears to himself. He'd never spoken of it until now. Never uttered a word of his misery but for these: lines of worry trenched crudely across his sagging face of clay—each night seemingly yielding yet another mark; the sharp tone of uneasiness wrestling with the soft flesh of intention surrounding his carefully chosen words, cracking through his warm sounding voice as if he were choking on jagged sheets of ice when he spoke of her and her liberty; and, of a dream, the protective forcefulness in the grip on her arm as she was blindly dangling one foot over, daring the vertical depths of death's edge—the century-footed cliff colored to mismatch his eyes only, for she, and all the rest..., were blind to it. But for these unforgettable things that defined her her brother, she wouldn't have known there was such a difference...in color. It was she who chose to believe that difference was good.

She smiled up at him. He squeezed her hand and smiled back in relief, though he wasn't entirely sure what for. Avi hadn't seen him truly smile in years. The wrinkles, settled in lazily across his face, sprang out flat in surprise. They scrambled in disarray, attempting to frame the expression, but were too late. Avi watched as the years just fell from his flesh like withered leaves. Invisible life had been stirring inside that dormant tree all along.

Dormant for a season. And seasons change.

.   .   .

And Avi was a believer. Who believed in the sanctity of life. Who respected its enigmatic ease. Should someone ask her directly, she'd tell them..., *one cannot hurry it, cannot discover its lessons ahead of schedule....* And she'd freely add, *that is why there is a command to judge not, for what is one judging but a process....* But like many, if not most, her gift, the true genius, remained locked inside, slowly drifting from her and away. But Life. She believed, however long, makes people who they were meant to be from the beginning, even if they're unaware of it all, even if they fight it every step of the way. It is much like a sculptor and His clay....

And of this belief, objectively reflected upon his skin, she prayed.... She prayed that her brother would see beyond his own frustration, his own exhaustion of failing to protect the seemingly vulnerable, for he was failing not by intent, but by Design..., a holy design that only angels are assigned.... She prayed he would come to value individuality..., freedom paths. See clear through it all and all loss, to the significance of caring while there is chance. Length of chance, length of stay, timed only by the Creator. She hoped he would become a father. Like the one he never had himself, but always dreamed of. She knew the boy lying beside them, outrunning his chance, his life..., would need one.

.   .   .

.

Drake rose slowly as if his joints were coated with a scabrous rust. When he
had steadied himself, he assisted Avi to her feet. The pair stood silently, watching reverently as Lemn took in shallow breaths, small and nearly nonexistent
like those of a newborn baby—so fragile, so soft that a cry would be preferable
to the disquieting peacefulness. As they exited the room, as gloomy and still as
an undertaker's parlor, Avi turned to shut the door. Her expression suddenly
broke mood as she winked and flashed a quick smile toward the boy who
thought he'd been spying covertly. Avi knew he was listening the entire time.
He was left to question why she had not tried to keep the personal conversation more private.

As Avi released the cool doorknob, Spencer's tangle of words remained
humming in her memory, growing progressively more specious amidst the
silence hovering between them. She was content…, she couldn't say she was-
n't…. Lemn was recovering rapidly, Spence was coming around, Mama was
healthy…, but of the question of she, the happiness seeped into blandness. She
began to feel its murkiness invade her persona. It tore at the weakened roots of
her unstable identity, threatening to crack her false air of confidence that was
built on shady ground prepared for her feet long ago. She had never been
afraid to tunnel through her history, to look down, she was just unsettled by
the fact that she could never grasp what held her—she couldn't see it. And so
hers evolved as not just a simple fear of the unknown, but as an acute anticipation of her own logically suspected ruin lying somewhere in the midst of her
future life. It lurked in the trenches of her soul, bringing the same old questions to surface with its uninvited daunting, continuous shoveling, eternal
chipping away…. Its presence became thorn-like…, infectious. *Is my life really
my own? Or is there someone else, something else, keeping me alive? And why do
I resent it so? Why won't it settle…?*
Avi had never been entirely sure what it was that kept her and her mother
safe. It forced her time and time again to ignore the chills racing up and down
her spine when she heard or saw another kindred soul brandished under the
White Hand professing Faith as it came down. In this world, that spun a million different directions around her, she couldn't trust what she couldn't still
with touch.

.   .   .

From that first hectic, panic-filled day, Mama was adamant that Avi drag her
favorite rocker into Lemn's room. Immediately. And perch it claustrophobically
close to his bed. But she didn't use it…. (Oddly, he would come to find the

closeness of it comforting and the incessant squeak to it, soothing. It lulled him into wonderful, protected sleep night after night, carrying on the steady and fluid rhythm of someone's eyes scanning over him, in distinct time with some-one's breath drawing in, drawing out—carefully matching each of his own. He was warm, he was wrapped securely, he was held tightly while an angel sang that lost melody older than his memory. The feeling of all this…, even when an internal tremble shook him awake to the sounds that stopped as soon as his unsettled gaze proved the chair unoccupied,…was enough.) Rather, she waited several days, then dusted its vacancy with her swaying hand—never touching its surface, before she sat down in it herself. The heavyset woman, topped with peppery hair turning saltier by the day, began to protest peacefully, refusing to let Lemn get up and on with his young life just yet.

"Young'uns is alway' in such a hurry to get on wit' they lives. Boy, someday, you'll wonder why it wen' so fast—thas why—'cuz everybody in such a hurry when they young."

Lemn was instantly reassured by her warm, inviting voice—then it snagged him. It drew him in and locked his attention deep inside her sparkling eyes while they read his soul. It was a strange feeling but one void of fear…he felt her draw out his own breath and refuse to give him another. Her warm hands were planted firmly, almost harshly, on either side of his dough-soft face, forc-ing his gaze to stay steady—but they really weren't there at all. He only *felt* them there. What he *knew* was that her hands were at rest, folded politely on her lap the entire time. And her eyes, set deep in her dark, weathered face…he read things there, about her, too. Of this she took note behind a raised eye-brow, then released her supernatural hold. He took a deep, calming breath like a nervous but contented boy after his very first kiss.

How amazingly refreshing…to find a blessed outlet for the churning essence everyone contains but can't quite reach—growing pearls locked in rigid shells held down under the weight of the world, we are.

His Spirit…. Like a stalled horse let loose in a springtime field, its legs scrambled, found rhythm and stretched. Beautifully….

To him, she seemed to be the type of elder who had seen it all, but still had the ability to embrace and encourage life, especially in someone young—and that took endurance, he figured. And compassion. And the way she interacted with Avi made him recognize a traversable bond more massive than that of mother and daughter. He suspected he hadn't seen the last of it, either. And the pain…. Before she broke it off with him, he had tasted just the surface of it. He couldn't believe that she still carried on.

She still carried on because this is who she was….

She had an intricate wisdom trickling delicately down through her like droplets of blood—where it came from she did not know, but she felt the pain and saw the odd color of proof when it escaped her. Quietly, humbly, by a power not her own, she'd know more about a stranger in five minutes than they'd ever know about themselves. She was a Reader. A Dreamer. An Oracle. While she used her gift to try to help others, the knowledge she possessed wasted her own life to an equivalent extent, therefore she breathed shallow in the top of her heavy bosom. Her joints cracked. Her body dragged behind her frame in constant, nagging complaint. Her old heart stumbled in place and was weary. You see, she could look into the soul.

And what she found there had three lives—the mind, the heart, the spirit.

And, oh, the things she saw….

Could be as merciless to its own as a three-headed beast—could it reach, it'd rip itself to bloody shreds with its gnashing teeth, but it's cursed, perhaps blessed, for it can't. So it continues to struggle, fighting its own nature, breathing vengeance, breeding torment during its wretched days.

Could fall into a pit of something else during that struggle. Viperous and low only to look up, then. Only to look up and see that the sky still hovers. Still watches over and accepts. And then there's the climb. The climb that takes every limb.

And that's the thing she lived for.

You see, she could see the whole mind, every subconscious, wandering tunnel of gluttonous addition and echo. She could hear the songs of the whole heart that sang of the pain and joy of counted beats lived, survived and passed. She could feel the measure of hope held there in silent lulls and waiting. And she could see the destiny planted in the spirit, the story written on the seed, the reason for being, the plan to be carried out before death. But these three roads of the soul, they often did not converge. The paths, instead, often wound their way into a twisted maze of darkness and confusion. But she could not alter them, nor shut up the logical lies of Satan.

You see, the soul has three lives—much like the Father, the Son, and the Holy Spirit.

And it is said, that for the Great God above to grant, the prayer must first be uttered from the lips of a body still walking the earth. So she prayed, not in tongues like the hopeful rest, but in words. In knowing. But she could not read God. This…this was her destiny. God placed her here to do what she did. And she paid the price for it. But every so often, an earthly reward would flood in. It lifted her spirits up and she found that she had toes that sprung out a dance as light and graceful as a feather floating on summer wind.

Today would be a day like that….

"Why you a gambler, boy?"

"Well, I guess I never thought about it much. My daddy died…, the farm's not makin' enough to live on, and my ma's not well, ma'am. Drake's helped me out a great deal by showin' me the ropes. Maybe I'll make enough to save our farm."

"But what good ya gonna be to yer mama dead, son?"

The question hung in the air like jagged icicles about to fall. The possibility that he might die before his mother had never occurred to him before.

"Not much, I reckon…. I guess I didn't know all this could happen just by bein' a gambler." Lemn's gaze scanned the handstitched quilts softly covering his mutilated body. For some reason, he was *so unbelievably cold*.

"Was yer daddy a gambler?"

And growing colder….

"No, ma'am. Daddy was a right good man—didn't agree with gamblin, drinkin', nothin," Lemn replied earnestly, not quite able to calm the shivers quivering up his throat. His teeth nearly broke into a nervous tap dance of chattering.

"What I'm sayin, boy, is you a righ' good man, too. Yer daddy din' go out a lookin' for trouble and he still dead. Neither did you go out a lookin', but ya gotta be smart when ya dealin' wit' the Evil cuz Evil's out fer anybody—me, you, yer daddy, yo' mama—don' mattah. It's out fer everybody, boy. The dif-f'rens is, you jus' *knows* you a lil' closer to IT then yer daddy *thought* he was—ya see, boy? Da Evil he come in many ways. Your mama git da evil in her min', others—well they's got the evil in they heart—make dey's core rotten. Puts a hole right through der," she said pounding her clenched fist to her chest, her voice taking on the sing-song intensity of a southern Baptist preacher.

"Das what them mens gots det come aftah you boy. You gotta be so smart, dealin' wit the evil—it take all shapes on dis earth. Smart mind and good heart thas op'n ta listen to the sweet Lord—thas yer key, boy. Smart c'n be fast, quick—wit' the practicin' to su'vive or it can be slow, layin' down playin' dead, actin' like you never be no harm, no harm. It ain't pretty—givin' a piece of yaself here ta dis' evil, there ta dat evil, but you mind dis, boy—da winners out-last—they outlast. They outlast dat evil, boy. You outlast it, Ya HEAR Boy? You outlast it, you d'feats it, boy—Praaaiiise Sweet Jesus—He hear me singin'. You outlastit, outlastit, boy, yous outlastit, praise JESUS, praise HIM! Yes, Jesus. YES, SWEE' JEEESUS!!!"

She finished her last phrase out in the hall as she twirled in bird-like circles, heavy-laden arms outstretched, now shameless and free. She might as well have been out on the open prairie with nothin' but simple Creation lookin', with that blanket of baby-blue sky dancing just past her fingertips, spinning gently closer and closer till she could reach out and, just like that, touch the entire universe.

Because she did.

Her voice trailed after her and riveted through every fiber of his being and he knew, if there ever was tell of it, that God's voice channeled directly through this woman like a tunnel pointed straight down from Heaven and he listened. He listened hard. He forever wanted to remember the frame of mind she intro-duced him to. All the crushing guilt, stemming from the fear of letting his par-ents down by making his own way, lifted off of his chest and he could finally breathe. He was first a child of God, after all.

And the fresh air that was God filtered through everywhere—even the smokey saloons, he knew. And God would bid His own reckoning.

.   .   .

It was that very night, he had a dream as the empty chair went on with its rocking....

She said, "Why you a gambler, boy?"

And he said, without excuse or hesitation, "Because it's in my blood."

And she smiled through shining eyes. And she nodded with her head full of wisdom. And she uttered, "Dat's right, boy. You got it right...."

Chapter Five

You need to do the right thing....

That didn't even *sound* good. It bumped sharp and foreign against the corners of his mind and was, frankly, giving him a hell of a headache. But he watched on as his own body lumbered through the motions of doing the right thing—like a hungry fly stuck in molasses, he'd brought this all on himself. He climbed Mama's staircase laboriously, on his way to ask Lemn if he was ready to visit his mother. *Dear, sweet Anne....* He almost felt remorse for the stream of sarcasm dripping off his inner voice...*Well, no I don't, not really.* Because he knew her blame would ripple through to him and it would land like a wagon load of bricks on top of the smothering pile of curses already befallen him—curses hurled from his own lips as sharply and mercilessly as a public stoning. And he would be commanded to give her an explanation which, of course, wouldn't be near good enough surrounded by the guilt stricken tone of his voice.

It was to Drake's veiled relief when Lemn immediately drew back from the question like it was a lit explosive. The boy simply wasn't prepared to witness the atrocious state his mother would be in—her vehemence fueled with anger and whatever else had possessed her lately. Lemn's hands were full managing the changes in his own life—he couldn't handle hers, too.

Lemn didn't want to admit it, but he'd begun to have a taste of the reasoning behind Drake's frequent departures. There was something to be said about the freedom of moving from one place to the next at your own whim. It had to be easier than facing constant pain and guilt associated with the people you loved—that you loved, sometimes, too much.

Drake heard Lemn's thoughts as clearly as if the boy had spoken them.

"You just stay here and rest a few more days. I'll ride out there and tell her yer okay, at least. It'll be fine. Don't worry 'bout that."

Drake didn't get up even when the conversation was clearly over. He stayed seated, as if he could rest in Mama's rocker for a year or better, comfortably hidden from life. He studied the boy. His skin color was richer, warmer, and he seemed more at peace with himself—certainly carried less guilt about Anne.... Drake figured a speech from Mama might have had something to do with it. *Good for him....* He'd rather duke it out with Anne in private, anyhow. The boy had seen enough of her mess, he was sure.

He turned to gaze out the window, watching a willow tree sway in the mild gusts like a pendulum in a sturdy, consistent clock. He wished life could be that way—boring, safely predictable. He thought,...*Must be what Heaven is like.*

"If ya don't mind my askin', Drake, how'd you all become family and why don't you live here with 'em?

A moment of silence passed before Drake gave a reply.

"It's a long story boy, with some details I don't think you ought to hear just yet. I don't mind your askin'. I'm sure that's a question on everybody's mind that at least you got the guts to speak out direct. Most just make up their own story. I've worked real hard tryin' ta keep my life a secret. I've misguided people for the purpose of survival."

"Yes, sir."

"You just rest. Try not to think about nothin' while you got the chance, boy."

Drake smiled a tired, uneasy smile and held it there a little too long. The lines of that expression told Lemn of the weariness coming up soon enough for him—the weariness blanketing the decisions forced upon a man. It was the kind of grueling sentence Drake had to escape when a town got too suffocating for him to think.

Or even breathe.

·   ·   ·

He sat still and steady, but for the waves of subtle breathing below him. He was dressed in black to blend as one with his horse and together they formed a pocket of darkness in the folds of swaying prairie. Like a senseless shadow in the bright, open sunlight, they hovered confidently as if they belonged there and had since the start of time. An unsuspecting eye would definitely have to look twice and focus long. But the cabin seemed to be staring right back, playing their game of frozen pose and winning. Or maybe it was someone inside the cabin, staring. Tiny hairs blanketing the scruff of his neck took notice, he could feel them rise almost one by one. It was a sure signal he was in line with someone's sights. But Anne wouldn't…couldn't possibly…. He was simply being ridiculous. So he urged his horse on, swallowing that familiar twinge rising up from his belly—he **never** ignored that feeling, the one that ever so slightly whispers that warning of possibility. The possibility of death. But this time, he did ignore it. He forced his only—and last—exception.

As he rode nearer, he couldn't divert his eyes from the loneliness swirling at the base of that barn, an unforgettable song still echoing its chills. There was no voice now, no Devon inside or around. Instead of pitching hay, milking the cow or harnessing the horses like he should have been, he was six feet under in that damn hole. The only thing left of him was that horrible stone marker. Drake knew it was up there in front of him somewhere, but he refused to let himself look. His heart sank, instead, into the middle of the barn as he watched a mirage of his transparent old friend wave enthusiastically, drop the pitchfork and jog up to greet him with a warm smile. But the image soon faded like fog lifting from a cold world, an early morning memory leaving only the bland background of the scene for reality. The emptiness was dry as dirt and Drake felt like giving up himself—meeting Devon in some other realm. But with a will not his own, his chin slowly lifted toward the house where a life still existed. That shivering warning, that gut feeling, quickly returned, but he knew Devon would want him to look out for her. His horse took dust stirring steps—Drake wished they would last an eternity—toward the porch. He dismounted with that uneasy feeling shouting now, grinding roughly against the pit of his upset stomach. He noticed the shake to his hands as he clumsily looped the rein loosely around the porch railing. The steps that struck him surreal in their existence loomed ahead of him. He tested their reality and strength with a tap of his foot before he trusted them with his entire weight.

In Remembrance….
A person lives their life striving to leave something behind. Something to be remembered by. And, often, it is that very thing that stares down the heart and presses pain from all the remaining days of their dearest survivor….

He knocked three times and waited a moment.

"Anne?"

There was no response.

"It's Drake, Anne. May I come in?"

Drake's mind slowly wrapped around the odd hue of his surroundings. Then the picture gripped him inside of itself and was sealed. He was a part of it and would be forever. His heart started to race—*Not a chicken in the yard, or a cat, not a single bird in any tree.* He'd never been in a place so starkly quiet—abandoned by *every* living thing. He had been so engrossed in memories…he felt like kicking himself for being so unobservant. There wasn't a single track, human or other-wise, in the dirt other than those he just made. No laundry was hanging in the breeze. Not a single animal around the barn…. *How could I not have noticed that…?* His knees went weak and an overwhelming feeling of consequence com-ing fired up in his churning stomach and was spreading up through his lungs like a blistering fever. It was ready to seize his heart with panic when he felt his ears straining for a sound—a single sound, the tiniest sound imaginable.

"Lullaby. And good night. Hum, hum, hum, hum—hum, hum, hum…"

(*buzzz-buzzz-hummmmm*…You t-t-take my b-baby an'
I'll k-k-kill you, y-you piece of t-trash-sh-sh. *buzzz-hummmmm*…I said,
G-G-GET OUT OF HERE!!!! *buzzz-buzzz-buzzzzz*…D-DADDY??? W-
W-Where d-d-did you p-put my D-Daddy? *hummmmm*….)

He recognized the faint noise as a tune, a soothing song he'd heard some-where in his past. Relief washed over him…. At least there was life.

He knocked quietly again, then opened the door ever so cautiously. He had to command his instincts to silence themselves—the ones feverishly whisper-ing for him to draw his gun. At that exact thought, something suddenly over-took him, not the sound of gunfire or the threat of violence, but a horrible *smell.* A heavy, engulfing stench that forced his body to wilt back a step in reflex. He had to push through its thick potency clinging to the air and as he did, oddly, the humming did not falter with his entrance. The only other sound in the room was the creaking of the wooden rocker on the planked floor.

"Anne…? **Annie!!**"

She did not respond. The woman seemed to be in a trance, fixated on a bundle held captive in her arms. She did not give any outward sign of the deafening, maddening reverberation shaking her brain with an intensity nearly rattling down through her teeth. Not a single indication or physical trace of the voracious cancer of voice and past taking over the corroded valleys of her mind like a wind fueled fire.

> (*hummm*...Y-Y-You c-commin' ta g-get him?? I-I'll kill you...*buzz, hummm*.... It-t's s-so LOUD in h-h-h-here! W-W-What are th-th-those n-noises....can't...think......my h-head hurt-t-ts. St-st-st-studd-d-d-dering...*buzz, buzz, buzz*.... T-T-Take it aw-w-way, t-take it away...away...take it-t-t!!! *buzz*.... I d-d-don't want to c-come out! Y-you can't t-t-take my b-baby, can't t-take m-my b-baby!!! *buzz, hummm*.... S-S-STOP THAT NOISE!!! I-I-I CAN'T-T B-BREATHE IN H-HERE!!! I-I CAN'T T-TAKE N-NO MORE!!! *buzz, hummm*....)

"What the..."

Drake had never laid eyes on a catatonic person, other than one he'd just shot. He wondered if she had been injured so he crept closer to her, scanning for blood while trying to determine what she was crudely coddling like a newborn baby. Suddenly, he ran into the source of the stink like a brick wall—it was wafting off of her in droves. Apparently, she had not been tending to her bodily functions and had soiled herself in a dress that he estimated she must have had on for better than a week. In all probability, she hadn't moved from the chair in as long, either.

He covered his nose and mouth with his bandana and sat down at the table contemplating his next move as he watched her under the rotating lighting of horror, then disbelief, and back.

His presence remained unacknowledged.

A low, terrified howl—almost in the tone of a question—dared to cry out from deep inside the bundle in her arms, perhaps it sensed an avenue of rescue. Drake lunged toward the source and pulled it free from her grasp in one swift movement. He stepped quickly onto the porch to get the creature some fresh air. He slowly opened the top of the cocoon of baby blankets and a barn cat peered out squinting in the bright sunlight. Drake turned to cast a quick glance toward Anne—she remained transfixed—then let the cat down to safety. It slowly wobbled out, sweat-streaked from the warm blankets and then, at the hint of freedom, took off running for the barn with such frantic speed that it startled his horse. Drake gazed back into the darkness of the house, stunned at Anne's bizarre behavior. She sat stiff as a rail with her arms held out in front of her, empty. The rocking had stopped, but she still hadn't noticed him. Hadn't noticed much of anything.

The cat's pitiful state prompted Drake on toward the other animals. He wandered to the barn in a mixed state of heightened cautiousness and dulling shock. He opened the large barn door afraid of what he might find. At his sight, the animals instantly started bleating and lowing with calls of hunger. He found himself teary-eyed from the rising ammonia as he pitched them some hay, found some grain for them and started carrying buckets to the well for water. *I should have come sooner. I should have figured as much from her....* From what he could tell, they were going to survive although they were extremely hungry and the pens and stalls were filthy. They were in a condition not unlike their caretaker's except their minds seemed in tact, at least. He opened up the Dutch doors of the barn to allow the animals the freedom to venture into the corral.

As he finished up the chores, he contemplated what to do for his best friend's wife. He could call on others for help but he sincerely hoped she would snap to her senses soon, saving herself the shame she would eternally torture herself with knowing others had witnessed her in such a disgraceful condition. He looked toward the motionless house and realized how much the house itself had aged. Although not much more than twelve years old, the weeds, sagging shudders and unrepaired roof made it look like it had been abandoned for years. It was as if the house knew of the emptiness inside and it refused to shelter pain for very much longer.

As Drake started back toward it, he noticed his horse was very rigid—unusually tense. Just then, the animal turned his head and tossed it nervously in Drake's direction then looked back to the house with full attention, the loose rein pulled tight. At that very second Drake realized he was in trouble, that he should have secured the Rileys' gun, but was too late in action to change the course of reality. Glass cracked and he felt the first shot invade his flesh as he dove for the ground and rolled under the nearby wagon. The shot wasn't fatal. In fact, he could hardly feel it. It had passed through surface flesh. He held his oozing side with one hand and drew his pistol with the other. He spit grains of dirt from his mouth while he considered the situation. Killing a woman would mean breaking the oath he made with himself. Killing Devon's wife...well, he might as well turn the gun on himself as live with that. He found he had no better plan than to stay put and breathe. As he ducked his head and took a deep breath he noticed that damn tombstone staring right at him. He could only manage a quick roll of his eyes before he focused back toward the house. He watched the black streak of horse and tail and dust thundering down the road and he hoped his stars were lined up, that help would come in time. *Godspeed, Sky....*

Anne sauntered off the porch like a risen cadaver rambling through a grim nightmare. Her arms were stretched out, feeling the air, groping as if she were blinded by the unfamiliar rays of sunlight. She meandered toward the wagon while aiming the revolver recklessly at passing entities only her imagination could see, cursing at them as she staggered along like an angry drunk leaving the saloon after an unlucky run of poker and a quart of bad whiskey. Suddenly, she glared in the direction of the wagon, as if the cause of her pain had just become crystal clear, and her gait took on more directness. Drake steadied his aim, ready to put a lead ball in her leg to stop her. It was his only choice. Mid-stride, she seemed to instantly change her course of anger and directed it at God instead and her aim followed. After she unloaded into the sky, she fell in a heap of rage, beating the ground like a spoiled child in a terrible tantrum. Drake ran to her and picked her up by the arms, ready to restrain her if needed. He tried to shake her to reality but she just fell limp and sobbed the most desperate sobs he had ever heard. *Keening—that's what Devon would have called it....*

He couldn't think of what to say, but his first concern was Lemn and his words tumbled out absentmindedly. He shouted them during the ebbing between her sobs. "Let's get you fixed up, Anne! Your boy is waiting...for his mother!"

"My boy??? I don't have a boy, you worthless sonofabitch!!!" she lashed out at him in a slur, screaming at the top of her lungs, spit flying in his face.

"*Lemn*, Anne?" Drake pleaded, searching her eyes for someone or—thing he recognized.

Her tone got deathly quiet and just as serious. She leaned in close to him and hissed....

"You killed him, didn't you. You took him away from me. You killed my husband first so you could kill my boy. Then me.... Don't think I don't know who you really are, you worthless bastard. It's all your fault, you've taken everything from me so go ahead! Go ahead and kill me—that's what you want, isn't it?"

He released his hold on her like she was a human vat of infectious poison. Her body slid to the ground like liquid as waves of sobs overtook her then seeped into the bland grey of the thirsty sand. Drake had happened upon many tragedies in his lifetime, but he had no idea how to stop a war inside a single, broken person. He'd never been able to stop the one raging on inside himself. He felt annoyed, angry, saddened and guilty all at the same time as he stared down at her. Slight tears leaked from his eyes as if he were attending a funeral, only this was the most hopeless sight he had ever witnessed—someone who still had a chance to live but didn't want it.

He couldn't help but wish Emma could have Anne's body somehow, could overtake her wasted chance at life. Emma wasn't ready to leave when they took her. And Emma was the only person who didn't make him feel worthless—he knew she never thought that of him, not once. He envisioned the body down at his feet rising up and revealing Emma's face, Emma's eyes, Emma's smile— thankful to be back…reaching up to him….

"I miss you, Emma."

He closed his eyes, felt the breeze, turned his face toward it, and knew what Emma would want him to do. He opened his eyes slowly. And as they focused, he realized he was looking directly at it—Devon's tombstone. He didn't turn away this time, didn't roll his eyes. Instead, he cried for his friend. Cried for him through Anne's tears.

She laid there sobbing at Drake's feet—her tear-streaked face collecting a thin blanket of dust and mud—until she was comatose with exhaustion. Her sunken waist and slightly protruding spine led him to believe that she had not eaten for weeks. He half-carried, half-drug her soiled body into the house and commenced to open windows, stoke a fire, warm some water for a bath. He undressed her, forcing himself to continue after each gagging response triggered from the engulfing stench and the appalling sight, both inescapable if he was to finish the task. He bathed her, dressed her in a cotton nightshirt, then encouraged her to drink some fresh water. Against the protest of his own pain, he held her limp frame upright in the bed, but the water trickled obstinately out of the corner of her mouth as blood oozed from his side. Her head rolled and snapped cruelly as it reached the extent of her thin neck, bobbing like a daisy lolling around on the top of a wilted stem, succumbing to the breeze with diffidence, no longer beautiful as intended. She fell asleep while still leaning against his arm. He quickly covered her with blankets then commenced to burn her soiled clothes as he knew help would be coming soon. He didn't want them to discover just how bad her condition had been. He boiled water to sterilize cotton cloths. They dried rapidly over the fire and he layered them carefully over his wound. He found an old shirt of Devon's to slide on and he tossed his blood-stained one in the flames. As it unraveled and seared beyond recognition he thought, *No one need know about that either.*

At the execution of that thought, Doc and Avi came charging down the road at a hell-for-leather pace, with a rumbling force backing them, equaled to that of a thousand angels. "Poor Avi." Drake spoke aloud as he watched them approach with jaws set like steel under urgent expressions, joints fixated in postures so rigid they were floating over the wagon rather than riding on it. "You spend the core of your existence trying to save me. And for what return…. For what return, Avi…?"

He watched them approach and, as if looking through a picture album of their lives, he reviewed the many times he had seen Avi's face twisted in worry, her determination voluntarily chipping pieces away from her own life in an effort to construct his: the first time they met…she was such a small child and she found him digging through restaurant scraps under the stairwell on the street like a stray dog—only an innocent child would have shunned fear for compassion when she decided to bring him home to ask Mama to help him…he thought it was worth a shot, although no one had helped him in six-teen years, including church-goers (*Maybe Negroes are different from the rest of folk,* he remembered thinking); when she found him beaten up after coming out the "winner" of many fights; when she learned, wide-eyed and breathless with awe-struck concern, how much cash he could bring home from one night of playing; when Emma died….

"Spence…? Spence!?"

"It's okay, Avi. I'm alright," he winked to soften her inquisitiveness about his arm held tightly against his side.

"Avi saw your horse come a chargin' straight through town, son. Ya gotta quit frettin' us so. We thought today was the day you might not 'a been so lucky."

"Cat scared 'im off. But I'm not the one that needs the frettin' Doc. Anne's in a bad way. Somethin's just not the same about her and I know she can't stay here by 'erself."

"Do you think seein' Lemn would help her? We could put her up in the other bedroom," Avi offered hastily.

"Well, maybe not just yet…." Doc took the liberty granted by seniority and thought for a long, unapologetic moment amidst silent respect. His aged fin-gers, knotted noticeably with stiff, swollen knuckles, stroked his chin then ceased, waiting in midair, as he shook his head. Those fragile hands had healed so much. "I don't know if that would be good for Lemn. With what the boy's been through…I'll keep her at my place just for a couple days for observations and so forth."

"Thanks Doc." Drake had become so concerned about masking Anne's severity, hoping she would wake to her senses, that he hadn't considered his own demeanor. He instantly scolded himself, embarrassed and threatened by the sweat collecting on his brow like a rookie at a poker table—a dead giveaway. Its source had been flawlessly concealed, tucked neatly in the folds of second nature for years, but never mastered in this type of circumstance. *Never been this transparent except when Emma….* He forced the thought to delete itself and looked to find a reason for his current weakness….*Must be the loss of blood.*

"Just glad it's not you, son," Doc smiled and patted him on the shoulder, knobby fingers clenching with a surprisingly fierce grip, deliberately testing for pain, but Drake pressed his teeth together like a vise and didn't wince.

They loaded Anne into the back of the wagon and Drake watched as the empty farm swallowed the day's events down with distance. The diminishing animals in the corral concurrently looked up in thankfulness as the wagon turned the bend. Drake nodded acknowledgment toward the animals' expressions that he believed were intended, in part, from the two protective souls left hovering there.

Chapter Six

"Lemn…? Son, wake up. I'm afraid I've got some bad news. It's your ma—she's not doin' too good. When I found her…, well, she hadn't eaten or cared for herself in a while. The animals weren't looked after either. But Doc's got her at his place now and he's gonna make it better for her. What do you suppose we should do with the livestock? They need to be tended to and if you're not feelin' up to it, then…"

Gushing his words like liquid, Drake would have sold his soul and let it go cheap if only he could drown the shakiness in his damnable voice. His speech was swift, erratic and slurred like his heart was beating in his mouth. His mind had difficulty monitoring what he was saying…. He felt like a fool.

He wanted—*so* wanted—to force the chill in his message beyond the boy's senses. He didn't want him to grasp it fully—the shock, the brilliance—he would have preferred it otherwise…, gushing blood of the sixth sin diluted to scrape and washed downstream. As nothing. Nothing at all. For when one dies, in the event of it, colors blend, they brighten to blinding. Momentum flies, swings with the force reserved to turn the world, everything rushes by, then through and the essence within is suddenly gone…. But on that day, he only felt death moving—restless, exhaling breath of disappointment…. It had passed by him, this time, as a magic rainbow of wind, it blew close enough that his own senses were humbled with everything heightened in its prism and, in his entire drab lifetime, missed…, somehow, thankfully. The experience, witnessed this side, provided him a valid excuse to fear its return. It was awesome, made one left behind shaky in skin and unstable of mind, at the very least. It was the image of these phenomenal things, and the reason for their summoning, he desired to keep from Lemn…, should he not have to second-guess the level of his own sanity so early, should he not have to visualize his mother with a gun, wandering beneath the splintered sun…, the sheer hell she raised falling in behind her, there, open jawed and awaiting the backlash….

If only…. He thought if he could only sashay around its fullness with grace, minimize the weight of impact with eloquence and ease, he would not have to grapple with a series of glazed over explanations on Anne's behalf. He didn't have any anyhow, not today. He didn't trust himself. And he didn't much question the why of it. He only knew he could not cover Anne under the kid's eyes, not for long…. For it was under the light in those soft eyes that even an unholy man could swear he'd seen the very color of Omniscience. It was warm and calm and yet moving on. It was a flaming rich but pure amber sparkling and seeping through the jewel-cut slits of chestnut brown like glints off the universal sun. It was similar to all that he saw that illusory day…, it was a suffocating place for dishonesty to be found creeping and low.

There were days Drake truly hated himself. Days he detested his birth.

And, as if to claim this day as such, an autonomous memory stepped up in Drake's ear and took liberty to whisper its twofold opinion, uninvited words leaving more questions than answers. She said, *You cain't never tell what kinda repulsions might come out a mouth with that much hatred pushin' 'gainst soft gut like black disease.* He weakly figured, then and now, he best not open his and find out…. How his mind had preserved her words so perfectly was a mystery to him—no taint, no distortion…. Could he have admitted it to himself—just once, in his entire lifetime—he would have admitted it here. For it was his mother's voice, rambling on to another girl while she was braiding her thick hair…, she was referring to the blue-eyed man who would later bring her end. The blue-eyed man…, mirrored to Drake with more reflections than these….

He couldn't stomach the contrast today, the contrast so evident between Lemn and he. He felt the bloodless gap…. His libelous, illiterate tongue licking libations from the timeless vessels of the saints…, wine, to an alcoholic, does not resemble Remembrance…. His polluted breath, let loose, coughing up seeds of corruption beneath the golden blanket of purity and light shining down. He listened to his mother's words again, took the blow they delivered like a grown-up—hitting his knees only inside…in the darkest place he could find. No, he would not admit it. Ever. That man wasn't his father, was nothing like him at all….

Drake knew death had seen him…, liked what it saw…, it'd be back for him. Soon. And even knowing this, Drake could not seem to salvage his chances. Couldn't seem to decide what, exactly, was righteous….

Lemn watched the turmoil rotating inside the man's mind, boiling the cool air sick and black-green like a High-Plains twister comin' down to dance. They were threatening, those unpredictable storms of Drake's…, could cause a lot of destruction if given a sliver off chance. The electric ebb and flow about the room seemed zinging on the guestimate of weaker bone, last-minute proof of the vulnerability in luck, but Lemn remained still as it rumbled on over.

"Drake…." Lemn paused and let the directness in his quiet voice bring Drake's attention back. And his voice sliced through the emotion, dispersed it, smooth and easy as warm butter spread on a lazy afternoon biscuit. "I'm gettin' better now. What happened with Ma isn't your fault. I'll go an' look after the place. It's time I went home anyhow."

The warmth of his own voice matched the safe comfort of sleep that had not yet evaporated from his being. Hell's bells had fallen imperfect and late, not yet clanging out the summons, so smugness and guilt still lay asleep at the foot of the bed. He couldn't help the way he felt, there under that blanket of security, one heartbeat ahead of the torments assigned his life. If only for the moment, he felt free. Realized the possibility that every socially shunned human notion may not be a sin…. He found the truth revealed, then. The truth of the lingering prediction of his mother's collapse…, it provided him with the unusual feeling of self-assuredness, the kind of unembellished pride that fulfilled prophecy delivers in those peaceful moments before modesty suggests mere coincidence. Before guilt condemns. Were his spiritual persecutors punctual, he wouldn't have breathed a single breath of naturalness his entire life. Never tasted the fruit of a serpentless Eden. He would never have known there was a difference.

This moment of freedom…, it was only a moment. But pure enough to last him….

When it passed by, he was oblivious to the changes that ensued amidst its distraction. Perhaps he should have noticed that his heart skipped a beat while his maturity advanced. That someone had moved him up in rank. Stuck the honorary pin into his skin. Perhaps he should have noticed he was marked. That the watching eyes of the world no longer looked upon him as a boy.

Perhaps he should have noticed the onset of the end.

·   ·   ·

Was it a holy distraction, his moment of serenity? A gift. A glitch. A tactic. A maneuver in favor of the peaceful side of the war? Perhaps, yes. Perhaps it was for the best that he did not notice…, for there are some things lurking out there.

Things for which human perception is not designed....

.   .   .

While he studied the concern draped across Drake's face, he got lost in the traversable lines there. The persuasive current of them pulled him beneath, bounced his mind along like a loose pebble under the river. He found himself being swept deeper into a sea of what Drake had seen, feeling like he was almost dreaming, floating, but with his eyes wide open. His body down, but ungrounded. He could see her. So plain, as if she were lying in his body's space on the bed and he had risen above it now. Her fire-red hair, while tame an apocalypse show of fierce color, was mussed and hellbent on angry rampage. Her worn clothes painted the room's air with the dank stench of her sorrow. That relentless rocking of hers continued like an inescapable song. A daylong cord struck and creeping in from the sea spirits' bagpipe, grating raw and tingling against the dry nerves of the brain. Sirens wailing, dancing with white flowing gowns atop foam covered rocks. They drew her in..., lighthouses of beckoning deception. Any hope of a boy's comfort was lost to the storm, squeaks and groans uttered not of structural sense. There it was coming..., the end. No promise of resurfacing did she give, and in those placid, sea-green eyes, no indication for him of soft shore....

The chair in his room was as still as her catatonic body but he felt it, somehow, as her brain continued rocking. With the waves. The bones buckled in his own neck, cracking with a pain such as hers—chipping joints down to sinking sand unable to hold up the weight of her skull and the worries within. He saw how she was. She matched perfectly with the segments that had conjured themselves up in his mind over a month ago, that unforgettable night, when the circle dropped.

Simplicity....
The wisdom of youthfulness is simplicity. So concurrent with the naturalness of gifts of being and blessing, that to reason internal notions into silence would appear the most childish form of ignorance.

And so it was clear, now, why God had told him to stay away....

As his body fell back into itself, he felt a slight chill strumming across it and it felt like the cold whisper of truth breathing down.

And It said….

The course of the river is hidden…
> from springtime water and light filling it.
> And the summer skipping stone,
>> Over stagnant winter's squander,
> is ceased by changing seasons' falls that we,
> somehow,
>> surface up from
>>> and survive
>>> to flow on.

Full circle…. He pondered it. The shape of the world. The path that it turns. He decided that the difference between those who die of body or of soul amidst the suffering and those who sustain beyond it, is in the desire of fulfillment of purpose for which each is destined by God to one day find. When it is finished, death be a peaceful dream.

…Hoop dance to eternal thunder, we glide on lightning, unburned and blazoning….

Lemn was comfortable with the nature of truth and life. The path to his purpose was well lit through his soul and he trusted it, leaned forward into it, as it led him through inevitable obscurity. Its comfort was its promise. Its promise, the reward of clarification upon completion. He respected the elusiveness of what everyone alive seeks after. It's like listening to the sheer color of sunrise, the taste of its vibrance impossible to summon. Some refuse to accept that they will never process the moment until it's become a memory. The expectation will go unmet until it is only a comparison. Life will not be understood until it chooses to explain. And, thusly, many struggle, exhausting themselves, trying to control the very essence of purity. But they will never grasp it until it is no longer, for it would be tainted, then, with touch. Lemn had watched people. Voyagers fighting the river. Travelers blocking their own way, studying and stumbling over a maze of angular trails around themselves rather than walking upright inside of themselves—one foot in front of the other, the heart then becomes a compass. The security is the constant feeling of going and being Home.
    —Not the perfection…, nor the ease, of path. Followed or blazed falls away irrelevant.

Drift along, the River will carry you as you are
and you shall come
full circle....

.   .   .

Drake waited, but there were no questions. He listened as his inner voice finished his rehearsed message in silence, its delivery intended to console a fragile boy who, by rights, shouldn't have been able to take much more. His stereotypical notions flaked away under the boy's direct gaze and the awesome, resilient spirit of youth—*or something more*—was left to stand between them. As Lemn continued to watch Drake with steady calmness, the man's shoulders softened permitting his frame to succumb to the comforting gravity of accepted insecurity. Drake continued to wait, but still there were no questions. In his recollection, he could not detect the tone of blame hidden under the waves of the boy's voice. In the stagnant silence, his yielding body forced out a deep breath that released itself, gently gliding through unclenching teeth. The wrinkles between his curious eyes evened out as the muscle behind them relaxed—youthful skin awakened, filling the dramatic gullies of frustration like gentle rain-washed sand seeking dry desert crevices. His entire mind flowed onto a smoother plane, fully relieved to be excused from a sprawling, rambling attempt to achieve the emotional maturity that this thirteen-year-old boy already seemed to have. It wasn't a lack of experience that made the kid innocent, it was the integrity he chose.

Drake, on the other hand, avoided internal choices. He had refused to deal with his own crucifixion—the guilt, sadness and shame—for so long, it had fallen away from him and left his shadow standing. But now it was resurrecting its wicked self. And knocking. Comin' ta get hisself. Again. Surprisingly, he wanted to experience—to go through, sacrifice to see, hold the bleeding hand of his other side, but he was stationary as stone. A connection with any emotion but anger had not been traversed for years. And his anger would not be allowed. Not now. *There's the boy to think about....*

But all the other roads leading out of his heart forced him to walk through *her* memory like a blood-saturated fog, a crimson cloud covering hollow ground. And he could not go there. So severed was his walk through that memory, his subconscious couldn't even dream it now. He burned those powder-floored bridges rotting beneath the elements of punishing thought so he could live with himself. So he could draw a single breath amidst a reminder..., so he could throw a manly punch without slashing his fist, curled around that double-edged blade reserved only for the unforgiven to carry. Forgiveness…, unforgiveness…, the battle became monotonous. He had his reasons for ending it. They nearly resurfaced in his recollection. Climbing, again, from the bottomless pit of him, along with her…. But his mind's eye closed that heavy door—hundredth, thousandth time…? Left her unfinished memory alone to struggle on behind it. *What would have she become…?*

Her eyes drifted into Lemn's—their ages were fused to a still and equaled point within Drake's mind. And it was sharp. And piercing….

He remained in silence. Was left to stand in front of the boy with no direction, such that a confident man would easily demonstrate. He felt unguarded, as if his mind could be seen in its array of disappointments and shameful incapacitation. He stood there in that room, hard and calloused, teetering on the verge of a free fall into an embarrassing display of relief. A display coupled with the release of years of pain verses the familiar nothingness, dammed up, forever encased in stone.

And it was habit he chose. Movement was not his…, and time passed him by.

Drake grabbed his handkerchief and turned away to blow his nose. He took a long moment to stare out the window and uncomfortably force things back into himself, talk himself back down. The voice of reason always brought him back into the expected role he had constructed for himself. But it was getting more difficult, like he was too full and just one more blow before he was ready would cause a rupture. Bottling his emotions became like a barn raising without neighbors, the winds of change forcing failure. He did need someone…. What was left of him needed someone. In all his imperfections, he turned back toward Lemn and the boy was still looking at him patiently waiting, unchanged. And the kid saw him, just as he was. And those innocent eyes did not look away.

Somehow, Drake managed a smile.

The things one expects of a father are often given by a Son….

"…It's not a good idea for you to be out there by yourself just yet. I'll keep ya company for a few days."

"Sure…I could use the help. I need to go see my ma."

.   .   .

The dreary, solidified expression hanging on Doc's face was downright disturbing. Beneath it, his ashen skin was strikingly detailed with dark purple streaks smeared under the protruding cheek bones and slashed here and there along the deep wrinkle valleys. Thin swirls of charcoal and black accented the sharp curve of his jaw line and dropped down to surround his Adam's apple, some bruise blue hovered beneath the corners of his backslidden lips. It was the color a corpse might wear after the entire body has turned to a weighted, rubbery mask, or at least someone toward the latter midst of suffocation. That's how he looked when Lemn happened upon him, it caused the boy to swallow the breath he'd just finished taking, and then…, *Thank God. His eyes are moving. He's blinking…. Thank God.* It was a horrid look to have to take in, but a look, nonetheless, that blended in with the surroundings somehow, seemed fitting for the occasion. And it complimented the faded, teal paint splashed on the walls—a strange, dense shade that flooded the office like a nauseating tide rolling in off a displaced ocean. It gave way to an immediate headache. As Lemn shut the door behind him, the sickly color of the room closed in tighter, soaking up the oxygen of light left sealed off and lingering in the world just outside, and he felt his own skin draining, falling pale under a cold, tingling sweat.

Doc didn't offer anything—a nod of the head for greeting, a sweep of the arm in invitation…, nothing. He just rose, shuffled along silently, leading Lemn up to her room with each ascending step of the staircase pulling him down deeper into his insecurity and age. He unlocked the door to the light-filled room and paused in the doorway waiting for the weak boy to catch up. He turned toward Lemn for a moment as if searching for an introduction, a kind way to announce his new mother and soften the change, but he got sidetracked by the boy's wobbling knees, hunched back and wheezing breath. He hedged back around and his eyes fell directly upon her. Upon her and the way she was…. (And the way she was could stop the heart of anyone, seize it and set it to spasm, hold it just under the surface, panicking and fluttering, then finally shove it up onto a jagged and rocky course, onto a long road of painful rhythm that just wasn't natural to follow. Anyone who'd seen her like she was would never be able to forget, and their heart—it would beat out odd numbers for the rest of its haunted days. For her undisciplined eyes—with bizarre and random and possessed and fleeting intentions behind them—would pop up from a night cloud roaming their unsuspecting sky of sleep. And those of the dreams would be sorrowed and stricken still with no bedside company other than the offset chambers of the heart beating backward and inverted in their chests….) The good doctor suddenly felt trapped in his own home, helpless and hoping that he could move away from the two other lives in the room—away at a distance of forever, and rise above the two bodies waiting there that he had let perish and sink to a level far below his own lofty expectations of healing. A level far below his practice as it was…, when he was a younger man. With arthritic, trembling hands, he noisily drug a chair from the corner to Anne's bedside and put a pillow on the backrest for Lemn to lean against. He patted the pillow heartily as he spoke as if trying to toughen his perplexed tone into one of lucidity, but the tears behind his voice pummeled through like an uneven, sheeting rain.

"You need to take it real easy, son. Those ribs take a while to heal."

"Yes sir. Any change in her?"

"'Fraid not…. I'm so sorry."

Lemn could see the truth behind the words mirrored in Doc's troubled eyes. But hidden beyond was something more. Something like pity. And, at that moment, Lemn was introduced to the slap of scrutiny following affliction. He found himself the imprisoned base under the merciless gavel of small town misunderstanding. Friends, acquaintances, strangers danced together, twirled and rolled into a single black-robed judge—judgement of immense proportions, beside the lonesome reality of the accused, and with a trapdoor mouth running constantly at the base of its ugly skull. Lemn's mother had taught him well when he was a young boy…, taught him saying, "Every assumption too inappropriate to utter at the source reeks with human error…." And at his perplexed and childish gaze, "Watch what ya say, Lemn. Don't believe most of what ya hear."
For leaking out between busy, self-righteous tongues, is a gross underestimation of the intense spiritual struggle raging on over just one soul. Take heed, lest you are caught idly standing in the midst of its battlefield….

It was as if, not only Doc, but all the townsfolk that eyed Lemn on his slow, painful walk over to the office were labeling him in their minds. That at the end of their gaze, they saw an "orphan" in the worst possible light. Being orphaned was his destiny, yes. But what they didn't know was that Lemn had been waiting. Innocently. But waiting still. And he was ready for it. And it felt as right as it could under the dire circumstances. He had always been more of a parent and a partner than a child and his life had been designed like this for a reason. Some people were simply born to raise themselves.

He looked on as the ghost resembling his unresponsive mother stared blankly toward the window. He did not expect anything more. He had been the only one to see it coming.

Some storm clouds are too wide to dodge, so let it rain….

"Ma?"

(*buzz…hummm…*)

"It's alright, Ma. You don't have to say anything."

(*hum…buzz…*)

Lemn took her hand and he could feel it—whatever it was—drowning the inside of her. He waited by her side for an hour. And in that time, he couldn't think of anyone his age without both parents or blood kin who had taken them in. He'd heard of an orphanage 'cross river in Evansville and suddenly he understood how circumstance could cause someone to hate the world they lived in. To work all their life, fighting to forge their plans, only to have fate lock them away behind another blank slate as they watch, hands shaking, sweating into question mark chalk.

"It's alright, Ma. You don't have to worry no more."

(*buzz…*)

Their touch turned to electric ice, then fell dead. His heart thumped crudely against his chest, knocking futilely like a mute messenger. It was no news any-how, the fact that she would never be back.

"This is your last slate, Anne Riley. Do good, Ma."

He hastily wiped a tear from his cheek and grimaced at the slice of pain that punished his thoughtless, swift movement. He got up to leave his mother for-ever and she didn't—she couldn't—even notice. The pain in his ribs and the pain in his heart commingled as he slowly descended the stairs and the over-whelming combination made him feel like crying right there in Doc's office. Like an orphan….

"I've got to go run some errands, boy. You wouldn't mind watching the place?" Doc's absence fell blank but necessary, like punctuation unmentioned in speech. Before Lemn could utter a syllable, the old man was already out the door and out of sight.

Lemn stood by the window, his presence on earth defining emptiness to its fullest extent. It hurt too much to try to sit down again and he feared the confinement of a chair would cause him to implode. He could easily turn inside out. Unleash the screams suffocating and scratching against his own flesh. He could sacrifice his body and destroy the entire office with his rage. He felt he could blow the whole house to splinters, tiny, floating flecks of teal dust, with one consecrated look. He forced his eyes to move, forced his brain to think—*Breathe...*—distracting himself with anything and everything until something of meaning snagged him. Reeled him in. It was a framed paper on Doc's ill-colored wall. It was from some kind of medicine school from some other kind of world. The handwriting was so elegant, pleasant and proper that it seemed to represent a beauty Lemn's life would never touch.

> *... University of Pennsylvania Presents on this, the Thirteenth Day of the Month of June, Eighteen Hundred and Tenth Year of Our Lord, a Proper Certificate of Honor Awarding the Title of Medical Doctor to Sir Charles DeFrancis Miles. ...*

Farmer. Gambler. He chuckled to himself though he found it wasn't all that funny. He was not amused with the lack of respect both his own occupations invited—dirty hands, dirty means....

He glanced back out the window and saw Drake and Doc talking with the town sheriff. The concern was equally spread across each face..., faces plastered stiff and pale with wired age. They gazed back toward Lemn's direction with gray unblinking eyes, studying what they thought they saw there like black-robed scholars perched upon a platform and whispering, *I didn't think that one was capable. But let us not forget, it's ultimately the test of time he must pass....*

The scene was just another sign. A sign that the colors of the world are capricious. They take on the dark blending of the shadows with whimsical fluidity. They dance passively while led in a wild frenzy, twirling closer and closer to the browning storms that swallow them. They bend down, roll over without preference to an eye they do not themselves have. They turn sour in an instant and clash against that foul breath of borrowed air seeping from the lungs of an artist known only as Evil. Every liberty is taken. Every spirit in the path of stroke, vulnerable, weak and changed, as he dips his corrosive brush, reaches in and invades the even canvas as his own. Takes advantage of the blank spaces in people's lives, coating them with some type of lethal tonic that traps time.

Frames it in rigidity. Illuminates its memory with a haunting pull, elongated and distorted light. Shameful to have lived it. And ugly, forever so..., in the eyes of all who had seen....

In this emotional vertigo, Lemn was brought back to evenness with a glimpse..., he took it through a spiritualistic eagle eye and he witnessed the reality of it. The truth of the tragic portrait that was in the process of being created without any say from the real subjects involved. He looked up the stairs toward the tomb of his mother and decided it would not win. It could not win. And he closed the door on his own pity as he stepped back into the honest light.

.   .   .

The stock cattle were casually milling around the water tank, taking turns with calm and contented sips. Lemn's horse was dozing in the sunshine against the warmest side of the barn with drowsy eyes and a droopy lower lip. The milk cow was happy to contribute to the peace and quiet by dropping her milk easily, back on schedule again. There was a warm and earthy smell of fresh bedding, oats, molasses and salt floating on the sunbeams of barn dust. And the cat, no longer suspicious of her surroundings, lapped the skimmed milk offered her without twitching an ear or raising her head in worry.

Drake had begun to slow down. Lemn figured he was tired. Full-time gamblers weren't used to pitching anything heavier than a playing card for very long and Lemn's broken down body hadn't contributed much. They worked all day to restore normalcy to the farm and it appeared they'd accomplished their goal. Lemn turned toward Drake intending to offer his gratitude, but stopped short when he noticed the look on his face.

Just then, the man began to speak. He started out real slow like he was thinking of staying quiet, then a fever—a fever of something like fierce loyalty, maybe hatred—it caught. Lit him up. His words fuel for the burning, a clear liquid line of them shooting straight into the sky and his eye dogged them like flame.

"Lemn, those boys that got the best 'a ya ain't likely gonna stop. Maybe they got it out of their veins for a while, but some more just like 'em will come along. I'll help ya the best I can.... I'll help you learn how to fight. But I know Devon wouldn't approve, so it seems to me you got a choice. I can teach ya what I know—what's kept me alive this long—but you take your chances. Sometimes, there's just plain evil people that come along and seem to get joy out of killin' and do it for no other reason. Don't matter if it's gamblin', a sack a' flour or you just happen to be the one there when they feel like doin' somebody in....

"I think it *is* partly luck, but mostly will. If you got a stronger will and you think of all the angles, they get intimidated, see? And they make a mistake. Don't matter who makes the first move, it's kill or be killed. That's what it comes down to—always. It's a hard choice to make, Lemn. A choice like that c'n tear ya up inside. But you gotta sort it out and let me know if you want me to teach you my way, or if you want to make it your own way. I'll leave you to think about all this…. Either way, you're a hell of a kid, Lemn. Hell of a kid."

Drake tossed his pitchfork onto the straw pile to signify his finish and only then did his gaze cool and meet the ground. He walked to the house so slowly, it was almost painful for Lemn to watch. His shuffling footsteps lifted a little higher, then a little higher, with each stride. His shoulders squared off and his back began to straighten with distance. It was as if he'd just walked out an invisible jail cell. When he reached the porch swing, he sat down, stared off toward the prairie for a moment, then rolled a cigarette in that precise way that was second nature to him. From the barn, Lemn could feel the magnitude of the breath he released—the tension, the weight, carried off by grey swirls of smoke to the sky and forgotten. Lemn stood still. He felt awkward just standing there, like a schoolboy stricken with stage fright, but his feet had turned to directionless lead and there was no exit from this stage anyhow. He wished he could take a long ride, but his ribs weren't ready, so he stood. With his head swimming, he stood. A million voices invaded his thoughts—his father, his mother, Avi, Doc, Drake and Mama all telling him something different. He directed a question to his father via his heart, *If he was such a terrible man, why did you like him so well?* Lemn waited to feel an answer back from his father's spirit and received nothing but a feeling of emptiness in the pit of his stomach. He took this feeling as disapproval. He was getting confused, so he simply stopped his mind. He'd do what he always did—follow his gut. He knew what his answer would be. He knew it weeks ago.

He limped along to catch up, managing his crooked and wayward stride as best he could.

Chapter Seven

As the sun proceeded to fall, it hushed the many boisterous hues of orange and pink that had magnified themselves with splendor against the low layer of dusky, deep-blue fog grazing the cool, golden prairie air. The silent ball of brilliant flame commanded attention as it conducted its routine labors with a uniqueness, a genuineness, as beautifully, and as breathtakingly—reflected gloriously there amidst the drifting cloud designs—as it had for all time and all seeing eyes that had passed below it. Lugged over its rounded and quivering shoulder of tireless strength was a vast blanket of twilight dotted with an applique of select and friendly stars, covering everything as it went down, finally tucking the earth into black. The gift given by its sweet existence became only a recent memory—the memory of warmth, the memory of life—and the hope of the coming of another day fell there in its place rendering everything living dependent and spiritual, full of wonder and why.

This sun, that watches over all like the eye of God, its magnificence was swallowed by the dark, its radiant touch consumed drop by chilling drop fallen of the wetness of the night as it checked on the other half of the world. Disorientation was left swirling by the air and space and blindness and tricks dripping down from the mysterious Milky Way—a crosshatching reflected off the afterglow of the sun's path to make a galaxy, form a bond, much like that of a man and a woman. She is elusive but loyal, this Milky Way. A ribbon of hoax that cannot be seen even when watched, for something would, and will always, be missed no matter how many centuries man studies her—her distance and depth and resplendence and creation grossly misjudged while her smiling eyes twinkle. She is laughing. At all, around all. Dancing and having some fun. (She doesn't care who is watching, judging, evaluating, condemning or praising.) And laughing some more. And only the bravest of the spiritual, those unselfish enough to believe and wise enough to admit they know nothing—only those few will she embrace with the celebration for in them she feels more like herself. And in return they will learn of the fullness of laughter and its freedoms whispered there.

Because they learn to laugh at themselves. Mistakes, regrets become smaller and smaller and smaller floating away into the abyss of time…, into this elusive sky of stars that must be a woman.

And those dancing with her are glad to have been alive. They are glad to be alive.

As they slide….

·   ·   ·

Lemn's energy had drained from him, trailed off after the sun, and the magic that occurs in the night tickled him alert with a vague fear, an uncertainty and unsteadiness, as it sometimes does, and he jerked. Lurched there in his chair. And he found that his head had been bobbing, his eyelids drooping—for how long now, he didn't know. The words…*a rainbow of One* drifting in off a dream he was having. Perhaps he had spoken them out loud. If he had, Drake seemed not to have noticed, as mesmerized by the flames in the fireplace as he was. There was no warmth in the room, regardless of the vigorous fire, no warmth to be found underneath the entire night sky and Lemn could almost feel it. Almost see it, or *them*…. The shifting of the spirits. Their fervor and activity prior to change—it was happening. They were circling. And Lemn could think of no place safer than to be sealed off from it all, from the powers that be, hidden under the covers on his bed with his hands folded in an all-night, silent prayer. Those heavy quilts, that his mother had sewn for him while he was just a baby, and his own tightly folded hands—together they had always kept him safe. So he uttered a slurred good-night to an unresponsive Drake and shuffled back toward his room, skirting around the wide aura of the still and quiet rocker that sat forever shocked with its emptiness like a giant, gaping jaw. *How unattractive is that?* The words brushed against his cheek with a strange callousness spoken of the dark. He quietly shut his bedroom door, hoping to dismiss them, hoping for an angel to guard him against their intention, and embraced his bed like a long, lost friend, instantly reminded of the sheer comfort its softness and scent held for him. The shape of the matted feathers cradled his body perfectly and soothed his aching side. As he closed his heavy eyes and drew and released his first few satisfying breaths of rest, he realized his true comfort was derived from something else. From his mother's absence.

And Drake's presence.

At that thought, his eyes popped open. Wide.

He felt a twinge of guilt, a thorn working its way under his skin then into the center of his chest. And it was driven in deep with a ramming stab of pain as he twisted, shifted and settled his body into a position a little closer to pain-free sleep. He rolled his eyes, irritated and wishing, more than anything, that the mold of bed would reform his soft physique and have it set firm and normal by morning. He folded his hands and forced a deep breath then, trying to recapture those first few moments of safe comfort, but he was left disappointed by the detailed churning of his brain that signaled the polar opposite of prayer, of contentment. The rotation of his mind was picking up speed and the momentum of it began to engulf more and more thought—the kinds of thoughts that turn themselves over and over again during long and sleepless nights. They are thoughts that dance outside of peaceful dreams and feed on the energy of emotions stifled during the day—sadness, injustice, loneliness. Counting sheep or any other furry critter had never worked for Lemn. He found himself following the bleating puffs of wool over the fence of his imagination to make sure they had plenty of pasture to eat, clean water, a good watch dog, on and on…. In fact, he figured the very idea of counting sheep a cruel, centuries-old Scotsmen's prank, for anyone who has ever attempted to count a respectful herd of sheep knows he is soon ridden with anxiety, optical illusions and, eventually, a number no one counting can agree on, so why not add "insomnia for the masses" to the lovely list as well? Especially for those outside the joke, kept cozy under woolen blankets, unaware of the ceaseless labor involved in keeping bands of confused and innocently ignorant, suicidal creatures alive and flourishing and sticking together—the honorable title *Good Shepard* completely lost on them….

And so he surrendered—choosing to believe his subconscious had a significant point to bring to his awareness—and followed his mind wherever it saw fit to lead him.

He thought on the day they buried his father. *Dismal.* That dismal day when somebody threw out a stone. It rose high up in the air, twirling and twirling for what seemed like eons and baby breaths at the same time. Eventually it had to come down. And it came down too quick. And it landed upon him. And it choked him, nearly killed him. He had no choice but to swallow it and it dropped. And it dropped farther still. Dropped all the way down to the bottom of his heart so that it made it rest heavy on his chest. A weight he'd never be able to cough up and out of himself. And who threw it…, he'd never be sure.

Anne's expression, every passing hour, minute and second leading up to the funeral, had been taut and fixed just like that dark gray unchanging stone. *Haunting.* It was so still. *So* still. Only her body moved, here to do this, there to do that…, moved carrying her face of gray stone like dead weight. Like an iron mask. Crushing. Suffocating. For a brief while, during the service, there had been misty air to breathe. It was cold and damp and stinging against the lining deep inside the lungs, like breathing in the sky's own salty tears, but it was air, nonetheless. Air to breathe…, that was until Lemn glanced over at her from the corner of his teary eye and saw the look on her face. It pulled his full gaze to her like only instantaneous disbelief does. Like only shock does. As his pre-shed tears continued to roll down the damp paths streaked on his cold, reddened cheeks and then dropped in turn, in silence, from his soft jaw line onto the arm of his Sunday coat, he looked. His heart and his breathing had stopped for what seemed an unnaturally long, surreal moment. His tears stopped, too. It held no comfort, that look of hers, only fear was found there—not in it, but because of it. Not a tear had been shed down it, he was certain. No raining down of hurt, healing or hope. Nothing of feeling emanated from behind the eyes—they may as well have been lifeless, sunken emeralds trapped forever at the bottom of the sea for they shifted and looked hard and unchanged back at him like they were animated not of their own force, but of some eerie under-current. They sliced through the atmosphere with a jagged line straight to him, the jade color of them illuminated with ripples of harsh indifference. Something beyond those eyes was unreachable, unthinkable. His skin shivered in waves over his tense muscles. The fear in him caused his young eyes to drop down and away from whatever it was. Then he knew what it was…. *How is it that a boy can read a book of meaning behind a single line in his mother's face?* She may not have been aware—the things she was telling him by that crease lifted too close to smirk, to smugness, to victory, to condescension, lifted beneath those emerald eyes that had lost their worth. Lost it by joining in with the murderer. What remained of her essence salvaged cheap peace by claim-ing…, *If given time, I'd have done it myself.* And to her child, she offered no apologies, no signal that she preferred not to be sinking.

But more than all this, beyond the possibilities of a grief-stricken boy's overactive imagination, was the fact that her eyes looked dead. Like an appari-tion. Like a sign, a warning from God meant only for him. He remembered turning away, swallowing hard, breathing deep and laboriously. He remem-bered looking to the preacher, then frantically scanning the crowd until he found uplifted eyes that were sane. He blinked his own to clarify them. He did all these things to regain the composure he may have lost, to gather enough courage to look at her again. And when he did, her eyes looked dead and nothing else. They looked like the glassy, vacant, open eyes of someone drowned and dead. And Lemn knew, on that day, his mother was not, and would never be, the same. She scared him. Beyond the depth of his own bones, she scared him. The fear was ingrained there, inside of him. Any growth in him from there on out could only layer itself on top. What was buried in him—buried deeper than that mucky, drooling hole waiting to swallow his father forever— could never be erased. He remembered the slanted drizzle trickling down heavier, then heavier still—another barrier between Heaven and the cruel goings-on around him. He remembered looking up into the sky, into the drops that seemed to be falling up, up away from him, beyond his grasp or recognition, carrying with them bits of Devon—his words, his memories, his smile. He felt it as each tiny speck of security that he tried to hold onto was taken from him, torn from him, snapping the sinewy strings of his bleeding heart one by one by one, pulling away what was once held so close, pulling it away, miles and miles up into the gray. He remembered wishing the funeral would last for days, weeks, months. He prayed for the preacher to be unbelievably long winded. He wanted his father to be with him—even if it was just his cold, settling body in a box. At least he'd be there, with him, above ground. At least it wouldn't be just the two of them, Anne and him, together. Alone.

But the preacher ran out of breath, words, time, will, necessity. And the day ran out of light. And the space that was their farm ran out of visitors. And Lemn ran out of help from anything beyond himself. For all the days thereafter, she was so hollow inside that to look at her face, glance at her posture— how she carried herself, was like looking into a shadow cast off something half-dead and stinking. Whatever was inside her was taking over her soul, rotting it. And she was letting it. As he watched. And she, or something like her, watched him. He'd catch her eyes staring back at him from the edge of a nightmare. The dreams he had…, dreams like standing on a sliver of rotting board, teetering there, peering down into a dark, mysterious well. A bottomless well nearly deep as hell that might have swallowed him whole and forever if he tiptoed too close and lost his balance, grew older and heavier than allowed or just happened upon it in inclement weather. A well he had to fetch from in order to survive. And he knew that way down in there, down at the bottom of that well, something evil lurked. A growing, climbing mildew of disease. And, at their worst, the dreams would offer her up…her flaming red hair bleeding out like liquid behind her, pale skin covering veins stretched and swollen too-blue without oxygen, emerald, blank and bloodshot eyes…her, all of it, drowning amidst filthy, blackened well water—water he'd just drank from. And just when it reached his trembling throat and he was about to throw it up, he'd waken amidst sweat-soaked sheets and silence.

He remembered other nights, lying awake, just listening to her rocker squeak back and forth, back and forth on the floor and when it stopped, his heart would skip a beat and his mind would run loose and wild with the fantasy maybes just past his door. He would see her try to take her own life—in a variety of ways. Or, other times, he would see her enter his room intending to take his—his only hope that she would recognize a trace of the love she'd stitched into those quilts covering him and stop. And he punished himself for such heinous thinking. Such grave imagination. And he would repent. Then repent again when the scenes would return. She had never attempted anything of the kind. But, still, it was happening. He couldn't explain it to anyone. No other human being would understand, would believe how serious it was. He couldn't even explain it to himself. Because the next morning, the very next morning, the rawness, the gruesomeness of it, would all be gone. Just like the bad dreams. But on those eerie nights, in the darkness all around him and down deep in his heart and at the bottom of his mind, things were rising. Rising from the ashes of his childhood. And things were happening to his mother. Things were happening. He knew it.

But they were happening, in human regard, either too fast or too slow, with the forces that be deeming a quick end too merciful (its impact soon forgotten) and a gradual change too slight, too risky (the plan easily deterred or unnoticed as necessary, accepted, mistakenly, as a vague, depressing, fixed lot in life). Therefore, the misery was real and it was noticeable and it was drawn out longer than any frontier winter—drawn out so it'd stick. It was cold, hard and unrelenting and no matter how far Lemn tried to distance himself from the changes, the chill hung on. It clung to his growing and layering bones. And those vengeful looks she threw between them…, the last one still hovering like a dagger hurled and hanging in midair waiting for a chance to strike. He remembered the night one of them had hit, he'd seen her reflection in the twilight glass as she glared straight into his back. He looked into the surface of the window at his own face and saw his father staring back at him, then blinking away the shock they shared for a fleeting moment…. The wisdom there in those identical eyes reminded him how often it was that Devon would stand in the very same place and posture, silent, lost to private thoughts, right hand level with his shoulder and resting on the window pane, just so, as he looked out the very same window—looking out into the deepness found in nothing. Lemn was his father's son, apparently growing more so in his absence….And his mother hated him for it. Of that day, the day they put Devon in the ground, Lemn still feared. He feared her unspoken confession. And in her wavering mental state, Lemn couldn't be sure she wouldn't mistake him for the man already dead.

That familiar thought sent him to shuddering, even now, under the covers of a safe night, far removed.

He realized he was no closer to answers, or sleep, than he'd been when he started. He forced himself to think of the good things in her. The times when traces of the *real* her did shine through. He thought of warm milk and honey after winter chores. Whenever he'd made the simple concoction himself, it never tasted quite as sweet. She'd sit with him by the fire while he drank it down slow, reading him particular segments from books she had brought with her years before—it was the sound of her voice that warmed him. And her green eyes would light up with those books, sparkle and dance across the dull pages with firelight their lead. She was always discovering some universal truth, whether blatantly brought forward or hidden behind the words, and she thought it her duty to pass every bit of it on to her only child. When she had finished reading whatever excerpt, she would ask his opinion and mistake the look of admiration in his glistening, dark eyes for the pride behind newly acquired knowledge. And on those nights when the prairie had delivered her a weariness too deep for respectable reading, she'd just sit quietly near him, sometimes smiling over at him for no reason. These were the kind of unsuspecting smiles that show only love—nearly the purest form of it. How precious and long-lasting they had proven themselves to be, with absence and with the distance of time…. But Lemn had to reach way back in his mind for these visions of her. She had changed so very much, his stomach turned when he thought on it. He couldn't recall a smile or warm gesture at all in the last year—nothing. She had isolated herself from everything and everyone. The books sat untouched on the shelf, night after night, as hurt transcribed itself on the inside of her and eventually replaced the pages of her own mind. Consumed the person she had been. Memories fallen together into mere ashes…from all those distant fires. Sad, sad story of her ending….

A tear fell to his pillow and his mind followed behind it, down, down, deeper into the finite crevices of cherished sleep.

.   .   .

Drake was relieved when Lemn had finally tuckered out. He needed to tend to the secret wound in his side—he'd let it go too long as it was. He slowly made his way to the bedroom, lantern in hand. As he surveyed the injury in the flickering lamplight, he saw some new swelling—an indication that infection had set in. He poured some whiskey over it, but felt nothing. He rubbed down his knife with the liquor, let it dry, then set the razor-sharp blade against the pocket of sealed puss and drew it down through the delicate, scarring skin. He forced his face into the feather bed to stifle any sound that might escape while he poured the burning liquid over his side. It mixed with his own and oozed out watery-pink, set a slow sting of fire to his open flesh. After several gasping breaths, the pain died down and the heat of his body was lifted by a string of chills ascending his spine. He wiped the sprinkling of sweat from his brow and hoisted himself up off his knees. One of them popped under his exhausted and heavy weight—bones in unruly disarray, blurting out his true age like a wise-crack. He wondered when it was exactly, that his own body began to rebel against him, all of its parts cooperating so efficiently, dedicated to the mission of making him feel miserable. He shook each of his hands vigorously, hoping to throw the tremble from them before he bandaged his side, looping the cotton dressing snugly around his torso and tying the frayed ends off with a knot. He unclenched his teeth, then flexed his jaw to help loosen it. As he rubbed his tense neck muscles, he chuckled to himself finding a twinge of humor in their predicaments. *What a sight we must be…retreating to separate corners of this lonely little shack, both of us too proud to admit how much it hurts.*

He tried to fall asleep but lying there in the dark, in Devon's bed, he felt like he was being watched. His late, best friend's wife would like to see him dead, at least in her current state of mind. (He glanced at his loaded revolvers tucked away in their custom-made holster belt and hanging on the bedpost…, the handles shined, seemed to come alive as they gleamed against the dwindling fire.…*Just a precaution*, he told himself.) This feeling of being watched reminded him of growing up, of that long stretch of stumbling and sorrow. He'd never been welcomed or trusted anywhere he went. Until Avi.…

"GET OUT OF HERE, ya theavin' bastard!!!"

"I'm just not sure we should let him stay in our barn, John. What if he steals the horses? And what about our girls.…"

"Sorry, son. I know you'd be a hard worker, and God knows this farm could use ya, but we just ain't got the means to take on one more mouth ta feed. Good luck to ya.…"

"What a disgrace! Ethel, did you see that boy? How dirty! And those *clothes!* God have mercy. Well, we'd better go, don't want to be late for Meetin' now.…"

"Well, well…what do we have us here? Look here at this dirty street rat. Ya think he'll fit the bill?"

"Yeah! 'Bout the right height as you, Jethro. We'll jus' turn his ass in ta the sheriff and collect our reward. We'll git paid twice an' no one'll be the wiser. His word agains' ours. Get up *punk*."

Drake hated this time of night. His mind wrestled with memories he wished he could erase, wished he could slice away like infected flesh. And he would. But, thank goodness, at the painful end of their course he always heard Avi's still, small voice....

A soft voice that parted rain clouds like the warm sun. Sound that sent his only rainbow down, his only promise yet unbroken. He'd hear it forever, that tiny voice, echoing. Saying just one enormous word. One simple word. *Hey....*

"Hey.... Hey, Mis'uh. Why you eat outta that waste barr'uh? My mama's gots the bes' fried chicken these pahts. She'll give ya some. Come on."

"Thanks, but I don't wanna fright your mama none, little girl."

"You ain't seen Mama. She not be scared a you! Not no more 'den a lil' itty bitty mice. COME ON!"

Avi grabbed Drake up by her tiny hand with so much determination he couldn't say no. This little girl made him smile more in five minutes than he had in his whole life.

She led him down the street and, oh, what looks they got. Drake felt like he was committing two crimes at once—a crime against his gender and a crime against his race. He had gotten so used to people calling him derogatory names..., "Thief..., Bastard..., Lowlife Punk...," that eighty percent of his mind was in agreement and amidst this, his birth name became lost on him..., could hardly remember it anymore.... *But what does it matter....* He had walked for years with his shoulders so slumped over in shame that his back never did completely straighten out.

She led him right up to the front door of the most substantial house in town. A house with presence surrounded by a whitewashed picket fence and rose trellises, perched at the end of the dusty main road like an oasis, a para-dise—no place for someone like him. He felt his legs begin to tense up, ready to run away out of habit. People on the street were shading their strained eyes, still staring at them. His mind raced trying to protect itself from another let-down that he knew, all too well, was waiting for him behind the heavy oak door looming in front of him. He tried to think of the most justifiable way to tell why he was with a little girl, begging for a decent meal....

"Well, go 'head. Knock on deh door. Mama says 'bein' proper git you a long way."

Drake smiled down at the little bank of knowledge with a different way of talking, put aside his insecurity and followed directions. She was the only honest person who had noticed him in months.

With white knuckles, he tapped the door three times. Three times so lightly, he figured no one could possibly hear.

Five seconds later, just as Drake's nerves started to take hold again, a sturdy black woman opened the door, slowly peaking out. When she saw her daughter, she smiled broadly at her, then apologetically at him—not because of him, but in good-humored excuse for her daughter. She was the only adult who hadn't given him the once over and a look of disgust regarding his poor condition. She looked him straight in the eye with a pleasant, comfortable expression and talked to him with respect, with kindness, like he was in a three-piece suit of the finest material. What was more, after a few moments, she had Drake feeling confident enough to look *her* in the eye.

"Did my Avi bothuh' you any? She's a go-gettuh,' she is. Avi, honay, go on in an' git 'nother place sat fo' yo' frein' heeah. You are stayin' fo dinnuh, ain't ya? Got plen'y."

And that was Mama. She didn't put Drake on the spot about a single thing as if she knew his whole story and he had finally come home. And what an elaborate home it was and she wasn't the hired help.

Drake stayed for dinner and, as it come about, for another two years.

"Wha's y' name, young man?"

"'Is name's Spencah," Avi spoke out without hesitation. She glanced at Drake with big and honest eyes while her cheeks ballooned around a large bite of mashed potatoes. Drake stayed silent, figuring his gambling name was worse than a lie.... *Best not to utter it in here....* He then nodded reassurance to Mama..., her daughter had it right. *Spencer....* Sounded as good a name as any to him.

.   .   .

The next morning, Drake was up early making coffee with Devon's cast iron pot, then drinking it from one of Devon's cups, on Devon's porch. It wasn't entirely Devon's porch—Drake helped build it. He sat on the swing, shivering slightly, listening to the resurrected conversations the two shared while working all those years ago. Their lighthearted chuckles, strained grunts and sighs of accomplishment from surveying a job well-done were recorded deep in Drake's memory and their playback grew increasingly louder, echoing inside his head, intensifying with each millimeter the sun rose. He tried to focus on the birdsongs exploding all around him, but painful memories and associations persistently invaded his thought patterns to the point that he questioned how long he would be able to stay on the place without going mad himself.

Everything was hitting him at once. He recalled the weather on the day he'd heard the news, it was the very same day Devon was killed. He remembered exactly where he was. He could read the shape of the clouds floating across the deep blue sky like today's Tribune, but they may as well have been rocks covering the ground, as much sense as the world made to him at that moment, as much permanence as they rendered in his mind. He remembered he stood there speechless for some time. He looked down at his boots, then turned to glance over his shoulder toward his horse. The gelding turned his head toward the east, then lowered his gaze and craned his neck more toward the south. Out there's where it happened. Out of town. He'd missed his friend's life by less than two hours. As he stood there in his boots—the messenger, Doc, waiting for some kind of response—he felt the blast deafening his own ears, then the gunshot wound tunneling through the center of his own chest. He felt it as his own blood drained. *I should've been the one....* That was all he could mumble. He got on his horse and left the way he came..., plunged into gambling way down river, kept himself busy, adopted a different culture, all so he would not have to deal with the loss of his friend. He couldn't stomach it—even now. The terrible things always happen sooner than they should. Injustice shouldn't have a season.

Lemn stumbled out onto the porch with sleepy eyes and a crooked stance, ribs still stiff and aching. His offset frame was counterbalanced with a spirited smile. The combinations of his very essence seemed ironic.... He was an old man in a child's body with a beautiful mind tucked somewhere between its tortures.

"Mornin.'"

"Good one."

"Sleep good?"

"Yep. You?"

"Uh huh."

The silence hung there like the morning air, clear but tangible. There was so much to talk about that it seemed awkward to even start on any subject of importance.

"How's the coffee?"

"Real good. Want some?"

"Naw."

Lemn knew it was his turn since Drake was waiting for the big answer and all. He did his best to push himself past a haze of sleepiness.

"I've got a lot of questions, Drake…. I guess I'll jus' go ahead an' ask 'em and if I'm outta line, well, jus' say so, allright? And I'll try not to ask 'em all at once."

"Sounds fair, boy."

"How did you and Pa get to be such good friends?"

"Ya mean, 'specially since we're different as day and night?"

"Well, that too."

"It all started out that Devon, Anne and you—you were too little to remember—were comin' through town an' y'all stuck out like a fly in milk. It was dusk—bad timin'—and I saw some boys eyein' your Pa's rig—probably for lootin' and God knows what else. I hadn't started a game yet and I thought, 'Ah, hell. I don't feel like watchin' this again.' So, I went over to your Pa—he was gettin' ready to leave you two alone in that wagon with all your goods to go find a room—and I told him straight out, 'Mister, due respect, but you oughtn't leave your wife and baby alone after dark. Not in this town.'"

"What happened then?" burst Lemn with heightened interest.

"Well, yer ma shot your pa a look that could have lynched him on the spot and he took me aside a little and he said, 'I don't know you, but you have no right to scare my wife.' And I said, 'Better scared than sorry, Mister. I know where you can stay that's more fittin' for a family than this trashy saloon hotel. Follow me.'"

"And then?"

"You all spent the night with Mama an' Avi."

"You mean ta tell me that I knew Mama and Avi when I was a baby?"

"Yeah…You sure did, boy! I remember Avi playin' with you like one of her dolls…oh, she must 'a been 'bout ten or eleven years grown."

Lemn's expression was like a child getting his first taste of sugar.

"I can't hardly believe that, Drake!"

Drake chuckled at the boy's surprise and realized how much information he would need to know to fill in the holes.

"Drake, I don't understand how all this time could pass and Avi and I never talked or nothin.' I mean if she liked playin' with me so much, why didn't we get ta be friends?"

Drake took on a look of dry seriousness mixed with sadness and shame.

"Well, son, I don't feel completely alright tellin' you this, but I guess you have a right to know. Your mama's already real upset with me for meddlin' with you as much as I have. You understand?"

"Yeah."

"So, some things that I'm gonna tell ya, you best not take them up with her…I mean if…"

"It's alright, Drake. Go ahead. I'd like to know."

"Well, back then your ma was a woman set in her beliefs and there wasn't no changin' her. I'm sure you know that. But understand that both your parents were good people for the most part—real good—but every person on this earth has things that ain't perfectly right about 'em. Your parents are no different.

They're 'jus people like you and I, and they make mistakes like you and I. Do ya get my meanin?"

"Yeah…What mistakes did they make?"

"Before I answer that, how much do you know about your ma and pa before you were born?"

"Well…I know they were from Ireland and Pa wanted to move out here to have freedom to do as he pleased and to live a good life. I know they traveled a lot of miles to get here. I never knew of any kin—I mean cousins and such—I guess they are all still in Ireland. That's about all I know. Ma and Pa never liked to talk about the past much. When I'd ask they'd both get real quiet. Ma usually got upset and that made Pa nervous, so I stopped askin.'"

"Well, you're right for the most part, boy. But did you ever wonder why yer ma don't talk like your pa did? I mean ta say her accent isn't the same. Your daddy was straight from Ireland—that's true. The way he told it to me, the fighting there was worse than anything you can imagine. He lost so many of his friends and kin to fightin' and hardship…, he just couldn't take it no more, so he left. He said everyone he knew called him a traitor and a coward for not staying to fight for freedom. He knew when he left to get on that ship that he could never go back, no matter what he found here. He said he just couldn't make sense of that much anger and hatred growin' inside of people for years and years and he didn't want to start a family there and pass the hatred on. I think you should be very proud of your father, boy. At least he tried to find a good place to live his life and he did what he thought was right. And he had a lot of good times here, son.

"Yer ma, on the other hand, he met after he got here to the states. She is from New York. Yer pa met her—I guess she was in a heck of a spot—with no family and no place to go. She hung around where the immigrants came into the harbor. She traveled clear up to Boston to try to figure out how they do it, you know, find a place to go. Well, there was some kinda shuffle with yer pa…some thugs were stealin' from the people commin' in off the boat an' yer pa meant ta put a stop to it. Yer ma saw it—he was by himself, she by herself—and somehow they kinda hooked up. Your pa said yer ma stood out like a rose in the winter. She was in perfect clothes and he said she was beautiful. She must'a been kindhearted too, cuz he was hurt and she mended him up. I guess they recognized the same kinda lonely fear in each other's eyes. They stayed on till yer pa got his travel paid off, then they got married and decided to start a farmstead, so they headed west. Right when they got out here, you were about a year old as I recall, they bought a chunk of land from the great lord of the Gallatin Salines. He owned most all the land around here. Of course he over-charged for it, you know that, but they were both so tired…yer ma' insisted they stop at the next habitable spot or your pa couldn't have one more red cent of her inheritance. She said it wouldn't a mattered anyhow as they'd both be dead if they went on any fu'ther. They were both real tired, I could see that plain, and yer ma was upset for bein' troubled with on the ferry boat th't crossed 'em o'er the Ohio—more thieves of some kind. Yer Ma was sure a fiery lady…."

Drake's voice broke a little, hoping he hadn't caused any more sadness for the boy.

"That's about all I know about 'em before they lived here. The reason you and Avi weren't friends is because yer ma had a way of thinkin' that white folks shouldn't be around black folks. I could tell it the very night you all rolled into town. She was right shocked when she saw Mama for the first time. I guess she didn't think she'd see any black folk out here, much less depend on 'em fer help. She even thought Mama's house belonged to a white family, she just couldn't get over that…."

"I don't understand. Why does Ma think like that?"

"Well, yer pa told that the reason your ma didn't have any family was because her father and her only brother got killed tryin' to help some folks escape from down south. They were against the slavery and had seen some unspeakable sights and decided to do something about it. So, every so often, they would go down—they worked with some kind of underground outfit—and bring a couple people escaped from slavery up north to a safe place to hide. One night they all got ambushed by some posse and were lynched right on the spot. Somebody knew where to look for them and they came back to your mother in pine boxes."

"My grandfather…."

"Yes, son. And your uncle. You come from a long line of folks with true character. They live out what's right an' have no fear about it. But you can imagine what that must have been like for your mother. Anne seemed to blame it more on the blacks than the whites and your pa said she never got past that, wouldn't talk about it at all, jus' clam up with hatred."

"But it wasn't the slave's doin'. None of it was."

"Exactly right. Your pa said she was even close friends to a girl that her family helped free when she was younger. But sometimes when people are put through so much, they twist it in their mind so they can deal with it somehow. It doesn't mean they're right, but I guess it lets 'em go on livin.'"

"But Mama helped her out."

"That's how your pa and I got to be such good friends. He was very grateful to Mama and me. Yer ma hardly ever came to town but for church meetin.' She didn't feel safe, so each time your pa came to town alone and I was 'round, he'd stop and visit. I offered to help him build the place and it went from there. I'll never forget how Anne threw a fit that she had ta live out of a wagon on her own land—we built this place as fast as we could, believe me! Your pa was a good man, son. I'd never seen a man so spirited to start a new life. He was unsettled at times, especially as he aged—you know this place ain't paradise— but truly in the beginning, he was a happy man. You would'a thought he'd landed on a goldmine. This place has been crass and wild for as long as I can remember, but, boy, to see your father so proud to be here made me realize there are worse places in this world. Worse by far…

"…You look a little taken' over, boy. I think that's enough talk for now. We'd better tend to the livestock, maybe round up somethin' ta eat. You look like you need fed."

"Yeah, Drake. And, Drake…, thanks."

"Sure, boy. A man has a right to know where he comes from."

Drake winked reassurance and Lemn caught the gesture, returning it with a sheepish grin before sauntering off the porch to feed the livestock. Drake stayed behind, resting on the porch swing, not finding the energy to get up just yet. He was naively concerned that he had put too much on the boy's shoulders. He couldn't live with himself knowing he was responsible for hurting the boy further, but Lemn seemed to take the story of his folks just fine. Drake's fears appeared to be unfounded. He just couldn't believe how resilient Lemn was. He thought, as he watched Lemn's curved silhouette grow smaller with distance, *That kid is armored with something.*

His gaze turned toward the road and he wondered how many times it was, in past days, that his old friend sat in the very same spot, watching him ride off.

He wondered what Devon must have been thinking all of those times knowing he might never come back alive, getting shot over a card game or other foolish, sinning ways. Drake chuckled and looked up at the brand-new, wispy clouds setting off for their morning sail under the sea of blue sky.

"Life doesn't make much sense down here, Devon. I should be the one dead, you know that. It's like fate switched us for some reason. You should be with your fam'ly.... I think I need a little help with all this. Help me do what you're not able to. Help me for the sake of your boy, Devon. I hope I don't shame ya."

Drake poured his remaining coffee out beside the sturdy porch steps and was able to look at all the aspects of their familiarity without feeling regret. He smiled as his thumb grazed the smooth, cool side of the tin cup, his skin feeling comfortably warm against it.

Chapter Eight

The early morning evolved through shades of pastel. Sweet softness rested lightly upon the world like a baby's blanket. It was the kind of morning one remembers for holding the last breath of innocence....

The clanging of pots and pans seemed almost uncivilized, so obtrusive to the quietness outside. After much ado, they sat down to a generous breakfast of salt pork, eggs and fried bread sliced from a loaf Avi had sent with them. Lemn swore he could smell her presence in the aroma of that airy bread, at least until they soaked it, fried it and smothered it with melted butter and maple syrup. As they came toward the end of the meal, Lemn's heart began to pound forcefully. The beats grew louder the longer he sat in bashful silence, wondering if it would be better not to ask. The heat of his blood rose in waves of swirling pressure, brushing against the inside of his temples. Suddenly, his stomach felt overly full. Then, without making a clear choice, he heard the words after they'd already slid out of his mouth.

"Why did they come after me, Drake?"

After he asked, he realized his tone was almost accusatory. A cold silence stood between them like a fortress wall. The vigorous pulse in his veins subsided and his mouth went dry. As he took a sip of cooling coffee, he figured the question must have hit a raw nerve. But Drake could be a hard man to read.... Lemn prayed he hadn't offended him.

Drake looked down at his tin plate hoping to see Devon's reflection there amidst the sticky crumbs—as if it could provide him with the right words to say, anyhow—but nothing appeared. His throat felt the massive restriction of the noose of guilt, tightening, starting to burn his skin and squelch his breath.

The reality of the responsibility he was taking on presented itself in full, unforgiving force.

"Lemn, you know I wasn't a part of the worthless sons a…of the *men* that busted you up…. They nearly beat you to death, but I feel it's my fault. Don't you see, boy…? I'm the one to blame."

"But, Drake…"

Drake held up a silencing hand and Lemn noticed it was not nearly as steady as usual. He began to talk slowly, carefully rolling the words over in his mind before letting them escape. His rigid face and piercing eyes took on a strange expression of vulnerability, a wavering uncertainty that made him appear reassuringly human.

"Lemn, I don't have a son, but…well…, to me, you are my son—as close 's a son could get. I'm not sure how you feel towards it, but watchin' a youngin' grow from a baby causes somethin' ta happen in a man's heart, I guess. But I've got a problem…."

Drake's eyes reverted back to a cold seriousness, as if he were reminded once again of the macabre source relentlessly griping the fixed end of his chains.

"I live a life that's dangerous to anyone who gets close to me. When I was younger, I used to think that my life didn't touch anyone else's. I figured that no one cared about me and that I was alone in this world—desolate an' worthless. And that was the case for a long, long time, but don't ever settle for feelin' that way, boy. Fact is, it ain't the truth. A man cain't get to be much more of a loner than I am, and some of the finest people I've ever heard tell of have crossed my path…. But even so, I never did place much value on my own life. I figured if I got killed in a fight, well…that's jus' the way it was supposed to end. I started out unwanted but, as I grew on, I came upon the grace of Avi and Mama who took me in as their own. Later, I came upon a woman who…"

Drake's voice cracked off and his hands started quivering noticeably, spilling a trace of black coffee that quickly seeped into the thirsty dryness of the rough, gray table right along with Lemn's diminishing curiosity. *I should tell him to stop, that it's okay not to talk about it….* Lemn had never seen Drake so unsettled. He suddenly looked fragile…, so much older than he really was. Lemn began clearing the dishes, clumsily clanking them together.

"Drake…, it's alright. I should get to cleanin' this up anyhow."

Drake tried to control his emotions the best he could without losing the magnitude of what he was trying so hard to say. The boy needed to know. He gestured back toward Lemn's empty chair indicating him to sit.

"Let me end it, boy."

Lemn sat back down peering shyly over the awkwardly balanced stack of dirty dishes.

"When I came across your pa…. Well, I'd never met a man that honest—not before and not since. I guess I pale in comparison to him. He didn't mean to leave ya, Lemn. What I'm tryin' ta say is that I don't know if I'll be able to do much better. In fact, I might make things a whole lot worse. This is a grave world we live in and I have to admit that I'm a little taken over. Now don't get me wrong, it's fine to have you with me an' all…. It's just that I've never done anything like this my whole life and I might bring ya more harm than good. I'm gettin' to be an old man by my own measure. I've done a lot of hard livin' an' most of it's been around the wrong kind of people and that can age a man. Age 'im real quick. And I cain't jus' leave it all behind…. They'd never let me…. See, there's this curse they call legend, follows you around if you want it to or not. And you don't even know the half of what people are sayin'. They won't ever leave me alone, Lemn, and it's just a matter of time before one of 'em gets to me. I just don't know when that time will come. Do you understand, boy? I'm gettin' slower. I'm past my prime. I jus' don't know when my time is comin', but it is comin', boy. And if you decide to stay around me, chances are it'll come after you, too. Jus' like it already has, only worse."

Lemn sat, speechless and numb. This was a side of Drake he hadn't expected to see and knew he'd never see again. It was a side that looked a lot like Devon—worried…, almost *scared*.

"I know this ain't easy to hear. I would be willin' to quit gamblin' if it would make a better life for you but I know, without question, that they will keep comin' anyway, boy. And I'm sorry now that I didn't make better choices earlier in my life. I'm not sorry for me—I'm sorry for you…. Sorry for a lot of things."

Lemn recalled what Mama had said about Devon not looking for evil, for death, and he struggled to find the right words. He had never had such a serious conversation with a grown man before.

"…Um, Drake?"

"Yeah, boy."

"My pa was a good man. He did what he thought was right, and…well…, he still died and left me and Ma, God rest him. If you get killed, it won't be your fault, Drake, just your time. I'm smart enough to know that people don't deserve some of the things that happen, they just happen. I know you won't fail me. My father trusted you. I trust you. I appreciate your help, Drake. You don't need to be worried about it, just do your best—you know, play your cards out."

All Drake could do was stare at the boy and let what he just heard soak through the calloused layers forged around his heart, rock hard walls keeping him safe and alone for years. No one had ever trusted him that much, except Emma….

"What I mean to say, Drake, is that I have known the answer to your question since you asked it—the one about if I want to make it my own way, or with you…? I know I'm young but I feel a lot older than I am…. I'll likely make some mistakes but I know they'll be mine, not yours. No one is forcin' me, but I belong here, Drake. I belong with you now. That is, if you'll have me."

Drake's smile began with a tiny sparkle shining from behind his weathered, ice-cold eyes, warming them, then spreading joy throughout his entire expression. As he nodded his head and breathed a slight chuckle of amazement, he knew he had been blessed. Again.

"Yeah, boy. I'll have ya…, be honored to."

They shook hands to seal the deal, but Drake didn't let go right away. Instead, he covered their grasp with his free hand, trying to ignore the tear that he believed was half a release of tension, half happiness. He was horribly ashamed of being so emotional, but it was the only time in his life that he had a glimmer of what it felt like to be somebody's "Pa." He thought for a moment, astonished by the fact that his own father forfeited the most wonderful gift in life. For a split second, Drake began to realize how perfect he'd been as a child—he'd once been pure, flawless…, the fault **could not** have been his own.

"Well, if that's the case, we've got a lot of work to do. How much do you know about guns, boy?"

Drake barely waited for an answer before he grabbed the Colt down off the fireplace mantel and released his own revolvers from the holster slung across his side. The dishes were thrown in the wash tub to be dealt with later as they made room for the guns and ammunition on the table.

"We need to start practicin' quick draws and ya gotta be right on. Are you a good shot, boy? If not, we'll need to work on it and in between times, how 'bout we fix this place up a little? I was noticin' the shudders and the roof need tendin'. We might have to sell a steer or two or I'll play a few more games so you can get a set of your own guns. You use and care for your own an' over time, they'll get ta be just like another arm. And your horse…, what kinda trainin' you done with your horse? Does he have speed? Is he gun-shy? A good horse'll save your life, Lemn. Your horse is your best friend…, don't ever forget that…."

Lemn was pleased with Drake's enthusiastic response toward their newly found union. He was relieved at the elevation in mood—he certainly didn't want to be anyone's burden. He sat, calmly watching, while Drake finagled various pieces of artillery around on his mother's table. Then the moment broke and Lemn shuddered just a little, it was as if he were watching Drake through his father's eyes—Devon's spirit was definitely hovering, almost tangible, and it wasn't floating peacefully. Drake's guns were glistening in the morning light like one would imagine pure veins of sliver trapped amidst dark, bland rock. They were clean and beautiful. Lemn noticed the "D" professionally carved into the ivory handle of one of them. He reached out and picked up the other, carefully turning it over in his hand. He slowly slid his finger over the cool, crisp "S."

•   •   •

Later on that evening, when the all-consuming sky was painted a riveting orange and iridescent pink with a backdrop of dusty blues and deep purples that made those under it lose a breath, Lemn said good-bye to Drake and watched him ride off toward town. Lemn was sitting on the porch swing with a rifle across his lap and a hope across his mind that peace would cover the earth that night. The early ghost of moon, hanging by a string of faith in the eastern sky, made him feel more at ease and he knew God's eye was turned toward him.

Although Drake said he was going to visit Mama and Avi, Lemn knew he was going into town to settle the score. Drake didn't utter a word for three hours before he left, he just sat on the porch steps and cleaned his guns to where one would think they would be thin as paper. When he was finally done with that, he started polishing on his horse. Drake had the most beautiful, well cared for horse Lemn had ever seen. He was a trace over sixteen hands, tall enough that Lemn had a better chance seeing under him instead of over, and he was coal black with only one white spot under his belly and one tiny star in the middle of his forehead, conveniently concealed by a full jet-black forelock—neither of these markings showed up in the dark. The horse had good muscling and a stable mind—very cool, but smart—you could see it in his wise, rich-brown eyes.... He was always watching Drake.

Lemn prayed that God would lead his friend to make the right choices, the right moves, and that he would return safely. Lemn continued, asking God if he was doing the right thing, following Drake and all. Lemn got a warm feeling in his heart as he watched the sky turn to black and the first and brightest stars winked at him, twinkling out a silent, soothing lullaby. He knew if he listened to his heart, he would be alright and his heart confirmed his choice to be with Drake, even though logic didn't..., even Christian logic. Finally, he prayed for his mother's spirit, that it find peace somewhere, if not in this world, then in the next.

Lemn thought of his regressing mother lying in her sick bed as he walked back into the house. He envisioned her strained, blood-shot eyes wildly shifting from one imaginary thing to another, yet never meeting his own. He noticed the weight of his body hanging more heavily on his bones, each step he was taking concurrently marking his troubled thoughts.

*Should I be at her side?...*step...*Is she talking sense yet?...*step...*Will she snap out of it?...*creak...

With the negative internal answers he felt, he bolted the door with too much force, slamming the stronger, doubled boards they had cut earlier that day loudly into their iron bracket. He was surprised by his sudden flash of anger, but pleased with the noticeable increase in his strength. He went to his bedroom and laid the gun on the floor beside his bed. He stared at the quiet killer for a while amazed at how the inanimate object was useless, meaningless, without human problems. Problems feeding the confusion that rendered it deadly, final, wicked. Lemn covered himself with his mother's patchwork quilt, folded his hands and awaited Drake's secret series of knocks.

While he rested, he contemplated the state of the first mind behind the creation of the first weapon…, the first human ever to use a tool to kill beyond food. He figured people today were no better, no further civilized than that first angry or fearful or lazy or greedy, ignorant man.

.   .   .

"Well, well. Would ya look who's back, girls."

A provocatively dressed woman, wearing an almost painful amount of paint on her face, trailed Drake to the end of the prominent oak bar, leaving her disciples to watch and learn.

"Drake, darlin', you've been gone so long I thought those boys done scart' you off, my handsome man."

"No, they didn't scare me off. But don't you have other things to worry about, ma'am?"

"Well, you know, I've always kept my eye on you, Drake," she said, tracing his stiff shoulder with her long, coral-colored fingernail.

"I appreciate that, Eve. But, with all due respect, maybe you should keep your eye on your girls a little better. Those rough marks ain't too attractive to me."

Drake cast a glance toward the girl to whom he was referring. She would have been beautiful but for the black eye and purple cheek bones that clashed boldly against her red satin dress, all covering a body that couldn't have seen more than fifteen years innocent, but had put on well over forty by now.

"Oh, well, that's just a little fall down the stairs, that's all…. Clumsy girl. She'll be alright."

"I hope you're sure about that, ma'am. Good evenin'."

Drake tipped his hat to the woman and she returned the gesture by rolling her heavily made-up eyes and casting a sideways glance at the girl with the beaten face. As she walked off to solicit other men in the saloon, Drake finished his drink at the bar, then ordered another and drank it down nice and slow. He watched as the abhorrent child with dark eyes looked into the bar mirror. She started to offer herself a look of despair, then refused it, accentuating her choice by hastily and unforgivingly applying more powder to her tender bruises. He wondered where her folks were…, if she had any kin a step above worthless. She reminded Drake of someone he once knew and he absentmindedly raised his glass to signal another drink.

Suddenly, a loathsome voice exiled his plummeting thoughts which were found trapped, for the thousandth time, sunk into an unsalvageable, dead end memory.

"Well, well, well. Did ya git my little message at yer doorstep, Drake?"

Drake didn't have to look at the man to recognize the filth, so he continued to drink his whiskey and look straight ahead at nothing.

"What's the matter, Drake? Not gonna talk to us? Look here, Jed. Drake's not talkin.'"

"Might could be ya hurt his feelin's, Slim?"

Drake knew they would present their offer soon enough and to directly ask them to reveal what their shallow, weak minds yielded for a truce would result in a lie or, worse, a reason for them to shield their fragile egos with a standoff showing reckless improvisation. Drake had ample ability to wait out the impatient…. He kept quiet.

"Ya know Jethro here is the one that hurt your little buddy's feelin's the most. Ain't that right, Jethro?"

"Com' on…. Y'all's the ones thit beat the little guy to a pulp, I's jus' tryin' ta scare 'im a little."

"Bullshit! All of us 'is got a problem with you teachin' a bastard kid to cheat us outta our money, Drake. So here's the damn deal. You bring your little Irish punk in, if 'es still alive, and we'll promise not ta kill 'im. He plays us fair an' square, you sit yer ass out of it fer once. If he wins, we leave 'im alone. If he loses, well, let's just say you pay me ever' penny you've swindled me fer and we'll decide if we want the bonus of havin' some more fun with 'im. Ain't that right, boys?"

Drake remained seated for the moment, his mind snuffing the choir of laughs turning torpid with an evil familiarity. He saw himself kill them—Slim and Jed anyway. He sat right there in their midst and planned it—grab the whiskey bottle, knock Jethro unconscious, shoot Jed with the left hand, Slim with the right. In less than five seconds, they would be lying motionless at his feet instead of hovering over him. But he knew how a life of gambling played out. There would always be others…. And there was a difference—albeit only the finest of lines some days—between a gunman and a murderer…, he knew that fickle line well.

If he chose to be decent…, if he chose not to kill them in cold blood, he was agreeing to a bargain, a gamble, on the kid's life. He knew if Lemn won, and he would, trouble would never cease. These men had too much pride to be proven losers to a kid twice in public view, but Lemn had to learn *all* sides of the game. Even if Lemn lost, it would never end…. They'd have a hunch it was put on, that they'd finally found a way to control Drake…. They would never leave well enough alone, always trying to get more money, using Lemn for leverage. If Drake were a younger man, he would take the boy and head west—get as far away from this life as the land would let him run. Then he thought of leaving Avi and Mama…. *God help us.*

"Here's **MY** deal."

Drake stood suddenly and turned toward them with such a cold lifeless glare, that his look, his *presence* seemed powered by an outside entity. All three men immediately shrunk back from it, crowding each other awkwardly. Jed fumbled nervously for the comfort of his revolver, but his duster caught on the hammer, preventing the relief of that false reassurance, proving that in another circumstance….

"He'll play **you**, Slim…. Your company here stays out and so will I. Understand? This here's between you and the boy. Thirty days from today, right here."

"Thirty days!!! You think I'm gonna wait that long when ya cheat'd me out all th…"

"You will if you're a smart man, Slim."

With that, Drake brushed by and left them standing, staring at each other. He never looked back, as that was a sign of fear, but he gave Eve a sideways glance as he tipped his hat. She winked subtly in reply as she strolled over and offered the three men a drink on the house. One small step outside the swinging doors, Drake let the fresh air completely fill his lungs and he released it in thankfulness. The hair on the back of his neck settled down as he shook off the heightened intensity that rises with the possibility of being shot square in the back. He walked to the hitching post, unraveled the soft leather reins, turned the stirrup slightly toward his foot and mounted his horse, glad he could do all that one more time. He gently clucked to his horse and took off at a slow secure walk out of town. He looked up at the pure moon and thanked God for whatever forces held those men in reasonable temper, since he knew it couldn't have been contributed to their own character or intelligence. He tapped his tobacco tin, laid down a line on a single sheet of light paper, rolled his cigarette, licked the edge for a seal…, all with rock-steady hands. About the time the cigarette was gone, he circled off the trail as he always did. Taking a little different route each time, he eventually arrived back at Mama and Avi's stead on the opposite end of town from which he'd just departed. He approached it through a back grove of trees that led directly to their modest and windowless barn that stood behind the massive house.

There was good reason he chose this black, surefooted horse—stealth. Picked him out of a band of twenty or so as a two-year-old colt. He'd been the quietest. Stood off alone, but not by force. He wasn't shunned, but rather respected. Drake studied them for hours from the crest of the hill. Sky was the one watching out for the rest…, constantly. When Drake rose, snapped a good sized branch off a nearby tree, Sky didn't tense, didn't cry out a warning but, rather, circled the herd, got 'em moving. With barely a sound.

.   .   .

Mama and Avi were sitting at the oversized oak table that looked out of place somehow—too sturdy with expert crafting and enduring survival to be bound by his eyes. Each time Drake entered their house he entered a dream. Some insignificant item that had always been there leapt out at his senses, its detailed existence witnessed (for what seemed like the very first time) as surrounded by an aura, a threatening wraith that could sense secrets. He was always on edge when entering that house, as if his tainted past invited Evil to float in behind him and steal his future. Of course this feeling was not brought on by Mama's warm eyes or Avi's kind smile, but by the dangers that lurked at the foundation of the house and their lives like a child patiently licking at ice cream only to devour it as soon as it becomes soft enough. He was afraid of waking up to the ominous enemy one day, having it shatter his illusion via the worst figment of his imagination.

"Hey, Spence…. How's the boy?"

Avi's butter-smooth voice and beautiful smile presented proof that his illusion was somehow real. He went over to the table, removed his black hat, pulled out a chair perfectly constructed to match the daunting table sprawled out in front of him, seemingly, for miles.

"Good, Avi. The boy's doin' real good."

"How 'bout ya'self, son?"

Drake nervously cleared his throat and forced his eyes to stay focused on either Mama or Avi, ignoring the house and whatever lurked therein.

"Well, Mama, I got ta tell ya, I never thought for one minute that I'd be takin' on this kind of task, but I feel good about it. Like I'm doin' the right thing. I wanted to tell you, Mama—and you, Avi—I couldn't a' dreamt when ya took me in all those years ago, that I would still be livin' now, much less have a boy lookin' up to me. And I owe it all to you two, I guess."

"I's a jus' tellin' Avi chil' here, 'Praise da Swe' Lord, He done sen' a Angel of Glory.' Send 'im straight to you, my son."

"Thank you, Mama. There's times I could swear that very thing…. He's quite a kid." Drake took Mama's hand and she smiled at him with all the warmth of Goodness. He put his head down on his arm while still clasping her hand and he slowly closed his eyes. She had a healing presence, a gift, that surpassed any physical rest in this world. Her touch felt as if she could be leading him into another life, but he would not change heart if he opened his eyes to it. He felt safe, he felt accepted, and he felt that she was proud of him for just breathing…, just…breathing….

This transformation of comfort happened nearly every visit Drake had with Mama. He knew this woman must have been carried by the good Lord himself for her to withstand all that she had. She was timeless and evil could not quite reach her. She seemed his only salvation.

"Spencah, chil', wake uhp youhr eyes…. Feahl the han' of God. He lead ya now, chil'."

Drake opened his groggy eyes leisurely. The lids fluttered and he blinked them to regain control as if he'd just awakened from a deep sleep. Everything looked brighter and better to him. Avi winked and squeezed his forearm. She had the most comforting angelic voice at times like these.

"See, Spence, you're not alone."

Drake regained his composure and cleared his throat—everyone in the room knew he didn't truly believe it.

"I know, Avi. I know. How y'all been holdin' up? Any trouble?"

"No trouble for us, a' course, but our brothuhs an' sistuhs…. That's always been a whole nother story, ain't it? God have mercy, Spence. An' justice."

Avi shook her head and concern draped across her soft face…, it was obvious she was in one of her "moods." She temperamentally slapped both hands down on the table—everyone else jumped—and pushed herself up, she then sloppily poured some coffee into a cup, sitting the china pot down with a strong thud, the spills intensifying her irritation.

"I jus' don't know how much longer I can sit aroun' here and watch horrible things happen and count myself lucky, ya know, Spence?"

Drake heard that word "lucky" echo in his head. *Lucky…lucky….*

"What makes me immune to the hateful things goin' on out there?…Not that either of you will answer me."

Drake took a deep breath, let it out easy before he began, because he knew she was right.

"I know it's a tragedy, Avi. A downright shame. It ain't right…, it's not fair…, but Mama loves you, Avi. Neither of us want anything to happen to you, jus' like you wouldn't want that for us. You've got freedom here, Avi. About as much as anyone…. I know it's confusing for you, but the rest of the world…hell, it's on fire, Avi. There ain't no where you could go without hidin', without runnin' like some kinda criminal. This is the best there is for right now. I know ya got spirit, Lord, how I know that…, but try and understand that it's spirit in this town, or a broken spirit out of this town…. I'm sorry, Avi, but that's the way it is. The world has so much hate. If I could change it, I would. Hell, if I could jus' change myself, I'd be amazed."

Mama soaked in Drake's words like a sponge, feeling every ounce of pain in them, then sending it all up to her Maker.

"Um-hm. Swee' Jesus, wahch our bruhthuhs an' our sistahs, they yo' children, God. Bring 'em up, deah Lor', bring 'em up to yuh Grace. Soothe the suffrin', deah Lor', make us outlas' it, deah Lor', outlas'…."

Mama let the tears fall from her uplifted eyes watching scenes of something Avi and Drake could not. When Mama talked to God, she was with Him, not on the earth. She got up without another word to either of them and went upstairs to her rocker. Her aged and gentle hand grazed the smoothness of the elaborate banister as it guided her burdened soul up higher, a little closer toward her Heaven.

"Amen," Avi quietly finished. As soon as Mama was out of sight, Avi grabbed Drake's arm signaling him to sit down promptly and listen to her urgent news.

"Spence, Mama told me 'bout Daddy."

Drake was shocked. Struck dumb. This had always been an inquisition to which Mama would never offer any answers or suggestions and for good reason.

"Spence, my daddy is a…. Well, uh…, he's a *white* man."

Chapter Nine

Lemn woke to light sounds tapping against a black dream.

Six knocks, wait till the count of three....

Then he was sure he'd heard them.

Then three more. An' don't feel ya need to hurry to the door. We don't need you to spring another giblet....

Lemn tried to clarify his somnolent eyes as he reluctantly rolled out of the comfortable position he so coveted, slightly wincing at the catch in his spine. He took the gun up off the floor—*Just in case....*—and noticed that it was starting to have a familiar feel to it, not so obtrusive and foreign in his hand. He gently tossed it in his palm, feeling the weight of it. He would be a natural but the cold lifeless metal reminded him of the *principle* and that, he knew, would never fit. He made his way to the window and peered out to ensure recognition of the tall dark outline, then he opened the door for Drake who ducked under the low door frame and nodded his thanks.

"Everything go along alright, Drake?"

"Just fine, boy. Just fine. Now go on 'n get some sleep, we got a lot to do tomorrow an' you need to be rested."

"Alright. Good-night, Drake."

Drake tossed his hat on the table and shed his coat. The moonlight leaking through the front windows revealed the gun hanging heavily on the end of Lemn's wiry arm like dead weight and Drake was proud that he was doing as instructed—carrying the gun with him at all times, especially when it seemed unnecessary. As Drake's eyes adjusted further, his mood deteriorated and his moment of contentment dispersed like the flecks of darkness floating from his penetrating sight. The boy had his free hand pinned against his side like a brace, supporting it. And his back was as crooked and twisted as a winding snake. Ever since the attack, Lemn's frame had veered off to one side and whenever he got up from resting, it took him a few steps to get the more severe kinks out. And it didn't seem to be getting any better. As Lemn shut his door, Drake wondered if the kid would ever recover and he couldn't help but feel immediate rage.

Damn those bastards....

.   .   .

Drake's body was tired along with his mind which was failing to find an easy place to store Avi's newly found discovery and the ramifications that would unfurl because of it. As his eyes stared into the vast nothingness floating above Devon's feather bed, he was unable to stop viewing the pictures flooding the screen of his mind. The thoughts rolled around in his head like a milling wheel, crushing and grinding on because the pull of the current was just too strong. His heart was heavy and swollen with fear..., he envisioned a miller with his sleeve caught between the unyielding stones with no one close enough to hear his screams for help.

"My daddy's a *white* man, Spence. Can you b'lieve it? *White, Spence?* Mama said she'd been real young, an' she was a slave to this man, ta my fa...*father.* Well, I guess more so ta his daddy...my *grandfather.* My *grandfather* owned my mama, Spence, an', in fact, her whole family. I mean *this? This* is what I come from, Spence?"

The way Avi's contorted face took on a sour look at the very thought of it, like she had just bitten into a rotten apple, halfway swallowed it, and then out would come these slimy choking words that gurgled underneath like whys— "*white*," "*father*," and "*grandfather*"—it just made Drake soul sick. Though the news had been no surprise to him....

Throughout her story, her pleading eyes had been begging him to reach back in time and erase it, or at least erase skin color and all the opportunity for human evil it covers, all the embarrassing shows of mental incapacity it reveals. She was asking him to wipe out the shady boundaries between class, the trails stupidity forged through a deserted Eden and back around by simply following sin's sloppy footprints—right judgement, left insecurity. The stepping stones of it all seemed to rise up as the world's children. She didn't ask to be a part of all this....

"Spence, I'm just not sure how I feel about all this. I'm lost in my own thoughts, like I'm spinnin' an' if I cain't get ground' I'm gonna lose m'self.... I hate what is happenin' around me—in people's lives—an' I've always tried ta heed Mama's word by stayin' open-minded, prayin', and helpin' out, much as I can. But sometimes, Spence, it jus' don't seem like enough, ya know? It's just not *enough*. And now..., oh, Spence, I feel like a damn hypa'crite, sheltah'd here all my life like some play-doll in a big, *fannncy* house, an' all dis time, *half a' me's part of 'em*. Y' couldn't have an idea of how horrible that *feels*...."

But he did have an idea. An idea of the first time a person discovers evil..., that it doesn't just exist outside. An idea of the first time a person realizes their own critical, ignorant spirit looks just as dirty and damaged to their target's eyes—it takes seeing that before the clean and flawless can show its shy and beautiful face mirrored there, deep inside of both. And he couldn't do enough for his sister at that moment. So he didn't do a thing. He couldn't take her pain away..., it was that simple. She'd always been so confident, but now...now she would have a sense of the self-loathing Drake carried around his neck like an oxen yoke, chaining him to the ground, never letting him rise above anything very far before it nearly strangled him all over again. He wondered what she would do with it—if she would ever look at him the same way. If the fire would consume her of if she'd turn it back to walking dust.

He could do nothing, but cross back over into himself. As punishment for the unrepentant, he resided there. At the spiritual graveyard, he rambled through his years. And it was a desolate place to be even though it was cheaply overcrowded and overflowing with distractions. He filled some of the space in his hollow chest with the kickbacks of Legend, like pride—it came easy. And power—it was free. As he walked the streets of his world, he saw injustices there, dancing, drifting..., and he believed that to stop them would cost. Would be the purchase of a ticket stamped "Early Death". He'd stood in line, stared at those ominous doors many times..., but still they remained closed and he, indifferent. So he turned his back—on all the things he could have, should have stopped, continued to roam the earth, sometimes vacant and half dead and deathly quiet. Sometimes outriding the flame, letting it burn, larger than life. Sometimes he'd join it—it and all its hell—because he'd grown tired of waiting for it to consume him, and because he agreed with the forces that be..., it was what he deserved.

Drake's exhaustion grew…, heavier, harder to fight off as the echoing voice of his sister reclaimed his unruly memory….

"But if I let my spirit git consumed by hate, I'm no bettah, no bettah than they are, understan'? I gotta stay above it, stay above it and learn from it. I gotta learn fr'm all this, or I'll die, Spence. I already feel like I don' have enough air ta breathe an' I cain't let this take mo' away. An' Mama won't tell me no mo' than what I already told you. She said tha's enough for now and ta not be discouraged, that she'll tell me more tomorrow…."

more tomorrow…

more *tomorrow*…

more tomorrow…

the wagons came through fast. stirred up night dust. grains of sand silently ground between teeth no one knew about. but somebody's always there, watching…it was so dark, everything was black, how is it, then, color still lingered…? not one left breathing wore skin that fit like it should….

"*Wherah's my baby goin' suh? C'n I keep my baby, suh? Suh?*"

"*Shut ya face b'for I shut it for ya.*"

"*Keep it down over there, you fool….*"

"*Yessir, Mr. Crenshaw.*"

"*The next time you use my name, you're a dead man.*"

"*Yessir, Mr…, a' yessir….*"

don't move, breathe small, act like you're not here, relax, blend in, try to fall asleep, you're alright, they'll leave soon, they'll leave, they'll leave

the most sadistic sound carried through all the ages, only a few can hear…it is a final sound, followed by sound no more…the wagons took them back to Slavery, traveling along the veins of America, but only in her sleep did they rape her, forcing her spirit back into the dark shadows of her soul, while you stayed, and stayed…, and stayed…forever, covering the steam rising from minute magnificence…covered from light and all eyes, *its earthly existence no more but for the trace of*

sorrow and crimson painting your own being
that even you could not see....
but White-blue Eyes
can See in the DArk,
CAN't THEY, BOY???

Drake pitched straight up out of bed, his heart lunging against his chest so erratically he swore he was waking up in the middle of his own murder. He clutched at his heaving chest as his eyes wildly searched to find the source of the condescending threats. His hand grabbed for his gun with instinctive precision and, for an instant, he was certain the walls had a voice.

He listened to the deafening words as they echoed against unfamiliar walls,
"Can't they, boy?
White-blue eyes...
Can't they, boy?
You can see in the dark...."

He felt steam breathe in soft puffs against the side of his face. His lungs squeezed, drawing his chest inward until he felt it would implode from the pressure of fear, painfully stretching and snapping obscure muscles as he panicked, searching through the opaque shadows, his brain not giving him a place to connect to. Desperately, he demanded internal control, forcing his failing eyes shut, willing the voices to stop. As his body slid back into itself and his senses became grounded, his eyes took the risk and fell upon the gleaming handles of *Devon's trunk...*, the same two, shining images that had deceived his perception and appeared like eyes *searching for him* moments before—the soft, secret eyes of an infant.

"Devon's trunk, of course, I saw it in the back of Devon's wagon.... Yes, Devon's house...."

Devon's house.... Drake let out a breath and drew another shaky one back into its place, enough to fill his quivering body down to his toes. Then he held it in quietly as he watched the traces of reappearing moonlight bounce off the dancing revolver gripped painfully in his tremulous hand.

"You're alright. Your hands are clean...."

.   .   .

The next morning, Drake woke slightly startled as if his mind had been replaying the events of his last awakening without his conscious consent. This time he was thankful to wake up to the welcoming sunlight innocently draped across Devon's trunk, its jubilant rays adding a bit more comfortable familiarity to the object by presenting the details plainly, rather than in dark cowardice. Devon's initials were carved in the wood just under the lock. Drake sat up in bed carefully imagining a younger version of his friend's strong hand guiding the knife that steadily etched out symbols representative of himself and his future.

What did you expect to find, old friend? I hope you were not disappointed with the course your life took on. And you've left quite a legacy in that boy of yours. Quite a legacy....

Drake tried to make this light conversation within himself linger, causing the darker thoughts looming ahead of him to remain trapped somewhere in future time. Soon enough they would invade his delicate psyche, probably have his renewed energy ripped to shreds before he even placed his feet on the cold floor beneath the bed. He knew things were spinning too fast—Lemn's uncertain life and injuries, the ignorant gamblers out for a boy's blood and easy money,...*a white man, Spence?*—and that he had to force them to stop in order to see each clearly. He chuckled to himself as he remembered hearing someone say that age brings experience. He was beginning to wonder exactly what experience brings besides immense amounts of fear and confusion coupled with the inability to handle what was taken in stride as a young man. The only thing he knew for sure was that *nothing* goes away....

Drake's eye caught a glimpse of Lemn on the other side of the bedroom window. As he poured buckets of water into the cattle trough, his youthful image was divided by the small, wooden squares Drake remembered helping Devon fill with store-bought glass and hang proudly in the frame. He noticed one pane had a crack in it and made a mental note to replace it later, then he focused his sharp eyes back on Lemn as he finished dumping the water in for the thankful stock, standing upright slowly, holding his back and looking on while the thirsty cattle drank. There was a sense of kindness, or maybe peace, across his face.

"Maybe that boy is stronger than I've ever been. I hope for his sake he is, Devon. But if you are floatin' around up there, ya best come back down and start lookin' out for him. He's gonna need it."

Drake commenced to rise and draw some water for his bath. He gathered Devon's old shaving brush and bowl to prepare to give himself a trim. He took off his shirt and bandage and placed them in the corner along with the other clothes he needed to wash and hang dry that afternoon. He looked down at his side and inspected the gunshot wound that was transforming itself into a dark purple scar. It was still soft, very tender to the touch. He was momentarily struck by how quickly his body could heal, but how slowly his mind—he'd all but given up hope on that. He took a deep and contented sigh—he was finally beginning to feel comfortable, this place was feeling more like home. He stoked the fire and left to quickly tend to his horse while the water heated.

"Mornin'!" Lemn called from clear across the yard and slowly raised a hand in greeting.

"Mornin', Lemn! Chilly, ain't it? How ya holdin' up?"

"Good. I got the chores finished early, but I figured you'd like to take care of Sky y'self, so I just gave him fresh wa…some fresh…water." After forcing out his last three words, Lemn's voice trailed off into a stark silence Drake did not heed.

"Good choice, boy. If he's my best friend, I oughta take care of him, hadn't I? Seems only right."

Drake winked at Lemn and Lemn tried to smile back but couldn't seem to think how for the distraction. As Drake had made his way closer toward him, Lemn's eyes were pulled into the maze of white and pink marks drawn across Drake's flesh like a recess chalkboard in the dead of winter. Lemn tried to turn away, but he couldn't help himself. He knew Drake could sense him staring. There were, what seemed like, hundreds of scars marring Drake's neck and chest—mostly straight cuts and, in the center of them, bullet wounds…, two or three maybe. Drake started walking and Lemn bowed his head in shame and wonder, following. When the two silently entered the barn, Drake reached down into a wooden barrel to retrieve a scoop of oats, self-conscious and irritated with himself for forgetting to throw on a shirt. He hoped the boy wouldn't ask questions about his butchered chest. As Lemn's eyes adjusted to the dimness, he noticed what began as a shadow proceed to reveal itself as a long, wicked scar darting across Drake's side—darker and more recent than the rest. Lemn wondered if its source could have been the bar fight a while back, then he reached up, touching his fingers to his own scar—it was completely healed. His train of thought led him to his father's empty revolver—the only gun the man ever left loaded. That gun had never been fired before and the tin of twenty lead balls, left untouched since the day of their purchase, was still missing the five that filled the chambers Lemn had found empty the day before. There were powder marks inside the barrel, scratches in the finish, grit in the workings. Fighting his bashful tendency to stay quiet, Lemn forced out the question.

"Did my mother shoot you, Drake?"

Drake dropped the scoop of oats back into the barrel and grabbed the rough edge of the container for support. His head was swimming with things from the night before and how horrible a five minute morning it'd been. He cursed himself for being so thoughtless, for allowing himself to get too comfortable—his shirt tossed in a corner inside the house just after he examined the very wound he was trying to hide. He looked straight forward at a patient Sky, remaining bent over as if the wind were knocked out of him by someone's unexpected fist. He slowly and painfully turned his gaze to meet Lemn's young eyes....

"Yeah, boy. Yes, she did. And I didn't want to tell you that."

"Maybe I shouldn't of asked, Drake...."

"You have a right to know. Most people wouldn't want ta know the truth.... You're not like that, boy. You seem to see things as they are an' you don't run away from 'em. That's bravery, boy. It is...."

"Drake, I'd like to say the same to you. You helped Ma even after she did that to you. Now I know why you and Pa were such good friends."

Lemn walked back toward the house and Drake was left standing, watching the boy depart. He looked up at the blue morning sky and smiled. At God. For the first time in years, finally glad once again..., glad that he was made.

.   .   .

(*buzz...buzz*...NO-n-n-nobody w-w-will ev-*buzz*...ev-v-er h-help me. G-g-get aw-w-way f-from-*buzz* m-my d-daddy. D-D-Daddy, th-they l-l-l-ock-cked m-me in-n here!! *buzz*...D-D-Daddy h-help-p me!! H-help m-me, D-Daddy!!! *hum...hum..buzzz*)

'They killed your father, they killed your husband, they killed your brother, they killed your son, they killed your mother, they killed your Father, they killed your Husband, they killed your Brother, they killed your Son, they killed your Mother, They Killed Your FATHER, They Killed Your HUSBAND, They Killed Your BROTHER, They Killed Your SON, They Killed Your MOTHER, THEY KILLED....'

(S-S-Silence!!! You b-bastards.... Y-You c-c-can-cannot-t-t k-keep m-me h-here y-your s-s-slave.... C-Can't k-k-keep m-me l-l-locked aw-away—*buzz...hum...buzzz*
D-D-Daddy?? D-D-Daddy, is-s that-t-t-t y-you???
D-D-Daddy, op-pen the d-d-door. O-Open th-the d-door, Daddy. *buzzz...buzzz...*
I c-can see it-t! *buzz...*Daddy! D-Daddy d-d-don't g-go!!!!! *buzzz*

SH-SHUT-T-T UP-P YOU B-BASTARD-DS!! *buzzz...*)

'THEY KILLED YOUR FATHER, THEY KILLED YOUR FATHER, THEY KILLED YOUR FATHER, THEY KILLED YOUR FATHER, THEY KILLED YOUR FATHER....come here, girl. don't you listen
to 'em, girl. hey, daddy's girl...there she is. come here, g-
THEY KILLED YOUR FATHER, THEY KILLED YOUR FATHER,
THEY KILLED YOUR FATHER, THEY...'

"Daddy...? Daddy, wait! Don't close the door Daddy! DADDY, I'M COMIN' WITH YOU!!!!"

As Doc heard the screams, he vaulted off his chair, spilling a fresh cup of coffee across his desk and onto the floor. He heard the crash of glass as his foot hit the upstairs landing. The thud of something soft but heavy struck outside the house as his hand frantically fumbled with the uncooperative key that refused to enter the lock of the bedroom door.

"God bless it! Anne! ANNE!!!!!"

Doc knew he would not get a response and as soon as he allowed himself to believe that a tragedy had already taken place, the key glided in and seemed to turn itself. His quivering hand pivoted the doorknob and the slow swing of the door revealed his worst fear…the window. Its glass broken with such force, there was hardly evidence that the cracked wooden frame ever held any. He glanced at the empty bed and silently walked to the window to peer at the ground outside. He willed that he would see only the boardwalk and the dried rose bushes forever in need of a pruning. His heart sank when his eyes revealed the truth. He saw her draped over the earth in such a contorted shape, motionless—the life snuffed out like a candle's light, still so needed. A dark pool of her thickening blood fanning out under her severed neck, oozing slow, like cooling wax. Folks from the street and Ellie—oh, especially Ellie, who had provided clean linen for Anne day after day—were looking up at Doc seeking answers. He waved at them apologetically, signaling he was leaving the window to join them.

He'd actually thought she was coming out of it. She had acknowledged his presence for the first time that very morning—made eye contact, nodded her head. Then, just like that….

His descent down the stairs was a sluggish, laborious one and once he reached the bottom, he stared at the coffee escaping his desktop, dripping drop by painful drop onto a pile of newly acquired textbooks bearing information on how to treat the insane.

Chapter Ten

The end of the day was approaching, creeping its way through horizon's door uninvited. It was as it was. And it offered no apology. Its brazenness went unnoticed for it noticed not itself. The marriage of pride and shame worshiped in some other kind of church as the color of ever-marching time evolved with natural ease along the road called Predestined. And it was a peaceful brand of beautiful. And the clouds pardoned the progression like mountains bowed down, humbled and moved. And the smooth yet brilliant sky taught Lemn an immediate lesson as he stood, staring out his father's window into nothing and everything at the same time. It took his envy and handed him strength and mitigation. In an instant, his mandated mannerisms fell from him like the withered leaves of a fig tree. He realized there is a time and a place and a reason for every single heartfelt human emotion.

Soul's Song....

Seasons change and our Creator, He makes no mistake in this.... Strumming across the erratic then flowing spectrum of feeling that keeps us alive and moving toward something we know not, but know the same, we make our music. Our soul sings its own song. And God seems the only One patient enough, enduring enough to discover, or to recognize, the unique melody resounding from inside each one of us.

No one else even listens. No one else can even hear the sound....

No one else was there in that moment when He first touched us, reached deep inside the darkness and set our tiny hearts to beating....

At this particular moment in time, Lemn felt darkly erratic, the sky inside him rumbled broad and deep with storm. Disgust mixed with the blood pounding against his temples till he felt a scream surfacing. If he had to suffer through one second more, he wouldn't be able to help himself...there'd be no telling what he might do. He turned to survey the usually empty table, awkwardly overloaded with the weight of breads, pies and numerous other foods no two men could eat before the staleness set in, and he saw himself attack it like a madman. He saw fragments of food hurling across the room coating all the best-dressed snobs in the disclosed filth that generally resided inside their shallow minds. *If they want to see how the insane live….* He could just feel the insincerity dripping from their lips and eyes, their tongues wagging with Anne this, Anne that…droning on like a swarm of stinging bees. *Did they even know her?* He highly doubted…, he'd never seen them before. *What kind of a sick practice is this*, he wondered. *What form of adulthood trickery invites strangers to invade someone's home after a tragedy?* "Paying respects," they labeled it—their ticket for sticking their damn noses where they didn't belong and the purchase price was a pie. A loaf of crusty bread. Small towns…, they're just plain suffocating. Relentless with social rudeness deemed proper custom by majority. Is it possible to feel free in a box…? *Probably only in a pine box*, he determined—not the translucent one that seemed to be closing in upon him while everyone studied and stared at the pitiful specimen locked inside.

Drake sensed it from across the room. Must have been something in the boy's bloodshot eyes, the heated way he was looking through them like a stir-crazy prisoner locked behind a thin sheet of glass. And Drake knew that feeling, knew it all too well. He quickly walked over and put a warm and strong hand on the boy's shoulder—enough force to startle him a little so he wouldn't react in anger. So he wouldn't break through and fall onto the long and lonely free-road that leads to Regret.

"Come on, son. I need a little air."

Drake put his arm around Lemn and silently led him to the barn, to his horse. Because Drake knew….

Nothing centers a man's thoughts like his horse. A horse offers choice. Always. A horse can carry you out of anywhere and anything at anytime and he don't ask ya no questions. He just trusts. Just standing in the presence of a horse calms. Cures pur'neart everything. Time spent with a horse even seals up a broke heart, sets it ta beatin' almost good as new.

Lemn felt like talking, but he didn't feel like speaking. He was clear full of almost every heavy feeling there was, but it wouldn't come out in words, he knew….

Words just serve to solidify, to prove it factual. Permanent. The only way this kind of pain comes out is little by little, day by day. Drop by drop in the silence of solitary tears. You can cry a raging river at first, if you feel it will help. You can press the agony out through your soul, tear it from your clinging guts, and it'll bleed out, leak and squeeze out, just barely an ounce. It sticks like poison to bone, it settles that deep. Like unforgiven sin it leaves a stain that time tries its best to cover, but, somehow, it just seeps back though and resurfaces. Becomes the color of your skin. And that's all you can see when you look in the mirror.

It's all you can see until a new hope arrives—one you can grab onto, one that doesn't reflect near as direct.

It's all you can see 'til you adjust to the darkness and the light drifts back into your eyes.

All you can see 'til you've made peace with God.

…He'd learned that much about loss last year.

The warmth of Drake's absent arm slowly lifted from his shoulders. He shuddered a little, began to shiver, but was detached from his own body. He felt something moist and bright and new flooding his Irish veins. He could feel it weeping for him. Raining down. Cleansing. It summoned the spirit of keening to rise up from the spiritual center of him and his blood started to churn like a slow, prairie twister. This force had Power. He felt it calling on him to join in— a string of wordless mourning that pulled continents together, connected centuries of sorrow, somehow stole the cold loneliness borne of life away and dashed it against the rocks for the sea to swallow. He could wail at the top of the hill, at the top of his lungs, for hours, but he didn't want to draw further attention to himself—the realistic rigidity surrounding him might start to crack. Rupture. Might break him in two. So he kicked at a pebble in the dirt. A cloud of dust rose like a slow, silent scream.

His blood fell cold and still. He could see he'd already gotten the toe of his polished boot dirty.

His horse let out a warm, friendly whisper of a nicker—the sound of simplicity. Lemn turned back toward Drake, but he was gone. The horse felt warm under touch. His face, soft like a living blanket. Lemn was drawn along a faint ray of light into the gaze of the sorrel's kind eye, into a miniature secret pool that slowly revealed tales of immense proportions in its depths and layers and circling, widening ripples. There was caring there in the revolving chestnut browns, it transformed into a welcome place to fall, to rest, like a bed of leaves tucked away in the wilderness—damp and cool but dry still, soft above and firm beneath—it transported him beyond his narrow life without the burden of journey. The darker shades etched softly there against a phenomenal mix of color formed the most perfect of all distant and earthly mountains with equitable majestic awe and grandeur emanating around and down them, trickling and flowing into lighter embers of gentle beige sand woven between them—miles and decades of sand. To gallop on. Free. In young body and unbound spirit. The center of the eye was twinged with a midnight blue like the dusky twilight of a desert sky—it could see everything there was and everything there should have been. Those eyes were delicate dimensions of jewels, precious jewels from Spain, from Arabia, from Iceland, from the seven sea trade winds and from the thunder fallen of the slit in the sky in a booming Voice commanding their kind to rise up—*Rise up!*—from the grains of shifting sand burying the prairie spirit, pounding with the blood of the massacred yet undefeated, drawing on the open air made of the last breath of many, hooves that still, and will forever, trample on history paved awry as they make their own way. Those eyes told him the story of where they have all been and where they are all quietly going, where all their hearts are aimed while they graze whatever is left of the Plains.

A tired tear trailed Lemn's cheek—a person could see the peace and stance and sweet sadness of Heaven right there in the simplicity of a horse's eye. Right there, a horse's magnificent spirit joined It somehow. Heart. Wisdom. And Timelessness. That eye was like a looking glass into a blessed world most people never find. A map. A sign. A promise. Acceptance. What a cherished gift from God given to the ones fallen awestruck in the presence of a horse, to the pain-filled children wrapped up in the presence of a horse.

It's a presence grander than all the problems they can hold.

His crooked body nearly gave out. He slunk down in the corner of the box stall, crossed his arms over his knees and bowed his head to rest. The gelding stood over him a fierce protector. Quiet. And sure. And still. Would have stood over him forever, loyal, like the strongest and most considerate of the Kingdom's sent guardians…a noble being, lowering himself only for a higher calling, portraying ultimate freedom just standing there. In a box.

The Lord of Lords shall one day ride in on a white horse….

While resting there, Lemn recalled Doc's feeble attempt at an explanation. The old man's tumultuous words kept rolling through his mind. The feeling beneath the message was certainly more sincere than that of the folks who clawed themselves out of the woodwork like roaches, scrambling in droves in order to dart their beady eyes here and there scanning the very cabin in which an unknown ill woman (condemned to eternal hell) initially lost her mind. Their shaking heads and clicking tongues indicated condescending judgement of a situation none of them understood or realized how close they, themselves, could be with the turn of a few events, with the strike of hell's merciless heel. Lemn barely paid heed to the useless words that drifted out of their mouths, but he did listen to Doc. The old man's manner was one he could not dismiss—the downcast eyes and quivering voice trying poorly to offer solace but instead, behind the words, asking the boy's forgiveness for his personal shortcomings as well as the failure of medical science to meet the human condition at some point that rendered all the scholarly entourage befitting.

At least the good doctor had tried. He tried long after everyone else had given up.

"Doc, I understand…. You don't need to explain. I know you did the best you could, we all did. At least you gave her care when she was alive—when it mattered…."

Lemn said those words, but they hit the air with someone else's voice lifting them—a man's voice. One used to shuffling through sorrow. One adept at handling the awkward aftermath of death. Becoming a man, by having family ruthlessly stripped away one by one, was exhausting…, nearly pushed him on over into the realm of elderly. The sheer effort it took to deliver the simple statement had depleted his last reserve of energy, swallowed the very last drop of his resiliency. And it didn't comfort Doc as he'd intended. In fact, Doc walked away looking worse, as if he'd been denied accusation, as if he'd been refused the only unforgettable outburst that would publicly solidify his failure and mandate his retirement. He was clearly carrying all the responsibility for a situation none of them could have rendered and he clearly did not want that responsibility again. The old man wanted to be punished—maybe to bring closure to his nightmare so he could once again sleep through the night. Maybe to exorcize Anne's crazed spirit from the echoing chambers of his house. Or his mind. (Probably one in the same….) But Doc didn't know Anne—not really. If that woman wanted something, it was already a memory.

Thank God Drake had the foresight to request that the minister hold the service late in the day. The herd of strangers had no choice but to leave early—townsfolk hated to travel the countryside at night for fear of secret-coded coyote calls and an occasional molted feather caught twirling across the lamplight on a breeze of black braid and those greedy bandits on stake-out—hundreds of them all filthy madmen, clothes and skin and wild eyes the exact shade of the shadows. Primarily, it was their own overactive and

undereducated imaginations pertaining to savagery that did them in—
episodes of trigger-happy men and swooning women were grounds for
yearlong jeering at best, though none were immune. Though first and last
carriage honors always went to the lowest of the pecking order. Lemn
watched them all through a sliver of space between two stall boards while
his horse blew puffs of comforting, warm breath against the back of his
neck. He studied Crenshaw's outline, complete with silk top hat and polished ebony cane, as it absentmindedly ushered a stiff frame of a wife. He
was a man who regarded funerals as proof of a successful business venture.
He had a slight spring to his step, his manner was quick and light as if oblivious to the black aura rising from his pretentiousness like a sin-cloud. The
soot above him dispersed and vanished for a moment then settled hard and
swift against Lemn's stomach. Like a kick. Thick sickness rose and bled
slowly out onto his tongue. The horrid aftertaste that man left could cure all
the hunger in hell. Lemn spat on the ground and breathed deep as the rest of
the nameless crowd trickled slowly from his tiny home, leaving behind a
dirty trail of unanswered questions he was sure they'd answer amongst
themselves. Why wasn't the boy ashamed of his mother's behavior? Why
didn't he apologize to the township for her sinful act? Beg God's forgiveness
of her in the presence of witnesses? Of the minister?

He had a question of his own…

When you are standing before God and your blabbering bank of useless
hearsay burns up as it hits the pure air there, what will you have left to say?

Lemn found himself back inside the house, walking aimlessly around the
table of offerings with no rhythm. His legs felt numb and his mind fell blank.
He was vaguely aware of only one thing—a warm cloud engulfing him like a
blanket of neutrality. It made him invisible, tucked him away inside its hazy
bubble. And it kept him safe from the repercussions of change. He felt he could
just drift. Like cottonwood seeds high up on a breeze. Just drift…. Above his
life. And out of sync with time.

He felt free, like a soul just passed on. But freedom never seems real unless
it's freedom outside. It was drawing him back out into the coolness of itself.
Out and under the air of a falling evening where the wide prairie slips into a
black ocean without depth, without shores, and the moon becomes an island.
It's dark and ominous out there—a place to get lost in, a place never to be
found. And freedom holds no fear. It has no walls. No boundaries. And no
family….

Thoughtlessly, he stepped out alone.

"Spence, jus' let him go. He'll be alright. Ya gotta let 'im heal on his own time. Thank God he's got us, Spence. Thank God."

Lemn's dulled senses managed to detect Avi's voice penetrating through his cloud as he shuffled dazedly off the porch and he thanked God for her. She was so beautiful, he wanted to turn back and bring her out with him, out into freedom and the mysteriousness of night that makes love bolder. Out to taste of the bittersweet loneliness he held himself in. Out to run through those tender fields of yearning found behind a single touch of desperation. He wanted to bring her out so she could walk quietly beside him. Walk quietly through the peacefulness in being and talk with a language left natural, a language free flowing and unbridled of the bane of two-faced words. Quietly. And beside him. All through his life. But he wasn't…wasn't a lot of things. Like old enough. Like strong enough. Like wealthy enough.

Like Destined.

So he drifted on alone—hungry and displaced and floating like he imagined a specter might creep—up the hill behind the house toward the black, daunting oak tree. The thousands of rippling leaves it was balancing on its limbs like sacred pieces of glass were reflecting some faint traces of color, of *life*, as he moved closer to it, thereby appearing safer, perhaps a little warmer, almost human. It seemed to be standing ageless guard over his parents' graves—one black and fresh, the other brown, dull and crusted over, more empty somehow. Fallen further into the unreachable, into forever, somehow. The branches seemed to be weeping out over both of them, raining down tears of sorrow suspended in time, frozen in a moment of constant remembrance. Perhaps the old tree held a window behind its withered face of bark, a hidden passageway they'd both stepped through. He wondered if they would meet on the other side, if his father would take his mother's hand, help her make the long climb up to Heaven—maybe that's what tall, tall trees are for.

Lemn was troubled that the common thought among people was that his mother would not enter Heaven because she had taken her own life. He was afraid to search the Bible for a scripture of proof and did not know that he would have grown old and died himself trying to find it. But he understood the sin she had committed against the Spirit, against God, against God-given Purpose. He understood that sin is self-abuse. He also understood she was mentally ill. That Satan brings disease. And that the Lord has ultimate power over Satan. So with this understanding, He spoke with every grain of will his existence could conceive, focusing on the *ask and ye shall receive* passage with everything he had….

"God, I understand You may be disappointed in my mother. She was sick, as you already know. She didn't understand what she was doing. She ran out of faith. And she ran out of time before she could repent of a broken Commandment. She's one of Your lost sheep…. Please find her, Lord. Please forgive both of us, for I let her down. And when you find her, tell her that I love her. I love both my parents. I can feel them. I know they can see me. Help me so I don't let You down anymore, any of You….

"'Now I see but a poor reflection as in a mirror; then I shall see face to face. Now I know in part; then I shall know fully, even as I am fully known.' God, You know us more than we know ourselves…. Show me what you want from me. Keep me protected so that I may succeed. Give me a purpose, God, and have mercy on all our souls. Amen."

The words his father read to him from the Good Book many years ago were spoken to him in full from a different domain and the crystal clear memory of his father's unique voice, breath, actions and physical warmth comforted him between racking sobs. Lemn felt his father's arms holding him now, they seemed so much stronger somehow, rocking him back and forth as if he were a small child—he felt terrified but safe at the same time. As tears eased down his young face, he followed them to the cold ground where he curled into the shape of the moon, smelled the damp earth against his cheek and listened to the oak tree breathe. It took deep, sweeping, enormous breaths—in and out, in and out—filling his own lungs with the wind of universal acceptance. The fresh and warm breaths were forced into his tired body by God Himself. It was a miracle, but his imagination could not fathom it. He felt his parents watching. They'd both been transformed into Awareness by now. They'd become perfect. The rising moon illuminated a path from itself directly to him. The tears flooding his eyes played with the faint light and it danced around her. Her ribbon of flaming red hair flowed behind her. He saw Anne walking slowly up to God. He thought he saw the Heavens open to receive her. Swore he heard His words. Words filtered down through thousands of voices spanning thousands of years to reach his ears, "I will not leave you as orphans; I will come to you…."

He forced the tears from his eyes, rubbed them hard, rose from the ground. He saw that the doorway to Heaven was just a rounded cloud. Just a circling cloud hovering in front of the moon. But that voice was still echoing through his mind, whispering through the leaves of the tree. And the last word spoken was not of verse. The last word he heard had been louder than the rest. God had told him. "Soon."

.   .   .

"Spence, jus' let 'im go. He'll be alright. Ya gotta let him heal on his own time. Thank God he's got us, Spence. Thank God."

"Thank God, Avi? Thank God! *Damn*, Avi! How much shit do ya think he should have ta take? I'm sorry, Avi, but these pompous fools showed up here for no other reason than exhibition. It's enough to make me sick! Weak people seem to flock to a suicide for the thrill of it. It's like they have to reaffirm that ever'one else thinks it's a disgrace so that they won't mistakenly slip up and do it to themselves one day. I'd do it ta myself if I was them. If I was that petty. It's pathetic."

"I know it's not fair for the boy, Spence, but 'least we're here ta help. We need ta help make 'im strong, not give him an excuse ta be angry or feel sorry for himself. Even if he does have the right to…. It'll only ruin the rest of his life.

"Look at all dis food! Mercy, mercy, mercy…. Is it alright if I give some to those hungry youngens that keep comin' to our back door?"

Drake looked at Avi with contemptuous, paper-thin eyes. As he glared straight through the narrow slits at her, he knew she was right. Her answer was simple and it was right. And he hated it. Sometimes the way she and Mama were always right turned his stomach. He always felt ashamed for the resentment, but he wondered why God couldn't directly lead everyone else to the Truth like he led those two—there'd be a lot less hell on the earth, that's sure. What made them so special? He'd been around Mama and Avi for years now. Years. And he still felt like he would never quite make It. He fought and he struggled to find It—inner peace, calmness, a righteous attitude, love of your neighbor. But people like John Crenshaw were his neighbors so obviously Mama and Avi's Jesus had mis-spoken. And there were things Avi didn't know about. There were a lot of things Avi didn't know. Maybe it was high time somebody told her.

Whenever he got this feeling, he knew he should leave. But not this time…. No.

"Avi, what in the *hell* makes you think you know everything?"

Avi stopped covering the cherry pie with the lattice-top crust she was fussing over and sat it gently down on the red and white plaid tablecloth she had brought from home early that morning. She noticed the similar pattern of the two objects—the vivid design crisscrossed like iron bars on a fortress, like millions of pairs of bloody swords, displayed proudly, dripping coldly, as if they had just finished slashing through the soft, simplistic backdrop of peace. In it, she saw them—makeshift knots of brother and sister. It was a dizzying facade they both threw up to the world as if the struggle were something desirable. And it wasn't.... As if their strife was something more dignified than just the ways of the world bending them down. And they were.... Both of them were succumbing. And she noticed the two of them could not be any more mismatched, any more contrasting, any more opposing and repelling—while still on the same side. It was a repulsive combination, woven there together, trapped in distaste until they'd been rendered antiques, tossed aside and immobilized just above eye-level on a dreary, dusty shelf. All of the sudden she felt tired. She felt very old. This was how she was spending her life. Opportunity could not find her. For the first time it occurred to her that her very breath might be contributing to that dusky odor she despised. That she might even be the collector, stashing junk in her big, soft heart. Hoarding the stinking pile of trash that had become the heated dialogue they'd both been rummaging through to find their worthless jewel. Their worthless trinket, their rusty, lockless key, signifying the value of the cheap answer they'd both been hunting while trouncing and grinding one another's limbs into dust. They'd wasted hours like this, years..., horns locked and growing twisted together 'til neither could find a self-respecting way to part.

She realized they were never going to find what they were looking for.

Not like this....

For a moment, she appeared to be contemplating running away or breaking into tears, but she just sighed and looked up at him with a half-hearted smile and said nothing. She chose to say nothing. The arrogance and sarcasm evident in his question lingered in the air between them longer than he would have liked and all the secrets he was about to reveal dissolved and blended back into their safe hiding places. He couldn't excavate them now if he wanted to—he was just walking blind on shifting sand.

"I'm sorry, Avi. Shit...It's been a long day for the both of us. Sometimes I feel that I should jus' keep my mouth shut—always. I understand that when I'm playin' I have ta think, I have ta choose wisely, but with fam'ly...I jus' make mistakes. No matter how hard I try to be a decent person and do and say the right things, espec'lly now that I have to be a good model, I always slip up—make a mess a' things. I've got a lot of anger in me and it don't take much ta light it. No matter what I do to try to get rid of it, it always seems to flare right back up like it never went away in the firs' place. I used ta be more in control, Avi. Everythin's changin' so fast. I'm tired, Avi.... Tired of a lot of things."

The room fell silent as the meaning of his words fell flat and hollow, their message void of hope. Avi could hold up the palm of her hand and almost touch the pain emanating off him like wafts of heat from a blazing and hungry fire. His pitiful expression poured inside her and wrenched against her gut like acid. Drake was the kind of man you could not touch, dared not hold, in his deep despair—no matter how much you wanted to. He was the kind of man that turned into Hate itself when he was angry enough, when he stumbled across that invisible line and on into hell. He was calloused from the burns he'd suffered and he could not heal—inside was just a deep and festering wound, a pitch-dark cavern just hollow enough to hold all the lost boys of the world and stunt their growth. She stood stricken and stood warned. She did not move toward him. She offered no utterance. Her spirit could not afford the sacrifice. His face twisted into grimace as it revealed the silent punishments he was screaming at himself while he fought some kind of internal holy war. His body slouched deeper and deeper into the crudely built chair beneath it as if it were hoping to take on the object's identity and, therefore, forfeit its own, escaping the murderous cruelty of the soul it encased. (*Rejection of self is the ultimate form of betrayal.*) His self-perception was plunging into some poisonous abyss in his clogged and sooted mind. Avi watched with familiarity. Like a reoccurring nightmare, she dreamt as the poltergeist danced through his internal halls, trouncing the buds of color, of newly sprouted hope, kicking down the weakening scabs clinging desperately to the rotting walls.

Drake had grown up hating himself for being born such an abomination and his adult personality could not shake the forlorn foundation on which it was created.

For what man would sever the feet on which he'd always stood, no matter how crippled?

> *Only the man limping along the twisted and cruel path of disease.*
> *Only the man crawling in the savage cold, forced to huddle at the doorway of death.*
> *And then, only the man with a violent will to live....*

But Avi was losing patience, God help her. He was a severely strong man, lethal in fact, but he couldn't comprehend the battle and that marked him. Marked him as one of the feared sons, born and bred among the most dangerous kind, beaten and blinded then left barely breathing the vacant air. Alone. To crawl, stand, fall, bleed. Alone. To drift, cry, kill, be killed. Alone. Except for her. She had always been the one. The one who lifted him up and out of his self-constructed, loathsome rut many times over the years, carried him through to safety, showed him the light shining against the sweet shore of the other side, and it was starting to drain her. Anger her. *Dear Lord, is this man stubborn! Why can't he just see it? Why can't he see what everyone else sees?*

And she remembered how things looked through her curious, young eyes....

The scourge of the earth that crawled on their bellies like forked-tongued serpents and fed on the scum of sin found in saloons generally couldn't care less about *anything*. But they TOOK NOTICE when HE walked into the room. The energy level of their heated, scattered voices revealed the very moment his presence had flowed in through the swinging doors like an all-consuming, infectious potion. *"Look who just walked in...well, don't stare, ya dumb ass! Ya got a death wish or somethin' fool?"* They WATCHED HIM as he inconspicuously surveyed the location of the tables and considered the combination of skill the clustered occupants offered while he had a drink at the bar. They ENVIED HIS assumed, unparalleled intelligence as he went over the habits and the amount, or lack, of will each player possessed in his mind. *"Fine, if ya think yer so smart then what do you think he's thinkin'?"* When he made a carefully calculated choice, they watched men of caliber MAKE ROOM FOR HIM with leery glances as they released varying amounts of tension—a loud sigh, elbows on the table, rolling up sleeves, elbows off the table, wiping sweat from a brow with the wife's embroidered handkerchief—because the stakes..., they instantly got higher. Then they CONFIRMED HIS location with each other, *"Drake's in on that three-hundred table. That Crenshaw fella don't know who he's up 'gainst. I thought Crenshaw gave up gamblin' fer religious ways...humph.... Religion my ass."* They ADMIRED Drake's confident aura, his walk, his moves, his ability to handle anything unshaken—seemingly untouched—even after a fight. *"Does that man breathe the same air 's us? Doesn't he bleed...? I mean, he did get punched, didn't he? Got punched damn hard.... Didn't he?"* Their drunken, jealous egos would ask the questions before their own lack of integrity slapped them on the back of the head leaving the bruise of embarrassment because they could never compare. Just to *look at the man* told them that. Just to *look at him,* even way back, when he was half their age. They all wanted a piece of whatever it was he had. *"What kinda gun's he got...?"* Just a tiny piece, just once, during their lifetime....

Way back then she'd already been thinking, *He c'n save the whole world. He c'n save us all if he'd just love Jesus. If he'd jus' love Jesus, he'd see. I'll make him see.* She'd witnessed it all back then—the way people looked at him. Rich and powerful people looked at him that way, too. She'd seen it with her own eyes, heard it with her own two ears while peering into the open barroom window, teetering on a foundation of recklessness, perched on the very tip-top of poorly balanced, empty whiskey barrels stacked out back in the dark, dirty alley. She'd seen it all up there at the top of the world just before her death-defying circus act crumbled. It made a horrendous crashing noise louder than thunder. Her legs flew her home faster than a bolt of zinging lightning. She didn't feel the sharp, singeing complaint from her twisted ankle until she was under her bed covers, breathing hard. The commotion she'd made in the alley crash was still ringing in her ears there in the dark silence. It kept on ringing while the blood in her ankle pounded and her flesh swelled up around it. That ankle was the size of a Granny Smith by the time it was all done but it was worth it—she'd found her people's savior. She'd found him.

But time and age marched on and wore down like it always does and Avi remembered other things. She remembered that of all the earnest, laudable men Miss Emma Thompson could have married, she dismissed them without a care and chose Drake, battling her distinguished father's wishes to do so. (The few times she reprimanded him, she would address him firmly as "Drake Spencer!" which got his undivided attention immediately. As his eyes gingerly climbed up space to meet her look, they relaxed the very moment he witnessed her patient sense of humor shining through her sea-green eyes—playful eyes framed with the silkiest white and golden curls. His heart would melt right into her sweet, dimpled smile as she politely continued on with her point that he was not adhering to prior.)

And now…. Now there was Lemn. And Lemn had no qualms about trusting Drake. In fact, the boy was taking to him like he was his own father.

How much proof does he need? Dear God! When will he ever learn that he is a strong and beautiful human being worth just as much as anyone else? Worthy of seeking forgiveness, Lord. Worthy of changing whatever it is he hates so much about himself. Worthy of closeness, of love…. Worthy of being alive.

And she prayed, right there in front of Drake, right there in the silence. She pulled herself down deep and God sent her a butterfly. A butterfly flying backwards, back…, back to where it came from. And as it folded, she finally realized. And her eyes held the chrysalis at a reverential and delicate distance. A simple, bland, calloused cocoon that scratched hard against her mind. And her heart fell down. And then down. She backed away from what she saw there. Backed away from the lesson hidden and so, so tiny in there—miracles are botched by human touch. *Humility.* The struggle was not hers. *Watch. And take care. That you do not overstep your bounds, creature sent walking softly. And I will care for you....* It was a battle *she* did not understand, nor did she have the right to—she had her own. And He said in a whisper light as wings, *Let be and be still. And know that I am God.*

Now fly....

And she turned away and left him lightly even though her heart..., it was breaking—split and bleeding and heavily beating. And, just as soon as she walked through that dark door, the cool night air held in waiting a kiss just for her lips. A sweet, soft surprise..., the lighted taste of pure joy. She smiled. The fairy-dust breeze brushed her high cheek bones and wrapped itself around her shoulders, lifting them up. It had strength. She heard a warm voice whisper freedom softly against her ears. She had finally found it. There, under the brave stars, she found freedom. But she was the only one who could hear it. She was the only one there when it finally happened.

Drake sat there in the emptiness with nothing but himself. Alone. He covered his face with both hands and rubbed his exhausted eyes, his stiff whiskers, then his eyes again, wondering why he was a mass of contradictions. He loved Avi, but he sure didn't feel loved. He liked Lemn, but he couldn't stand people. He wanted his wife more now than he did when she was alive, standing right next to him and it was enough to pull him apart. A little meaning in his life would be nice, make it worthwhile, but responsibility just tied him down. He could feel himself itching to leave Lemn already. And sure, he'd like to see the ways of the world change—*Who wouldn't?*—but he considered himself worse that anything he'd seen in it. God had some answers, he figured, because he'd looked everywhere else, but he was too terrified to ask the questions.

He needed to take a ride.... Needed a stiff drink. Better yet, the whole damn bottle. More than anything, he needed to clear his mind of all this useless thought.

Chapter Eleven

Two weeks had disintegrated into historic dust, the first in a depressing haze and the second in a despondent panic, but the particles of both had aged and died and dissipated beyond matter, the air of want clinging about them had evaporated like a dream, all of it weakened and sucked through some sullen void called Too Late Now. Sucked through and on into Never Again. And it was cursed to a miserable, secluded depth reserved for the misunderstood.

Lemn stood staring lost chance down without tear, but weeping still. *It's so unfair….* Reaching out, but arms dangling down, paralyzed, because everything was moving so fast…, nothing else in the universe noticed him. He stood waiting for them to come back—the moments that had escaped and betrayed him, stood waiting in the dry rain like a cheated lover with a coetaneous pure, now broken, heart. He stood there fearing the grey was suffocating the dawn because he could no longer see what he once saw in her. His thin, nicked skin bled testimony to how cruel the razored world was to the soft and kind. He stood there until he perceived nothing but the cavernous depth of ramification burrowing beneath the quivering shale surface of the shallowest of sins….

Covetousness….
It's time. Time spent in reckless spree as if it were nothing more than liquid gold trickling through the delicate fingers of an insecure rich man diseased with fame, enticed into a room full of suited vultures displaying trumped-up trinkets and societal must-haves, currency flowing like a river of saliva while dirty and starving children remain locked outside behind vacant eyes. Covetousness….
Not so sweet a choice, missing the mark.

No one alive has it easy. He had to move on alone or risk falling through yet another layer of deprivation. Perhaps it was harsh, but it was necessary. He had to grow thicker scars over the frail tissue of his soft heart without slowing its passionate beating, somehow. Without altering its strong desire, its genuine compassion, for these things were of greater importance, far more challenging and rewarding than mere survival. And to go on in pursuit of these things, he had no choice but to grope around in the sharp darkness his own failing pair of eyes provided him. They were the only eyes, the only windows to the soul, he had through which to attempt sighted endurance. And he could not eradicate the diseases they'd openly scanned and soaked up in their short time, could not delete the horrors they'd recorded that triggered their skeptic squinting and stole their blind faith. There was no longer any part of him that trusted the world that sustained him, but he'd die before he let himself lose hope for it. The heart inside him was that big. He'd not been victimized more than any other, to feel such marring depth of pain…, perhaps he just believed a little more in goodness, in true connection. Perhaps he had a little farther to fall before hitting the sad, manmade reality below. And lying there at the bottom, broken, he became filled and swollen with shock. Appalled and saddened by the coldness of his own kind. Because he would have been there for someone else—he would have sensed it, would have *felt* it, and he would have been there. He would have picked someone like himself up, sheltered them with love. He would have stayed with them as long as it took, even forever, without a second thought. He would have given them his life. He was the kind of person rare enough to do that. He would have. But no one else like him was there this time around…, and would never be. He was the only one who knew the nature of the struggle inside, or so it seemed. They all just left him the bloody mess that he was. No one dared come close. But still, even broken, he was who he was. And they were who they were…, what could they—what could the jagged, misplaced fragments of them—do.

.   .   .

"Mama, we gotta help 'im…, too much time 'is passed. He needs somebody ta talk to."

Avi's mother looked inattentive—lost to a daydream—as she had all morning.

"Mama!"

The old woman didn't change her stolid expression. Not even one degree of her peppery, thinning brow line rose in response to Avi's sharp tone. She just began to speak groggily, almost remorsefully, while she rocked in her chair.

"Had a chick'n one time. Had me some chick'ns ta look aftah, I did. Fox, paintah, wild dog maybe…, don't know, chil', but some kinda devil got in t'rew de gate one evenin'. Musta been my doin', leavin' a hole der fo' de devil ta crawl on t'rew like 'e done dit. Shoulda watched over 'em bettah. He stole what 'e wanted. But 'e bustet up dat chick'n's leg, bustet up dat one 'e left b'hind. An' the blood scare't me stiff. But dat chick'n still breathin'. Real shallow like she done. Tremblin' like she w's colt. I stole me a blanket. Wrapped dat chick'n up tight. Thought I was helplin' ya see, but she didn't get any bettah. Couldn't use dat leg dit was a hurtin'. Couldn't use dat leg….

"Got m'self thirty fo' stealin' dat blanket….

"He'll talk when he talk, chil'. No need ta peck 'is wounds ta death…jus' ain't no need."

       .   .   .

He was lost in a cloud risen of his own implosion. Someone had taken his hand unbeknownst to him and guided him through. Coddled him in a dark, underwater womb removed from the light of marked time and the invasiveness of clan—that place that holds the silent miracle of healing no one birthed forward from can clearly recall. He now found himself standing—weakened, oblivious, though stronger somehow. More experienced. But terrified….

To Breathe for a Season….
Seasons rotate beneath the sun and the moon. Feathers molt, twirling down through the shifting sky. Skin, leaves and rotted fruit and flesh are shed and turned to soil and seed. And it is in this fresh and vulnerable state of uncertainty, this nakedness, where man is revolted to learn firsthand that he is not in control of nature, nor is he immune to it. It is in this state of confounded delusion that the mind opens the door to take in a brand new world before it's springtime and steps straight into frigid snare. It is in these few chilling moments that he solidifies his enduring failure to trust. He fears what he cannot discern, he despises what he cannot manipulate. And, as the snow melts and the flowers bloom and the birds sing sweetly, he remains locked inside a dark lie. Though he feels out of his element and—as if life is passing him by—stiff and unnatural like a concrete riverbed, he remains rigid and soaks up his own bright ideas as if they were the sun—What's wrong with me…? And he proceeds to use his pent-up energies to decay and wither from within rather than rest and wait until he is called forth to blossom once again. Blossom and live life vivaciously. Full of clarity and purpose. And true to soul.

It's an effective tactic the forces of evil reserve for the tenderhearted.
For those with high expectations regarding their own intelligence, their
own excellence in conduct, their own ability to prove they are worthy
enough for the world. For those who want to do well at living but believe,
for some whimsical, malleable reason, that they are not. They are not
doing enough, well enough…, just breathing for a season constitutes fail-
ure. They believe their freedom lies in controlling circumstance, perfect-
ing it, and this belief is indeed their prison. Their poison. For we are all
creatures of change in a world that is turning.

We do the work of the devil. We do it to ourselves. While he is sleeping,
his belly…, it grows.

…Lemn *believed* he was flawed—and what wasted power lies in the hysteria
that typically follows this revelation. He *believed* that this flaw of his had
caused him to falter initially and that it needed to be discovered and eradi-
cated. Immediately. For he'd already wasted too much time and this, of course,
left no time to consider anything antithetical. And his brutal excavation was
fueled on its misguided course by anxiety. *If it happened once….* He didn't
want to feel that assailable again. Ever…. So he set himself to thinking.
Reasoning and planning. Working in himself. For himself. Disrupting everything about himself in a feeble, erroneous attempt to protect himself.
Completely incognizant of the very Hands that delivered him and set him
upright. The same Hands that would undoubtably deliver him again and again
and again through the processes of life, death and resurrection—the very
processes that keep the soul renewed. And flourishing.

It seems ignorance and independence are the elements that age us….

So in this season of numbness, in this obliviousness seemingly brought on
of his own accord, it had been simply inevitable—the passing of each hour and
the expectations they let fall. He could no more retrieve time from the past
than his parents' breath from the atmosphere and it would be redundant to try.
And now, the seconds were screaming by his ears in the tiny rush of air as he
walked. He just walked…. With no particular destination other than peace of
mind, solace, the few simple answers he was craving, but his steps were leading
him deceptively backwards onto deeper and darker trails, onto backsliding spirals that wound around tightly and tunneled down through his twisted imagination. He wondered how a journey through the inside of himself could be so
strange—*I should know myself by now…, I should know who I am and I should*

be stronger by now—wondered how it could be that such a large part of him had been set aside and rotting for so long, the stench wafting off so overpowering, so infectious. *I should have known, should have seen it coming....* And discovering this wicked pit of confusion circulating down deep within drew the scent of fear out of his glands on a cold sweat. But he was barely there.

He was barely aware of all the things he would never come to know.

He moved on. In the physical. In the mental. It was the spiritual side that had left him. *Sufficient for each day is its own trouble...*was less than a whisper in his manic crowd of thought. His guts churned. They seemed to struggle and twist amongst themselves like a pail of nightcrawlers. They began to knot up. This was a hyperactive upset of a magnitude he'd never felt before. The rumbling quake rising up inside him threatened to rupture and fray his delicate web of nerves to the end. His hands began to tremble. He had nothing with which to compare this episode other than an encounter alone with Avi—and this felt much worse for there seemed to be no *cause*. Its source was intangible, unavoidable. No way to run away from it. No way to separate. *If only I could buy myself more time.* More time to do what, he wasn't sure. And suddenly, he heard the bullet zing beside his ear leaving the air against his cheek to linger still, tense and void of wake. He followed its hiss backwards through some sort of atmospheric warp while his eardrum throbbed. He followed it for miles until it was sucked back inside the quiet, sheathed gun, sucked back into its holstered brand of short-lived innocence. He was left staring at the barn, staring at the disturbing peacefulness of it, while the memory of his father played out the events of the days prior—secret, unassuming days that were reversed, sunset to sunrise. The subconscious recesses of Lemn's mind unfurled, rewinding back through all the delicate and painful moments before his father was shot..., if the man would have been given the chance, he probably wouldn't have changed a single thing. Because it didn't matter. Some of the things a person hopes and prays for 'til they just can't live without, or things a person regrets so severely they wished they were dead—they're things that don't even matter. They just don't matter.... Because something inside his father knew what was coming. It was in the way the man carefully ordered everything—*everything*. It was in the way he caressed and studied ordinary, uninteresting things, studied them *too* long—an axe blade, a wildflower. It was the way he oiled each and every piece of harness leather he ever owned, painstakingly, almost mournfully. Oiled them twice in the same week. It was in the way he went to town that fateful day, stocking up with extras..., stocking up a surplus of things that his family already had. He knew.

At this, Lemn's muscles started to slacken. Coolness filled his veins. He was letting go of his father. His heart was solidifying around the impurity of it all while it was cutting off the tender ties one by one. (How he knew this was happening he couldn't, and would never be able, to say.) He literally felt himself giving up—meaning, purpose, and every reason under God—and, for a moment, he was lighter somehow, at the absolute mercy of another driving current. But as his line of thinking continued to sink to a depth beyond caring, as it drifted on out into a sea of blandness, unknowingly, he had tossed the carnal man deep within him life. His mind had offered this new brand of man a series of footholds—flaws all strung out, woven together for collective strength and sway, sent wild and unfurling...the end of a rope. The grip and vigor of this massive climbing frame caught him off guard. He surrendered slightly as it pushed on through the surface with survival's greed. It held up a strong, tempting hand that he tried to join but soon discovered the bottomless debt that ensued, the impossible weight of void inside where integrity once stirred and overflowed. As he fed its ambition with curiosity and poured its empty complaints full of pity, this gluttonous persona grew and drained him dry. It was broad-shouldered and crass and gave no thought to crushing the vulnerability of its own youth. It lumbered through fragile lessons learned and tossed them aside—shattered. It trampled on the worthless piles of rubble it made of previous years—wasted dreams and things, important things, once strived after for change, for dignity, for preservation because they were right and good—and it rose up higher in its own domination. It held regard for nothing, for no one, but itself.

Lemn was repulsed by this possible version of himself that he'd conjured up. The familiar taste of regret that swirled in his mouth devastated him—he spat in the sand. Like oceans of saltwater tossing the thirsty closer toward the sun, more sorrow ground into his wounds he did not need. Yet he'd never seen anything so clearly before. The disappointment clung painfully to his eyes as he recognized something, something unmistakable—the taut lines that tied him to this virile premonition were the very same lines dripping from the hardened faces of many men, real men he knew and loved. And he'd never stood so close to choice before—how easy it would be to step into a shell of callousness and brutality. How easy it'd be to strap it on, but he wouldn't be able to move. He'd have no freedom. The weight would pull him down and all the fresh spring water in the world wouldn't soften the red eyes he stared out through—dry and listless, chilling raw and rubbery eyes. He'd become a blank soul without vision..., rambling around a sunken grave, waiting to die a more permanent death while hauling drudgery upon his streamlined back.

That's not how it's gonna be....

Fresh air assaulted his face. He found himself standing still but couldn't recall when he'd stopped moving. He felt dizzy…, too hot for the early time of day. A sense of vertigo slid up beside him, then beyond him, and the world seemed to usher his body forward without his consent—blatantly. He knew he'd have to be very careful, that he was in an extremely delicate state. Then like another realm of a night-long dream, something new rotated within and around him. Another turn in the road he was winding down, another roll of the dice tossed in a shady gamble—a word that slyly suggests it's not much more than a harmless game, but victims know it's a game with the hint of blame, blasphemy and blood tucked inside its borders. This suave new thing fell heavy but polished at the pit of his stomach. It rocked. It was there. It let off an air that whispered to him. Whispered the possibility, the probability, that everyone was possessed. At one time or another, every single one of us is seized by the devil and possessed…some longer than others. *And the one thing Satan has, my young boy, is expertise in manipulating his minions....*

This hissing whispering woke him up. He started. He felt something unyielding lodged in his throat—it burned, felt snake-bit from the inside. He could not breathe and his eyes sprung open wide.

Put not your trust in man....

He bent down and it loosened. He gagged and coughed it up, his tongue sensed the tiny, spherical indentations—seven on one flat side—but, when he spit it out, there wasn't anything there. He drew in shallow, rapid breaths but none of them took, his throat throbbed and his mind wondered, his eyes fluttered and gazed upward…. *How is one to know when the man not to be trusted is himself?* His only answer was the fact that something sane within him had asked the question. His air slowly returned to him. And it seemed that his time had come. For things had shifted. Nothing felt the same. His instincts could not be discerned. But he knew there was a part of him, living inside of him, that he did not want to be. And when he turned back inside to face his demons, he found himself standing not in familiar green pastures at the still water's edge, but at the mouth of a murky pit, a sticky rimmed cavern swirling with the spirit of fear, dripping with assurances torn. Where had his integrity gone? He was starkly alone—and yet accompanied by multitudes passed unknowingly by—in his bewilderment. And in his search, he traveled beyond himself and could feel the gateway to hell looming just ahead. And the path on which the core of him stood was smooth with wear, steep and slanted. Slick like black

ice. There was a howling wind pressed in deep at his back and the barren trees
flanking him were out of reach, brittle and dead. The dominion of wicked sky
was clouded black beneath deep streaks of blood-red that somehow flowed
into a rancid smoke that stole his natural sight. Air was being sucked from his
lungs, from the hollowness within him, from this entire place. And how suddenly it was that he'd found himself transported there. How unexpectedly the
course of a life could turn inside out and bleed.

*Every man but One has been tricked and confused and blinded beyond his
shallow circumstance. Backed into a corner of liquid walls. Reality bites until the
blood it draws looks just as real..., until your mind joins in the cry of the victimized and strengthens the facade.*

Blood-red soon turned to sky blue. Trees sprouted leaves quicker than eyes
can adjust. The breeze beyond the crystal sunshine blew at his face and, this
time, he was fully awake to his world. He tried to make sense of it all, to fit
these visions into his life.... He could escape death of body for a while. He
could escape death of soul if he sold the best piece of it. He could leave this
place, the farm on which he stood, but it was the only part of his father—and
now his mother—he had left. This is what they had given him. This is what
they died for.... He could keep running back to the ease of his boyhood, but he
had seen how efficiently age paves the road in-between. No, it was time he
made his own way. Time to turn forward and face the things that lie ahead.
And he didn't know what that would hold, what that would mean.... It
seemed, that for now, he needed to find a way to move while standing still.
Find a way to fight without sinning. And it seemed impossible..., Slim wanted
him dead. Slim was merciless. Slim's was a blinded soul. He looked to his parents' graves—two slits in the still ground that were beginning to look like the
margins of his destiny. They were just ten steps in front of him.

*If only the spirit of the Father could whisper from beyond them just a little
louder. Just a little clearer. Just enough that we would need no faith....*

Suddenly, Drake emerged from behind the far corner of the house. It
shouldn't have startled Lemn, but for some reason his body jerked. His heart
lurched. He just wasn't himself today and nothing looked the same. Nothing
seemed right. He watched on as Drake placed some secondary tools on the
ground and then worked himself between Anne's favorite shrub—a spindly,
crimson bush so vibrantly colored it appeared to be burning—and a window.
He was absorbed in the task of hanging replacement shutters and he wore a

look of controlled determination on his face. His hands and forearms were strong and accurate in their skill. The muscles most responsible for the force behind them moved with a cool, steady confidence, with the free fuel that comes from enjoying the work at hand. Yes, Drake looked fine. He looked just fine. And he acted fine…, and he had the whole time. Not a care in the world did that man carry. But Lemn had been anything but fine. The only thing in the past week the boy could think about with any degree of rationality was the wife he was never going to have. The girl, wandering around lost out there, that he'd never find. It almost made him sick, thinking of her. He knew she was out there. He could feel it…. But now he'd probably never reach her. Never know her. Or worse, if he survived, he might reach her and not be any good for her. And that did matter. Mattered more than anything to him.

All the pressure'd been on Drake before. But Drake could handle it. He was used to it. It even seemed like he *enjoyed* it, like he was *made* for it. The last time Lemn set foot in the Shawneetown bar, he'd been naive. He assumed that it was all for fun. A joke. Something that the older men would laugh at. He figured they'd cut him some slack if, by some small chance, he did win. But there weren't no slack cut…*Maybe he'll think twice 'bout usin' a kid ta cheat with, ya lil' Irish punk*…. Little Irish Punk. Lemn mouthed the words as he rubbed his aching muscles fighting their cursed location against his crooked spine. Tremors rose from his lower back to his skull setting his hair on end and he could hear a hissing noise leaking out from inside his bones. He felt a sudden chill just before the queasiness in his stomach washed over his entire body. Before he knew it, Drake was jogging over to him with a strong concern in his eyes.

"You alright, boy?"

"No, Drake. Don't know as if I am."

Drake dropped his hammer in the dust and looped an arm around Lemn's waist just before he faltered.

"Come on…. Let's go up to the house so you can get rested…."

If the truth be known, Drake had been hiding it all along (and he hid it well—it was second nature for him to be a walking, breathing deception). Deep underneath, he had been tormented over the upcoming fight for Lemn's life since the sick scheme was forced upon him exactly twenty-five days and twelve hours ago. He was tired of counting the days. The passing hours enraged him, nearly dithered him up into full-blown fits. He wished he'd have told them sixty days. The kid's mother wasn't well…. *What was I thinking?* He wished he'd 'a just killed 'em all. Right then and there. They were throwing down threat. They were implying the murder of a thirteen-year-old boy. Rolling the idea around on their tongues like cheap whiskey. They were gambling with a consecrated life like it was worthless. They had no idea what kind of flame they were playing with. He should just hunt 'em down now. Kill 'em all in cold blood and broad daylight…. It was tempting. Heat rose from his back, straight up through his shoulder blades and down his quickest arm. The muscles of the right side of his upper lip contracted and twitched slightly like they'd instinctively done before each and every draw while his weaker right eye squinted and his left focused on the target like a hawk's. His mouth watered then went dry. His tenseness slacked off some and left a dull, throbbing ache at the base of his neck. He needed to stay around for the duration, for Lemn's sake. He needed patience, needed to stick to his plan, because the sheriff couldn't cover him for everything…. There were always too many witnesses around those fools anyhow—they all flocked together like a bunch of loudmouthed, drunken loons. Their saviors were in numbers and dumb luck. And aggressor's pity.

And after all this time, Drake still hadn't come up with the words to lay out the stakes for the boy. Lay 'em out honest and ugly as they truly were. They were damn high, damn pricey, and Lemn was so young—had no experience with throwin' out the trash and leaving the whys unanswered. A game like this could have repercussions that traveled for miles, lasted for years, if the kid was lucky enough to be left standin' after the wake. The what-ifs alone could craze a man.

Drake stood aside as Lemn curled up on the feather bed. The boy whimpered a little then took a few deep breaths, letting each one out long and easy. It made him look even younger, balled up like he was. He seemed weak. Real weak, like a hatchling swallow knocked out of its nest. Drake covered him up with a quilt and stepped back again. Devon was probably rolling and clawing in his grave just out back, probably brewin' up an Irish storm. But Drake just stood there. Silent with his arms crossed and unchanging. *Ta hell with it…*, this thing already had momentum. Had a force all its own. The fall would be inevitable. And when it hit, it wouldn't land pretty—that was the only thing he was certain of. That and the fact that the kid would win. He would win the game of poker easy. They had practiced for hours on end, not so much to sharpen skill, but to test Lemn's phenomenal gift. Its improbable reality portrayed itself hand after hand, humbling Drake's normally consistent, cut-throat tactics and wounding his pride (he didn't *let* the kid win once). He'd win the card game easy. It was the bigger game that had Drake worried. They'd practiced target shooting and quick reloading, too. Lemn's horse was no longer scared of the shots even when Lemn fired from his back. It was Lemn who still flinched. The kid didn't have the will to hunt for his own food.

"You jus' take it easy today…. Just take it easy. You don't have anything to worry about, you're more th'n ready."

Drake stopped himself just before stepping out the door. He kept his back to Lemn and a look of clouded uncertainty crossed his face as he spoke to the floor, voice steady and smooth as the sun.

"I don't know how to tell ya this, boy, so I guess I'll just say it. Slim's gonna have ta die…. Ain't no other way."

The door closed, sealing the light from Lemn's life. He was locked in and waiting, the dark room an early prison that captured him for a crime not yet committed. He'd never felt further removed from himself. From God. Lemn's mind was cursed—in itself, in reality, in its realms of dizzying sickness and in its dreams where the gateway to hell creaked back open, inviting him to slide on in.

Chapter Twelve

"Well, well…what in thee hell have we here, Drake?"

They found Slim nestled in behind a game table in the back of the saloon, glassy-eyed and different—no booze, no pretentious airs. He'd literally backed himself into a corner and seemed oblivious to the eerie aura rising from his own skin, warning of something poisonous collecting within him…. Drake could sense it on him. Immediately. It hissed out a premature elegy through coils that rattled beneath illusory scales. It moaned, trembled and rose up through cracks in the man's flaky layers of cast care—cracks that were itching like hives. And his breath of breezy easiness turned foul just past his lips, his tongue swam in babbling streams of venom—acidic sewage bubbling up through rusty veins and infected glands. The lucid casing binding his flesh was stretching thin, barely keeping his being contained, barely keeping lard from rendering and insides from boiling over—all of it oozing down around and inside his own boots, a thick, pink and glossy pool…raspberry swirl collecting in Drake's mind.

But Slim was simply smiling—an overly-confident and sickening smile, but a purely authentic one. He was completely content with himself and everything that stood for…, anything that stood for—stupidity and crudity proudly counted and concluded as, basically, the sum. And he had those dusty and water-cracked boots of his resting upon the table's edge, ankles firm but nonchalantly crossed, and one of his spurs held a tiny strand of thread entangled in its rusted rowel—taut, green thread still hooked to an unattractive arc he'd managed to snag through the cloth that covered the table. Drake doubted Slim would even notice—Slim wasn't a highly polished man. (He needed a good soak, actually. Needed to be taken out back with a stiff brush and a bar of soap, stripped down, dunked into a trough, scrubbed, shaved, trimmed, then stuffed into storekeepers' garb, a three-piece suit or maybe a circus costume to see if one of those looked any better on him. He just didn't fit the profile—whatever sloppy, undefined profile it was he was trying to fit. He wasn't particularly *good* at anything he did except for getting under people's skin. He made gamblers, cowboys and even outlaws look bad and he had irritated nearly all of them in the territory at some point.) And he wasn't especially ambitious. Nor could he be accused of being observant. (Maybe having the undisputed knack of honing in on the nearest hashish or opiate could be plausible, but never could he be accused of being too observant. If something did catch his bloodshot and watery eye it was written all over his scraggly face though, in the end, he could usually care less one way or the other—he probably forgot about it before he could decide. But it was, typically, odd and minuscule things that ignited that explosive, insatiable temper of his—things *no one* would notice, much less have an opinion about. And this gullible, passive, yet unpredictable personality made for a miserable poker player…, seemed to make for a miserable existence all the way around.) But he'd readied himself for this night, however. His personality seemed to have shifted. Overnight. And he stood firmly grounded in it—fortified. And to Drake, his eyes appeared clearer—more focused and noticeably *dis*-jaundiced—and his affectation, more alert. He wasn't liquored up—not at all. And this genuine sobriety was a first. As was his punctuality, his preparedness. He had been on time…, *he* had been waiting for *them* and with his own deck of cards. His fingers had been strumming atop the crisp, brand-new deck when Drake and Lemn happened upon him and those fingers were not shaking—their rhythm was methodical, calm and steady. And just as soon as he had recognized his hostage opponent, his lips curved upward into a smile so revolting it took restraint for Drake not to slap it off his irritating face—even at his best, Slim was still the lowest lifeform creeping the earth.

"I didn't think yer lil' Irish punk cheater'd even show up." He spoke the sentence upward as if addressing the clueless air and finding understanding there in a floating world with no noise and no relevance. And he seemed more surprised than anyone when he came back down and realized he'd spoken out loud. His soft foundation sagged disgracefully as he stood back and witnessed the blatant layers of foolish haste plastered atop his amateur design. His mismatched vision, his crude, sloughing sculpture, his life's work sorrowfully evaluated with disbelief while his words, his breath, his inexperienced, tearful eye, they pelted against this fragile dream of his like a horrific rain. The ominous silence was lingering overhead like a saturated storm cloud. The intensity was growing muscle. He didn't have the patience to build it all back up again. To lower himself, to blend in, to become one again with the mud on his hands…, he would go mad. Fully. He needed to salvage it…. He shifted in his chair alongside last chance. He did his best to nominate his partners as lingual receivers, hoping like hell the idiots would at least support him with a chuckle. Lighten the mood…. They didn't. So hoisting up a wobbly front of confidence, a concealing stretch of dirty canvas for skin, he hunkered down inside it. But cowardice peeked up through the ragged moth holes eaten in his decrepit persona anyhow. And it was as yellow as daffodils defying a mound of dirt-traced, melting snow. A plastered grin rose up and spread across his askew face—so fake it was insulting. It was an afterthought. A weak and unpunctual expression obviously and pointlessly rehearsed in an attempt to pull off good-natured humor during off-set, heated moments such as these. "How was that bet, boys? I b'lieve you jackasses need ta pay up."

Classic Slim. Diverting attention. Uncomfortable—itchy—in his own skin…. Already. Drake's anger stepped aside, opened the door for a released breath he didn't know his lungs were holding. His analytical nature took over, noting Slim's first sign of weakness—he had pointed out, just as sure as if he'd said it aloud, that Jed and Jethro were his crutches. Take them away and he'd crumble atop his broken splinters for legs.

And the game hadn't even begun.

Slim lifted his torso as he repositioned his lower body deeper in the chair. While bringing his feet to the floor, he unraveled a little more material before the thread snapped. And he did notice. He noticed the snag and he noticed the thread. He bent down to unwind it from his spur while Drake belittled him.

"Did your mama teach you how to talk like that, Slim?"

It wasn't the words so much as Drake's hardened tone of voice—a voice that suggested Slim's humanness had already been removed, that his chance, his life, had already been deemed null and void by a man brash enough to step between massive, colliding worlds and silence God. But wrapped up in the softening innocence of Lemn's presence over these final days, Drake had been breathing in an aura of goodness, fresh air and honest work. He had sensed upon his strength and muscle the faintest brush against purity and had found the delicate edge of peacefulness inside his own soul. He'd simply forgotten all about lost hope—it had trickled out of his system on a sweet, healthy sweat. He'd simply forgotten the calloused, deadened feeling attached to certain things, certain choices. He'd forgotten, that to some men, there is absolutely no God. There's only one dark world on which to strive and then fall off of. Into blind nothing. He'd forgotten the possibility, the downright proof, that the concept of humanness, of life, never crosses the mind in some, never reenters their conscience in the miles of hours after midnight. And, to those men, there is no form of intimidation severe enough, not when inflicted by another mortal man. No, their intimidation must follow..., for their wasted belief in the expendable value of life only holds true for others if they live recklessly themselves. He'd simply forgotten all this. And so that voice and that sheer look of hatred he threw down, that pumped-up effort..., that unmistakable, blatant ploy—it fell flat. For some reason, it was void of power.

There were layers and depths of things Drake couldn't see.... His dare to push Slim straight to the end of the dual might have worked had it happened on a different night. But tonight the moon was not set quite right in the eastern sky as if the spirits had tilted it to peer out from behind. And, tonight, it wasn't Drake's blood Slim was thirsty for—it was the onset of his drawn-out misery, it was the basis, the very reason, for years of his self-inflicting torment. It was the slow weakening, the humiliating downfall, of a legend. These were the things that he craved. And if there had to be a sacrifice to spawn it, so be it.... (If there was a net of hell beneath Slim's corroded version of the world, he couldn't hear it calling out for its chosen boy to come back home. Not yet. Not tonight. And he would be waiting, still and patient. Ear tilted, listening. Because Slim was that man—the very man born to push Drake over the edge.)

Before Lemn was attacked, Drake never really sensed the vast perversion in Slim-he must have had more important, or more trivial, things on his mind. Perhaps he'd grown vain inside his own surreal and suffocating image. Perhaps he was guilty of taking all the coincidences at face value—a type of denial, a hopeful fantasy that there was no iron chain growing link by link, waiting to bind him, waiting to string him up, in public, as he really was. He never stopped and wondered *why*.... Perhaps he'd just grown older, too tired to care anymore, and he settled—too easily—for ignorance, hoping to forge innocence. For whatever reason, he wouldn't allow himself to ask why. But he should have. He should have explored *why* Slim wasn't particularly good at anything and *why* Slim didn't have any useful, notable purpose. Instead, he just allowed himself to judge lazily. Allowed himself to assume Slim was slow, brought up backwards and a little more twisted than most. The man always appeared to be more of a joke than a threat. And that's all the thought Drake gave to it. All the thought he gave to Slim's loitering, the creepiness behind the man's drunken gaze, the deadened atmosphere between them. He always knew something about Slim wasn't right, but he never once considered the magnitude. (Never once considered that Slim's time, Slim's thoughts, Slim's drinking and hustling..., none of it revolved around anything—but Drake.) And, logically, there was never any reason to suspect anything further. Drake didn't really know Slim, didn't recognize him from years gone by. He'd never done him especially wrong.... The man was a nuisance to *everyone*, but he seemed to respect the social order of crime well enough, seemed to flow within the shifting physical boundaries of territorial dominance well enough. He'd kept himself unassuming enough to drift alongside the law. He was still standing.... So even after losing, it was highly unlikely..., downright shocking, that he would target and victimize Lemn to the extent that he did. And then not leave town. Lemn—a kid obviously tied to the most feared, the most notorious, gambler in Illinois. *Why...?*

After that first game, that first fight, Drake was banking on his own inflated ghost of a reputation to shoot Slim's hostility down, to liquify and drain Slim's plan for revenge, but he made a drastic error in judgement—instead, he found himself rudely awakened and wallowing in a humbling morning light that proved his gambling habit had discreetly crossed over and consumed his personal life again. (He would never forget how *broken*, how *disfigured* Lemn looked the first time he saw the damage Slim had done—that tiny, busted body, that young, struggling life interrupted, manipulated and frozen as the tarnishing focal point in that umber, sealed-off and breathless room.) He had simply overestimated himself and overestimated his ability to protect what was his. He'd always prided himself on being able to read people. And he assumed Slim was nothing but a simpleton, a pushover drunk who avoided challenge and sought out defenseless loners—the elderly, tramps, estranged travelers, the downtrodden. And Lemn was supposed to be at home, out of sight and safe.... Drake had dismissed his uneasiness about leaving mother and child alone that first night. He'd grown impatient with his confusion, with the sideways state of affairs, so he blocked them out of his mind—the two of them with all their stifling conditions, and especially her with all her flailing, unhinged emotions. And he did what he always did when things got too complicated. He left. And Lemn paid the price. And now, tonight, Drake thought he had all of his misguided judgements corrected. Now he believed Slim was nothing more than a *sick* simpleton who had overstepped the most sacred of Drake's laws. And there would be Drake's brand of justice comin' on.

But still, Slim held something more. He held on to his one-dimensional interpretation of Drake's life like the Holy Grail. Held it in a silent, aging and reverential obsession like most men hold to a family or to a cherished way of life. And the horror and distortion he envisioned in the dull reflections of antiquity…, how *could* anyone else have known?

Slim's face was gathered and creased in intense concentration. But he remained fixated in this dried-up, raisin-like manner for such a prolonged moment, the question of seizure activity, possibly liver failure, grazed Drake's thoughts. Slim was still and silent, in a blank stupor for an unnatural length of time before his eyes and body language suggested varying degrees of coherency. It was obvious he was stumped in an unhealthy way. He was strongly considering a rebuttal, a reaction, to Drake's lingering insult about his mama—Drake's words had definitely cut his pride somewhere deep inside—but, though his mouth was beginning to water vengefully, it didn't fit into his plan. He had that blessed plan painstakingly etched on the roof of his mind. Although the lighting was dim and the script tiny, it was engraved there in his skull meticulously. And his outward expression revealed the exact instant he recalled the frailest dendrite of an addendum appropriate for the current crushing circumstance. Only then did he allow himself to become fully animated. He forced himself to oblige Drake's mood with a false humility, with a dogged determination—as such that was in his intellectual power to maintain. He forced himself to follow Drake's open-ended, witty sarcasm with a controlled, somewhat embarrassing, silence. He'd prepared himself for something like this, for the awkward moments that would inevitably befall him when he didn't trust his own ability to speak. It was impossible to rein in his own anger once it took off—he was aware of that much at least—and he needed to keep it tightly caged. He needed to wait it out, needed to suffer a little, even if it meant he'd make himself look like a fool. A complete, bumbling idiot. He was pretty much used to this anyhow. And, tonight, none of that mattered. Because he *could not* lose this once in a lifetime chance…. He'd come way too close already.

So he feigned total social absorption while his sidekicks fumbled around for the petty cash they probably didn't even bet, or if they did, likely succumbed only to meet their babysitting quota for Slim's weekly ego trip. Drake noticed the look in Jed's eye—complete and apathetic disdain. He disrespectfully pitched two coins out onto the table so that Slim had to grab for one before it rolled off. There was no loyalty there. And certainly no fear. Which wasn't surprising given Jed's true motive…he circled Drake's showdowns like a ravenous scavenger showing more and more bone. Drake also noticed the sheepish manner that Jethro handed over his poke of savings. He looked like a whipped pup. While Slim was rummaging through his sparse collection of coins, Jethro cast a quick glance in Lemn's direction and he smiled shyly at the boy. He tipped his hat for a fleeting moment as if to say, "Glad you're alright." When Slim was finished, he didn't even bother to check how much was taken from him. No, Jethro wouldn't be a problem far as Drake could tell. He wouldn't have the heart to shoot the boy when it came down to it. He probably saved Lemn's life once already. Drake made a mental note not to shoot Jethro either…, if he could manage it. And he doubted he'd be lucky enough to do Jed in. Jed was too smart, too removed from responsibility, too concerned with his public image. He'd been taught by the best and tossed just enough steak to keep him loyal.

Lemn was oblivious to most everything but his own nerves. He chose the chair directly across from Slim and quietly sat down. He hoped, futilely, that no one would notice him much. He wished he were invisible, maybe never even born. He wanted more than anything to continue staring down at his folded hands sweating and mock-resting there on the table, clutching time. He wanted desperately to avoid that dreaded, confrontational moment when their eyes would meet, signaling the onset of their fate. This game was crucial, he could feel it—above and beyond the measure determined by the men surrounding him. It was not a selfish crucial, but a sacrificial one. He needed to survive this day—it was his destiny. Someone was counting on him. Someone in his future was held in waiting for him. For all his confusion and torment, this was the only thing he knew for sure and he'd stand at the gates of hell—naked but for mercy—just to see it through.

Suddenly, the risk and the depth of it all hit him in the center of his chest, tried to knock the heart in him down. *There seems to be no choice at all here….* The slap of this stayed long on his skin and it stung clear through him. It wasn't the knowing of it, but the living of it that caused his heartbeat to accelerate, caused panic to grip at his throat. He swallowed hard. He'd never felt so ill-prepared…, yet so responsible for the insane chaos swirling around him. He was caught up in the middle. Helpless. And just plain dirty. And the words *God's will* kept rolling through his mind, dragging abrasively over his soul carving shavings of guilt from its surface. Kindling…. They were words not of his own. *God's will….* And the dry, crackling sound of them emptied him. The rim of his lowered hat became a protective wall, a psychological shield, a fortress, guarding his too soft and boyish eyes from the evil soon to be violating his field of vision. He'd rather not look into Slim's face, rather not look at the reflection in those vacant eyes and see his own reality coming for him, but he'd have to. And soon. He'd have to look all of it square in the eye. Face the evil borne of his own and stand upon the pyre. The conversation of his Judgement Day was rising, holy whispers on smoke—the consummation could not be reversed. Devon's discerning face crossed between the flames in his racing mind and it looked non-complacent, but said nothing—just stared—arms and tongue tied. A father removed. Lemn suddenly felt the true magnitude drop fully into his hands—heavy, smooth and six-sided. It rolled there again—the threat, but this time it rolled real and burned. The corners were piercing to the sensitive skin on his palms and the spin ran opposite the course of the pure blood surging through his veins. He was gambling with his life, with his afterlife. Disheveling his own innocence as God and his father looked on. Both were watching with a slow sadness in their eyes, crying without tear, without sound. As he was branded.

If Drake was right, the one left standing—standing close enough to steal the air expelled from Slim's sunken lungs—would be him.

Still, he did nothing.

And that was a choice.

He felt like the body he was wearing didn't fit—skin stretched too tight, flesh swollen and obese. He felt like he was trapped inside someone else entirely and he wasn't sure who he was anymore. *Is Lemn the kind of kid who would be doing this?* It was becoming a challenge just to breathe. The man sitting across from him had beaten him brutally and Lemn's entire being cringed in his presence—he wanted to run. He was on the verge of hyperventilating. But he was expected to sit still and face his demons. He was expected to play civilly, calmly, in order to survive this second uncivilized circumstance. It was just plain unfair. But he could not allow himself to be craven—he'd attempted escape once before. He certainly couldn't become indignant, not with Slim's freakish temper. And most importantly, if things went his way, he could not act smug. If he wanted to continue, he had to command his body and mind to relax—to be denied, neglected and forced to nearly disappear into oblivion, into weightlessness, blandness and near-sleep. He took a deep but quiet breath, centering himself warmly and fully between his stingy lungs. And then he said to himself, "If God wants me Home, I'll be there soon. If He wants me to stay, I'll be staying…. God have mercy." Suddenly, Drake's adamant, downright traumatic form of coaching returned to him. *Look right into his eyes when you sit down and I don't care if they start stingin' terrible, YOU DON'T BLINK…YOU DON'T LOOK AWAY…and, sure as hell, YOU DON'T LOOK DOWN 'till he does it first. You got that? I'll be watching you, Lemn….* So with his regained composure, Lemn lifted his determined, unflinching eyes for the first time. He caught Slim's gaze, drew it in and held it as the man's superior smile slowly drooped into silent contempt, absorbing Lemn's seriousness. And Lemn's eyes did start to sting. The air was drafty, smokey and dry. He was afraid he'd tear up and become the brunt of cruel jokes the entire night. Yet, at the same time, Lemn did feel like crying—unnecessary evil is what keeps evil alive. He honestly felt like curling up, rolling over like an inch worm, and crying. He'd never seen anyone die before.

And then it happened. Slim did it. He caved and he caved first. Slim looked down at the cards and his voice held the shaky tone of barely controlled irritation.

"Well, let's git this show on the road. Let's see how well ya do without Drake holdin' yer hand, boy."

Jed and Jethro were seated on a hard bench against the wall. They stretched and slouched their bodies getting ready for a long, boring haul. Jed propped his feet up on a nearby chair and readjusted his sweat-stained leather hat by nearly taking it off twice then sliding it back to where it was before. Then he folded his arms, resting only an instant before he changed position again, this time locking his fingers together and twirling his thumbs impatiently, hands perched atop his outstretched belly. He yawned. Took another exaggerated breath that let itself out as a heavy sigh suggesting he needed days worth of sleep. And he seemed about that interested in matters. He just couldn't get comfortable, but then again something about being around Slim had always rubbed him the wrong way. The man was ignorant. And plumb crazy. *Ta hell with this....* He stood up, laced his fingers, stretched his arms out in front of his chest, and took a good look around. A saloon girl from across the room caught his eye and as soon as she delivered her round of drinks, he was gone.

Drake smiled to himself as he watched Jed quietly disappear into the crowd. If Slim noticed, he didn't let on..., he was a little *too* focused on Lemn.

"Hold up just a minute there, Slim."

Drake stepped up to the table and lifted the deck of cards before Slim had a chance to protest. He shuffled them back and forth lightly for a moment then spread them out on the tabletop with one instantaneous, fluid motion forming a neatly arched display. He checked the back side of the deck for marks then, flipping each card over in another smooth maneuver that sounded like a kitten purring, he examined the other side for duplicate or missing cards.

"Alright, go ahead."

"Now hold on, Drake. With all that fancy card trickin' how's I ta know ya didn't slip somethin' in that there deck, huh?" So Slim did his own clumsy inspection of his own deck. Drake rolled his eyes but once they settled on Slim's sincere manner, he felt embarrassment *for* him. He just couldn't help but feel a twinge of pity for the man—Slim's ignorance had an innocence about it. Something childlike behind it…. The foreseen ending of a life always made Drake a little sentimental.

"Alright. *Now* we can go ahead."

Slim finally looked satisfied that he had gained the upper hand. He shuffled the cards under Drake's critical eye, "Cut, boy." Lemn's hand steadied at the cool feel of his delicate fingers uniting with the deck and a sudden surge of power ran up through his arm as if the cards were a innate extension of himself, like Drake had talked of guns—…*another arm.* Slim took his cut and flicked the card out on the table—four of hearts. Lemn cast a shaky glance at Drake who nodded the go ahead. The card sailed through the air, twirling once before landing. The ace of diamonds.

"What the…oh, what-the-hell-ever. Call the game then, punk."

Lemn was instantly relieved. Relieved Slim had taken the cut without accusing him of cheating again. He noticed that Slim's mind seemed to be on something else, seemed to be a bit more detached than usual. The man's body had succumbed to the chair, its language voicing a form of casual retreat. At this observation, the muscles along Lemn's spine let go. His back relaxed and stretched upward, his neck bones popped slightly and he sat a little taller in his chair. But Slim didn't notice. His eyes were scanning the barroom for an image the likes of Jed and Lemn could tell the moment he gave up the search—his face turned a shade closer to the color of anger. Lemn looked over to Drake who nodded once and Lemn knew he was done reassuring. Something in the way Drake's jaw was set told him. Lemn understood that Drake didn't want to trigger a hostile reaction in Slim before it was time so he fixed his mind on the game and gathered up the cards. He stated his indisputable choice with an even tone, "Five card stud." He took off his hat, tossed it on the seat of an empty chair, and ran his fingers through his thick hair momentarily lifting the wispy bangs that concealed his plum-colored scar. He brought his brown eyes up to face his opponent and found Slim staring at him, relentlessly. But Lemn didn't look away. He did as instructed and maintained aloof eye contact with Slim while shuffling the deck with precision and comfort—no fumbling or clumsily misguided actions that one would typically expect from a boy of thirteen. Not a single hesitant motion, not a single card had strayed, and he didn't look down once. With his skilled hands, with his blatant confidence, he seemed to be making a mockery of Slim. Again. Seemed to have something to prove….

Little punk.

Build of Your Own....

The colossal power that emanates from reputation can be an invisible shield of armor or the very sword that slays you.... Which...When...That is the twisted tactic left untold to the soldier. Therefore, build of your own no reputation with man. For its foundation is of sand, its brick of judgement, its mortar of gossip, its roof—the very wind of the world's falsehoods.

Slim opened his mouth to say something sarcastic but his brain fell short of delivering anything more innovative than "punk." He got chills as he realized he was face to face with a smaller version of Drake. Perhaps, with someone even more powerful than Drake. He was damn spooky—this little punk. And Slim had no other choice but to back down from the kid's stare. A second time. He shifted uncomfortably in his chair. He didn't have much of a supportive audience, no witnesses to testify to the kid's cocky attitude, to this outright, disrespectful goading going on, damn them—he cast a glare towards the bar hoping it was in Jed's direction. Jethro probably got lost on his way back from the john. This kid could really handle a deck of cards, no doubt about that. *But just who does he think he is? He'll get his soon enough.... Damn punk.*

But Lemn wasn't mocking anyone. He didn't have anything to prove. He was simply trying to play the game the way Drake had told him to. He was just trying to survive and be an adequate opponent under the bizarre circumstances imposed on him. And he was struggling under the weight of his own guilty conscious. (Which, to those unfamiliar, can appear outwardly as any vast array of physical or linguistic illusions. Illusions which can be exponentially misinterpreted and absorbed as God's truth and relayed feverishly, utterly convincingly, though the transference is nothing but gross inadequacy. *Judge not...do not snag yourself on the free flowing hook of offense.*) He dealt out five cards each and he was just getting comfortable with the game when he realized what he held in his hand. He stopped breathing. *A royal flush.* He forced his lungs to move, to do something besides sit in his chest stiff with shock and burning. His face grew increasingly warm until it felt like it was on fire. He figured he was beat red. He glanced—barely one millimeter over the rim of his cards—at Slim who was studying his own with no particular interest. Lemn folded his cards and tossed them down immediately in a nervous, stiff gesture. He didn't have to check Drake's expression, didn't have to hear a sound. He could feel him screaming underneath his breath, "Play 'em out.... **Go on, boy!!!**"

He picked the cards back up and saw that his hand was trembling. Slim was still rearranging his own, oblivious.

After this first hand, Slim lost his patience. After the second hand, he was ready to see somebody pay. And as the game wore on, Lemn was typically just one card higher than Slim or he blew him out of the water every third or fourth hand with some unbelievable combination…four of a kind, straight flush, four aces, royal flush. Slim's stack of a hundred mock chips had quickly dwindled to less than forty. He'd begun to sweat and seethe with rage. He ordered Jethro to get him a drink from the bar and when he brought it, Slim slammed it down acrimoniously and rammed the shot glass into Jethro's hand with tenfold the force necessary, ordering him to get another and to find that bastard coward Jed. The only thing keeping Slim in his seat and keeping his hands on the cards instead of around the little Irish punk's neck was Drake's constant and full attention raining down, his hands…, steady and constantly—all too conveniently—free, his blue eyes monitoring every move. This imposed claustrophobia angered Slim further. Spectators had cropped up one-by-one to watch the comical show. They were uninvited and unwelcome and Slim would have liked nothing better than to kill them all. But then he remembered the object of his plan. He only needed one to die, just one—the one most important to Drake. *Yeah, this little punk's dead, one way or another he ain't gonna be breathin' for long….*

Slim's concentration was no longer on the game. The details of his plan had grown hazy and amounted to nothing more than a piercing headache in need of numbness and booze. He could care less about his chips, about his cards, about the spectators, about Jed. He was no longer feeling the pain of defeat, of humiliation, but rather, was imagining ways he could murder the kid. It was so sweet a thought he could barely contain the urge not to jump up and do it right now and a sickening smile spread across his lips—dried, chapped lips that were trembling with a mixture of contempt, perversion and those damnable shakes that had come back from outta nowhere—and it was a slanted smile that spread itself just enough to show his coffee and tobacco stained teeth. He smiled even wider, wiped a trickle of drool off the corner of a mouth preparing itself for another evening of siphoning whiskey, then laughed openly with the onlookers—a shallow, twisted snicker. He was nodding encouragement and false acceptance toward them as if he were playing a friendly, cutesy game. As if he were a mentor, a gracious doormat on which this youth could wipe his brand-new shoes. And no one was the wiser. He began to enjoy watching the boy, filling his head with evil thoughts that fueled his obsession, *You ain't gonna get no older th'n ya are right now, Irish trash. Just like*

*yer worthless daddy, you're a weakling. Born a weakling. And you're gonna die a
weakling. And there ain't nothin' Drake can do about it....*

Drake's eyes were burning a hole in the side of Lemn's brain. He could feel it
tunneling there. It was making him sweat though the air in the room had
turned cold. *Dear God, have mercy on our souls....* He'd do the sign of the cross
on his chest if he were brought up Catholic. But he wasn't. He put his right fist
over his heart and held it there for a time. Something didn't feel right in there.
His soul didn't feel settled like he hoped it would. Slim was walking right into
the pit they'd dug for him. He was playing right into it. And it was just downright unnatural, the feeling hanging over the room. It was like a death-green,
springtime sky and Drake had it timed perfectly as if unclenching his own fist
were breaking the seal and he knew the exact path the twister would take as if
the very lines on his palm were a sign leading up to this day. All he had to do
was blow out over his hand.... There had to be another way. Lemn just needed
to find it. Needed time to think. He would try to shift his luck on this deal, try
to cut Slim some slack. Just as the last card fell, Jethro brought a bottle of
whiskey for Slim and, after surveying Slim's small pile of chips, said, "You ain't
doin' s' good, boss."

Lemn shot a look over to Drake who appeared cool and steady, yet his tightened, quivering muscles were prepared to fill Slim's side full of lead—his eyes
never moved from his target to address Lemn's inquisitiveness. And Lemn got
spooked. Drake's anticipation, his flexible rigidity, told him hell was about to
sing. He thoughtlessly laid his cards down—face up—without looking at
them. He wanted no part in this. He meant to fold. Meant to walk away a quit-
ter. Meant to humble himself. But that's not what he'd done.... What he did
looked to everyone else like another perfectly ordered straight flush...looked
to Slim like another straight flush after an odd hand signal. Who puts a fist up
to their chest during a poker game...?

Slim jumped up, bumping the table, and cards, chips and whiskey flew to
the floor, "What in the HELL are you two thievin' bastards tryin' ta pull here?"

The friendly crowd dispersed clumsily and as quickly as possible, in perfect
sync with the liquor chugging from the upset bottle on the floor. Some of them
had pushed and shoved in a brash panic, others, further away, took a little time
to judge Slim with condescending expressions, head shaking, pointing fingers
and comments too quiet to hear specifically, but their meaning, crystal clear.
The saloon girls fled—some upstairs, some out the back—and the bartender
ducked behind the bar, covering himself with a woolen blanket reserved for
such occasions—he'd been pelted with flying glass many times before. Lemn
wanted to explain, but his air was cut off. Slim's hands were wrapped around

his throat. The grip was so tight, so fierce, it was crushing his windpipe where a man's Adam's apple would be.

Draw your gun, you piece of shit...draw your damn gun. Sweat beads were bubbling up on Drake's forehead and a few seconds seemed to last forever. *Hold your breath. Slide your gun up, finger on the trigger, but don't draw 'till...*

Lemn was wide-eyed, but Drake was beyond his range of vision. And he didn't have to look at Drake to know what Drake wanted. The blood in his head began to surge, he was growing dizzy, faint, as he realized that he was the one who had to give Slim a push. He was the one who had to sway the pendulum, the one to set in motion the ending of a life. The power and the choice were his and his alone.

He could simply close his eyes and die here....

Before he made a conscious decision, he felt his soft hand imprinted on rough, sweaty flesh. He felt skin and warm, sticky liquid under each of his nails. He realized it was blood...he had blood on his hands. As his air returned, he heard the hoarse words float up out of himself. And those words would make him ponder their cost for the rest of his life....

He said, "What are ya gonna do about it, ya drunken, low-life **PUNK**?"

Chapter Thirteen

By the time Lemn's horse was unsaddled, inadequately brushed and put in his stall for what was left of the night, it seemed as if two weeks had passed, maybe two years…and under the wave of this reverie, Lemn would be able to draw in something deeper, something near to a full breath. Then a faint ray of moonlight would mercilessly glint off the splattered blood stains on *his very own shirt* and the sight would send him into hysterics so gripping he had to grab onto whatever was near him, cling to it to keep from collapsing—this time it was the barn door. He tried to steady himself as he gasped for air (his lungs were wheezing, pulling the faintest trace of oxygen through an invisible, yet seemingly tangible glove covering his face like the hand of the ghost of the dead come 'a callin', demonstrating to the little punk exactly what losing life could feel like). Lemn had already lost the slim contents of his stomach several times over and now, recognizing the blood as proof that *it did happen* only two irreversible hours ago, he was forced to suffer through yet another bout of hyperventilation. (Something close to a panic attack, something like going through unexpected death with no assailant other than the mind, no circumstantial trap other than guilty conscience, with all the gruesome scenes retrievable from memory, salvageable for the mere shock factor, redisplayed as rapidly and as forcefully as a realistic nightmare—yet one cannot wake from this…. It is a nightmare void of sleep. Beneath pressed and sealed eyes the visions, the sounds, they don't go away…, they come alive. Before open eyes will they come all the closer…. Powerfully, vividly, they threaten the very core of vitality as the heart tries to outrun itself, as greedy lungs spend themselves of precious, life-giving air….) In a fight to recover, Lemn wished—willed—that it hadn't happened at all and part of his mind granted this in occasional sweeps of illusory relief, blocking reality out and making the atrocity seem grossly vague and unfamiliar…for a moment. But his intelligence could not deny him the fact that his own eyes had witnessed the bloody truth, that the spark of his own voice had ignited the flame—the sound of it kept ringing garishly in his ears. Reminding him again and again. His voice, then the blast…then another answering the first. It all echoed there still. In his mind. And on his skin. That's the funny thing about a memory—it keeps its own collection, there is no selective erasing…. And this torture…, it's what he deserved.

He defiantly tore his shirt off as he staggered toward the house still sucking tiny, rapid breaths within the top tenth of his lungs. He wadded it up in his hands…, hands that he'd washed at least ten times in the trough behind the saloon but he was sure they were still dirty—dried blood in the cracks, in the folds of skin at his knuckles, under his nails. He wanted to rip them off one by one and scrub beneath them. He entered the house and threw the outer layer of flimsy, non-thinking, innocent evidence into the dark fireplace. With his violent shakes, he managed to splinter and crumble three matches into uselessness before the fourth took off. He lit the inside fringe of the hem but the flame was as weak as his own soul and it turned blue, void of air, then it died. He sat in the dark room straining against his shallow breath, trembling and crying, shedding tears and fragments of broken matches upon the hearth until the blasted thing caught on fire and disintegrated between two logs. He was irritated with himself for ruining a perfectly good shirt, one of the few that still fit his broadening body, and he watched passively through blurry eyes as the laughing flames stole every trace of his happiness away. Burned up his youth. It's what he deserved….

His mom made that shirt.

He sat there, falling deeper and deeper into a daze that lasted well over an hour. And only as the fire turned to embers did he acknowledge how tired he was (he was tired in every way that a human being can be tired). He stumbled into his room. Drake had been standing in the shadows, at attention, the entire time. He followed Lemn with a distant, cautious, closeness like that of a mother encouraging her toddler to explore autonomously but nerve-racked with worry that the child would be in danger if her powerful gaze failed to envelop them for one instant, if her attempt to proof the room failed, if…. It was like mothering, but then again it wasn't. It was a perversion of it. And Drake stumbled over his heart and over his tongue trying to make the horror seem a little softer than it was, trying like hell to make the poisonous medicine go down quick. When he spoke into the dark, it almost seemed that he broke it in two. Cracked it like a mirror.

Maybe that was the sound of his hope dying.

"I know the feelin' you got, boy, and it ain't exactly gonna get any better than it is right now. I guess I've just gotten used to it over the years. A fella like

Slim don't deserve ta live. Now you might disagree but, either way, you didn't kill Slim, boy. I did. And don't you forget that."

Drake turned and shut Lemn's bedroom door. He couldn't take much more. Couldn't stand to see that kid so shook up.

"Drake?"

Drake wanted to pretend he didn't hear that tiny sound. He wanted to walk away. But he didn't. He opened the door and spoke softly around the lump in his throat.

"Yeah, boy."

"When you kill someone, you only draw after they do, right?"

Lemn's voice sounded so strange. So different and distant and cold.

"Yeah. I try to, 'specially if there's witnesses. That's why I waited so long tonight…Slim had to draw on you first."

"And that's why the sheriff doesn't put you in jail?"

"Well, that's a whole 'nother story."

"Tell me, Drake." Lemn's command was dry and unyielding.

"Alright…. Sheriff is an old friend of mine. He's a different kind of man…, not exactly suited to his line of work. We have a little understanding that way. I help him with his job, he helps me with mine. Take Slim for instance. You ain't the first person Slim's hurt. There's no question in my mind that he would have killed you, boy. He's robbed, raped, harassed…, made a menace of himself. And now he can't hurt any more folks, includin' you, and the sheriff didn't have to do a thing."

The silence lingered. Drake could tell Lemn was thinking, taking it all in, so he waited patiently giving him ample time—the boy had been through a lot. But the question that arose from this gift of peace burrowed up from underneath his superficial level of expectation and shattered it. Blew it away.

"Are you ever afraid that you will go to hell, Drake?"

The air flowing on top of the world simply seemed to stop, particles held and frozen for no plausible reason. Like that strange moment of suspension prior to plummet. That teetering up there on the ledge overlooking gravity as if God were preoccupied with a thousand other deaths and needed a time warp. Everyone—every soul, every spirit in every cloud, in every crevice below—everyone was holding their breath. Waiting.

"Yeah, boy. Yes I am...."

The world jumped back into its natural momentum, into its chaos circling the stillness, as Drake closed the bedroom door a little too abruptly. He'd had enough. And he was done. *Hell....* That was one subject he couldn't talk about—not tonight. He went out on the porch to roll a cigarette. He sat down heavily on the porch swing which creaked loudly in complaint. He rested his feet up on the railing, followed their direction out into the sky and gazed up at the tail end of the rising moon. He said a prayer. A nearly hopeless, frigid string of words sent out into the blackness. *Forgive me for what I've done. And help that boy in there.* He took a draw, let it out slow and easy when a statement suddenly entered his mind, *Get out of this life.* He spit a trace of tobacco off the tip of his tongue and dismissed the thought as rapidly as it had presented itself. It didn't occur to him that the Almighty God had spoken. To him.

Lemn would have been tossing and turning had it not been too painful to change positions. Instead, he lay still and gently caressed the perfectly round bump on his forehead where the barrel of Slim's gun had been roughly pressed. It would leave a bruise the shape of a wedding band. His throat burned. His right ear was still ringing. His back ached as always. Events of the evening grazed his mind, but he was so ridden with exhaustion, so disturbed with guilt that he couldn't concentrate on any one incident long enough to form an accurate, sequential account of what happened.

"What are ya gonna do about it, ya drunken, low-life **PUNK?**"
"It's not your fault, boy."
"Sheriff's here!"
"What in the HELL are you two thievin' bastards tryin' ta pull here?"
"It's Not Your Fault, Boy."
"So you say he drew his gun first and pointed it at the boy?"
"Got proof, look at the knot on Lemn's head."
"Don't look at him, boy. Try not to look at him. He ain't comin' back."
"IT'S NOT YOUR FAULT, BOY."
"What are ya gonna do about it, ya DRUNKEN, LOW-LIFE **PUNK?**"

Lemn had watched from a confining, suffocating distance as Slim's brown, bloodshot eyes switched from wild anger and hate to childlike hurt and fear. He watched the desperate expression, watched the shock settle in as Slim's fist slowly released the fierce hold it had on his shirt collar. He saw Slim's weakening hand let the gun drop to the floor—he counted the spirals 'til it hit. Two and one-quarter. He felt relieved when it did not go off. He watched as Slim's life-draining body followed it, the fluid motion interrupted by one last feeble attempt at redemption, a struggle to hold onto the table for a second chance not to be seen. Lemn watched Slim's fingers slide until they were able to grip the snag at the table's edge—Lemn saw that the snag was shaped exactly like the scar on his own forehead. He shivered. While he sweat. The fingertips were white while they were gripping so fiercely, then the color pink flooded in as they began to let go. They quickly slid up and over the rim of the table as Slim's body collapsed behind it. The same fingers that would later swell and turn a dark, shadowy purple. Lemn could no longer say that he'd never seen a man die. He'd seen it a thousand times now. He could not stop seeing it. Couldn't stop the splotches, drops and spots of crimson blood floating in front of his eyes, even in the dark—there seemed to be miles of it and he could not move, seas of it and he could not swim. At times it seemed to become the very air and he could not breathe it in. And the words *It's not your fault…*would never ring true to him. *It's not your fault…*smeared across the pool of blood fanning out over Slim's frumpy clothes, leaking from beneath Slim's stiffening corpse. Words written with his hands, letters traced by his fingers. He needed to wash them again. And again. And again. They would never be clean…. And Slim's lungs. They released his last breath long after he was dead. Long after anyone was expecting it. A hefty sigh escaped his sleeping body, an unsettling gurgle at the end. People jumped, men startled, a woman shrieked and every eye held that body for a long, silent moment. The sheriff maintained gracious distance from it. Everyone addressed it oddly until they were sure he was as dead as he was supposed to be. Jethro had been the only one to kneel beside the body, take off his hat and whisper, "Boss? Boss…?"

That empty, ragged breath stole something from Lemn's soul that he would search a lifetime for but never find again.

Innocence….

Chapter Fourteen

Nothing settled in that night. The soul had hardened while the heart still bled. It was drowning in its own pool of loneliness. Separateness. *So-this. Is-how. It-feels.* It drummed without voice in a tomb without ear. *Bro-ken. Spir-it.* And, although it was a blue dawn…, a spiritual thing rolling in off a soft embroidered cloud, encouraging dream to die with reality breeze, with warm birdsong it held the voice of a mother—*See, it's not so bad here, boy*—gently offering hope, lighting the way beyond the sorrow inside to the strength found in that next feeble step like magic, *I promise…*, whispering what sounded like universal truth, it spoke that meaning, that understanding was surely waiting just over that next hill there like a pot of gold…. *Rise, son…. Go see.* And he did try. Oh, how he wanted to believe it could be his. But he looked around the world and, although it was a blue dawn, time was lost to it. Lost to it all. He could see that with his matching eyes. The things he felt down deep had become the air. His thoughts, the sky. *Sometimes the weight is just too heavy, Mama….*

Some crosses are made of iron, my son….

And the tiny bit of knowledge trapped in his foreign, dumbstruck mind was younger somehow. Regressed. Inexperienced and flighty. Certainly not to be trusted. Because it wasn't just any dream. It's never just a dream…. *I said it's never just a dream.* Not to the dreamer. And of his dream the common ground had been stripped down while they both watched on—he and the boy, it was stolen from beneath their feet and the bond between their hands had been broken. Kicked off the earth but unable to fly was he as a man. His desire'd been busted up like the limp and featherless wings he never learned how to use. Undeveloped…, his helpless, inanimate arms. They should be holding something. And as he walked along the undulating shoreline of sleep, he absorbed the dead space left of division. It seeped in through his toes and filled him. How could something so immense settle inside a man's chest? He was bloated. Comatose with the misery of it. Where was his sweet open prairie? His swift horse? Where were his broke-in boots? Another shaky step and something buried beneath the sands of his dream pierced through his naked flesh, injected his life with the costly solution of segregation—oh, how it burned beneath the skin. It swam through his body. He was high but still not flying. Never flying. Beautiful strength, majestic wingspan, icy eyes on fire, cry of the soul of the earth—they were not his. Not ever again. He was floatin' up there limp, lost to the colossal shadow of an unanswered *why*, its talons sunk deep in his back, clench unyielding. He felt it now, sitting up in the middle of a bed big enough for two. Cold sweat dripping. He placed his hand on her empty pillow. So quiet. His soul…. Gone. It'd been shattered like glass when the dam ruptured. The shards were swimming in the flood, scraping along inside his bulging veins. He didn't have long now. *Don't have long now, Mama….* He looked down at his arms. Rubbery. Weak. Nothing to reach for anymore.

He was drinking a cup of coffee at the table, slowly, now about as awake as he was going to get. He thought about Mama, wished she were here with him. He hated the dawn. Hated facing the daylight after a kill. (It would be some time before he could look into a mirror. Some time before the gentle reflecting surface of trapped liquid would mesmerize him and bring him calmness and comfort rather than alienation. Delusion. Several uneasy nights would drift over his life before he could allow the corner of his eye to pull him further into the vacant image turning toward him on a pane of glass—a ghastly being, distorted and dancing with the flames…, many darkened moons would creep unseen before his mind could recognize the silent phantom's face and allow it to flow into his own. That's the way it always was with him, after a kill.) He wished that for once in his life he could have slept soundly, unaware of the intrusive morning sunlight and the consequences it delivered like spring hail. He'd sleep for weeks at a time, months if he could. *I surely would….* He brought the mug of acrid brew to his lips and blew across the surface to cool it. He made certain his gaze did not slide onto the beckoning ripples as they played with the light and all its elucidations for they could easily seduce him, carry him out to a place that would take far, far too long to come back from, a journey with much too much travesty for a man of his age to weather all over again. He closed his eyes and took a slow, deep breath from the midst of the rising steam hoping to soak up the earthy aroma and the elements of simplicity folded therein, but he couldn't smell a thing. He took a sip and found it disappointing. Tasteless. He thought it odd that he couldn't feel it burning slightly as it trickled down his throat, that he couldn't feel much of anything at all. His entire physical existence had fallen numb, muscle stolid and grey under lucid skin. He considered that he may be experiencing a slow heart attack..., and that that would be fine. Thirty-six years would suit him just fine.

He sat there robed in the pastel stillness as his mind proceeded to bathe itself in the red aftermath of Slim's death. In its eye, he watched as the undertaker gently pushed the lids down and then, with the same pudgy finger, pushed the rim of his bowed, wire spectacles up the sweaty bridge of his own flattened nose though only for momentary avail. Drake started there in his chair, jumping slightly as he heard the crisp linen snap somewhere behind him..., somewhere in the back of his mind. It cracked in stages through the varying thicknesses of his skull like pond ice. Like razored branches of horizontal lightning, its force seemed to come from miles away yet he felt himself being moved dangerously closer, then closer still toward its luckless destination just as its wicked prize ricocheted up through his feet and off his spine. Then, just as suddenly, it left him. The slight breeze from its backlash flowed on up the back of his neck, chilling him as he sat there, now, in the quiet. Stunned. But he refused to turn around. Oh, he felt it there. Indeed. Some sort of presence breathing over him as if hell had belched it back up. Unmistakable, it was. But giving in to these glitches of the mind, offering them the slightest bit of merit..., it's what caused madness. He reminded himself that he was far too strong, far too dignified, for games such as these (as he had to do, frequently, after a kill). So he took a merciless gulp of the scalding liquid connecting him to his empty morning and he stubbornly pressed on, recalling how the plump little man unfurled the sheet, how he covered Slim from view as if death were naked. A good deal of blood spotted that sheet like little backward rain drops. They embraced one another quickly, multiplied, then flowed together like a miniature burgundy flood. An eighth of the cover was soaked through, looking like the limp, makeshift battle flag of some godforsaken island country, by the time Drake walked out.

He contemplated these things not in remembrance of the man erased, but for the stamp they placed across the future. For those secret things unseen being whispered and sown this very moment inside a sleeping boy.

The wind of dreams....

A sprinkling of seeds....

Tears of a hard life....

And the rain, or the sun, of his own choosing....
With these things, the boy's fate would be sealed. And too soon he'd
be sent off into this world....

Drake forced his mind back inside, before the sheet had been stained. He
forced the mass of memories colliding in his brain to come to order within
that gloomy, smoke-filled room. He scanned each and every minute detail surrounding the stiffening corpse—the faces, the comments, the blood, the traffic
flow, the assumptions, the mood.... Like a vulture, his mind encircled it all.
Ravenously, his eyes searched..., something was missing. He hovered overhead, dove into the recessed corners, but he could not find Lemn. Lemn was
not locked inside after the shots were fired—not inside Drake's memory, not
inside the saloon. It was like he died with them. Like Slim's ghost had up and
spirited the kid's soul, too sore a loser to just let it go. Drake's jumbled
thoughts and vivid imaginations suddenly converged upon the blank sheet
and fell silent. They remained there, looking on, while the crimson spread....
Drake was somewhat frazzled this morning and he found himself momentarily wondering exactly which body that sheet covered, wondering if he had acci-
dentally murdered Lemn. He was getting confused. A little panicked. And that
rarely happened when he was evaluating his work....

Drake *knew* he'd spoken to Lemn afterwards—he *must* have—he just
couldn't recall it. The boy was completely removed from the circle of his mind,
the hollow circle inside that barroom where Lemn should have stayed and
grown into a man. This was detrimental, a critical point that determined
everything to follow. And to ruin it once meant to ruin it forever (like bucking
out a colt..., the cinch *has* to be snug enough). Because second chance? There
was no such thing. Not with this. Not as far as Drake was concerned. This was
the only form of claiming manhood that he understood. He understood it
inside and out—this blatant stance of triumph over the first man down, this
breathing deep and free in the realm of the dying—and it was essential. Like
betting to a poker game, like bullets to a gun. Its outcome was key. Because
walking the streets and riding the trails without it was a sign of weakness, of
emptiness..., a death warrant. Signed. And people see *it* first on a man—not
the gun, not the face, not the clothes...it. Drake's life had taught him this,
taught him to face death fearlessly. It was his only assurance of living another
day. And these first few moments after Slim's death—Lemn's initial reaction,
the look in his eye, what he did with his hands—they would have told Drake
volumes about the kid. But he just couldn't recall....

This stone philosophy of his, this circle drawn around the dying on which
to stand tall, it was the only inner life that Drake knew. It was his memorized

and limited form of introspection. It was familiar. Easy. It fit with the ways of the world when everything else was just plain puzzling. It was the only line of living that enabled him to join his years of struggle—years bought and paid for with blood…some tears…a few near lethal lessons—to meaning. It *made* it all make sense, dammit. And it was in this same mind that the chaos of one up close and unhinged existence swirled into a cyclone headed straight for Lemn. And Drake wanted to cram it all down the kid's throat—experience, wisdom, skill. It was hard earned. And it was damn valuable. And it caused Drake anxiety when Lemn could not be found pacing within *his* rock borders. When the boy's spirit could not be bound by *his* time, *his* strength, *his* choice, could not be caged by *his* forged survival. It felt like rejection to him when the boy's existence, when his future, could not be stuffed neatly and safely and permanently into the hole *he* carved out of life. And this youthful, passive defiance made Drake angry. Made him resentful. If the boy were his own son, he wouldn't think twice. And isn't that the tragedy of it…. The pure sadness of it. The landslide of lineage. If the boy were his own he would not ask himself, wouldn't *think* to ask himself, if what he had was worth passing on.

There comes a time when the struggle stops. When the clouds part and the sky is clear. And the sun shines down upon different colors. And it is a feast for the eyes.
Just as it is.
Acceptance….

Like treading through the forest only to reach the clearing with nothing to hold to but the five-mile memory of dirty toes, Drake stopped himself. And he looked up. He turned around. And he saw all the things he was about to miss. He saw the sun was setting on time. He knew nothing about this. It threatened him and he was tired. But he had something to pay for. Something to atone for. And he was going back through…. A man of his age.

A man of his age knows about blankness. That hollow place that echos no answer. That space left unfilled and useless that blame likes to creep into. Anger likes to nestle in desolate corners like that, likes to huddle under the layers of coldness and cruelty and then harden with time. It takes root. *What grows there…?* Whatever it was, it would take years to emerge from Lemn's personality. It would need to crack through the surface that the young man had designed, had painstakingly built with his own blood, sweat, tears, his own dust of bone. It would need to get out in the open air, into the light of day and feed on circumstance. What it could produce would be anyone's guess. And Drake doubted he'd be alive to see it. But he felt responsible for it, now. After everything that had happened.

Yes, Drake knew about blankness after everything that had happened. To him. His parasitic fears burrowed in deep and stayed hidden—unexposed—for survival. The color of flesh, he could not see them when he took a good hard look at himself. They kept themselves a mystery and, to him, the confusion, the anxiety they spawned was more persuasive than a loaded gun cocked and pressed against a sweaty temple. They writhed around in the dark, on the undisclosed side of a slithering line, while they whispered things. While they hissed fate. A pit of sickness swirling in the stomach, feeding on the very life that sustains them. Drake's journey had been far. And desert dry. Nothing with which to cleanse himself. Nothing with which to purge his demons.

His journey had been tiring…. Exhausting…. And his chin fell into his chest.

And the free and easy spirit of convenient abasement went breezing by him like a shiny government locomotive that didn't bother to stop, his dusty boots holding the last valuable thing in this ghost town life. And he dropped the gun and the white buffalo skull and ran like the wind 'till he caught his cheap salvation…, slid down into the red velvet seat, then down some more through the hellfired escape hatch—come out the other side gleaming in white leather gloves, white cowboy hat and a white suit jacket that covered the blood of his crime. He was damn-near't invisible…, no one trapped on the same ride seemed to have the time to notice him breathing. So he bought a nice meal, a thick juicy steak, and he grew fatter while the caboose of flames cleared the prairie behind, while the world turned upside down and the birds fell and the coal flew, blackening the sky and spreading seeds of starvation, distributing the vaccine of an epidemic. How spineless. How gutless. He was born with no eyes. And as the track stretched on and the machine wound around on the ground like a silvery serpent, he realized the contraption had no brakes. He turned grey through the seasons. His belly burned hollow and his heart slowed with rusted disease. And he found, in time, that it was his own blood fueling this fast-moving, demoniacal train destined for Nowhere.

Laden….
How shallow a world laden deep with shallow souls….
Where anything disproving inclusive imperfection is saving grace.
There be no need of God, then—no God bigger than our own religion. There be no need for forgiveness, then. No need for love. No need to ever speak candidly of these awkward things. Or hold someone's hand while they stumble through the fire we may have started.

And isn't it lovely….

Isn't it brilliant, incredibly genius, that smothered in our layers of subconscious defense mechanisms, trodden and fossilized beneath our millenniums of evolution, that we still know not what we do…?

*We've got the most intricate and colossal eyes yet it seems we prefer to go blind. We've got the most tender, merciful hearts with which to feel love…. If it is not so, what is that sound I hear calling out from somewhere deep inside you? That voice begging your attention that you leave unanswered year after year? What is that yearning there in your soul, I can see it reaching out for understanding, for belonging, for something deeper, for something **more**…. If it is not so, what is that tear there at your eye, oh precious and worthy leader? What is that strong daughter, what is that beautiful son, what is that amazing child yours for…? If you have no love to give….*

Drake's neck snapped. He opened his eyes, straightened himself in his chair and cleared his throat. He knew what his responsibilities were. He knew what the challenge was. And to look at it all at once was overwhelming. He had no idea where he'd get the energy, the skill—no one had bothered to raise him, after all…. He knew it was wrong to play with thoughts of desertion. But he gave into the freedom fantasy just a little bit, into the torturous daydreams and the "if only's" that whisper false promises as if the key to salvation is in the luck of the draw, the 50/50 chance at the fork in the road. He listened, just a while, to the hissing lie that he'd be younger somehow, if he were just somewhere else—anywhere else. He wouldn't be empty or lonely there. Of course not. He wouldn't disintegrate. Not there. No. He'd be more relaxed, more comfortable, more *Drake*, if he could just wash his hands of this entire thing. *What can I do for the kid, anyway?* And fatherhood. He just didn't need to mess with it. All he needed was a good excuse: Lemn's gift with cards, it was just plain unsettling. Unheard-of. His advanced level of maturity was freakish. And the kid talked to himself. Probably praying, but still. It was downright disturbing. And after Lemn's overreaction—*He knew what was coming*—after his outright breakdown, it seemed the boy was a loose cannon. Unstable, maybe insane, already. After the long ride home, stopping so he could puke, so he could catch his own breath—more than once, and then the whole episode by the fireplace…, well, it seemed he was his mother's son after all. He was acting so near death with fits and such, one would have thought him gut shot. Or undulant fevered. And if he wasn't gonna amount to nothin' more than that…, if all he was gonna do was follow ever' single one of Anne's crazy footsteps, well, it'd just be best to move on. And soon…. Because Drake could deal with a lot of things, but not this. Not anymore. It just wasn't natural, the way that boy was. He was off-center and it was about time somebody said so....

It was just about then that Lemn entered the room. He didn't say a word, just sat himself down across from Drake and rubbed the sleep from his eyes. Looked like he needed to rub it from his entire existence, but couldn't reach it. He looked dog tired. Old, almost. And it occurred to Drake that not half the hell on earth would have ever had a chance to happen if the two main people involved had just sit their sorry butts down at a table without guns. Without money. Without booze or power. Or colleagues or friends. And without words. Or age. Or color. Or gender. Just sat there and looked one another in the eye. *My, my, my.... Because,* he thought, *least a man be half dead an' hellbent already, he'd see somethin' there. Somethin' in that other person thit looks an awful lot like himself.* If he just would've done this one simple thing, he doubted he'd a' killed a soul all his life. And now that he'd done it, he knew he wasn't ever gonna leave this one.

And that was all there was to it.

He tilted his cup to take a drink and realized his coffee was ice cold. He sat it back down. He tried to think of something to say, something not so harsh, so abrupt, but he couldn't think of anything. It was hard to look at Lemn. It was harder still to allow himself to be looked at. But as for the first, he'd rather not peer into those deep brown eyes of Lemn's and see hollowed out glass—that glazed over cavernous look that follows things like these here…, like death and killin' and such. Things that leave a person shifted and stained for what seems like forever. Drake didn't want to look at that because he knew exactly what it felt like. And he'd never had the guts to ride out a sorrow that low. But he knew Lemn would. Lemn would let it take him to the bottom of the ocean if it wanted to and he wouldn't fight it, wouldn't come up for air until it let him. Until he'd done his time. Drake's mind jumped to his fondness of trees. That's the closest he'd ever come to feeling the pain he'd caused himself by his own hand—standing at the base of a tree. Not saplings, not pines or cedars, but big old burly oaks. The ones that a decent-sized man couldn't hope to get both arms around. The ones that stood tall, twisted and scarred and unashamed. Knots and bumps and cancerous growths boilin' up outta their hide like leprosy. To Drake, those trees stood there in broad daylight and told anyone who'd listen what it felt like to kill someone. To hurt someone. *To never forgive, never let loose whatever it is inside yourself thit up and caused that shit to come out of ya. A' course a tree never done nothin' but try to survive. But a man. A man should know better. And there ain't a thing you can do with that kinda pain other than grow around its ugliness, try an' grow a hard, brittle shell around those hol-*

low parts eatin' the core of you away. Drake had always stood in awe of a hundred-year-old tree.... He'd never be that proud. He'd never make it that far. And if he ever come across somebody cuttin' one down, he'd be liable to shoot 'em in the back.

He tried to get his unruly mind back on the kid. As far as he could tell, Lemn was nothing like Anne—*or so what if he was?* He was still the shadow of a friend. All these little things Drake could see in him—they were the shadow of his friend. Lemn was like Devon's spirit reborn. Like chance given out plain and honest, all over again. Lemn was sensitive. So was Devon. So what. And he had emotion. Had heart—a strong heart that would appear to most men as shamefully weak. Almost embarrassing. It was a special trait and not something to be made light of, but it sure was different..., 'specially on a boy.

There was a truth buried beneath all this analyzing, all these rambling thoughts and second guessing..., Drake couldn't see the heart in this kid killed without shattering what little was left of his own.

And Drake didn't have the slightest idea what he was doing. He'd never been able to live any kind of life and keep his soul untouched. In fact, searching back to his earliest memory, he'd never really had a kind heart to begin with. He'd never been anything like Lemn, he'd never been *pure.* The only thing he knew for sure, the only thing he would never forget, was that baby. Burying that lady's murdered baby broke the only heart he ever had. Broke it straight in two and he'd lost both halves like they bled out through his hands that horrid night. That was the night he changed....

He wondered if somethin' in that baby'd circled back to this earth as Slim..., and how bizarre a thought....

The poor kid was just sitting there, forlorn, looking out the window for what he'd lost like it'd come floating by any second, as if Anne, Devon and Slim were the best of friends, just standing outside talking like adults are supposed to do. They're not supposed to drop like flies in the fall. And Drake knew he wasn't of much help. He was such a mess himself he couldn't so much as speak. He didn't know where to start anyhow. He guessed the story to be told, the first line of the rest of their lives, would have to come from the boy's mouth. Sure as the world, their plan would be written there in his eyes. He just needed to give the boy a little time. Drake choked down the remainder of his cold coffee, wincing slightly at the bitterness of the trailing grinds. He followed Lemn's gaze out the window half expecting to see Devon out there himself. The day had decided to turn grey. It was befitting, he supposed. It had just barely begun yet his mind was spent. He didn't even have the capacity to order it to stay still.

It wound up and took off again, blatantly, proving that it answered to no one, and it recalled how—before all hell busted loose—Lemn's eyes held a certain trust. A warmth and an honesty that could not be duplicated by anyone. It was so much more than an expression and so sincere that Drake had had to stop whatever it was he was doing just to wonder at it. Just to stand there in the path of it, regarding it in awe as if he were beneath one of his trees. It was pleasantly different—that look of eternal hope mixed with a quiet joy, contentment with his lot, a little mischievous humor. Drake remembered thinking, *How can a child own that look?* Because there was a wisdom to it, as if Lemn knew everything that was to come, everything there had ever been, and he knew that none of it would defeat him. Yet he was humble. His attitude toward a person was sweetly nonjudgmental. But he wasn't naive nor was he blinded by transgressions as if to him flaws served for no other purpose than the magnification of goodness. They were a welcome, fresh opportunity for redemption. His was a look so real and so, so *light*. After the first few times he'd experienced it, Drake summed it up for Mama like this—*It's something to guide yourself toward regardless of age, of your experiences or condition. Imagine being looked at like that, Mama. Imagine being **able** to look at someone like that. To inspire somebody old and worn out like me. I've never seen anything like it. It's completely selfless. I wonder if he even knows the power he's got....*

Drake nodded off, his sluggish body as reluctant as the slow-moving morning, but his mind kept going....

Lemn's eyes would sing. Yes, that was the word he should have used to describe it for her. Sing. Those eyes would sing in a silence. In that amazing way that eyes shine like they do. That amazing way they shine out from the heart, like light coming up from an underground heaven. A person wouldn't expect to find it there, in that instant. But there it is, quick as a wink. It wouldn't be thought possible, that the meaning of it would be so clear, so unmistakable, and without a single word uttered.... In fact, words would tarnish it, wouldn't they. Words would bring reality rushing back in and reality would break it into pieces, shatter the delicacy like an interrupted sun ray. And then, just like that, it flees. It's gone. And it's hard to remember if it was even there, unless...*unless you are blessed enough to live your days out with a person so free and so grounded, Drake. So peaceful. Here, but not. A person like that lives more inside you, in your heart, rather than beside you. Imagine what a shot through the air can do to a soul like that, Drake. Imagine what spilled blood can do to eyes like that. It's why you yourself are broken this day....*

He awoke quickly to the embarrassing lurch of his own body. And Lemn looked cold. It was the first thing he focused on—Lemn was cold. In fact, he looked so cold he was nearly as grey as the thick sky lumbering outside. It was a color too damn close to death.

It had been a long night to suffer. It should have been over with by now. It was like the dawn saw what was comin', turned around and went back to bed. Drake's mind had started in on the self-torture while his sins and flaws could still be covered with a thick blanket of darkness, could still be eased by a state of semiconsciousness, but there was no mercy now. The punishment was full-blown and relentless here at this table. It seemed penance would drag him through itself again and again if he was sorry or not. Since the shooting, every single one of his thoughts had been tainted the color red, each one polluted with the old, familiar feelings of suffocation—when he shot someone he ran. It's what he did. He needed to escape himself after a kill and the closest he'd ever come was in a different town, any town where he could trade in his persona for something a little shinier. And this loss of freedom was overwhelming, its injustice was creeping into his bones. This was the first time in a decade that he'd had to fight his natural tendency to leave. He'd always catered to it before. Denying the impulse of flight was unsettling—shook him where he stood 'til he was about out of his mind. The lack of motion, the lack of distraction actually caused him to tremble. Because all he had was himself—it was all he had to think about. And there in the middle of the night on the cold floor in the dark, after taking out his bedroll and saddle bags just to stare at them, caress them and feel the freedom they carried, the release, he uncovered his addiction, surprised and somewhat ashamed to find it every bit as detrimental as any drug or drink. His frailty disgusted him and, inevitably, he shoved his gear back under the bed. Then the dreams came.... He tossed, turned, felt his guts were hanging on the outside of his swallowed skin, slabs of his soul curing on broken bone. Peaceful sleep became something precious—a crown of jewels passed before the unworthy son. It became something that was too much to ask, too peaceful a blessing for someone like him, and he needed to get out of that bloody room. So he rose, dressed, quietly lit a fire in the stove, and he figured, as he boiled his coffee, that the night had been the only thing to win out. Logic told him that he'd just grown too exhausted to leave. That's what he thought earlier this morning. Earlier this morning, he reassured himself that what he discovered was nonsense. That he could always pack up, always leave and rejoin his coveted world at anytime—*ain't no shame in that.* He found comfort hidden in this choice. He saved it, savored it as a last resort. Held onto its promise, kept it in his back pocket for most of the miserable morning, until this....

"God doesn't think you're a bad person."

Drake was relieved to see some sign of life. He was about to jump up and shake Lemn by the arms. The kid's lips were nearly blue. Drake was thankful for the hint of normalcy breaking though Lemn's gloomy shell, but irritated by the words. His chair groaned loudly as he slid it back from the table and stood up. He got a fire going in the fireplace—partly for heat, partly for escape. He didn't want to reply. He'd grown used to patronizing Avi, he expected that sort of talk from her, but for some reason, this morning it made him angry. He was tired of every single family member he ever had thinking they had the right to preach to him. Thinking they saw a need. Seemed to him the whole lot of 'em was hypocrites…, judgin' him all the time. And now a thirteen-year-old. *Do they all meet under the full moon in the middle of the night? They can sniff heathenism out like a pack of wild dogs. Then they corner ya, go to gnawin' on ya….* When he was finished at the fireplace, he stoked the wood stove and added another log, lingering there for several unnecessary minutes wondering if he should cook something. He rubbed his forehead. He had a headache and beads of sweat had erupted at his brow. He unbuttoned his shirt slowly, slid it off his shoulders and threw it over the back of the rocker no one sat in anymore. Lemn had spoken his words like they were ash. As if the taste of them were as gritty as a mouthful of Drake's cold coffee grounds. His tone was as grey as the day and as sullen as his skin. And Drake couldn't even think what he meant, exactly. And, anyhow, such a time of silence had passed, he assumed, he *hoped* that Lemn wanted to take it back or, at the very least, that he was finished with the poppycock.

"He just doesn't like what you do."

The words came out cold, hard, like they were written on a heavy stone tablets locked inside Lemn's chest. His voice cracked again.

"You think you have no choice. But you do. That's why I'm here with you now."

Drake was too tired for this. Through the entire night, then this morning…, well, his mind had plain wore his patience to a nub. One prophesyin' woman in his life was enough. There were times she blew his mind. Downright spooked him. And Emma, and Avi…, all their concern, their tears, their pleadin' and their prayin'. He just couldn't take anymore of it. And now it was comin' from Lemn, too. Lemn of all people….

"Stop complaining."

Drake's breath stopped inside his lungs. He had to check for a minute.... He didn't speak out loud. He was sure he didn't speak....

"You need to listen to this, Drake. It's your last chance."

Lemn's eyes came up to meet his. Dark circles were hanging beneath them like he'd cried two black stones. His skin was loose, aged and sagging, like he'd seen every horror in hell and each sighting had stolen a piece of flesh from beneath his face. It was a look no one would dare fight. It was unexplainable—possession by an angry and haggard God would come the closest.

Lemn got up from the table, body still sunken and frozen, skin ashen, and when out into the chilly morning without overclothes or a coat. Just walked out the door barefoot, in his longjohns, not bothering to close it behind him. A five-minute-younger Drake would have been convinced the boy was going insane, would have taken this as proof that he'd swung over to Anne's ways—all fears and suspicions confirmed. But not this Drake. This Drake was speechless. His headache had cleared. His mind was at rest. This Drake had been explicitly warned.

.   .   .

Time passed them by. But time, like everything else, has a dual nature. And this time it was different. There was no pleading. No crying. And no praying. And Drake missed these things terribly because there wasn't much of anything to take their place. And Lemn looked lost in the ice and snow, wind howling with the devil at its heel. He stopped talking to Drake altogether. He acted as if he couldn't even see him, or like he saw *through* him. Like the man was a breathing shadow. And the kid looked like hell. His hair was growing longer. Down past his shoulders already. Scraggly and unkempt like the exposed, dried roots of a withering tree. A tree perched there and pleading, watching the dried-up brook, waiting all day and all night for nothing—Lord pity the placement. His warm, chestnut eyes had grown as cold and dark and as bitter as an old man's. He didn't eat much. Didn't do much. Sat out there cross-legged between those graves for hours. Days. Blending into them. Clutching his chest. Doubled over and rocking, half-frozen. And, rather than filling out, it seemed his body was getting smaller, weaker by the minute. Drake tried to force him to come alive once, he feigned fun, poking him in the ribs to get a response and the response he got…, well, he never tried that again. The kid was obviously in pain and the look in his eyes…, they were dead. Dead.

Avi was beside herself with worry saying he should have snapped out of it by now, but Drake had given up weeks ago. Depression gives off an infectious stench. He'd packed his horse on several occasions, in the middle of the night. He nearly lit out once—the closest he'd come, but caught a glimpse of the boy's shadow in the window, the outline of that desolate face watching him. He sat there on his horse for what must have been a half-hour, stiff and staring through the mesmerizing, floating, falling snow 'til he couldn't tell if Lemn was there in the window or not. Perhaps it was an apparition. Perhaps it was only frost playing with his imagination. But either way, he ended up stepping down. He unsaddled, unpacked, went back to his sleepless bed and stared at the abysmal ceiling that felt an awful lot like his life.

But an energy, pure and sweet, was floating in on the air today. Finally. To Drake it smelled like poker and smoke and cheap whiskey. It made his blood flow a little easier, it surged a little smoother down through his cold veins. He kept looking hard toward the horizon, the one leading into town. It was whispering things to him. Calling. His soul itched and burned, thawing. After morning chores, he found Lemn seated on the porch layered in enough clothes to cook an Eskimo. He was holding in his hand, of all things, a looking glass.

"Whacha doin' boy?" Drake didn't expect any sort of answer from him.

"Look into this…, please."

Drake was taken aback, surprised that Lemn was actually talking to him, so he obliged—quickly. He took up the mirror and looked into the glass.

"Tell me what you want to see."

"What kind of a prank is that, boy?"

"Go ahead, Drake. I'm not foolin'. Please tell me what you want to see."

Drake swallowed. A mirror was not something he liked to look into and the reason why always seemed to be a mystery until now. Everything that was missing, everything that he wasn't was suddenly staring back at him.

"Your father."

His eyes remained averted as he put the mirror down on the porch swing beside Lemn and walked into the house. Lemn sat a moment, looking blankly into the sky. Drake's answer brought a tear to his eye—it wasn't what he expected. He didn't know what he expected Drake to say exactly, didn't really know why he'd done it in the first place. But he did. He rose slowly and entered the house, shedding layers of useless clothing like his sadness.

It was Easter Sunday, he'd nearly forgotten. They were all supposed to meet at Mama's for dinner.

"You know what I want to see in it, Drake...? Your son."

Chapter Fifteen

A year and a half had passed since Anne's death. Time running like liquid over them, they were the rocks of the falls, those graves. Both had cured and were identical in their loss, covered with a dry, cracked dirt that seemed bottomless, a thick slice of earth portraying all that was empty. Desolate down to the core. Like stone regret. Avi saw how Lemn looked when he passed by them, shoulders curved just a bit more. A woman's touch was rain to this place…. And, on her next visit, she brought a burlap bag, soaked and sealed. Divisions of perennials from her mother's garden. Without a word she kneeled down and began transplanting them over the graves. When she was finished, she stepped back, dusted the front of her dress, and smiled. Alive. Something was alive. Something new risen of the ashes. When he'd seen what she had done he said nothing. Turned and walked off. Left her guessing for a moment, unintentionally. Came back with a bucket. Watered them. Asked her if he could have more, thinking of Slim's patch of dirt floating outside the skirts of Shawneetown.

Glen was a neighbor whose character and deed fell under every intended pleasantry of the word. A decent man, late forties, honest, with loyalty steely enough to match his sturdy stature. He had a keen eye and a sixth sense about trouble—things Drake admired. He tended the place for them while they were gone gambling, off carousing in one of those faraway places that only existed for him on a floating map painted by disconnected lines pulled from their stories. Stories of blue on black, red veins through tan skin, jagged trails that bled into one another, rigid legends, dark characters that sometimes ran completely off his mind's page, but he liked hearing about them all. His eyes would twinkle, at times he was almost there. He'd listen to Drake go on for an hour or so while Lemn sheepishly added a detail here, a quiet comment there, then he'd hurry on back to his own chores, back to check on the missus to see if she might be in need of anything. He was the kind of man who would water flowers over the dead—asked or not. Lemn owed Glen some back pay from the last journey. He planned to settle the account today, a nice and pleasant day full of spring sunshine and promise, and headed to the barn to retrieve his sorrel gelding.

The heavy doors gaped open like the jaws of a lazy giant and swallowed him. The belly of the barn encased him like a private tomb—dank and cool, a space that held itself stubbornly unaccountable to the whims of the weather while its skin of planks popped under the sun's warmth like water blisters. He was temporarily blinded and he stopped moving, waiting for his eyes to adjust. As his horse slowly filtered into a recognizable image he noticed that the animal stood as solid as a statue, molded in a trance of rigidity. The only movement was the pulsing of his huge barrel, forcing air rapidly in and out, in and out of flared nostrils. He was searching ravenously for a familiar scent, something that could jog a memory or offer a trace of comfort. But he was finding none. If only he could run.... His attentive ears were pointed sharply forward and the whites of his eyes flashed a curious fear as he focused intensely on something other than his owner, ducking and tossing his head momentarily, then fixated again, muscles ready to explode. Lemn turned in the direction the horse was indicating and then it moved, stealing several of Lemn's heartbeats with its sudden revelation of identity and dynamic impulsion, dually shocking in their synchronicity.

The instant Lemn spotted her, she bolted like a wild cat and was gone. He belatedly jogged outside after her but realized, with a paralyzing twinge of back pain, that he would be severely outdistanced. As he watched her sprint—*fly*—for the river, he yelled, "Wait! I won't hurt you! You're safe here.... You're saaffee!"

She was close to his age—just a few years younger..., couldn't have been more than ten, eleven maybe—and how he craved that brand of companion. He figured she spoke English. There were very few Indians in Illinois anymore. In fact, he couldn't think of any offhand. And he'd heard the stories. Stories of degradation and bloodshed that made him shiver to the bone, made his stomach swell with an odd shame. Stories that made him glance over a shoulder when he felt the wind change on a still day. He recalled that strange sensation a few years back, unforgettable yet so hard to describe he had told no one—he could feel footsteps crossing before his path as he seeded the spring soil. Invisible, yet he *saw* them somehow..., or maybe just knew. There were men, women and children—the soft moccasin footsteps of a long, hard journey. They were crossing before him on an easterly breeze, hundreds of them as he worked the entire field. *Who were they? What did it mean?* He surmised them to be the spirits of those who had died on the reservations, returning.... Yes, he figured she'd understood him..., though she wasn't dressed white. He turned and went back inside. He became increasingly saddened as he went through the blank routine of brushing his horse, picking out the hooves one by one, saddling. He imagined the darkest of scenarios, the spectrum of wickedness that she could be running from and alongside. *Lord only knows....* There was an aching she left in his chest, a hollow homesickness for something spiritual that he didn't understand. How could he feel so lonely, so unfulfilled after four seconds with someone—someone with whom he'd never even had the chance to speak? It was a mystery. He wished she could have trusted him but at the same time knew why that was a preposterous expectation. Perhaps things would have been different if she'd waited until mid-summer. His hair would be a little longer by then and his skin, a rich golden brown.

·   ·   ·

In just one year of gambling, Lemn had made enough money to settle up with Crenshaw. He paid for the three year's worth of back farm payments, paid this year's payment in advance, plus all the interest. He could have paid toward next year's but didn't want to stir up any more attention. Crenshaw's bushy eyebrows raised high enough at the sight of those zeros on the note, his greedy cogs set to turning while his aging hand quivered with an angry curiosity. It was unsettling to say the least—a boy conducting a man's business. In a man's bank. In a man's world.

Somehow Drake eventually swallowed the fact that Lemn was no gunfighter. Never would be a gunfighter. This mode of self-preservation simply did not register with the kid's brain. They put a lot of distance between each game. Miles and rivers and hills and time. The stakes they were dealing with gave them no choice. The most profitable venture was the steamer trip from Louisville to New Orleans and back, which brought Lemn close to two thousand dollars. At the rate he was going, he figured he would have his farmstead paid off in three more years. Then he would be able to farm the land on his own. He'd tend livestock. Start making the honest living he was always chiding about.

They bought unusual clothes for their travels, tailored suits that made them look like city-folk rather than farmers. Drake was meticulous about the grooming of his mustache, the slim shadow of his beard, just so dark. Lemn's hair was long, the tip between his shoulder blades, but it was silky, soft to the touch with a golden sheen like candlelight. He often wore it tied back. The overall appearance of the duo was nothing short of sharp. The walk down Any Street was tall and seldom went unnoted. The ladies stared, transfixed. Long eyelashes fluttering over frilly lace fans of oleander ivory or dusty Dakota rose. Young girls ceased their games and giggling and Lemn ducked with a shy grin and blushed. He was becoming a man—a good-looking one. No detail of their profession went unattended. They took on the identity of father and son; Spencer and Devon McCollum, McCall, Montgomery or Jackson. They were from the city; Chicago, St. Louis, or Davenport. The adventure of traveling was theirs together and for Drake it was a heavenly retirement, a sabbatical of the sweetest swirl of flavors imaginable. He felt *alive* for the first time since Emma was by his side. Under a different name he was legendary no longer, just a mentor in the shadows, in the shade away from the blaring sun. He loved Lemn like he was his own and it was the longest he'd ever gone without killing a man.

.   .   .

"Mama, I jus' don't undahstan'. I don't see why I cain't at least *meet* my daddy."

"I's too dangrus, chil'. I's jus' too dangrus!"

"You said it y'self, Mama, he's a lot older 'n you. What if I never get to meet my own daddy? Mama, I love ya. Ya know that. I jus' want ta know more 'bout m'self's all."

"Avi, chil', ya's gots ta promise me, sweah ta me, chil', you won't go 'way. Not down der. Down der is so close ta hell, chil'! I cain't let ya throw y'self back into de fiah! Le's write 'im. Le's you an' me write 'im a lettah 'stead, child. Doc know' 'im. He help."

"You mean Doc knows my daddy? Mama! How is it that everybody knows who he is—everybody but me?"

"Oh, Avi. Tha's how's a come we stay safe heah. It ain't like dis no othah place else. Doc an' y' daddy, they's frien's. They's go back 'long ways, long ways. Yo' daddy knowed we'd be killed, we'd be killed, chil', if he di'n't move us on out. He knowed Doc from way back. Praise sweet Jesus, chil'. Da Lord done sen' a angel in Doc for us. An' we been safe heah, chil', all deese yeahs."

Mama's tear-filled eyes rolled back in her head and fluttered, finally falling still as they gazed up at the ceiling, locked on nothing that Avi could perceive. She was lost to her sea of visions—confusing flashes of hurt in the world, displaced in sequence and proximity—and God's will for it all. Avi wondered what one exhausted and feeble old woman was supposed to do about it…, didn't she have enough troubles of her own?

"Alright, Mama. We'll write. A lettah will do. For now."

Avi squeezed her mother's hand and bent down, lightly kissing her plump cheek. Mama knew things before they happened. What a curse. Anxiety grounded. She'd wept in the darkness for years. She carried the weight of the devil's work across her tired, scarred shoulders. Everyday. As she had for miles of time.

.   .   .

May 17, 1859

Dear Sir Elliot James Woodford,

I hope this letter finds you well and that you, in turn, find it in your heart to fondly remember these details to which I am referring. My mother's name is Aviona, a woman to whom you were once well acquainted. I am her daughter Avi, named respectfully after her. I have recently discovered that in all likelihood you are of my closest kin. Would you be so kind as to respond in regard to this matter, Sir? I could think of nothing greater than to speak with you face to face should the will of the Lord allow. I will be patiently awaiting your reply.

Sincerely yours,

Avi

During a private conversation about contacting Elliot, Doc suggested that Avi allow Ellie to help her with the formal details of the letter in a surreptitious attempt to kindle a friendship between the two, giving Avi more opportunity to feel comfortable in Shawneetown and perhaps avoid thoughts of traveling so far away (*and into a slave state, no less*). Doc always had a notion that the two young ladies would bond if given the opportunity and he hoped this would be good enough reason. When Avi reluctantly asked Ellie for assistance, the pale complected, blue-eyed woman appeared thrilled to help but, secretly, her enthusiasm was due to the fact that she was one of the first let in on a matter of official town gossip. After Ellie hastily wrote the letter, had Avi sign it, and flung the letter toward her husband, the postmaster, to be sent, she immediately paid a visit to Doc. She burst into his office out of breath, nearly hyperventilating as if she were reporting an emergency, ringlet curls bouncing around her intrigued, flushed face, "I didn't know Avi's father was from South Carolina! How on God's green earth did you get his address?"

"Well, this may come as a shock, Ellie my dear, but you don't know everything there is to know about this old man. Avi's father is a very respectable businessman and a good friend of mine and I would appreciate it if this stayed a private matter. Avi hasn't exactly had the easiest life, you know, and she trusted you to help her, Ellie. You. Which I have every confidence you have done a dutiful, Christian job at. Now good day, dear."

Ellie stammered a brief reply—more of a snort caught and squealing in a sinus cavity. She tugged up her skirts and spun on her polished heels to return to her home—a modest, two-story Victorian with the Shawneetown Post Office crammed in the entry. It was a house painted a white so glaringly plain it infuriated her to the bone, caused her to bang the screen door with each blasted entry signifying to her husband *you may have won **that** battle but this is a hundred-year war.* She haughtily breezed in through that damn door, slamming it so hard this time it bounced off the jamb twice. She pushed past her husband's patrons like a cow toward a water trough, a *My lands!* erupted up and out of a frail pair of astonished lips after she stomped across the little woman's toes. Finally up the stairs, she slammed her bedroom door to sulk like a spoiled child behind it. Her shallow sobs were an embellished drama for her own entertainment. No one else was listening. She defiantly pardoned the fact that she was over thirty and grabbed an embroidered handkerchief to dab her turned up nose before setting off on a new wave of wails. Life had always been so unfair to her. When she ran out of examples that depressed her, she checked her makeup in the mirror. *But Sweet Lord, I sure am beautiful....*

In his office, Doc smiled to himself in regard to Ellie's youthful mannerisms. He thought they were becoming, but not to such an extent that he would openly let her know for fear of encouragement. *What poor Postmaster Shaw must have to humor.* He allowed his mind to drift back to when she was a baby—already uncommonly attractive in feature, yet highly unattractive in temperament when she arrived on that midnight coach. *Can't you keep her quiet? This isn't a show for the entire town, you know....*

You give it a try, but I reckon if she ain't quit fussin' fer two weeks, she ain't 'bout ta quit now. Good luck, Doctor. You' gonna need it.... He recalled taking her up in his arms, thinking it was just a touch of colic—*poor little thing*—but that child fussed and carried on for years, was still fussing this very day, matter o' fact. He peered out the window to confirm her lasting departure then sat down to write a long overdue letter of his own.

·   ·   ·

Deah chil', don' go down to da hellfire. Hellfire's a burnin' down der, chil'. Burnin' it ta da groun'. Sweet Jesus, hell's a comin'. Hell's a comin' SweetJesus....

Chapter Sixteen

The harvest season dwindled frost after murderous frost as the color of the world was shrewdly stripped away, suffocated, forced to lie shackled in dormant grays. Ash until it felt the sun's touch of warm encouragement on those glorious days when it was acceptable to BE again, bold like green against a cotton-clouded sky. But those days would not come for a long time. The chill in the air caused the strained muscles blanketing Lemn's spine to grip tighter, balling up in painful knots. Nerves pinched under the rigid masses shot spears of debilitating misery down his left leg. See, his body was growing at a rapid rate but his back was still caught. Trapped and folded in against itself like contorted branches working to strangle their very own trunk. Mystical forest of nerve and bone foully enchanting, dark path of inescapable dread, stagnant pools of torture hidden within—these became his body. At an age that should know no pain. He favored that leg—had no choice, muscles atrophying little by little. Day by dismal day sickness fell like swamp rain on his drenched soul. But still he carried on. He held his leg straight at the knee when he moved, hobbling about like some pitiful and cursed creature, swinging it out from the hip at every step because straight pressure was unbearable—snapped him like a twig. When he mismanaged its awkwardness to escape a storm-spooked steer, when he misjudged the severity of the uneven, icy ground before him, he'd come near to collapse, a twinge of pain and all his youthful powers were gone. He'd fallen a few times, landed in the snow-framed mud on wounded pride. He learned to be especially careful around the cattle. They held little relationship to him and showed no mercy with winter on the air, but his horse seemed to understand. Seemed to forgive the boy's decrepit slowness at feeding time, attempted to counterbalance his dangerous leaning in the saddle.

Drake whittled a walking stick but didn't know how to present it to him, ended up pitching it in the trees. He constructed a two-step box for mounting a horse after he painfully witnessed the boy's sorry attempt; barely hoisting himself up

with that weak leg and after all that fuss. The effort, the strain, sweat and tears....
Dear God.... Left it set there just inside the barn door without a word.

.   .   .

From the river, she had been watching him with the eyes of a hawk. She knew
when he did sun chores and moon chores. She held the walking stick in her hand.
But it was not yet time for her. She would wait. Still like rock. She would wait until
the tall paleface with the horse black as a crow feather was gone.

.   .   .

Mama and Avi prepared a large supper for Drake, Lemn, Doc, the Sheriff
and his wife Ammie. The long table was filled with too much food: creamy
mashed potatoes, honey-glazed ham dripping with rich salted gravy, sugared
baby carrots, buttered green beans, buttermilk biscuits, dessert of warm cinna-
mon-candied apples drizzled with cream. It was a delicious meal. Every guest
partaking overate. The hint of winter was whispering reminders along their
tense spines, saying true things of seasons gone before—gray gales sweeping
over skeletal cabins encased in ice, layers of frost on the morning quilts, miniature drifts inside window sills, food supplies dwindling, dipping far below
what was initially feared. Even townsfolk got anxious and greedy, mercantile
only stocking what little trickled down through the frozen veins of distribu-
tion, half of that robbed away. There'd be a line of honest folk knee or waist-
deep in early morning drifts waiting for the shades to rise and the door to blow
open, pushing through and over one another like backward prisoners freed.
Prices hiked up further with the extra help, big brutes with clubs and guns paid
to beat off those that clung to the back alleys like thin shadows waiting to creep
up on supply wagons. But Mama and Avi were blessed. They would have been
the last in line but instead they were given enough pork and beef each fall
(semi-anonymously) to last them well through the endless winter, so they prepared meals for their closest friends—before winter and during when the cruel
string of weather broke for a time. They gave to needy families and loners alike,
shy and empty beings that blew up on the back stoop like ice-dusted spirits,
black-eyed lost and ragged angels. They also grew a wonderful garden every
year bordered by apple and cherry trees. It seemed to flourish effortlessly and
they canned and dried enough produce from it to stock the shelves of their
massive cellar. And their friends were thankful.

After the meal most of the group was relaxing, limbs shifting uncomfortably
around their overstretched bellies, chit-chatting a rocky road with occasional

peaks of laughter to climb and descend—first the circle of men talking over one another in the parlor, then the women fluttering about in the kitchen, voices dancing with clanging pots or dinging china…, tinkling silver, their considerate punctuation. Lemn deciphered no words but it was soothing and pleasant to him, just the rounding flow like the melody of distant and circling birds. He felt the arms of the house full and content in its sheltering, no creaks or moans gurgled of something life left behind. He was in a quiet room adjacent to the parlor lying on the floor in the dark attempting to flatten his crooked spoon of a back. Hoping it would crack and pop and offer a hint of relief. Avi nearly tripped over his body, screeching in surprise.

"Ooohhh…. My lands, boy! What 're ya doin' there on the floor?"

"Nothin' much, I reckon."

Lately, Lemn had been growing bashful, alarmingly introverted—even for his deeply reserved personality—around Avi. His fondness for her was becoming difficult to ignore. He was mortified that she had found him like this—strung out like a drunkard collapsed on the floor. He tried to get up but the pain shot through his back something fierce. It instantly crippled his leg sending him directly down, flat on the floor. Again. He groaned in agony, mostly from the sheer embarrassment of it. The pain he was used to.

"Lemn, are you alright…? Is it still your ribs? After all this time? Good Lord Almighty…."

Avi knelt down beside him, concern draped in the heavy outlines of her shadowed face like black cobwebs. Like charcoal smudges from school, the one day he remembered doing art…, little pressed sticks that came in a grey box, half of them already broken. It was on his fingers, his shirt, smeared across his cheek. The rain had ruined his picture before he got home. It reminded him of her look, like someone had colored her sad and haggard, rain falling down upon her. He was aging her, he could tell it. She called for Doc without taking her hand off Lemn's shoulder.

Doc entered the room as hastily as he could at that age. His breathing was rushed causing a slight wheezing noise to bubble up in his chest, phlegm trying to string its way toward escape. When he stiffly bent down on one knee, it creaked against gristle for a disturbing length of time. *He needs to be oiled*, Lemn was thinking.

"What is it?"

"The poor boy can't get up off the floor wit'out pain, Doc. He's so young."
She lit a lamp absentmindedly.

"You been havin' troubles, boy?"

"Yes, Doc. My back's crooked. And my leg gives out some from the pain."

"Get Drake in here, Avi…."

The tone carrying Doc's last statement was not intended to be merciful.
Drake quickly entered the room as if on cue, picking up on the hint of blame—
he understood the situation completely. He'd been dreading this day. His crystal eyes darted down to Lemn's upturned boots and stayed as if the map to
Sorry were found etched on the blankness of soles. He started wringing his
hands then he nervously stroked his mustache, eyes still chained to those
boots…. Lemn's back had been degenerating for a long time and Drake knew
it. He had no excuse for keeping quiet about it. It was only fear. For the boy—
what it would do to him if he knew how bad it really was.

"Drake, you're gonna have ta look out for the boy with his back here. Use a
hot water bottle, heat some rags…,'bed sheets'd be better, and lay them 'cross
his back where the pain is. That'll soften those muscles up. I'm afraid that's all
we can do right now, boy. I'm sorry, son. I was hopin' you'd grow out of it…,
heal up straight."

"It's not bad, Doc. I'm alright. There are plenty of times I don't feel the
pain…, can't feel anything at all."

Doc's professional background caused him to take Lemn's comment more
seriously than did others in the room and his expression fell as the probability
of the situation became clearer. Drake helped Lemn to his feet because he had
to. The boy was just too weak. Doc watched him walk awhile then lifted the
boy's shirt up, examining his back from an upright angle. He ran his cold,
tremulous hands up and down Lemn's spine. Didn't say a word. Not even the
occasional nasal *um-hm* that usually accompanies these awkward exams and
relays absolutely nothing. He slid the shirt back down slowly, patted Lemn
lightly on the back and glanced at Drake—a serious look suggesting the need
for a private meeting.

Lemn's feelings were conflicted throughout the ordeal, he couldn't understand why he was suddenly so sensitive around people. Certain people. He liked Avi's concern, how she touched his shoulder and held his hand. As he relived the memory, it made him smile to himself and his face flushed with heat. But he was also deeply hurt and angered toward himself that she had reason to take pity on him. His body was growing weaker by the day and the pain, more pronounced. Secretly, he was terrified. He worried that he would not live long enough to marry a girl, become a father..., and furthermore, that he'd be unable to care for them. He always knew, deep down, that he wanted to be a husband, a good husband to someone. He wanted to be a family man more than anything else, wanted to share the feelings he felt inside. He wanted someone to love. It seemed like his reason for being alive. He could dream about her, awake or asleep, had always felt her presence. *She's out there somewhere..., right now.* The stars were her stars, twinkling for her eyes and inside of them when she smiled. The clouds drifting over the moon were sailing to her..., they knew right where she was, they'd go like a blanket to cover her. Like a kiss, like a dream on her skin. He could run his fingers through her long hair—it was warm and smelled like the sun. He could reach up into the sky and feel her breath. Her sadness was rain. Curses against her, the storm. Snow was his waiting. Apart from her. Blankness. An absence of color to his world. Of course he never told these thoughts to anyone but God—he could barely put them into words. He'd be too embarrassed to tell them to anyone, probably even to her, when he did finally meet her. But he felt this way just the same. It was as real and solid inside as the color of his skin, the color of his eyes, the shape of his hands. It was a bigger part of him than anything else, this love for her. He had only to find her.... He'd almost forgotten where he was when he saw her coming toward him. It could never be her..., Avi. But his heart beat too fast when she looked at him like that. When she smiled. He couldn't help himself.

Drake decided it was best to stay the night, to travel by the morning light. Fresh snow had fallen, sprays of powder hissed before each hoof fell into it with a dull crunch—millions of priceless crystals broken, pieces of the finest art shattered. Graced the likes of this world completely unseen. During the ride back, they were both relatively quiet. Nothing to say and lost beneath heavy thoughts—Drake thinking over what Doc had said and Lemn thinking about what Mama had told him. The sky was active, a massive presence of dark grey depression that was as inescapable as the headache it gave those below. Panicked clouds rambled about with no particular pattern, swirling pointlessly like smoke that lost its fire. The winter drained life and the resiliency needed to live it with decency, drained it out of them and everything else trying so hard to survive. Lemn noticed the whites of Sky's eyes were showing.

"Drake?"

"Hum?"

"When spring gets here, after planting, I really need to hit a lot of big games."

"More than last year?"

"Yep. Maybe twice as many."

"Why's that, boy?"

"I don't know what Doc said to you, but there are things you just know about yourself. I know my back isn't going to last me very long and that means I won't be able to plow the field, or ride my horse very far, or take a stage very far. I'm going to have a hard time taking care of my family, Drake, so I want to start getting ready for that now."

Drake was silenced, stunned by what the boy said and Doc's words ran through his troubled mind for the thousandth time since they were irreversibly spoken....*There will come a day when the boy's not going to be able to walk anymore, Drake....* His icy-blue eyes glared out, victimized, over the snow drifts and the bare trees that seemed stark with death, just floating by. Nothing looked familiar but he had lived enough to know that time would flow on. That things would be alright again but he couldn't seem to stomach it now, he just couldn't wait that long. It hurt so bad he thought he was dying. The frozen world was turning away from him. Turning away and leaving behind everything unfair and forsaken for him to drudge through. Maybe he wouldn't make it this time.... He stopped his horse to roll a cigarette with shaky hands as tears began to leak out of his eyes, defiantly, clouding his ability to see what his frozen fingers were doing. Suddenly he dropped the tin of tobacco to the ground, thinly sliced papers gliding down on the other side of his horse, and he doubled over the saddle horn sobbing like an old child. That's what he'd become...nothing but an old child. The more his deteriorating mind learned, the less he could comprehend *(faith....)*. The more his tired eyes had seen, the less he could envision *(hope....)*. But he still had Lemn *(love....)*. At times that kid tore him apart. *(The greatest of these....)* He looked over at him..., his boy.

.   .   .

And Mama had told Lemn……

"Da sun, she bring life. But wit'out de rain ain't nothin' would grow. Alls be dead then, chil'. No fruit. An' de same 's wit' us. Now some don' learn to like de rain. Claim dey don' need it, others claim dey don' see it—they's blinded to it by der minds. Think they's doin' theyselves good, but dey get confuse', see. Don' know what it is if dey cain't see it, so dey b'come da rain theyselves. Undahstan'? Dey *b'come* da rain. Dat ain't what's intended, boy. I's a terr'ble storm when dat happens. Terr'ble life. Bu' strong folk, da ones ain't afraid ta see da rain fer what it is, they takes it as a less'n, chil'. Take it on easy like…, try 'n learn from it and den go on. Dat what make ya wise, chil'. It's jus' part a da livin', boy. Some rains, oh my lan', chil'! Dey go on an' on an' on, dey do. Mercy, dey do. Bu' ya take it, boy. Take da less'n it's tryin' ta give ya. Ya take da Lord's han', chil', He reachin' for ya from da cloud, see? You take it. An' ya keep aholt of it. You be a'right, boy. You strong kind…."

And these words he would not soon forget.

Chapter Seventeen

The sky had gone. And with it, all color. And buried beneath its feathered and downy absence were further layers of drab depression. Bottomless. Where one supposedly stood, took for granted their bearings, became a travesty. There was no solid surface on which to get grounded, no fine lines with which to gauge coherency. Or sanity. Avalanche of sin swept down through the spirit world was a prairie winter. And it had landed. Atop angels trapped and still. And the white wind behind its chaos and fury had a personality all its own— blood cold. Winding through icy corridors straight to the brain, it howled shrill and clear in the ear. Thrown down from a chain of distant mountain and jagged cliff, the call of the silver-backed wolf—must exist, some long-ago feared legend from the stories slain, some unheeded warning for these here parts drifting on a mingling of snow and dream, come near morning thaw with blood dripping on white imagination, some icicle dagger about to fall, then awake with clear sweat under white breath. *What does it mean?* answered by nothing but that howl. Constant and resonating over a blinded prairie gone as mad as the back side of reason. It could pounce, could lunge at anytime. May not have made sense but the bones of the body sure felt it. The eyes in one's back closed in prayer, sockets recoiling close to the heart, for the lonely made for easy prey…, all cloudy-minded and desperate, searchin' for that sky like they did everyday, why their jugulars'd be bared. Their sunless and haggard flesh'd be hungry and isolated. And their will, all empty like that…, their will'd be lagging far behind 'em, far, far behind those icy and drifting shells for souls. All things that creepeth the earth do not feel love. Cannot cultivate it for them- selves, no. They need some sort of sign. And while they are waiting, they will worship and adorn, touch, smell, embrace, even speak to and sing Old World songs about, evergreens.

How anything could survive a prairie winter was a mystery. A miracle. And, sometimes, only a mirage floating across sands of white time....

.   .   .

Grey days like these proved that the concept of owning land was a cursed venture, an ideal built on spilt blood. Shaky. Unclean. Jinxed. Downright brassy to ask God to bless it. These endless winter days compiled themselves into months of nothing to do besides stare out the frosty window, peering into one's own head—*a man could lose himself out here....* Lemn thought about the land as most farmers do, found himself holding back tears thinking of spring—not just his skin, but his muscles itched down to the bone. He craved fresh air in a world warmed by the sun and, therefore, he empathized with it— the ground, the earth, all buried under there, waiting, a jaded source of renewal. He thought on.... *She's got to be getting tired, but still, she gives of herself and lives. Though blood-soaked to saturated with genocide and war, though stripped, raped, of mining, logging, sod busting, though buried beneath the immense weight and cloaked in the poisonous stench of those hideous cities, she will outlive. Any man. A steward's fate is so very small compared to all the time she's seen. Hidden in her hollow crevices are the answers to his very fragile life. Holy places inside her cracked opened by the arduous changing of the seasons. She knows things. Loosed like spring, the secrets of her heart overflow but are only mere whispers to the heavens—no one else is listening—but they are requests wise beyond generation, visions bold beyond blood. A humble man can feel her watching his every move, a quiet man can hear her creak with age, a man begging of her his living can gauge her very breath for mood. And she's in a foul one today.... Paradoxical, isn't it. How war was born of this life-giving gift. How a thin slice of paper could prove possession of something so untouchable. How a grid of jagged veins could denote boundaries across her....* He could almost see the red brick wall looming in the snowy air over there, a bloody knife blade drawn down from some draftsman's table, sliced strait through the heart of the Ohio.

He'd waited long enough, was driving himself mad within the realms of his own predictable company. He'd finished every book in the house, including the Bible—every single book of it. On more than one occasion, he found himself thumbing through Noah Webster's 1828 edition, figured Noah himself must have been either snowed in or flooded out to take on such a dull, no..., *tedious* task. He layered his clothes looking forward to some physical activity, choosing to ignore the pain nagging out its never-ending list of warnings. His willing attitude sank as he measured the depth of the drifts beside the porch—shovel high. It was bitter cold, no time to waste. He quickly began to tunnel a track through the beautifully deadly snow, delicate as the breeze and multiplying into solid tons. He followed the blizzard rope, stopping twice to backtrack to the house, to the fire. His fingers and toes burned. His back ached. His sweat was freezing then thawing, his underclothes already soaked. He pressed on with the rusty shovel, finally reaching the barn door. He dug a trench around it, needing to slide it open just enough to squeeze through. He noticed the wind was picking up—the word *draconian* tapped against his slow-moving mind. The undefined sky seemed to be suddenly swallowed by a cave of early darkness. The hungry, shivering animals were waiting, depending on him, a chorus of pleading bellers and whinnies urging him on, thanks enough. As soon as he had finished feeding, he made his way back to the house for the melted snow. He made several trips with the smallest buckets he could find. The rising steam floating up his coat sleeves felt good for a moment before it showed its second face and joined in with the enemy. Lemn's body began to slow down, his mind belatedly realizing how exhausted he was. With all safe for the night, he stepped back out for the last time with empty buckets and the lantern. A gust of crystalized wind engulfed the tiny flame and choked it, snuffed it out, as it stole his next breath. He ducked his head and shielded his mouth from the northern gale, finally regaining his air. He pressed the buckets down into an expanding shelf of snow, carefully setting the fragile lantern upright inside of them. His hands and forearms were shaking violently, his chin jumping off his upper jaw uncontrollably. He began to struggle against the stubborn barn door telling himself he was almost done, just this one last thing to do. The winter night had completely folded down around him now, a swirling world of blindness where no one should be caught lost and out wandering.

Drake hadn't returned from town that afternoon as he avidly promised he would. (Lemn couldn't help but wonder what it was about grown men that made them swear to trivial, indefinite things as if false promise were the same as good intention. They just set themselves up to let people down. That's all it did. He wondered why they didn't just admit they weren't sure about something—there'd be no confusion, no disappointment. No one'd be misled. His father'd always done that to him, too—made statements of fact that never came about. Presented wishful thinking like it was the Ten Commandments. Did that clear up to the day he died. Sure was hard on a young boy's trusting mind.) And he was sorely missed. Lemn assumed he was warm. Dry. Comfortably perched in front of the fire at Mama and Avi's, rubbin' wheel grease or lard into his knees. Drake could always sense the severity of oncoming storms by the degree to which they made his knees stiffen up and crack like dried bark. There was no possible way he'd be out in this one. Not in his right mind. Lemn knew he should be more understanding but caught his own thoughts cursing Drake and his bloody absence anyhow. He could sure use the help about now…, but facts were as they were. He was on his own. He restrained his hostile mind, ignored the distasteful attitude spawned by his physical challenges and concentrated on the matter at hand. He couldn't just let snow drift into the barn and overtake the animals. He wouldn't sleep a wink if he allowed himself to be that irresponsible. So he faced the sliding door sized twice his height, straddling it with a foot on each side, determined. He straightened his weak back as much as possible, bent his knees and tugged with all his weight and strength in an attempt to slide it toward the center line of his body. No movement. Snow began swirling thicker, sharp flakes dotting his burning face. He leaned into the wind and waded through the piling snow awkwardly, trying to swing his leg outward to avoid pain. Some of the drift was up to his thigh by the time he sank to the bottom but somehow he managed to make his way to the opposite end of the barn door. He pushed hard, assuming his grandest effort wouldn't budge it. But the door jutted forward with an unexpected momentum so sudden, Lemn simultaneously heard and felt the crack of ice in horrific harmony with the popping of his bones. His back was forced into an unnatural, excruciating twist. Every vertebrae along his lower spine ground together, every muscle separated, every nerve screamed as it was pinched, paralyzing his lower body and his state of mind. He lay in the suffocating snow unable to move as the wind taunted him, making a mockery of his helplessness, freely spending each passing second of his life like stolen grains of sand draining slowly but inevitably from an ominous hour glass. *This can't be happening…. Not this way. Not yet, God.* Traces of snow began drifting, pouring over the edge of the hole he'd made with his fall, a grey tomb the exact shape of his body slowly filling up. He actually chuckled somewhere deep inside of himself, humbly admitting that a life of lexicography could be better than sod-busting. Safer…. He thought of Noah—warm, candlelight reflecting off wire-rimmed spectacles, tired eyes poring over golden piles of books…, his harvest…. Then his face was covered. It was hard to breathe. He could hear his horse between the gusts. Could hear the animal audaciously pawing the ground over and over protesting the confines of his stall. Lemn understood he was cursing the limitations of his own limbs—oh, he understood that. Imagined he heard snorting, in his mind's eye, saw the horse shaking his head low—violently—no longer interested in his previously coveted meal. Lemn thought he heard a bucket of slushy ice water spill just as his frontier dream fell dark.

·   ·   ·

"If you're gonna run down through hell and back against Mama's wishes, Avi, then I'm goin' with you. And that's that."

"Spence, you cain't leave that boy alone. You said y'self that Jed and Jethro might be self-righteous enough to seek revenge. They'll hear you're gone and be tempted for sure."

"Then we'll both go with ya, Avi...." With those words an awkward stillness settled heavily on the air as if it were a national moment of silence for the lovely boy everyone once knew, for the great and robust young man everyone expected to adore one day, to have the space and the time from which to glean their eternal inspiration. It was a dream now shattered. Held inside their beholden hearts forever for, soon, there would be constant living, breathing and painful reminders of the way things should have been. The way things still should be. It was too tragic to think about. To witness would buckle one's knees. It was as if the boy had died but only in part—he'd be dragging his dead pieces with him through this nearly impossible life, impossible in distance and grueling feat for a healthy man. In the back of many a stranger's mind as they passed by, as they saw with their eyes and empathized with their aching bodies, they couldn't help but have the notion that, maybe, *that boy* should have died. Completely. If such a terrible, wretched and horrible thing could bring some form of relief. Some forgetfulness. And then the punch of guilt that followed that thought, enough to cripple the one supposedly standing.... Drake's face burned with raw sorrow and contempt. He of all people. Asked to watch more hell being born in the body of his young and innocent savior—every single day anew. Of course Avi knew Lemn wouldn't be able to handle the travel, it was a preposterous statement on Drake's part. Utterly thoughtless. Downright embarrassing—the massive weight of it, blatantly suggesting the fog of denial he was still under. He always ended up feeling naked and perched on the front-row pew of Sunday mornin' church when he talked to Avi. She could see right through him but had the decency to cover it most times. He was thankful for that at least. There was no comment dignified enough to salvage, so he changed the subject with a long and weary sigh.

"Look, I know findin' your father is very important to you. I know how that is, Avi. There was a time I'd 'a given anything to find my pa, even my own life. But, after bein' on the other side of things, I mean seein' what it's like ta look out for someone, I've realized this—the one who ought to be doin' the riskin' isn't the child, Avi.... Not the child. And I don't care how grown up she is."

"Oh, Spence. I don't know…. I guess it's just a crazy, fool-hearted notion. Everybody's so dead set 'gainst me goin' I guess I can hold off for a while. Maybe in a year or two things will be safer in the South. And I know what you're sayin' to me. I undahstand that he—my father—knew 'bout me all my life and didn't once try to visit me. Didn't once write…. Maybe I should jus' let it go. But it looks like if I don't close this gap…, ain't nobody gonna close it for me. It hurts, Spence. It hurts havin' half a' ya gone."

Drake let out another sigh, this one concealed and full of relief—he'd managed to stall her. And maybe in a year or two things would be better. Maybe in a year or two the old bastard'd be dead.

He noticed that Avi's gaze had clouded over…, her own private rain. She had her head lowered in shame. He recognized it. Her shoulders were curved in defeat and loneliness, her thoughts were spinning downward in depressing alliance. Drake knew all about desertion. He knew exactly what she was feeling inside as if her unspoken words were written across his chest, as if her pain were branded there in his own gut…. *Who will want you when your own folks don't? What's wrong with you? Why were you even born? You don't belong…, and it won't matter where you go.*

> *He learned that you can run from that voice as fast and hard as you can until your bones are heavy with exhaustion and just when the minute arrives that someone confronts you, puts you down, threatens you, there it is lurking over your shoulder like a shadow that never left you for a second, screaming sedulously in your ear.*

Makes a strong man weak. Gunfire always silenced everything….

He took her hand.

"That kind of hurt will eat away at you, won't it. Rot your core much as you let it, but no more. Isn't that what you've always told me? Remember, girl?"

He got a faint smile. A trace of the familiar.

"You're stronger than it is, Avi. Don't you forget that. And don't you forget your mother…. That woman has loved you and feared for you more than five generations of reclaimed fathers ever could, Avi. If there's one thing I know, it's that a woman knows how to love. It's a woman knows that.

"Can't you see what you done? As a woman, Avi? You gave me my family. Jus' give it to me. For free. You walked right up to me in my filth and troubles in your little blue dress and braided pigtails like on a cloud. Out of the sky you fell one day. Handed me the best gift there is in life. And I love you for it, Avi. Always will."

For the first time since he took hers, Avi felt his hand—really *felt* his hand. It was warmer, stronger, more comforting than usual. The connection felt safe. It felt real. She would always remember that moment. It was hers. As her first and final teardrop of the conversation flowed down her cheek, she wiped it away with the back of her free hand and smiled up at him. Their private regard was quickly banished by Mama calling frantically for her daughter.

.   .   .

"I's bad, chil'. Da devil, he in on it."

"I've got to tell Spence, Mama!"

"No, chil'. No, Avi chil'. Hush, ya heah? I beg of ya. Don' ya see? It's da devil's plan, chil'! If Spencah go' out, it'll be 'is las' time. Ya heah, chil'? He'll breathe 'is las' 'an he ain't ready. Deah Lord Almighdy, chil'! Da Lord ain't reach' our Spence yet! Avi, honay, don' let 'im go. DON' LET 'IM GO, CHIL'!!!"

Mama was enraptured by her vehement vision, it held possession of her to the deepest degree—it had captured one of her children. Tears began streaming down her haggard face, her fingers were pressed pale, venomously gripping Avi's forearm, fixated there. She'd begged her daughter to save her son, but she knew better. As she paralytically watched the inescapable events play out before her eyes, unable to move save the trembling of shock, unable to speak save the whimpers of agony, she already knew. It was too late. And Avi sensed it—that she was doomed to fail just as soon as the request exited her mother's mouth. *Damn this living hell....* She felt weak, powerless to surpass a force greater than her own and she understood, that from this moment on, the scenes perceived would haunt her dreams forever. The words spoken would echo in her awakened mind inexhaustibly. *No rest, no rest....* An invasive horror overtook her as she forcefully loosened Mama's grasp and ran down the stairs, almost collapsing weak-kneed and breathless at the bottom where she witnessed Drake desperately thrusting an arm into his coat sleeve, throwing his hat lopsided atop his head. He was already wound into panic and reaching for the door. Couldn't get out fast enough. He had overheard. Enough to decipher Mama's tone of voice. Enough to realize something was seriously wrong. His fatherly instincts took over. Lemn was in danger. And Lemn was his son.

"You…cain't…go, Spence."

Avi spoke in a broken whisper then fell down on her knees at his feet—*those black boots*—looking up into his uncompromising, determined eyes for an instant before their locked gaze was severed. Her eyes closed and her hands folded for an instant as if she were in prayer but she was too stunned to speak it, then her body wilted and curled as she dropped to the floor sobbing. The burst of cold air against her rejected skin was her brother's final reply.

.   .   .

sssssssssssss—crunch, crunch—
    sssssssssss—crunch, crunch—
        sssssssssss—crunch, crunch…

Lemn's vision was limited. His mind, hazy. The night was black, but still he imagined—*or was it real?*—that he could see through a darkened tunnel straight into Heaven. But someone was pulling him back and away from It. Warmth. Painlessness. Light. He cried out, but had no body of his own. He made no sound. They pulled him back into his hell as he watched all things Beautiful disappear from him, completely helpless with empty grasp. As if towed by a chain—like stump clearing—his body returned to him, lifeless and dead and seared with misery. His rock-solid, frozen legs made a sleigh-like path through the snow by no power of their own. They just dangled there, trailing his body that started to burn and Burn and BURN until he wanted to jump out of his own skin—peal it off with a razor, a knife, an axe—but he couldn't move. As the fire inside him intensified, he wanted to cut off his fingers—bite them off—his hands, his arms. He couldn't breathe—something was cutting off his air. He wanted to scream like a wild animal, but tears transformed into instant icicles, tiny eyelashes stiff and frozen together were the only outward signs of pain that he could produce. His thoughts were racing and his brain became warm with a numbing hum growing louder, Louder and he started to feel claustrophobic of body and insane of mind. Then, instantly, a glowing-white, a picture, a vision—some of mind, some of snow—demanded his autonomous chaotic state to gravitate toward it, focus on it and its light, its heat. The image was of his mother, Anne, with a face that said nothing but spoke still. She understood....

ssssssssss—crunch, crunch—
       sssssssssssss—crunch, crunch...

Lemn detected, between waves of nausea, the limited strength of the person dragging him. She let out grunts and sighs of exhaustion, but continued to move desperately, quickly. She was afraid for his life....

"Avi?"

The attempted word was pursed out through chapped, blued lips and formed by a frozen, swollen tongue. In his critical state of semi-consciousness, the name sounded more like "Ahvah" and would have been indecipherable by a close friend, let alone a stranger.

.   .   .

Although the buried trail was etched on summertime stone in Drake's mind, somehow he miscalculated. He merely had to follow the Ohio south out of Shawneetown to the largest grove of oak trees and fork off to the west about one hundred yards but, at times, he could barely make out Sky's ears two feet in front of him. The forceful gusts were blinding, stirring up whirlwinds of engulfing snow. He was exhausted, half-frozen himself when he decided to turn back east to find the river again. *Hold on, Lemn. Just a while longer.* His horse was soaked in sweat, muscle and hide glazed over with ice on the surface, steam rising. The horse had come miles, treading through snow up to his belly. Drake knew the horse was drained but he also knew his own limitations—he wouldn't be able to make twenty feet on his own. He could not feel his hands or feet. He desperately wanted to give his horse a rest but knew they were caught, dealt the most wicked and miserable hand, and stillness would mean the death of both of them.

"I love ya', old buddy. You got a heart of gold.... 'Case I never told ya."

Drake's words were swept away on the wind. He felt the massive muscles of the horse's body trembling violently beneath him. The animal's steps were getting slower and more laborious, at times stopping in mid-step, hoof sliding and then resting on the crest of the four-foot snow. Drake pulled upward on the reins to encourage the horse to pick his head up, but Sky was finished—as was Drake's heart. It was tempting to try to force him, but Drake would not go out like that. He'd never laid a mean hand to a horse and never would—he'd burn in hell first. Drake mustered up enough strength to force his frozen body off the horse as the beautiful, black creature collapsed into a soft white pillow grave, his enormous body falling to the ground, his intelligent mind choosing the opposing direction in which to lean in one last declaration of honor and kindness toward man.

Just as Drake knelt down to comfort his best friend in his final moments of life, the earth screamed out a horrific quake that cracked wickedly, like only a bullwhip at the hand of Satan could, and the ice gave way beneath them—the river found.

     .   .   .

...She understood. Her vaguely familiar, long-unseen smile and out-stretched arms started to warm him slowly from the inside out, as only a mother could, while the unrecognizable, young girl with long, black hair worked like a horse to save his life. She started a fire, took off his wet clothes and wrapped him in blanket upon blanket while leaving room for her hands to enter the well-made cocoon to rub his arms and legs and bring the blood back. Blood like a river, she prayed....

     .   .   .

The ice was on fire and he felt like he had reached the depths of hell.

The agony of watching your noblest companion loose life and slip away, in part by your own hand, is unbearable, uncomparable, forever unforgettable, selfishly unforgivable....

He prayed he would strike his head on a rock or fallen tree to end his misery as he caught glimpses of a large, black mass floating just under the surface of the ice, but unaware—safe and warm in his new life; sun-drenched pastures, knee-high and dotted with sweet clover and shade trees, no bugs nor burrs, with an oxbow stream trickling down through it, always spring. Drake found sole comfort in knowing the animal was no longer suffering but, still, a shot of hope punctured his heart each time the massive body bobbed up to the surface, reaching through the river-worn ice as if it still contained a fighting spirit. Those dark eyes still seemed to be watching out for him, searching for him....

     .   .   .

Lemn's senses were returning despite the overwhelming pain sprouted of his cracked and blackening appendages. He could only manage one word with his ill-functioning tongue and chattering teeth. He thought he could taste blood.

"N-N-N-aamme?"

"Da-qua-dov...Sky Fea-ther."

Sky...Drake's horse. Instantly, strangely, Lemn understood something completely void of doubt, as solid to his mind as stone to the hearth. He realized Drake and Sky were not at Mama and Avi's at all. And he forced his eyes to gaze up into the girl's. They were large, dark eyes watching his every move with concern and kindness, eyes that held wisdom, more familiarity of him than they should have. They seemed to be searching for something.

•   •   •

Drake's frigid body was no longer controllable and his mind was dazed. His lungs were barely functioning and his heart fluttered a weak beat only every so often. His veins would not take the thickened blood. He could make out Lemn's face in his mind but the image was fading fast. *My boy.* As the two words collided together inside his failing heart, the river's undercurrent pulled him down, down, and the icy water filled his lungs. There was no fight. His earthly vessel had been consumed by the hard season, squelching any more chances he may have squandered or salvaged. No one would ever know....

•   •   •

Lemn's body ceased its trembling and his mind drifted off into blessed, peace-granting sleep. He'd have hell to suffer soon enough. *U-yo-i. E-hi-s-di.* Feather continued to wrap his feet and hands with warm cloths hung directly by the fire, wrapping and unwrapping tirelessly through the night. As she kindled the fire, she had a vision. There was no fear in her heart. The paleface would never return....

•   •   •

Spencah come up outta da other side 'a de river....
He climbed up the bank, no longer cold. He felt fine. He sat down on a fallen log—oak—not sure where to go next. He could see the snow blowing and the river rushing under and over the ice, weaving through it like the world

was a basket nearly done, but he was distant from it now, and everything it held. He reached into his vest pocket and found paper. He reached into the other pocket and found a tin. He rolled his cigarette, lit it with the one match he had left—a perfectly dry match, and began to think.

He thought for a long time. About all he had done in his life. It seemed that he'd spent his time endlessly trapped in the dark, caught up in the mystifying maze that was his mind. His mind alone. The snow lit up around him as if the dawn might just start right under his feet. Like he was sitting on the sun. From the midst came a rising. Of a different kind. He killed a lot of people in his day. No gettin' around that. Because of some confrontation of one type or another, the nature of which—his justification regarding any of them—well…, he could no longer recall. The thought of Judgement Day made him consider suicide, but there was no way out of it. And then they started…. Comin' up the river one by one. All the people he had killed. The line was eternal. They passed beside him standing still, floating like on a cloud. They stared straight though him with blank and sorrowful eyes. And behind each risen spirit trailed families. Babies. Fathers. Sons and Daughters. Wives and Mothers. Those people mattered. Their lives mattered. In enormous and intricate ways. He could painfully fathom that now. He saw women scarred (some beaten, battered, some bitter), children starved (he'd taken their fathers away from them—he, fatherless himself), brothers shaken (turned mean, turned to revenge, to alcohol, a gun) and souls scattered, all lost without direction, lives that had played out all wrong. Because of him. Because of his sense of control that really wasn't. It lacked wisdom, courage, faith and true integrity. It plain lacked decency. And it was done. Irreversible. His life was over. And his eternity was regret. A regret so sour it made his throat twist holding it all back. Made his skin crawl, his stomach harden and his heart ache with a pain so colossal he begged for a death that had already come.

Nature is spread out before you to look at, boy. But you chose to grow blind. Delicate webs dotted with dew drops in the morning sunlight. Don't you remember them, boy? When you were small yet, and unafraid—had your eyes open. Skinned knee, no shoes, no shirt, ragged overalls—yellow dandelion in the front pocket…, for your mother—soft summer skin. You knelt down in the tall grass and you studied your world—spiritual, often invisible, with Satan in the center, waiting for his prey…. You noticed those who see the signs, you noticed those who reflect the Son—they do not get snared. It was My design you decided to deny. I watched you as you grew too big in the world, thought yourself beneath or above it all. I watched you grow cold. Grow calloused. One drop of dew told you, little boy. But you forgot how to listen, how to live, like a child.

Human encounters, My son, are merely a meeting at one intersection in that web, but the span of meaning that follows…, no mortal walking the earth can envision. Only believe.

And Spencer shamefully understood that Drake deserved hell.

His cigarette had lasted for hours. It finally burned down to his yellowed fingertips. He listened to it hiss while the snow snuffed it out. As he looked up, he saw quite a sight. The only thing he'd ever really lived for. His blue eyes were bright and young and he could see clearly. Emma was riding Sky. Beautiful. Real. No saddle. No bridle. Just loping over to him like a gentle breeze, hooves effortlessly grazing the snow, leaving no tracks. They both looked so happy, so free and so light. He figured they'd glide right by him, figured they couldn't see him—all the hell he'd have to pay commenced. But they stopped. He was their destination. Emma slid down, coming to him with open arms and a smile that held no hurt, no hate or blame. It'd been so many years and that smile held a love that had never faltered, never faded, like it was new every day they'd been apart. Her arms felt more like home than any place he'd ever been, felt more like a mother and a father than any lost child can dream. Sky snorted his playful little signature snort. Spencer hadn't heard that sound since the horse was a two-year-old running the plains. He desperately hoped it was not too late as he stood there and he stared. He could spend eternity here and never want for a thing. But he didn't deserve it. It wasn't his choice. He had long since allowed that time to pass….

.   .   .

"Yes, Spencah come up outta da other side 'a de river, chil'. His eyes is cleansed. He see it all now. He in God's han's, child. He in God's han's…. Same as ever'body, chil. Same as ever'body else. Wouldn't hurt none ta pray for 'im one las' time."

Chapter Eighteen

A tomb is not for the dead. It is for the living. Something smooth and vacant—a stone, something solid, strong against time, something that keeps logic sealed from the mind. The imagination does its best not to creep there, six feet below. The heart does not want to grasp its own destiny, flesh becoming dust and all the gruesome stages therein. Those still standing on earth and in body need something of a memory—one that does not change. Something to cling to that hints of the eternal perfection in that soul gone—they themselves had seen it, hold a piece of it in their own. Something is needed of cleansing. And of hope. To protect the soft flesh loosely caging a naive spirit still trying to do its best, to perform smoothly in the dance while solving all the riddles *(not stepping on toes or unleashing any curses)*. To hold the innocence there in their cloudy eyes that are, as of yet, still warm *(and being thankful)*. And wandering..., wondering..., as they gaze the sky, then sweep over a name rarely spoken anymore, *Where are they now?* Why is this done..., it seems so forlorn from a distance of age. Why are these grounds held sacred?

To prove, my child, that death does not do a thing to love. Love. It is the only thing we hold that cannot be crucified....

No..., a tomb is not for the dead. A box is not for the spirit. Sin is not for the soul.

.   .   .

Still she had no stone. No body. No sign other than miles of winter cement that in the springtime would thaw and dissolve along with any trace of him. Sickening, almost as if he'd never been.... Her place of neutrality—the place where she could stand on the threshold of the spirit world, almost touching his hand—by then, it would have long sense vanished from her like it had so many times before. She should not think it funny. She should not take it selfishly. All she had to do was look at his life. Spencer would not have stayed in any one place, could not have rested in peace that way. To bury her brother would have been an outright blasphemy of all that was him.

But what about her, her empty hands. Her hollow heart where he used to be…alive.

"I'm so sorry, Avi. In this drifting snow, we jus' **can't** send men out to look. Surely, that would bring nothing but more tragedy. Drake's been 'round a long time. You jus' keep heart. He's been 'round a long time. If anybody could make it through, he could. We'll go out jus' a' soon as we can."

The sheriff tipped his hat, too abruptly. He was done talking and his show of compassion was finished and that was that because his inner voices were beginning to yell. His hands were shaking from nerves or from the cold, probably both. He backed out her door trying to avoid the look in her eyes. He wanted to grab on to her, wanted to break down and cry but he'd never stop. Instead he resumed his scooping, tossing the top layers of snow into the wind as he went hoping the white spray would cover his bloody insides like a shroud. He swore there were times he could feel them spilling out. Sometimes he had to run home and look into a mirror and, on rare occasion, even strip down to his bare skin—entirely, to make sure it hadn't become a newspaper of sorts revealing his hidden psychosis to the whole world. (With that much pressure, some law of physics would suggest a breaking point, a rupture from within…, seepage, at least, especially considering his age. It was logical to him that his pain should come out in words. It was words that first introduced it to him, words that delivered it still, words that kept it going when the world was a rarity with its peace and its silence and its lazy generosity….) As he scooped, his wild movements looked ridiculous. Something like a panicked man rowing a boat, barely dipping the oar in far enough to get it wet. He was aware of this, he was no idiot. He understood that he was getting nowhere. He perceived himself a mere dot on a sea of snow where, underneath, a dead man was lurking. He tried to look confident, strong and wise in both the useless task at hand and his conservative decision to do nothing for Avi, but he could almost see his own guilty conscience rushing up behind him about to clobber him, about to knock him out cold. Sometimes he wished it would. Anything would be better than its endless admonitions, its merciless criticisms rattling about his head. He wished other things too, all the time. Like he wished he could swallow the words he'd just spoken to her. They were as futile as the effort he was putting forth to temporarily open the hungry drifts waiting to be filled up with the next gust of wind. And he wished he were invisible. See, he was paid by the town, what was filtered through Crenshaw's sticky black glove anyhow, and it didn't take long before he saw everybody as The Town. He felt that he always needed to be doing something to prove his value, to apologize—without admittance of wrongdoing—because he'd botched up the job so much, the honor of it, but he had difficulty prioritizing. Or, rather, he just portrayed it that way…, he'd had to train himself to get into the habit of being irresponsible. It took him a while before sweeping the boardwalk could take precedence over a back-alley murder. He'd learned first hand just how keen a blind eye could be, how visiting the reclusive elderly could coincide perfectly with rampant crime sprees. He got to the point where he didn't even need fair warning. Human behavior has a lot to do with the phases of the moon and with the atmospheric pressure pressing down upon the brain, squeezing the sinus cavities. Storm fronts, hundreds of miles distant, are wired directly to the amount of tenseness in neck muscles that fuel short tempers that fire loaded guns. He'd observed this. By the time he got around to feigning an investigation it seemed to always be raining, sometimes hailing, sometimes there would come a blizzard, one time it was a tornado. He, too, was only human. And a lot of the time he just felt like vanishing.

She could no longer see him or his ten-foot sprays of snow. The glass before her was frosted over, dusted with confectioner's sugar from a little girl's dream maybe. Its magic drew her in. She could see the intricate designs of tiny snowflakes. Hundreds. Trapped. Hazily outlining her dual worlds of illusion. There was nowhere for her to go—outside, inside, it didn't seem to matter. Her thoughts were, at times, driving her into patterns of unfamiliarity within her own mind—ugly, terrifying places to be, but the real insanity had impacted her earlier that morning when her gaze magnetically locked into grips with the empty eyes of her mother. The life of Spencer seemed to fuel the woman's gift and now it too was gone. Proof of his death if anything was, probably more so than a body but Avi didn't want to believe. Her wounded spirit had left her chest gaping as if it had been split wide open with an ax. Cruelty was hacking away at her from within and her maimed heart was exposed to the elements. But there was no truth here. It seemed that nothing could heal this….

She didn't know what her life looked like without **him**…his worn vest, his dual nature, his fatherly advice, his scars—hidden, but always there—a reminder of something never shared, his preference to befriend a horse over a human, his blue eyes that seemed to see everything in front of them but *more* somehow. He could *perceive* so much in another man, in a complete stranger. Could sense his way straight to the reasons behind their choices even when they didn't know those reasons themselves. He understood "types" of people, their patterns, the errors in their judgement, their uneasiness, their weaknesses and triggers that led to automatic defensiveness and the probable string of events that more than likely caused them to function in their typical way. Or, on those rare occasions, when a man broke in two, when a personality cracked, when they up and killed someone, did something outlandish, something so out of character people gossiped about it for a lifetime—Drake was the one who was never taken by surprise. He could see it in their bloodshot eyes, veins flashing like lightning, change rolling in like a band of thunder heads. "It's fear," he told her once. "That's all it is…. Jus' comes out in different ways." He understood their obvious boyhood pain like it was his own. It was his own. If only he could have read himself that well, he might have healed himself, become whole. *Where are you now, Spence my brother? If only I knew you were Saved….*

.   .   .

"…Mama?…Mama, can you see anything at all about Lemn? Heav'n forbid, I'm afrait t' ask, but is the boy gone, too?"

"Don' know, chil'."

The dumb silence following was a good time for Avi to lean out the back door and retch. Mama had replied with reservedness, simply, quietly, all she could dare as if a flood would come if she oozed one drop. Her words lingered in the air, intrusively occupying space and time, giving the repercussions of her shaky voice opportunity to resonate her shame. Her inadequate reply sounded strange to her own ears as if she were a commonly responsible child being harshly interrogated for a lost mitten, it's whereabouts honestly unclear, her memory failing, her self-doubt convincing her *I must have done **something** wrong.…* She was telling the truth but after it was spoken it portrayed itself as an irretrievable falsehood. She Didn't Know and she didn't know during the time she was needed more than ever before. Her face burned and heated feelings rose up inside her as she sluggishly hoisted her stiff body (weighted with more than itself, heavily bearing down on cracking knees and swollen ankles) up the stairs to rest. If she slept…slept…, the anger and suffering wouldn't swallow her soul, not completely. She was exhausted but restraint kept her from breaking down and revealing her despair and emptiness to Avi, in whom she had persistently attempted to instill the humble ultra-wisdom that a child of God never questions their Father. Sometimes it's the only way to stay sane.

Deah God f'give me, bu' if You let the devil take tha' boy, I don' undahstan'. I won' undahstand, Lord. Please..., help that boy.

.   .   .

Avi had just nodded off at the table. Her mind had exhausted her, playing the last conversation she had with him word for word, over and over again—he had been seated where she rested (she had tried to feel, swore she felt, some of his body heat still emanating from that chair)—when, finally, she'd fallen into temporary peace. But it was shallow. Something had summoned her. She rubbed her eyes. Strained, but didn't hear anything unusual. And as her awakening mind convinced her it was nothing, the shock of her suppressed loss returned full force nearly knocking the wind out of her lungs. She felt like surrendering, never taking another breath of this cold world, then *tap...tap...tap....*

It was his knock. High up on the door. Forceful. Distinct. She knew it was his. If only it had all been a cruel joke, just a twisted nightmare, even inexorable insanity on her part..., she'd take *anything* so long as his death wasn't real. As she opened the door, her eye muscles were anticipating an outline only he could fill, her head was lifted just so to address his height. She tried to prepare her mind to take in the image of Spencer's face but it was fading from her memory. Already. Her gaze descended along with her expectation.

"Av-ah."

Not fully perceiving the image or deciphering the word just spoken, she asked perplexedly, "Y'name's what, child?"

"...SKY...FEA-THER."

Feather's dark eyes glistened above her red nose and cheeks and her tone of voice sounded as if she asked herself a question (Sky?) and answered it herself (Fea-ther.) with certainty and an accentuating nod of the head marking her finish. She blinked and waited.

"...Well, um...well...What c'n I do for you? I'm sorry, you mus' be frozen stiff.... Come on in...I'm not m'self today—this ev'nin'. Where y' come from?"

Avi tried to recall the girl's face, scanning the many children who knock on the back door asking for a hand out of food or warm blankets, but this girl was unfamiliar. Avi was sure she would have remembered an In...

"O-gi-na-li, LEM."

"Oh…OH! My goodness, chil'. MAMA!!!!!!!! MAMA!!!!!"

Feather felt frightened with Avi's excitement and had to fight her instinct to run, but she recalled Lemn's slurred words, "Avah…Doch…Feathah ShAFE." Instead she stared at her feet wrapped in bear hide and deer skin commanding them to stay still as they dripped, dripped, dripped, making a water puddle on the dead-tree ground. She started to sweat.

"Come heah by the fire, child. Warm y'self! You must be frozen. Is Lemn alright? LEMN, is he alright???"

"Doch."

"DOC!!!! Doc…. Stay here, chil'."

Avi flailed around trying to force her boots onto her feet as Feather calmly watched with a polite, expressionless face hiding a twinge of humor. *Tsi-s(a)du a(li)s-gi-s-di.* (Rabbit dance.) Avi was out the door with coat in hand and Feather waited a few moments taking in the enormous house for few people before she slipped back out into the darkening icy evening, disappearing on a gust of wind. Mama descended the flight of stairs to find an empty house and snow melting on the oak-planked floor.

A minute later, Avi and a winded Doc burst through the door.

"Where is she?…WHERE IS SHE, MAMA????"

"Who, chil'?'"

"She was right here! She said Lemn's name and asked for you, Doc. I told her…I told her to wait. Maybe she didn't understand…."

"Are you sure you really saw her, Avi? You said she walked to your door…in this weather? An Indian girl, Avi?"

"Yes, Doc! I'm not goin' crazy. Lemn needs help! We have to get out there, now! I'll get Sheriff and we'll find a way to get to that boy, Doc. Can you make it out there in this cold?"

"As much as I want to, Avi, I'm 'fraid not. I'm sorry, Avi. Truly sorry....'"

"Alright. I'm goin'. Bye, Mama."

"Avi, listen to me and listen good. If he can't walk, there's nothing you can do but comfort him. If he's been frozen, warm him up slow and keep him warm. Keep any blisters clean until it thaws some and I can get out there. If this storm lasts and God forbid gangrene sets in, you'll have to take the infected limb. Take this disinfectant. God be with you, Avi. You be careful and turn back if the weather's too bad, y' hear?" Under his breath he murmured, *No sense loosin' you, too.* And she was gone leaving the two old friends behind. Doc closed his black bag with a snap and stood still and silent for a moment as if trying to remember something.

"'Tween you and her daddy, she didn't have a prayer for bein' mild-willed, Aviona. She'll be alright. Your girl will be just fine." And they took each other's aged hand.

Avi made it across the drifted road dissecting the little town to the jail house. A faint light was peaking through the window and she was suddenly aware of the bitter, relentless cold especially where her body heat was beginning to melt the remaining snow adhered to her sheer, cotton undergarments—icy water against her bare skin. She silently cursed the female condition of proper and highly unfunctional dress. She banged on the door loudly, blatantly unlady-like, and was met with a questioning look from the sheriff.

"Lemn's in danger, Colton. We **have** to go."

No one—other than his wife—had called him by his real name in years and it caught him off guard. He looked at her lips, then back into her eyes—she was alive with determination. Her heated and steady look meant business and the wind had temporarily died down so, despite the silent discouragement of his concerned spouse, he quickly made the decision to help his *late* friend's would-be son and sister. He knew there was no stopping Avi anyhow. He was amazed that she'd taken as long as she had. Then it wound itself up..., when called to perform duties such as these, this *thought* played through the back of his mind almost subconsciously anymore (he could listen to it while thinking about something else) but always the same, always there, like reading from the same book over and over again. Put it in the closet, burn it, bury it deep, and every night there it is. The damn thing is on the bedside table, waiting.... This *thought* was: *I might not make it back but it's my job. My responsibility. I've got to stand up and be a man—a respectable death might make Ammie proud.* This thought comforted him, cheaply. Narrowly slid him past the guilt of leaving her alive and alone but for some reason, it was always spoken in his late father's voice—the only thing he found remotely disturbing about it.

Sometimes, when the weather was nice and his world was calm enough to BREATHE in, he would dare to ask himself a difficult and introspective question and find an answer that terrified him—*I don't know.* Oh, he was a smart man but running away from himself, inside of himself..., well, he never got very far. And what with his loud, volatile, persuaded and easily influenced self outwitting his meek but beautiful, untainted and true self—sometimes without even knowing—his brilliance never got the chance to shine through cracks clogged such as those. And his muscle and skin he stretched thin and used to hide it—his mass of imperfection churning inside, growing heavy. It physically hurt, being like he was. How, like he was, he couldn't exactly say. He just didn't accept it—no one did. Few people—actually no one that he could think of besides Ammie—ever really understood him. It'd take too long, he was far too complicated. He was so disappointingly different from birth—the way he felt, he thought, the way he wanted to straighten the crooked world, make it even for everyone. And try as he might, opening his mouth to explain just served to intensify his oddity. It crushed him to see that look of confusion, alarm, dismissal in someone's eyes and directed at him. Thusly, he escaped a lot of the time..., himself, the world, the thought of his lost and buried niche in it. He did this not with alcohol, never raised a hand to his wife or anyone. His mistress was one of a cool breeze of dream rather than flesh—the written word. Millions of them. Hours, years of them strung around his soul, helping to bind it. He was well read—too well read. Too knowledgeable. Too many facts colliding in his brain most of the time muddling his judgement, confusing him further, but sometimes so crystal clear he could have educated, or at least debated with, the experts in almost any given field—medicine, war, agriculture, blacksmithing, law, history, furniture making, U.S. or abroad patents (numbers and dates), geography, philosophy, psychology..., *How To Treat the Mentally Insane*—yes, he had to read those books, take them one at a time then strategically place them back on the good doctor's shelf, cover them with a fine coat of powdery dust so they looked untouched for the month and a half the old man couldn't bear to look at them...it wouldn't stop. He'd read to occupy his mind, then the additional facts he ingested would make his condition worse. And what was his condition? He didn't know. Couldn't seem to concentrate long enough.

His soul, his sleep had never been quieted enough to cradle certain notions befallen him, rather they slid down on cold sweat and combusted like star dust. He'd never entertained the whisper within long enough to watch it weave its story. Something to believe in, something almost proving that forces float in and around able bodies, forces designed to recognize and cage a spirit as powerful as his..., valid as anything written with the sweet aftermath of empowerment, hope, an individualism folded around value and married to peaceful unity..., finally, a place to be, a place to behold with an artist's eye—a horizon that looks something like Heaven. But no, he'd not yet tasted of things such as these. He only knew he was rapidly growing tired of hiding it—his deteriorating mind. He'd made quite a mess of it and it was beginning to slosh out. He was plain sick of trying to appear as "Sheriff"—such a bogus title it fit him about as comfortably as a barren maiden's corset. One day it would happen..., he'd crumble, explode, suffocate or scream so loud he'd bust his heart wide open. He had no idea how it would happen, he just knew he couldn't take anyone innocent with him when it did. Oh, how he hated the killing and death in and around his work. Drake had always protected him from doing most of it. For some reason, Drake *knew* when all the others thought good old Sheriff was just a regular fella. Saw right through him with those cool flaming eyes, but never once judged. Didn't condescend. Didn't ask any questions..., he just knew and was smooth about it, calm..., paid just enough attention to know when to shift the dynamic. But Colton couldn't count on Drake anymore. It was probable, inevitable really, that the risks of the job would snare him. And then it would stop—his mind. His life. He was quite sure of it. But he knew that passive suicide was still suicide and God would know. *Yes, God would know.* And he was terrified of that. He'd read his Bible exactly thirty-three times, each reading after the first spanning the time frame of forty days and forty nights—calculated exactly, but inside it, he found no earthly way out.

He realized he went through all this thinking in about one minute as he came back to reality. (At least it was some form of his reality—philosophy intrigued him in a dizzying way, on a tangible level.) Fear crept up in him as he quickly scanned the numerous events that could possibly occur on their journey and he surveyed, in depth and detail, the more difficult ones—what he would say, do, his options, his facial expressions, Avi's possible, probable, replies...requests. He wondered about encountering Drake (or, more than likely, Drake's *body*) on the way...a horse stumbling on his perfectly preserved, stone-solid corpse lying eerily under the snow—just *lurking* there, **waiting**. *Could I pretend it was a fallen tree limb, a rock? No, Avi's too quick.... Too smart. She would want me to check.* Heaven forbid, then they would have to haul it somewhere?—*the body*...? Drag it with ropes...? He would have to act like a SHERIFF, like a MAN. His palms started to sweat even though he could see his own breath in the air. *Dear God, don't let his eyes be open.* (*He was tired of the nightmares, cold sweats and panic attacks—dead men rising with blank, unblinking eyes, coming after him, some shot...dripping with blood. Blood of all colors...black and some kind of devilish purple that would turn to flaming orange then pale yellow like an oozing infection. It wouldn't come off his hands. The flowing blood...it spilled onto his hands, onto his bed, onto his wife—in her eyes, running into her mouth, then spilling out when she spoke to him...—she would say,* "Colton, Colton, Colton!!!" *but the rest was garbled and sickeningly juicy— ...bubbling out, running down her chin, her neck, soaking her night clothes. She never knew it was on her, all over her, she couldn't ever SEE IT.... His poor, sweet wife.*) No.... If he couldn't see him alive, then he didn't want to see him at all. Especially not his eyes....

.   .   .

While the sheriff got the horses saddled and located some rope (coiled discreetly, one in each side of his saddle bags that were strapped securely behind the cantle), Ammie helped Avi dress for the weather in her husband's long johns and wool trousers, deer skin gloves, hat, scarves, vest and coats. She packed some biscuits and sausage and poured them the winter usual—whiskey in a canteen.

"My lands, girl. You sure have a lot of grit. Stay alive and watch out for my husband, will ya? He's the only one I got, y' know."

From the doorway, Ammie smiled a good-natured smile at her departing friend hoping it would not be their last visit, then held up a steady hand in a mutual, lasting wave to her husband, whom she loved so much, as if they could touch each other through the air, connected by some invisible force. She hoped he would be able to calm his mind—he always managed to and did the best he could to help others. He looked at her and wondered if this was *it*. And he prayed silently for her and thought she would be better off without him. It was just his line of work she had said—why they avoided having children—trying to ease his mind. She would be terrified she told him, to raise a child on her own if something should happen. She was always selflessly looking out for his feelings. But he knew why they both agreed on the subject and he hated himself for it even though she would never want him to feel guilty—not for a second. She understood. But he couldn't help it. He could see the uneasiness in her when she was around him…careful, too careful, not to say anything that would cause him more worry. God bless her—because he couldn't. Little did he know that God already had. She was with child, just not sure how her husband would handle it. Not yet sure how to say it.

The bundled-up pair rode off into the night as three restless people in three different houses peered incessantly into the nothingness outside and prayed for the wind to stay calm.

.   .   .

Dear God, don't let him be out here. Dear God, don't let him be out here. Dear God, don't let him be out here. Dear God, don't let him be out here….

"I hope we find Spence, Sheriff. I'm prayin' we find him."

Shit. Shit! Shit!!!

"Alive. I want him to be alive."

"I want him to be alive, too, Avi. You have no idea how much. No idea…."

What if she asks, 'What if he's not?'….

"What if he's not? I mean if we find him an', God forbid the thought, he's not…*alive*…, what are we goin' to do? H-How?"

Shit!

"Don't worry about that, Avi. He'll be alive…. He-will-be-alive…."

Colton's distant attitude and heavy concentration on the waves of white-blue snow stretching out in front of them indicated his intense desire to stay on track. To waver more than a couple of yards off the assumed, buried trail could mean death for both of them. It was hard to calculate distance in the snow, in the dark. Avi decided she had better follow his lead and remain quiet, command her mind to stay on their course of travel, but she caught herself scanning the area every few seconds for a shape, a shadow, for anything that could be a sign of Spencer.

*She's looking around for the **body**. Shit!*

*Calm down...it's alright. Breathe, in...and out.... Slow—your—heart—down. Dear God, don't let him be out here. Not dead. Not a **BODY! PLEASE!!!!!***
Breathe...

'*...The mentally insane will often hear voices as if they are being spoken aloud, which no one else around them can hear. It may be described as another person or persons inside the brain. These voices may even carry on full conversations separate from the will of the host personality. Ancient practices referred to these voices as demons often exorcised by puncturing the individual's skull in order to bleed the demon out. Upon the demon leaving the brain, it was often claimed the angry entity took the life of the individual to hell as a final act of revenge, not considering the puncture inflicted in the name of healing as cause of death.*'

It's freezing out here. Can't feel my fingers. That's a good sign. Perfectly legitimate should I find my death of pneumonia.
'*...Pneumonia: an inflammatory disease of the lungs.*'

"Sheriff? Sheriff, what is *that*?"

.   .   .

Lemn watched by the hour as the fire slowly dwindled, its mission—transforming stout logs into weak pieces of glowing cinder crusted with grey ash—finished. *Dust to dust....* He dreaded the moment that he would have to hoist himself up onto his raw limbs to kindle the fire, but his breath began to frost the air and, as it fell, it formed momentary, miniature icicles across the dark wool blanket that composed the outer layer of many cocooning him up to his chin. He thought about lying there. Dying there. But blessed Feather had considerately left everything he needed within reasonable reach. There was plenty of firewood and kindling, water, clean cloths hung in front of the fire, blankets, a piece of bread, dried venison, Drake's whiskey and some concoction she mixed to rub on his sores. All signs that she believed he could...that she believed in him.

He felt a pressure in his crotch and realized he needed to relieve himself. He pushed his torso to a forty-five degree angle off the floor and rested, transfixed with fear, there on his elbows. His back didn't punish his position with twinges of pain as it would have in the past, but he knew the next step (pushing his body upward with one of his hands bearing all of his weight) would be excruciating. Undamaged muscle quivered beneath stifled layers of top-muscle, rousing his nerves, grating, daring them to deliver all the agony possible. His swollen tongue was engulfed by saliva and his neck tensed revealing protruding veins unnaturally straining against the flow of his own blood. Before he forced himself further, he began to weep in desperate exhaustion looking down through distorting tears, at the unfamiliar, leprous hands lying helplessly at his sides.

After a few moments of heavy disheartenment, he angrily wrapped his hands in the makeshift bandages, using the web of his elbow and clenched teeth, determined to get up no matter what torture his existence would serve him to swallow. He decided to use his right hand to lean on, which was not as blistered as the left, and he padded it fully. As he pushed himself up, he was surprised, amazed, that the pain was not as intense as he had imagined. He twisted his lower body, nudged the covers off with his left elbow and forearm, and began to drag himself toward the stack of wood, motionless legs trailing behind him.

. . .

"What is *what*, Avi???"

> *God help me, I think I can see…Not now, I'm awake!!! It never happens while I'm awake. What the…Oh dear God, don't let this happen. Don't let this happen…. I can't be going completely insane!!! No…no…!*
> '*But she can see it, too, Colton. Don't be a pansy. **You'll never make a man. You're a disappointment. Absolutely worthless. You're mother should have taken ill the very minute she told me about you….**'*
> *Father's voice. I guess he did say that, didn't he? When I was seven? Eight? I was no more than an eight-year-old. I would have been just a child…. Just a child. How could anyone…*
> '*Why don't you act like a man, for once? That lil' darkie woman over there's braver than you. **What a waste you are. A damn shame's all ya are.**'*
> *Father. Yes. He said that, too. All the time. Every time it wasn't Mama, it was me. I guess I'd forgotten how it was….*

"I—I cain't tell what it is f'sure, Sheriff. It cain't be…."

. . .

Lemn slid over to the neatly stacked firewood and attempted to gather his own legs up underneath himself in order to stand on his knees and reach the top log, but his foreign, fractious body failed him. His legs were like dead-weights bolting him to the ground—low as a snake—and he had no use of his fingers or hands for the pain. Lemn gathered some comfort from this thought…*low as a snake*…recalling the various animals he had seen while walking home from school, during Drake's unsuccessful hunting lessons and while plowing the fields. He remembered the tiny field mice scattering about him as he plowed through the spring sod, regretfully destroying their homes. *God, please protect them,* he'd pray. How low to the ground they were and they lived with it.

Lemn smiled weakly at his achievement of mental comfort and consolation, comparing himself with other creatures, but just as soon as it fell from his face he was sobbing gravely, remembering himself as an able-bodied being—whole—like he was meant to be. He was strong back then, during those quick and glorious years. Not as strong as a man, but strong in his own young body—thin arms strained tight as ropes, hands blistered like they are now, only from work—healthy work, not hellish misfortune—directing the convulsive plow as it pitched behind his sweaty horse, stepping high over the rough ground, legs aching, feet swelling in too-tight boots, thick, wide reins draped loosely over his shoulder then back around his sunken, boyish waist. He was building a foundation. Way back then, when he first managed the plow with his father's eyes watching, critiquing, proud, he understood that he was building something to support his family. His own family. But *now*…. Lemn screamed—keened—in frustration and smacked the side of his face hard against the wood pile, forcing the orderly logs onto the floor in scattered disarray—that's what life had done to him.

Instantly, he was infuriated beyond his character, recalling scenes from his past…, must have been triggered by the blow. They were the scenes of his beating—the beating that took his legs. Slim and *Jed* took his legs. He savagely raged against the unfairness in his life and against his own body, trying to tear free from its torturous grip via will alone. His head throbbed, a clear string of saliva dangled from his open lips and tears dropped from his eyes—many tears, his ear bled a stream of crimson, his cries were deafening but no one could hear them. No one could save him, help him, change him. No one.

He curled his upper body into a ball on the cold hard floor. He left his legs stretched out oddly right where they had stopped—he could care less about them anymore. As his body started to shiver, he realized he had accidently relieved himself in his own clothes and the wet cloth was starting to stiffen in the cold. He disgusted himself. No longer wanted himself. He laid there in fear, waiting for the merciful hand of God to rest upon him and give him permission to take his very last breath.

Chapter Nineteen

He wasn't completely delusional. He couldn't be…, Avi could see them, too. Those eyes ahead. Vacant of anything natural. Peering at him through the darkness. Tormenting him so directly, yet so silently. How they burned right through his chest as if to take his soul. Burned cold like the deceptive blue of a flickering flame. *Drake's eyes….* The thought smacked him and it stung, down his arm, through his jaw. When he looked away, they still glowed inside his own eyes—closed, open…didn't matter. No escape. He would have to pay. He would have to pay for all he had done. He told them—swore to them in his sleep—that he was sorry, but they kept coming for him. Maybe this time they would enforce the threat they carried about their disjointed necks like a weighted chain. This time it was all so redoubtable. So *surreal*—its concealed intention fast approaching the too late, embodying the horrid redolence of something lived but in a dream, so vivid, so revolting…, its visit swallowed by the vastness of subconscious brain as if it never was. His senses of the supernatural had fallen, left him dumbstruck and with his delicate spirit out in the open like that, his very essence was vulnerable. But his physical was a mystery fast dissolving, unraveling from within. The rapid spurts of beating followed by the dead space—a still drum and his body would quit the dance—then the odd flip-flop of his jellied heart, tired, haggard, lazy, no backup. It was shockingly abnormal behavior for his vitals, even compared to the unsettling hyperactivity racing within him during his episodes of panic. He was losing control of it all or rather, whatever amazing fragments weave themselves into the substance of life…, they were releasing him. The unique avenues which composed the many facets of him, they were no longer flowing into him, but turning, taking leave in explosive, erratic directions. He had nothing of himself to cling to. The forces were granting him his wish, the autonomous voices in his head, narrating….

'...Attack: a fit of sickness.'

The pain was not releasing him. He couldn't breathe. His lungs were stretching ever tighter in uselessness as if someone had fitted his torso with a noose, looped it around his chest, pulling, pinning one arm down, then jerking it, snapping it, cracking it. Clapping and cheering at it.

*Oh, I'm sorry. I'm so sorry, Edgar, Cole, Blaine, Perry, Samuel, James, and Derrik...Derrik, no more th'n a kid, you were. I'm sorry, but it's my job. Why'd you have to do what you did? Why did you have to go and have such a cursed streak of luck? I know you jus' made a fast mistake all at once, when most makes slow, secret ones all their life long. Who's ta say which is worse? And I believe you're sorry. I believe your story..., some loners' lives jus' get obliterated 'tween the grindstones, become sand sooner that way, dashin' betwixt the flow. Makes a soul awful tired.... Yes, I believe you read some of the Bible last night. And I do believe you would change, back to the way you was when you were younger.... But those people want justice. The judge.... They all want an eye for an eye...say it's from the Bible, from Jesus' lips. From the good Lord's Word. But if they would have read a little further.... Why didn't all those people just read a little further? All those hundreds of people who gathered from towns all around to watch you swing and twitch and leave your body, your world, they stole your boots, spit and cursed and paraded your pain, they didn't even know your name or the reasons why you did what you did 'sides from rumors, talk, gossip, razored tongues.... **Judge not, least ye be judged.** Now that was in the Bible.... They didn't even know you but I had to take you to EQUALITY. To hang. **Thou shalt not kill.** Now that WAS in the BIBLE.... **Let he who is without sin cast the first stone?** Yessir, boy. I believe I read that in there, too.*

Yes, this was different from the panic attacks. He leaned over the horn of the saddle. He didn't have to ask his horse to stop. The blue eyes kept buRNIng...buRnIng...buRNIng that hole right through the center of his chest. He wondered who would walk on in his empty boots.

"You alright, Sheriff...? Colton!?"

The level of intensity, the urgency she heard in her own voice made the situation that much worse. She was so alone. Her body, her mind, her soul—the three were displaced somehow. Scattered. She was falling apart with the world around her, grounded by nothing, befriended only by a spirit of panic. Colton's skin was lined in dark shadows, tracings with a thick ink of purple, ribbons of a poison in black, all seeping from within. He could not breathe. He was about to collapse and fall off his horse. And she was responsible. Ammie had told her specifically, *He's the only one I got, you know....* And now God had left her with her mess. Shown her how weak and miserable she was on her own. If only He'd come back. Her eyes strained through the cold air and darkness, quickly scanning for shadows of movement, outlines of spirits in the direction that she had seen the ghostly figure just moments before. She prayed that a miracle would reach her somehow, that Spencer would be alive, that he'd be able to help her. He was always so warm, safe and strong—unshaken by things like this. But Colton wheezed—a formidable, far-reaching sound, it dragged across the bottom of her soul. It was she alone who needed to provide that eerie sound an answer, dig far within her being and force out a heroism yet unseen of her, brave, stout enough to lift them both above and alive. It would take *him* to do something like that— Drake. She would have to steal his calloused identity, his cruel persona, his brash spirit—dead or alive, didn't much matter anymore. She'd trade her own soul for a slim piece of his if that's what it would take to save Colton.

"If you're in Heaven, if you're in hell..., you wake up and you answer me. You tell me what to do."

She fully expected his reply to float in off the thin air and, immediately, she felt confidence wrap around her and it lifted her spirits up. It warmed her and gave her a frame of determination stronger than bone. She stepped down off her horse and steadied the sheriff's weakening body. She reached up, removed his shawl, felt his face. His skin was like ice. He attempted to speak but his speech was slurred. He was in an excruciating amount of pain but was able to gesture, indicating that he wanted something from the saddle bag. Avi's numb fingers hastily groped the frozen leather tie, pulling at the delicate strings clinging stubbornly together until, at last, the knot gave way under her rushed, warm breath. She swung the flap up and saw the canteen strap. "Whiskey," is what he had said. *Of course.*

Colton's mind was slowing down, peculiarly, and it was effortlessly focusing on his bodily functions, on his own survival. *The heart is a muscle. Whiskey relaxes muscles. It's that simple. That's your chance.* Between gasping breaths, he struggled to remain alert and conscious enough to drink as much as he could. It was the only hope for his heart. That and Avi getting him to Lemn's quickly, before the exposure killed him. His heart began to slow, then it slowed too much. He forced himself to cough, deep, harsh and jagged, again and again. Just before he blacked out, he thought how ironic it was that he was getting his wish—this was *it* and he wasn't hurting anyone else to do it. It was absolutely perfect. Executed better than any plan, as if it were meant to be. But here he was at the end, wanting more time. All he had to do was let go but he was hanging on for dear life. For LIFE. Any measly part of it. Because he was not relieved as he had anticipated. He was distraught. Yearning. Through the pain, his mind's eye was scanning, searching, but not racing. No, this time his mind was slower, sharper, more accurate, seeing not the blank, eerie eyes or grotesque images that brought the antagonizing fear that had spawned his attack but, instead, the sweet face of his wife, smiling, and flashes of everything *worthy* he had left undone. It was *his* life. And he wasn't about to lose it, he wasn't going to squander it anymore. It was now something precious to him…. It was essential. It was all he had. *Ask and ye sha…*

"COLTON! Colton, don't you die on me! Don't you dare die on me!!!"

Avi spun around, a breathless circle. She had not been paying enough attention to the trail. She couldn't remember if they had already passed the grove off to the left that marked mile number four or if it was ahead of them. The snow twirled around her stiffening legs, rising up with the fear inside her. She began a sorrowful wail that ended in a full-blown panic-stricken scream reaching far out into the cold night, far beyond her vision, far beyond her hope. She offered up wordless, wretched screams of diffidence to the darkness, defeated pleas that trailed the lonesome wind for there was nothing else she could do. The poisonous pain held of her body retched itself up through noise until her throat cracked a strand of silence and her sinuses filled, sealing off the path to excess air. Tears began streaming down the cheeks that she could no longer feel. Her entire being shook. Her chin descended toward the white drifts around her and her knees began to buckle when someone from behind rested a hand on her weary shoulder, commanding her to find instant stillness, summoning the flow of her inner source of strength. It was hope that filled her—that she did feel. And the steely determination returned full force with the touch of that hand. It was warm, safe, strong…, unshaken. Instinctually familiar.

.   .   .

He was defeated. And ready to die. Life had beaten Lemn, though not deserted him. His version of mercy never arrived and so his heart, it just kept on beating…*bum-bum, bum-bum, bum-bum*. Persistently, gaining no reward, no recognition…*bum-bum*. His eyes opened. Again. Maybe that *was* his Mercy.

.   .   .

"Spen…"

Avi turned to embrace her brother but halted abruptly, shocked, mouth hushed mid-word. It was **undeniably** his hand that had reached for her, she felt it. *Didn't she?* He comforted her. She could *sense* him. She *smelled* him. *Heard his breathing*—the way it rushed past his whiskers, unmistakably. No doubt in her mind and there never would be. Spencer was with her, if only for a moment, he was there. *He truly was.*

She was absolutely astounded, standing there frozen, staring blankly at someone not at all like her brother—it was the same quiet child that had generated her convoluted journey.

.   .   .

Lemn's eyes slowly opened, scanning his surreal surroundings as best they could between moments of wincing and involuntary twitching. Rushes of blood and pain surged in feverish waves throughout his chilled body. He felt angry and, for the first time, truly abandoned by God. It took him a moment to remember, then realize that his request for death had not been granted.

He could answer his own prayer….

He considered this in detail as his late mother must have done. He looked at the knife lying less than two feet from him and he envisioned how he would try to slice his own blackened wrists, gashing them against the blade while holding the handle steady between his clenched teeth. If he succeeded, he would lie there, bleeding slowly, scared and alone, knowing he did the wrong thing, not sure he would be forgiven, his worthless limbs rendering him helpless to save himself if he changed his mind, if he panicked. While he was evaluating his own death he realized he was dangerously incoherent. *When you are tempted…*He understood his mother like never before, he'd never been this close to her in life. He could feel that cold and heavy steel door locked in her mind, in the darkness his healed hands explored the rusted bolts and fused hinges that sealed her off from her own life. He could see that mile-high cliff of shame looming beyond it, the one she never climbed. The clear wind upon it whispered of the glory she would have found if she'd only fought the battle. If she'd only pressed on, she would have seen the sun.…*He will provide a way out…*No, he could not let himself fall that far into nothing. Into uselessness. He would stop himself. Throw himself against challenge and die trying because he still had a vague sense of his belief—the substance of drive, of desire that made up his core.…*so you may stand up under it.* It was that hope, it was that *feeling* that God was watching him, caring for him and his purpose—it made that familiar strength of his start to filter through again and he got bold. *God, stop the pain…stop the pain so I can think! Now!!!*

In that pivotal moment, his desperate dispute between surrender and survival was silenced. In the midst of his decision to wrestle with the evils befallen him, a simple truth entered in. There was power in its comfort. Rest in its clarity. His hazed mind held onto it, thankfully. It said, *God must want me alive.*

"Gawdh—musth—whan—meh—ah-alhive."

He was aware of nothing more than a sweet blanket of peace, though so much more was happening. He'd never be able to explain it. Never be able to put it into a story for his wife, for his child, for himself. But the spirit is not of the body. His labored breathing began to subside. His future reward was starting to be fulfilled, ideas, dreams, trials planted inside separate souls, lives shifting, evolving, lining up in a mystery to face his kind direction. A new-found inspiration flowed in and out of him with each quiet breath and the young man experienced a miracle, yet he was unaware. God was with him and He was granting His mercy. Falling on into a deeper sleep, the color of white, golden yellow, peach pink, a trace of blue, warmth of a morning not yet dawning, the point of all beginnings, the tiniest spec of pure light that fuels life and the pain in his limbs had lessened. A Gift. With the dew raining down from His heart, drops of sweat trailed down clammy white skin as of clouds, breaking the fire that hell had incased him in— it would have taken his life for certain. In his slumber, the faintest of smiles spread across his cracked lips—a touch like a kiss of the innocent and they were that much softer. Healing. As the sun's rays, it spread out inside him. He was enveloped in it. And, from this moment on, his life would not be his own. That mountain in his distance would surely wait for him.

By the mighty hand of God.

.   .   .

"Sky. Sky Fea-ther."

"Yes, yes, chil'. I know your name. It's jus'…Well, it's jus' that…."

Avi wiped the crystalized remains of tears off her burning cheeks, finding it impossible to finish her sentence while lost in the warm eyes of the mysterious child standing in front of her. Avi noticed how calm the girl was and how the deadly weather had left her virtually unaffected.

"Tsu-ga-sa-wo-dv."

Avi did not have the time to translate languages, but she sensed a deep compassion in the child's voice.

"Chil'..., Sky, we have ta get 'dis man to a warm place.... Someplace WARM, chil'. H-Help...help me, please."

"E-s-ga-ni, Lem."

Feather pointed her glowing fire stick, indicating that Lemn's cabin was nearby. She promptly began walking, apparently preferring to travel on foot. Avi clumsily mounted Colton's horse as quickly as possible. She perched herself awkwardly behind the saddle, both her small arms stretched fully, encircling the broad man's torso in an attempt to keep him steady. Her heavily gloved hands managed to find the reins of both horses, directing one while leading the other. She counted the horse's footfalls. Every five or so, she leaned to the side all she dare, peering out from behind Colton's rounded back to ensure she was still following the child's blue flame. In Avi's state of exhaustion, the girl had assumed the properties of the wind, gliding over drifts with a smooth solicitude like an angel of burden floating. She rested a cheek against Colton's unresponsive back, closed her eyes and prayed, "God, save this gentle man."

·   ·   ·

Something in the wind had awakened Lemn and he lay there still, listening to it howl. His pain had been significantly alleviated—he was bound by a deep sense of peace that would shatter should he move an inch—but his life was waiting for him to rejoin the fight. He took a shaky breath, attempting to calm the waves of anxiety creeping up through his delicate mental state, a foul emotion multiplying like droves of grasshoppers preying upon a drought-stricken field. It was not his will—this fear that was bombarding his thoughts and weakening his hope. It was making a mockery of his minimized ability, magnifying his failures before he even had a chance to try. He was stiff and frightened, his body pinned to the floor. He imagined himself, every muscle, every sensation, as he painstakingly tried to force his victimized body to perform in awkward minute increments, millions of tiny measures that would provide him ample opportunity to prove his own frailty, commence the birth of his own demise—cruel things that would stack up against him and push him back into suicidal despair. But he also thought of something else....

"Gawdh, helph meh."

Restricting his mind from thinking one more tainted thought of its own, he tenaciously struck his elbow on the floor and ground it into the rough wooden surface for leverage, pulling his massive weight painfully, one inch at a time, toward his goal—a single piece of firewood. The more he moved, the more his pain returned but he knew it could not kill him. He wouldn't let it. As he reached the piece of wood, out of breath, he used his right forearm and chin to anchor it under his left arm, then he slowly slid himself back to the fireplace, carefully rolling the cherished log onto the cooled ashes with his wrapped forearm and bloodied face. After he succeeded and one log was in place, he stared at it, exhausted, realizing the shocking limitations of his strength. He placed kindling around the single log, grasping one small piece at a time using his elbows while grinding his ribs into a log on the floor for elevation and stability. Similarly, he struck a match taking care not to ignite his own bandages. After snapping three in half, one finally took and with that he started a fire. When the blue and orange flame hissed, snapped sparks into the air, sleep began to pull at his eyes—oh, what a sweet feeling accomplishment is....*Whoever trusts in the Lord is kept safe....* He shook lassitude off for a moment, slid himself over to the water bucket and broke through the thin layer of ice with his skinned and slightly burned elbow. He dipped his face into the bucket and took a slow cool drink, the ice water stinging his skin. He bit the corner of a blanket and rolled awkwardly, pulling it over himself as he lay down right where he was. This time he tried to adjust his lazy legs, aligning them with his spine as best he could before embracing the deep solace of warmth and rest.

.   .   .

Colton's horse was dog-tired. It seemed the gelding's only inspiration was the younger horse following at his flank, volunteering frequent nudges and nips sometimes mistakenly planted on Avi's calf—they were gestures of a strong and persistent *Don't give up.* Avi's arms were about to fall off at the sockets, her entire body was frozen and numb and she was certain her leg was bruised if not bleeding under the layers of clothing. A few more minutes of this, she'd collapse for sure. She'd held her tongue several times already but finally the urge overwhelmed her and the chain of restraint holding it snapped. Her fear broke free, unleashed out into the atmosphere, drifting on spoken word. She screeched it atop the strengthening wind, with power she pitched it over Colton's bobbing head.

"Chil'? SKY FEATHER??? Can you hear me!!?? We should be **there** by now! Are you sure…

Before the question could escape her lips, it was answered by her own misguided sense of direction. She was immediately humbled as Lemn's cabin began to emerge from the chill and the darkness not more than fifteen feet in front of her. But she was facing the *back* of the cabin. They had approached it from the opposite direction she had intended, the direction farthest from town. She realized it then…, that Sky Feather had somehow found them out in the storm, out on the blinding prairie, even though they must have been more than two miles off course.

"H-how…?"

Avi hastily decided that it was no time to be asking trivial questions as the child was already rounding the porch to check on Lemn. *Please, dear Lord. Please, help us….* Avi rode up tight against the house and dismounted in the shallow drifts that had been hollowed out by the strong winds whipping ferociously around the tiny cabin. She freed Colton's foot from his boot that had crusted over with ice and frozen solid to the stirrup it was wedged into, then she pushed her body in against the wind, making her way around to the right side of the spent horse. She loosened his other foot with her hands—hands that seemed to be comprised of tiny stones linked together with strings, dangling from the ends of her stick arms…, they were about that useful. She tried her best to ease his massive weight down off the horse but while struggling to slow the momentum, she found herself quickly overpowered and they both landed in the side of the drift, bodies instantly and completely dusted with powdery snow. Just as Colton's heavy body sank deeper into the drift, his horse's knees buckled and the animal went down with a thud, releasing a funereal moan. The younger horse stepped in closer, hanging his head down low over him, forlornly protecting his mentor from the cold. Avi turned to call out to Feather for help just to encounter the child standing directly behind her, silently waiting, blanket in hand. *She knows my every thought, almost like Mama….* Working in unison, the two rolled the stout man onto the blanket and drug his body over the snow. They lugged him up the steps, across the porch, through the door, finally allowing him to rest beside Lemn.

"We gotta get 'im warmed up. He's still breathin'.
"Don't die, Colton, not now. It's not your time. Think a' Ammie, Colton."

Lemn was lying on the floor awake but motionless, staring up at Avi. At the sight of her, he was momentarily embarrassed out of habit. That old adolescent crush of his brought an astonishing amount of heat into his cheeks while the rest of him continued to struggle for every degree of warmth it could muster. As he watched her fuss over Colton, it didn't take him long to realize, to filter things through his stressed, his *stretched* mind. Given the current circumstances, everything had a new and contrasting value. He was now detached from his former foolishness as if it had been separated from his soul, as if it had floated away on the crisp, wood-smoked air while he was sleeping. What was left was a blessing. A purification in every sense, for he was down to almost nothing..., but every spec of it was precious, vital and fitted. Perfectly. As if it were tailor-made. A sword through the chaff and he could see suddenly. And it showed itself essential and good. A lighted path straight to his purpose. A journey that, before, was always there in his heart but obscured. Vague. Sometimes almost hopeless. He had been freed inside, free to live and breathe and feel his dreams. His dreams—as real and as necessary to him as the sun, the air, clean water from the earth. And it was the first time he'd ever thought about what it must be like to love someone else. Deeply. Enough to see their dreams. And it was nothing like infatuation.

He only cared about her.

As he watched her struggle to remove Sheriff's wet clothes then cover him with blankets, he wasn't even wondering what had happened to the man as if another praying spirit covered that hellish situation. He could only see her. He said the words, but not audibly. *Are you too cold? You must be so tired, so drained, lie down here by the fire and rest. Let someone take care of you for a change. Let me take care of you....* He felt older than he was in a way that was wise. Pictured himself in a perfect body bringing her coffee, an extra pillow, touching her cheek, stroking her hair briefly, gently, looking her softly in the eye, never breaking. *How long since I've seen you? Has it been months? Years? Too long, you beautiful soul, what a smile you bring to mine. Like a breeze that goes right through me, I'm new again. I see things in you. Like nothing else I've ever seen and I will never see it again, Avi. It is an honor for me just to be near you.* A step outside of his daydream, she caught him staring at her and he was too beside himself, or too true to himself, to glance away. He could finally *see* her. After all this time. And what an amazing person he found standing before him. As he released the breath he was holding, so released was his chimera composed of an idealism she could never become. And what took its place was so much more. He could finally see it all through *her* eyes. He'd stumbled upon an unearthly vantage point, the only angle from which selfless eyes, windows to the soul could behold the true prism of compassion, of understanding. What a rainbow above everything. Everyone. What magnificent colors lie there in it and come pouring down. It was through **her eyes**…, eyes that had been wide open through her own trials to endure, lessons to learn, and emotions to feel that he had absolutely no concept of. *What about her world…?* And so it commenced, the seeds were planted in a man who grew to truly know how to love.

"My God, *why*?"

She would have fallen to her knees, looked up through the ceiling to beg of her Lord an answer but she couldn't tear her eyes away. The sight was shocking. So strange…, no breath of hers transpired and her eyes, they did not blink. An unspeakable moment. She'd never seen the work of the devil up close. To see the mangled and pitiful daemon Satan had thrown in Lemn's place, to see the decrepit creature who'd risen, come a clawin' out the pit, stealin' her boy's precious soul, the spirit to him, his light…, all of it…, it was just gone. Vacancy replaced with an answer of stone. Of course Satan would want him ruined. He was a walking angel. *Was….* Her heart hesitated, awaiting her permission to go on. Indeed, she questioned *what for* as she absorbed the awkward position his body was sprawled out in and how his hands were wrapped, the blisters and cuts, the dried blood on his face, the distance in his glassy eyes. He was so far away—a place too calloused, too far removed for a child. She covered her quivering lips with her gloved hand and heavy tears rapidly descended from her eyes even though she was ashamed—she cursed herself, allowing Lemn to witness her uncontrolled reaction…, inconsiderate and careless, she knew, but she just didn't have enough energy to stop. And to make matters worse, Doc's words of instruction rang like pharisaical sunrise bells on the Sabbath, frighteningly true but off-key to her haggard ears…, distasteful, impossible, a cruel joke to the ill at heart. *Avi, if he can't walk, there's nothing you can do but comfort him. If he's been frozen….*

"Dear God."

Never. Not even in her most vivid, odious and far-reaching nightmare could she have imagined this. How in the Lord's name could she amputate…. Her body stopped the thought for her as she turned away from him and gagged. Repeatedly. Blood rushed to her head and her vision was shrouded in white. Somehow, she steadied herself enough to stagger over and pick up a wool blanket Lemn had struggled out of earlier. She nearly collapsed as she laid down beside him amidst the scattered logs—if the only thing she could manage to do for him was die alongside him, so be it.

They fell asleep by the crackling fire as Feather quietly tended to it, the sheriff, Lemn's bandages and the bleary horses she'd put up in the barn. The wee hours passed by in seasons through the girl's mind, bringing her wisdom and vision, clarity through the storms. The dawn finally approached her, she met it alone as it offered up a renewed sprinkling of life. And she watched as it entered Colton's chest—a deep breath spreading the rib cage, a series of coughs, a drink of water from her cup, then back asleep. She envisioned it as it revived the old horse—a massive and aching body hefting itself up off the stall floor, muscles quivering, unsteady but standing once again, cold muzzle meeting a young friend's, head lowering, a parting of lips grasping for strands of hay. The circle had turned once again. Feather looked out at the morning sun with tired, yet shining eyes that held miles and realms and illusions full of silent stories.

"Ga li 'e li 'ga." She whispered her thankfulness and allowed her heavy eyelids to close.

Chapter Twenty

"Op'm ya eyes, chil'. Op'm 'em up now. Come on outtah it, chil'. Havin' a bad dream…, hush now, chil'. Come on back ta yo mama. Come on back, y'heah?"

The bright spring light dryly fingered Avi's wide-open eyes as she sprung out of her dream, lungs gasping, burning and sore, serving up layers of phlegm through a harsh cough that seemed to come from her toes. Her brow was speckled with a subtle sweat, the sheets, a twisted knot at her feet. She clamped her eyes back shut. Swallowed hard. Lemn had become her own. Her child. She held him inside her chest, a place near her heart for him alone and oh so fragile…, it felt cracked. Although—thank God he looked fine now except for a few scars and some discoloration (wouldn't have known it happened at all if she hadn't *counted and felt the loss of every reeking inch of his sloughing flesh)*— he didn't need protecting anymore. Somehow what had nearly crippled her made him into a man. He crawled through the fire and come out walkin'. A masterpiece. It happened only a few months ago, all that hell. And in her head she was followed by the brother of it—the same gruesome nightmare every night for over a month. Each time she woke from it she felt nearly possessed as if one second more and the poltergeist would've had her. She'd hurl her body up in blind madness, screaming forcefully enough to penetrate every earthly and spiritual realm, begging for Spencer's help though he never came. Lately, finally, there had been a silence. A blankness, a blackness to her nights. Those nightmares passed beneath her like a rumbling storm cloud, so far away no lightning could find her as she floated. She began to relax, to let go, assuming she'd pushed the inertial torture far beyond the fluid walls of her deepest sleep. She didn't feel useless there in a world full of nothing. She could escape her foolish self. See, she couldn't do a thing for Lemn…. In his time of need, she'd crumbled and risked Colton's life to do it. Then yesterday she'd heard that Feather left—just up and vanished. That girl was the one who…, well, she was

Sent. She surrounded Lemn with a quiet power so *amassed*…. Every spirit of every being that has ever lived, ever strived for purity—they were joined together there. If not for that little girl, he would have lost his legs…. *The gangrene*…. It was impossible. Unbelievable. But it happened. So much more than a miracle, so much more than his body was at stake. What took place was indescribable. Satan bowed down to her, slunk away. Now she was gone, too.

This time Avi didn't have to vomit right away, only after the fact, when she realized for the thousandth time that it *really did* happen. It happened to that sweet, sweet child—*her* child. Everybody's child. Lemn. Only when she thought of his tender and kind soul did she have dry heaves over the bed pan Mama's shaky hand held under her while the other rubbed her back. Small circles that could not wear it away. *The moaning* of something scared and dying that rose out of those angelic lips of his when Doc lanced and doused the worst of it—those red bubbles of infection looping his forearm…. She couldn't strip his horrid screams from her ears. They echoed there, over and over and over again. He was imploring them to stop. She couldn't stand to look at him…. She turned away. She turned her back on those pleading eyes….

Thank God he couldn't feel his legs back then. THANK GOD.

"…Thank God, Mama. He alright. Thank God, Mama…. He alright now."

.   .   .

But dreams are necessary…, they carry with them the secrets from within….

"Tell me."

"Well, there was a crackling fire, Avi. And someone else was there with me—outside of my field of vision—watching. Almost nervous or anxious…, *agitated* or something. They were pacing back and forth across the floor but the footsteps were ever so light and delicate. Soft, like a toddler's almost. Or like someone half floating, half angel…. And wringing her hands…. I never did *see* who it was exactly, but I have a pretty good idea. Anyhow, my dream led my gaze back to the fire—it seemed to be drawing me in but then there he was, blockin' my path, just standin' before the flames strong as iron. I think my heart must have stopped at the sight of it, Avi…. He was deathly quiet and still, petrified but for his eyes—they were boring straight into me, studying my mind, searching my broken body all concerned-like, looking inside of me for something…. He took the longest time and never did blink. When he had finished, the meaning inside his eyes turned dark and sad—a place absolutely void of hope, Avi. I've never seen or imagined anything so sullen. His whole being emanated *Why...?* just as plain as if he had cried it out, but he already knew the answer. His shoulders slumped, his cheeks turned ashen and fell in against sharpened bone, his whole body grew thin and it arched, drawn back against a single curved line but his shoulders, his arms..., they were still strong, the muscle rounded and defined, almost colossal. The transformation turned him dark, the color black was solid over him—his coat, his boots, his sleek hair—all of it grew to a new, shiny black and fit against him smooth, close to his body. It looked so bizarre. And the strangest thing about those eyes of his...they weren't blue anymore, but black as a crow's—*completely* black..., deep, thick and liquid like oil and they were no longer readable. He had some sort of a choice to make and he was running out of time. And I can't explain how I came to know that because he didn't speak the entire dream..., but I could tell the exact moment he made his decision. He spread his arms out in pain like he'd hung himself on a cross. These massive wings spread out beneath him like draping shadows then he folded in on himself. He looked right at me before he bowed his head and his eyes closed. Scared me near to death when the crow busted out of his chest and separated from his body—it was a messenger and it flew right into the flames..., let up an awful scream—a screeching..., a deafening sound, more than a second of it would drive you right out of your mind—and then it was gone. It left his normal self behind and he was so peaceful, Avi, exhausted but peaceful. I wish you could 'a dreamt the same thing because seeing him like that..., well, it made it all worth it. In my dream you did see him, you were sitting at the table waiting. He was jus' so sure of himself, Avi..., took the good with the bad and was finished with all of it. He was unlike I'd ever seen him in life. *Undivided* would describe him the best.

He sat down across from you and you took his hand. You both had these cups, they were round with no handles, a dark brown color like Indian pottery. And you drank some kinda brown liquid. I could smell it..., it sure smelled foul, Avi. Almost made me sick to my stomach but you two drank it down like sweetened coffee and the more you drank, the higher that fire rose in the fireplace. It got real hot, a heat that cracked like bone. It glistened on skin and rose through that room like humidity dancing across a summertime field. The only thing to breathe was raw steam.

You just sat there looking straight into one another's bloodshot eyes, sweat pouring down. You were both real quiet but you *knew* about the other one—knew *everything*. That part's a little hard to explain, I guess. You only asked him one question, 'Did you at least get to see Heaven?' He didn't answer right away so you said, 'The boy ought to know....'"

Lemn fell into a moment of silence that lasted a little too long for Avi's taste. The suspense regarding her brother's afterlife was something she found unbearable. "Is that *it*???"

"Yes'm. That's it. You didn't get the chance to finish…, it was like spoken words were morning sun to that dream—it just evaporated." A tear leaked out the corner of Lemn's eye and he ducked his head down while his throat grew a lump inside. Certain things were just meant to stay one step ahead of human understanding. And he supposed there was good reason.

"Then you woke up?"

"Well, Feather woke me for supper. And, Avi, so help me…. She had a bowl of stew sittin' on the table. She pulled out a chair and said something in her language, something like, 'A—le—dum….' No…no, that's not it…'A—le—di.' Yes, 'A—le—di' is what she said. She said it two or three times and just stood there, staring at me."

"And then?"

"I didn't understand. Every time before she would help me sit up and then she'd bring the food to me. I figured she'd grown tired, you know? That she'd gotten discouraged and was ready to give up on me. Just when I thought that, she said it again, 'A-le-di.' But this time I understood it, Avi. Or my body did…. And somehow, by the grace of God, Avi, I did it. I just stood up! I remember putting my hands out in front of me. I rolled the bandages off. I bent over and did the same with my legs. And what I saw…I couldn't believe it. And my back, Avi! My back…was *perfect*. When I stood back up, I was *tall*….I was **straight** again."

.   .   .

And some dreams lie in wait, sleeping. They need to be picked up, cradled, revisited and let go—a new breeze beneath still wings…, see where they soar….

"*You suffered a mild heart attack, Sheriff. You're lucky this one didn't get ya. 'Specially in that cold. But if you hadn't 'a went, that boy might be dead. You're a hero, son. A hero in anybody's book.*"

A hero. Colton sat in his rocker beside a stack of unopened books and rocked. *A hero....* His recovery was not only physical—he'd done a lot of thinking, the kind of fenced in thinking that allows a man room to grow, to move forward steadily, not sprint in downward spirals of panic, something parallel to that old saying *dance as if no one were watching....* What if he lived his life like that? What if.... He was going to be a father soon. He was already a hero but felt absolutely nothing as a result. But to be a father...? Well, there wasn't an emotion he didn't feel. His wife, *dear Ammie...,* she'd stood beside him at his worst. For years. She couldn't have seen everything going on inside his cursed mind, but she saw some. He figured her for a smart woman, she'd probably deduced the rest. And she'd never run off to her mother's upriver. Not one time. She thought not of her own well-being, her own future..., sure couldn't depend on a man hanging over the edge by a thin rope, knife in hand, but she stayed anyhow. She *stayed.* Must be what love is.

He stilled his rocker. Permanently. Slid the chest over to the wardrobe and began packing. He loaded the wagon, hitched the horses, went back into the house to cut up the apples too early and tart for eating—no time for baking—and returned to the barn, feeding each horse an equal amount. He stroked their necks, soft beneath the coarseness of dangling mane. He rubbed the space between their eyes affectionately—one star, one blaze—taking the time to ensure that neither choked on the treat as one had old teeth and the other was in the ongoing process of shedding his deciduous ones, both held a snaffle. He adjusted the blinders..., they had a long journey ahead of them—all of them did, but somehow he was certain they'd make it just fine if they kept their eyes on the horizon. He checked his mental list twice. He had everything, for the first time in his life, and an easy smile graced his face, leading the kindness in his soft heart ever so gently to the surface. Made for a beautiful and a very handsome man.

He took his keys off the wall-hook, they jingled an erratic melody while he twirled them around his index finger. He dropped his silver star in the spittoon. He waited until they rose to their feet, depressed bodies smelling of the filth of oppression, eyes glaring, expecting more. He opened the only book he would take with him and began to read....

"And He opened His mouth and taught them, saying,
　　Blessed are the poor in spirit: for theirs is the kingdom of Heaven.
　　Blessed are they that mourn: for they shall be comforted.
　　Blessed are the meek: for they shall inherit the earth.
　　Blessed are which do hunger and thirst after righteousness:
　　　　for they shall be filled.

Blessed are the merciful: for they shall obtain mercy.
Blessed are the pure in heart: for they shall see God.
Blessed are the peacemakers: for they shall be called the children of God.
Blessed are they which are persecuted for righteousness' sake:
     for theirs is the kingdom of Heaven.
And Blessed are ye...."

He tucked the Book under his arm and unlocked the barred door.

"Go on through the house. There is a wagon in the barn. Don't speak. Don't try to run. Slide under the canvas and stay deathly still. I'm going to wait for my wife to return. Then we will both get in the wagon, leave the back way out of town. I'll stop and say, 'It's time,' when we get to a place I can drop you off.... If you're puzzled, what's happening here—the best I can see it—is an act of God."

The only thing of value his dead father left him was a run-down homestead in Kentucky with a barn full of cobwebs and rusty woodworking tools. He would need to do some spring cleaning, would need to rewrite the dialogue that echoed its way down around the skeleton of that farm like a creeping mold. But it could be as it should have been. He was finally on his way Home....

Letter Two

What God Has Joined Together

Chapter Twenty-One

It was the spring of another year. In due season, come. And the glorious days given of it blew life over the prairie, poured smiles into the trickling streams, echoed joy through the river song. Its grace planted renewed strength along the sun beams, its mercy kissed the colors green with dew drops.

Hellfire may have been raging, but not here…here was just the hush of promised heaven swinging delicately beneath rainbows that blessed both ends of the earth.

.   .   .

Lemn thought of that majestic Soul often, the One who floated down amidst peaceful snowflakes to save him, but in the worldly blizzard of pain and change, dark mystery and displaced time he'd somehow lost hold of the proof of her. Her existence evanesced like so much summer rain. And it left behind rippling, belying memories like crystalline waves washing over a dispersing dream. Sand through his fingers…, to build something of it would take an integral faith. He never really could *read* her even when she was grounded and encased in flesh illuminated by common candlelight. He'd look into her eyes every chance offered back then but had gleaned shockingly little…, he still couldn't understand from where it was she came, couldn't imagine where it was she might be going. But the time she spent was so powerful, it made him who he was. And in his heart she left the answers to everything. Indeed he learned that angels walk the commonest places on earth.

The only thing he could compare her presence with in the natural was the companionship of a stray dog. Odd, but comforting in its association. He was thinking not of a pitiful creature—not by any means—but rather a beautiful one that trots into a lonely boy's life one day right out of the blue, filling every secret detail of a birthday wish long since overdue. Noble, head held high, coat slick and silky with a vanity given, not coveted and stolen and squandered. As instantly as he adopts that little boy, he becomes the most cherished part of the lad's day. Doodles and daydreams through hours of school, mixed between pages of blurred arithmetic fall wondrous stories full of rigged up fishing poles, curved columns of digits following familiar trails down by the river bank imprinted with two tracks, side by side. Adventure or nonevent…, no matter with a friend. But deep inside the little boy's heart, he knows. Knows there will come a day when that dog will not be waiting on the porch, tail thumping. Knows after calling just three times that a four-legged answer will not round the corner. But can he blame him? Never. For mutuality is not forced, respect not mandated. An animal's nature he does not conceal…, its pure honesty. Unforgettable, easily understood is a Teacher. Discovery is motion. Life is for the living.

And what it would be…, to live a life like that. No regret, no condemnation, no shame. The carriage of a body would be dignified. A smile would emerge almost too quickly. Laughter would be word. A lonely hand would not have to reach far. And the heart would offer no excuse, no apology for its rhythm and, therefore, would have the time to drink in love and press it back out with rays like sunshine, naturally. Attractive in its sight, noticeable, universally recognized. Restful purity surrounds. Ease of kindness spreads. The value, the rarity…, the proven possibility spurs an enthusiastic mimicry of achieving a life loosed from the harshest critic, the one that emanates from within. Fleshly cages rattle, bars begin to weaken at that decisive point between why and why not. Contagious like starlight, acceptance of this gifted visitor occurs without consideration, with silenced judgement, for to live next to one who is truly free, no matter how short of stay…, it offers a hope to the needy—the taste of choice granted by one's own…, it's called risk. If shot down it brings a standing ovation on stage before a theater full of the seated—a brilliant performance it is. And a step closer to the sky.

He didn't know if he would ever see her again. He thanked God for the time he had with her. He cried. A smile through the tears and then sad once again. He felt the gaze of the moon cloaked across his strong shoulders—"*Sv-no-yi e-hi nv-da,*" his chin lifted as her voice drifted in off the night clouds, brushed up against his cheek with the softness of her hand. As months then seasons passed, he thought he caught glimpses of her under the far oaks, assuming the spirit of the shadows, watching over him…. Her long, black hair flowing into nothing more than a whisper of midnight wind. But he could never be sure. Nor his searching eyes, hopeless. She'd offered him a second chance and he was going to take it…, just as soon as he could recognize it.

.   .   .

Avi practiced the speech in her head, a string of words that rolled together into a nervous ball of energy and bounced off her emotions like a ricocheting bullet. What she heard herself stumbling through was anything but coherent, the delivery anything but composed. And her reasoning certainly wasn't going to convince anyone, herself included. But if she didn't speak up now, if she didn't take this first step, she'd never get over that mountain. It had always been there in her distance, since childhood, blocking her view of the sunrise. But now it was looming before her, enormous in its size and shadowing her own ability to shine. The side she was facing didn't look so bad, stepping stones of possibility laced with tiny veins of regret. She wasn't naive to its viable elemental reversal, to, perhaps, its landslide waiting on the other side. There was only one way to find out. And with the entire country quivering to the core, passivity was something she could no longer accept.

"I received a letter, Lemn."

Tiny hairs shot up along the nape of his neck. A cold chill drifted across the landscape of muscling defining his strong and able back, flowing out onto broad and steady shoulders. Each layer tightened as the wind seemed to swirl then dive into a deserting current—the very nature of the world wanted no part in this. He could smell the freshness mixed with the dankness of the river, could hear Drake's voice rising from the past just as clear as day…. Drake had been livid, absolutely beside himself with rage…, why Doc would give Avi Elliot's address, he'd never know. He ranted and he raved, cursed a storm over Doc, then a hurricane over Avi's father. He seemed to lose his breath for a moment…, then continued on, adamant, though nearly inaudible. His thick tongue loosed a stranger's voice, laboriously low, stretching around hate's choke hold, grumbling about how he wished that old man, Avi's father, would just get it over with and die…, *ain't no good use for 'im, never was.* Drake had warned Lemn, told him to keep his eyes and ears open concerning that impending letter of reply. Now that it had finally presented itself, Lemn had no idea what to do about it.

"I hope you won't think poorly of me, Lemn…, that I'm desertin' you. I'd never do that. You mean more to me than anything, but you're a grown man, Lemn. Look at ya. Strong, young, good head on y' shouldahs. You don't need me…, it's time you start carryin' on with your life and I guess it's time I do the same. See, I know that I might not make it back from Carolina, I know that. There's all 'dis talk of war…, but it's high time I start seein' what my kind has ta go through—up close. I haven't done my part, Lemn. I know you'll come to understand that…, if not now, maybe someday. All my life, I've been hidin' behind somebody's, or some*thing*'s, petticoats. It's in my gut, Lemn. My gut feelin' says I need ta go…, get from outta this hole of secrets and find my own truth. An' tha's all I got to go on, Lemn, my gut and a prayer. It's all I got. Please understand…. My daddy's gettin' on in years. That letter said he might not be livin' much longer. He's a wealthy man, Lemn. Maybe I can talk 'im into doin' some*thin*'…convince him ta start freein' people. Send 'em up to the Lakes, to Canada. I know…, I'm prob'ly gettin' myself in a heap 'a trouble but I'm willing to take that risk. But I want your blessing, Lemn. That'll mean the world to me. Mama ain't gonna give me hers, that's sure. Mercy! That woman's been pleadin' with me for over two yeahs now. I *have* ta do it now or we're gonna drive one 'nother senseless. You'll look in on Mama for me? An' Doc? Because…, if you've got any notions that you're goin' with me, you get them out' your head 'dis minute, ya heah? I love you, boy. But this ain't your fight. Your life is here. You're supposed to do somethin' here. You need to find out what for y'self."

Lemn didn't listen to many of her words but he could hear the force behind them loud and clear—he could recognize the sweet sound of a dream when it sang. A chorus of the many voices found inside one angel…. She needed to fulfill her purpose same as anyone. He didn't agree with ducking, hiding…, it caused atrophy of a soul. This call on her life had lain patiently in wait, had fallen dormant over many parched seasons. Its concealment made everyone feel safe, everyone, that is, but the host. The dreamer. He had seen it rise to the surface, again and again, for over two years. Watched as she exhausted and bruised herself trying to stomp it out, to appease everyone else, but circumstance kept disheveling and cracking the soil. And its persistent agitation finally broke through her iron mold, set seed to a stone and windy world. Wasn't easy…, change. Certainly wasn't a science…, this mystic transformation. But somehow it's inevitable, an unexpected switch of the track toward Destiny when all the conductor sees is air space over passing cliff. The only thing to run on is pure heart. Excess nurtures into reality and it is written—a life's story. And hers had just begun. For some reason yet untold, the weight on Avi's heart and mind had stacked itself up against her concern for family, against the expectations dictated her by man and it tipped the scale, making her do something outlandish to counterbalance the force. *So she is going…going all the way to South Carolina. What's everybody doing with all that guilt, those chains, trying to hold her down? She's nobody's prisoner…let her fly.* Some birds fell right out of the sky, he knew…, fell just like that. But it wasn't his call. These things are better left tended by the One who plants them.

He was so distracted by his own thoughts he didn't realize what was asked of him for a few moments.

"I'm sorry...what? Oh.... Yeah, Avi. Sure I'll look out for both of them and when I'm gone playin' I'll get Glen to check. You know I will, Avi. You don't have to worry about that. I think all the worryin' needs ta stop. And as for my blessing, that's a given. It'll always be with you, Avi."

She reached out for his hand and found it strikingly cold against the warm afternoon. Chills rose from his fierce grip all the way up her spine. She glanced at him, but his expression was comfortable, his hand loose.... She gazed across the horizon, not looking at anything in particular, attempting to breathe her way out of the slight premonitions that had begun to invade her mind. They sat speechless and motionless on his porch swing—his mind scanning the possibilities of their separation, Avi's avoiding her inheritance—when her body suddenly tensed.

"What is it, Avi? You alright?"

"...Fine. Fine. You take care of y'self, y' heah? I'll see you again, b'fore I leave."

He stood quickly, his physique portraying balance, strength and precision to a degree easily matching that of any athlete. He was the picture of health, of newborn masculinity, comfortable and confident in his restored body—so much so he was already taking it for granted. But his mind was not on himself as he watched her walk away. He jogged after her, easily surpassing in time to help her into Doc's carriage. She smiled her thanks and he waved a hand to her as hooves and wheels roused up a shield of dust between them, some sort of line he knew better than to cross.

As she traveled back toward town, the wide driving lines began to slip across her palms—nervous perspiration repelling the oil-treated leather..., she'd forgotten her gloves on Lemn's porch. She tried to focus on her future, on the trail winding away in front of her slithering like a snake. She tried to hook her mind on the melody of a pleasant hymn but the end of each verse swiftly carried her back to the start of her vision, an unbearable image she so wanted to ignore. She took a deep breath and held it—drawing strength from that of her mother, she decided to surrender to whatever it was trying to tell her—then her lungs slowly emptied themselves. She stopped atop a hill, set the brake, closed her eyes and opened her mind..., she wanted to know who was inside. When her bird's-eye view swung down toward the coffin, her body tensed in apprehension but the lid was slammed shut, almost on her face—she jumped, she'd felt the force from it. And a foreboding feeling surrounded her, almost suffocated her as tenpenny nails sealed the lid down tight—no air, no light. She felt the bite of each one as it was skillfully hammered in by a white man's strong hands.

·   ·   ·

April 27th, 1860

Miss Avi Woodford,

My deepest regret and sincerest apology for responding in such an unpunctual and uncivil manner. I fear I have much to address in apology and regret, my dear. As you may be aware, I am nearing retirement from this life and my ways. I will send for you posthaste. Please prepare yourself to ready at a moment's notice. Your journey will be secure, although the means you may find somewhat unsettling. My heart to your mother, as always and forever will be.

Sincerely,

Elliot James Woodford

The letter had been read and folded, unfolded and reread so frequently, the creases had worn down to the delicacy of a single layer of onion skin, the points of the folded corners had disintegrated into pinholes. Avi had left the note behind as an avenue for her mother's cherished trips of reminiscence. Lemn sat at Mama's kitchen table, having difficulty returning the letter to her. He couldn't pluck his mind from the second-to-last line—*the means you may find...unsettling*. A bystander might interpret the statement as an innocent indication of the crude wagons, rough roads, calloused men with shameless vulgarities one meets on wayward travels but, with Avi going South—alone— and at a time like this, "unsettling means" took on a completely different hue. He read the letter again. And again.

"Mama? What does he mean here...? That the 'means may be unsettling'?"

"Don't ya worry none, not 'bout my Avi-chil', heah? She be alrigh'...she gots to."

"Can you see anything? I mean, do you have a vision that she's gonna be okay?"

"My vision done started ta transfah. Transfahin' on ovah wheah they needed, boy. Gif' of da Lord..., map a' da spirit world. See glory, son. See sin. Plain as da nose on y' face, um-hm."

Mama began to rock back and forth on her chair, clutching the letter to her bosom, eyes closed tight, peaceful smile spread across her face. It looked like freedom. If she did have some knowledge, she wasn't passing it on. Lemn understood it was out of his hands, but still he worried. He hadn't seen Avi since she left his farm that day and something about her hasty departure didn't set right with him. He began to reason excessively..., couldn't get Drake's angry voice out of his head and he'd been struggling with doubt and sleepless nights ever since. Maybe he should have tried to stop her..., or, at the very least, he should have accompanied her, helped her settle in, made sure she was safe for his own peace of mind. He squeezed Aviona's free hand as a good-bye gesture and started to leave her to rock with her thoughts that spanned the depths of ages. But he hesitated. Stood staring at her. Silent. He couldn't help but feel that she was hiding something. Pretending, maybe. Avoiding something. He reprimanded himself for being so ridiculous. Why, all the sudden, was he so suspicious of everyone? He turned toward the door disheartened, body slumped with its first taste of the weight Drake carried through this world. It was a massive contradiction, a source of unsurmountable frustration, to be human, forever beholden the pristine. Mere nearness and touch and time is coveted and cherished. It is also what tarnishes the beloved beyond recognition, pitifully diminishes the priceless value.... Responsibility spirals down as a two-edged sword. *How,* he wondered, *do you protect someone you love without bottling their life?* He felt restless. Helpless. Just as his boots pressed their mark into the dusty street, a heated anger flamed up inside of him as if someone struck a match by dragging it against the rough muscle of his heart. *Unsettling means....* He had no intention of becoming a killer, ever, but he could understand it now..., could see that clear line come into focus for the first time and he knew nothing more than the name of one of the men baiting him to cross it.

If anger's fire, fear is the fuel.

·   ·   ·

"I didn't realize Avi had such po' writin'. Well it's mis'rable, really."

Lemn jumped a little, startled by Ellie's shameless intrusion. She had been reading the letter over his shoulder—Avi's first letter, the first sign that she was alright—stretching every muscle, straining every ligament, overextending her toes, balanced way over the elevated mail room counter like a crane in flight, nose and derriere in the air.

"When she asked me to help her write to her daddy down in S' Car'lina, I reckoned she just wanted it to be proper an' all. Didn't know she couldn't write a speck on her own, poor thing...."
  "And what do you have to do with ol' Crenshaw's mines? Is that how you get all that money a' yours?"

She winked one eye over a flirtatious grin just as her husband cleared his throat. He shot her a reprimanding scowl before he went back to dryly sorting mail. The pair interacted more like father and daughter than husband and wife, a trait that could have been attributed to their thirteen year age differ- ence. Lemn made a mental note to refrain from marrying a child due to the fact they most likely stay that way. He tipped his hat and walked out the door on his way to report the news to Mama and Doc.

                    .   .   .

"It's in some sort of code, I guess. She's hinting about Crenshaw's outfit, for sure. See? Here…where she talks about the salt mines—none of us have a thing to do with them, but she mentioned 'em anyhow. Twice. And look at how she wrote it, like she doesn't want anyone to know she's learned. She's traveling with the others Crenshaw kidnaped to send back into slavery—I know it. And I don't like it. Not one bit."

Doc nervously glanced over at Aviona and found her studying her bare feet, appearing ashamed, lips sealed over years and years and years of nothing to report. Doc started to fidget, to rub the wrinkles momentarily off his fore- head..., there's nothing like watching elderly respect die. It's what they both wanted to avoid, but there was no stopping Avi. She probably didn't even real- ize it herself—yet. She would when the others went straight to her father's plantation with her. She would....
  Lemn read their body language like an age-old, keyless diary, forbidding lock finally rusted through. It dawned on him that they knew everything. It

was like the skeletons of Shawneetown weren't skeletons at all. They weren't hidden in the closet, they made up the damn framework. Storybook sidewalks rolled out for everyone to stroll across in broad daylight. Everybody had seen it. Everybody but Avi and Lemn—the only outcasts who looked, with trusting eyes, to the writing on the wall and perceived it unanimously cryptic.

"Do you two mean to tell me that Avi's father is in with Crenshaw and Kuykendall? You mean he's in the *business?*"

Silence. Doc's mouth opened, but the languages of the universe had no words that could explain. He shut it again, tight. His heavy, timeworn eyes misted over as he watched the contempt expand. And they had caused it. They had simply shattered Lemn's faith in them, in people.

Lemn was distraught enough, holding in his hands the proof, more or less, that Avi was traveling the Reverse with Lewis Kuykendall, Crenshaw's most cutthroat trader, but he never suspected her *father* to be the **buyer**. He thought he was going to be sick.

"This is going to crush her! And what do you two suppose the Lord thinks of all this? You two especially! Coverin' for the devil's work…, a *prophet*…and a *healer*???"

Lemn spat the labels out and nearly gagged on the aftertaste. He absolutely hated confrontation, hated to condemn others, so he immediately turned from them and left town looking a lot like his second father, thirsting after the haze too much whiskey would offer.

He rode out toward Glen's to inform him of his departure—he was going gambling. He was missing Drake's company like never before and deep in the game is where he seemed to get closest to it. He felt so lost and alone, jagged points of a compass rose spinning…, amazed that one could walk the straight and narrow path and still the world falls apart around them. He was struggling for a sign, yearning for some sort of clue regarding the locations of Drake's unpredictable sources of strength, desperately searching for waning traces of the leads that guided the man toward decisions for which he offered no apology…. Drake was never overly concerned with doing the right thing and was certainly not about to bounce his choices off the fickle reflections in other's haughty eyes. Because, Lemn was discovering, something happens in the wee hours between youth and manhood, something in the weather changes. The journey suddenly slants, rises continuously upward over jagged and slippery rock. Trails bleed down and vanish. The sun fades, stars homogenize. The right thing seems to have fallen far behind, somewhere down in the foothills maybe, hidden in softer pastures of the mind, and it's replaced with something harsh, ugly and worth so much less for the effort—the lesser of two evils. And with forked choices like that, he figured 'twas understandable why a man would offer up no apology—to start would end all silence....All this, and today a cold rain..., fellow travelers can seldom be trusted—the most disappointing, pathetically crippling leg of any voyage.

As he reached Glen's turnoff, something told him to keep riding past. He urged his horse up to a lengthy lope. The gelding wanted to stretch his legs..., *thrump, thrump, thrump*.... The cooling breeze caressed Lemn's skin, tickled forth tears a touch too close to the surface, awaiting any feeble excuse to release and flow. He couldn't see the trail all that well...he let himself go and trusted his horse. They reached a bend that swung to the left and the horse automatically switched leads in midair to stay in graceful balance, not missing a beat. *Thrump, thrump, thrump*.... The animal's nostrils expanded to take in deep, even breaths—a healthy draw of oxygen to keep powerful muscles fueled. A quail popped out of the prairie grass—*chu-chu-chu-chu-chu*—seeming to aim for the gelding's belly, his back arched as he skipped sideways two or three strides, mane flowing out over his rounded neck, then, regaining composure, he flattened back out, holding a steady, relaxed rhythm seamless as liquid all the way to his own barn.

Lemn swung his leg down, his body's memory flinching, bringing him into awareness once again of his strong, pain-free back, of his miracle. He smiled in spite of everything as he looped the halter loosely around the sorrel's neck and slid the headstall carefully over the ears, allowing the horse to spit the snaffle bit out on his own. He fastened the halter in place, tossed the lead over the hitching post, securing it with a horseman's knot, and unbuckled the back, then front cinches. Steam curled up off the sweat-soaked back as the saddle and blankets were removed. Lemn untied the gelding and commenced to walk him in large circles around the place to cool him down. He realized the ride had cooled his emotions as well. As he circled, he searched the horizons, scanned his parent's graves, glanced to the oak grove. It was going to be a glorious sunset. It wasn't his place to judge, just forgive.

He sat outside for a long while. The horse was groomed, all the livestock fed and watered. Himself, he didn't have an appetite—not for whiskey, not for Drake's take on life. He had his own. And was thankful he'd passed the temptation. He looked out at the farmstead John Crenshaw still owned three yearly payments on. He listened to the birds of spring warble out their quiet goodnights. He knew Doc and Mama were good-hearted people, their choices were exactly that—their own. But God help Avi.… His thoughts floated back to Crenshaw. That man seemed to have his stamp on every household in the territory. It was no wonder he was untouchable with everyone in on his *plan*, sustained by his *plan*—with the alternative being death. The only one who seemed to have any authority over him was Elliot. Of course, that's why Mama and Avi stayed safe. Crenshaw kept them safe at all costs or Sir Elliot Woodford would ruin his business—the *reverse* Underground Railroad. Evil had its cancerous fingers nestled into every fiber of life, it seemed. And Lemn couldn't help but wonder what would happen when Elliot passed away.

He dropped down to his knees and prayed with his Entire Soul. Because miracles do happen. When he was finished, he went into the house to light a candle and search for answers in the only reliable place he'd found.….

It's what his father would have done.

.   .   .

Crenshaw's money was dirty money—as dirty as money could get. Lemn's talent had saturated the area leaving few, if any, who would take the financial risk of playing him. But still, he found himself in Equality, again, for only one reason but that *reason* had him a little too intimidated to admit it openly. Just yet. And poker was a nice cover while he studied his reason.

"Well, look at you. Farmer/Rancher/Gambler."

Lemn shuffled sideways in his chair. It made him squirm uncomfortably thinking of all the unpleasantries Crenshaw's occupational list would reveal—*murderer, kidnapper, hypocrite, monopolizer, slave driver*.….

He looked down in silence, contemplating Mama sitting in her rocker, alone.

"With your legendary talent, let's say we up the anti, shall we? How about your farm payments. You win, you're free and clear. Three years wiped clean. You lose, you owe on six years. Now how 'bout it, Legend Boy?"

"Call it."

Of Crenshaw's response, Lemn only caught a wiry eyebrow beginning to raise, for then *she* appeared. Out on the balcony, gazing down into a room full of emptiness, her expression heavily laden…, something like Jesus must have looked as He surveyed the crowd fanning out from the base of His cross. Her low-cut scarlet dress was satiny underneath, covered with delicate lace of the same color. It flowed all the way down to her bare feet. The memory of Feather glistened through her dark eyes, reflected through her shimmering, black hair that lay smooth against her face, framing flawless olive skin and high prominent cheek bones. It was as if Feather, the child, had miraculously grown into this beautiful woman. But Lemn knew she wasn't Feather. Their spirits were so very…different. As she descended the stairs she looked right through *him* with a hollow hatred. The walls were going up. Completely up by the time she stepped out onto the main floor. And that's when it always started.

"Hey, lookie there—it's the squaw."

"Oi—yoi—yoi—yoi."

"Whatcha think, maybe I oughta scalp her tonight, huh?"

A collective wave of filthy mockery mucked its way through the atmosphere like thick coal dust. She—*beautiful, graceful she*—was the brunt of racist jokes, perverted evil, harsh cruelty. The other whores betrayed her, laughed along, covering their cheap insecurity. Loathsome men placed their hands of gruesome smut upon her, pushed her, pulled her roughly. Clamoring along in a sadistic, group joke, their individual intentions read aloud as their humored expressions fell rapidly into despising glances, touches, gestures, striking hatefully against her and each one counted, each one left a mark.

Lemn's stomach churned. He was disgusted with himself for agreeing to Crenshaw's ridiculous game. He wasn't worried about losing, he was worried the timing would be off. Some sorry excuse for a man would try to take her…he couldn't let that happen. Not again.

Not ever again.

"Ya gonna deal or not, boy?"

"Yessir."

Crenshaw easily honed in on the subject preoccupying the majority of Lemn's attention.

"You know a piece 'a trash like that ain't worth nothin' better. Don't ya, son?"

"No. I **don't** know that, sir."

A saucy sarcasm spread through Lemn's voice—thick and brandished, heated emotion trailed it, fed with fragmented memories. Memories cheated their initial shock, horror fallen void upon the indolence of youth, now drawing the meaning out of those silent years, pooling deep, then bleeding toward the edge of a deep-seated anger. It was a hate permanently fixated within and at times, a wicked churning barely controlled—the seal becoming worn with age. His parents' coveted life of freedom seemed another cheap form of slavery, toiling all those years toward an early death. The old man sitting before him had played a satanic god, lording over every move they dared to make. He had a knack for regarding human beings as trash. Anne and Devon, to him, were refuse. Lives used up and no longer profitable, bodies to be tossed aside in his dirty world. And what Lemn hated even more than this was the fear revisited—Crenshaw in the same room as she. The old man's ace in the hole was Lemn's land and his parents' dream resting upon it—he'd only use her, too. It seemed inevitable and creeping ever closer, a plan churning behind those mischievous eyes—Crenshaw's attention could be downright eerie. Lemn started to sweat, the smoke was beginning to burn his eyes. His adult life seemed to be emerging from the depths of some destructive lava pit, piece by jagged piece forged by a stranger's hand and becoming buoyant in the dark coolness of reality—a floating puzzle reflecting itself there, an image likened to the suicidal king of hearts.

"Easy, now. Didn't mean ta step on any toes."

Crenshaw openly enjoyed the irritation he'd caused, eyes beaming over a contemptuous grin. He assumed he'd just gained a gambling edge, but he didn't assume for long. Lemn raised the bets to staggering amounts in a hurry. A crowd drew near, blocking Lemn's view of her, so he rushed the outcome all the more. Royal flushes, straights, four-of-a-kinds, and full houses flying phenomenally across the green tabletop. Crenshaw was wiped clean in exactly ten, crisp rounds. Lemn sprung up and grabbed the old man's hand, nervously shaking on the game while his scanning gaze targeted that red dress. She was climbing the stairs with a drunk.

"Now wait just a minute…."

"Deal's a deal, sir. I'm sure a respectable businessman such as yourself would agree. Enjoy your evening."

Lemn cordially tipped his hat—leaving Crenshaw with his mouth gaping, his empty hands lifted in bewilderment—and pushed through the crowd with his broad shoulders, apologizing repeatedly for his haste as he bumped unsuspecting arms left steadying sloshing liquor. He took the stairs two at a time and reached her toward the top of the staircase, out of breath. He stood under her vengeful glare, panting like a dog, for what seemed like an eternity of embarrassment. He took his hat off as soon as he thought of it. He held it over his heart. The man standing beside her looked mildly amused and rather tipsy.

"Sir, I don't mean disrespect. I won't waste your time. Here's a hundred dollar note in exchange for the lady."

The man straightened himself at once then narrowed his vision, his squinting eyes focusing in on more money than they'd seen all year. He was obviously impressed—it was one of those bank notes, printed up all proper and dangling right before his nose like a juicy carrot. He managed to peel his eyes away from it and he looked her up and down. He wasn't blind. Nor was he so far removed that he couldn't recall those wonder years, that block of sweet time where wild ideas rule the lives of young men…, and somewhere deep inside he hoped this boy's would actually work out.

"That ain't gonna nowhere near pay for the trouble you got in store salvagin' this dirty tramp, kid."

And with that he snatched the paper bill quickly, swaying with the delayed momentum of his own hasty motion. He held it up to the light, doing his best to rule out counterfeiting, snapped it twice, then tottered back down the stairs to get on with drinking it away. That's when Lemn's heart started to beat hard and his palms turned cold and wet—this was the first time, in reality, he'd been alone with her. He'd never even spoken to her before…, they'd not been formally introduced. Before he panicked further, he needed to get his feet on more solid ground or he would swoon straight away. Probably reach his death falling backward down the stairs. He sheepishly turned his face, lifted his kind eyes to look up at her. She was still glaring right through him.

"Well, uh…should we go on in? I mean, after you…. That is if you *want* to go in, I mean."

Her eyes immediately dove to the floor at his statement. He wondered what he said wrong. As she turned toward her bedroom, he noticed that the mark at the base of her neck was not a necklace as he had presumed from across the room. It was a scar. A clean cut healed over. It was done slow with a sharp blade, clear across her delicate neck. She turned from him and looked like she was swallowing more tears, but she hadn't cried. *Oh, she was **beautiful**....* And she went on in.

She walked silently, almost like she wasn't there. She went over and stood by the foot of the bed with her back turned to him, head angled down. She just stood there. She was the only color in that depressed room. The ribbons of red running through her satin dress rippled in delicate waves against the light of a flickering candle. She stood out from the dark like a single rose resting across a coffin, the only thing alive, but not for long. The tiny room held a heavy, repulsive odor. Dank. Musty. Smokey. It smelled like sin.

He didn't want to scare her. She seemed terrified like a wild colt, strapped still with some kind of chains around the ankles of her being. A sudden move would ricochet and his intent would be lost. She didn't belong here but was too beaten to fight it. Too defeated to run. She had it written all over her now. She looked like steel going into that barroom but now, she just looked..., *bruised.*

He was at a loss for words so he walked slowly and quietly over to the window—it wouldn't give. He tapped on the stubborn frame with the ball of his hand—glancing back..., she hadn't moved—and continued to work the stiff window up. Fresh air poured in on a slight breeze. The night was growing cold. His voice broke through the bars of too-quiet.

"You wanna come look at the moon?"

.   .   .

"I'll be damned. I will be damned. The kid's just like him and I'm not talkin' about his father, too holy to live, no, no.... I'm talkin' about Drake. That kid's just like him. Arrogant. Disrespectful. Brassy. Smart, real smart. And we sure as hell don't need another one like that..., some big-name gambler that thinks he's got somethin' to prove."

Crenshaw took another drink, looked at his timepiece and let out a heavy sigh.

"Funny thing..., 'bout that damn Drake. When a man takes a moment, considers all the times he should have been dead..., and what gets him? The galldamn river. The river!! Don't that beat all."

He rose from the table chuckling to himself, tossing down enough coins to cover both tabs.

"I'll be in touch."

He shook his head, reminiscing, as he disappeared through the saloon doors.

Chapter Twenty-Two

"That girl's sealed up like a caved coal mine. With no survivors."

"What do you 'spect from an Injun' in these here parts? Shoot…, she don't belong. Shouldn't she 'a gone on with the rest of 'em? I mean I ain't seen an Injun' for I don't know how long 'til she drug her sorry-assed self on in here. An' it's no wonder she's all 'lone. Why she ain't said one word ta any of us since she came! Don't she even know no English?"

Madame Jackson sat back in the shade with her feet propped up on a liquor crate, squinting into the bright light of day, drawing long and thoughtful on a cigarette, fingers still reeking from the last one. She watched while the girls hung bed sheets out to dry, passively listening as they rambled incessantly, spinning useless talk around the newest outcast, predictably unaccounted for. But then she didn't expect kindness from any of them. None of them had ever received any. A hard life it surely was…. Did they choose it or had they been chosen…? Her answer depended on the weather, on the shape of the clouds. She sat quietly, recalling memories of her long, lost self, back when she had once been obliviously young. How desperate, down-on-her-luck she felt before forcing herself into that filthy shack on the back edge of town asking for work the devil himself wouldn't do. It was the last chance to survive for a girl already tainted and shunned—by choice or no, didn't matter.

She absentmindedly flicked her snubbed cigarette into the sandy alley. It landed near the other discarded three.

She walked into the saloon. It was empty and quiet, dark and refreshingly cool. She poured herself a double, drank it down fast. She was breaking her promise to herself. She was getting involved. She climbed the stairs as the liquor burned its way down. She knocked hastily on the door.

"It's Madam', girl. Open up."

The door swung halfway open but she already had her back turned and head lowered, retreating from any form of human contact by the time Madame Jackson could enter.

"You gotta come down and eat somethin'. Ya look sorrier than a damn bean pole after frost."

Gentleness was a trait as foreign to Madame Jackson as walking a church aisle. She decided to step in, close the door and get comfortable. The girl stood at the window, staring out silently—her outline of skeleton seemed to emerge through dissolving flesh right before Madame's eyes. The kid looked half starved and the dresses were no longer hiding it. It was the one thing Madame detested—a girl who wouldn't eat—it reflected poorly on how she ran her business. She released a long unhindered sigh, the utter exasperation behind it was anything but masked—politeness, feminine etiquette as lost to her as toes beyond a bulging, inelastic waistline.

"Look. I don't make it a habit ta get in other's affairs. I'm not good at talkin' but I'm gonna anyways, so listen up. That boy that's been savin' ya every night— he ain't the regular kind, ya hear me? He's been comin' here playin' cards for years now. Started pretty young. He ain't never been with no other whore but you. And I know you ain't workin'. He's layin' down that money for free.

"What I'm sayin' is *notice* the way that boy looks at you, girl! Don't be no damn fool. You pass that up, you'll spend your whole useless life waitin' for a chance jus' ta see a glimmer of that look again. And you know what? You never will. You *hear* me!? You **never will**."

She hadn't moved from the window. She was standing stiff as if trying to ignore back lashes slicing right through her, not giving the assailant the satisfaction of knowing how deep.

"Dammit, kid! You don't wanna listen? I'll *make* you listen."

With that, Madame Jackson exited, slamming the door with such force it rattled the window that the girl continued to stare through, blankly absorbed into the vacantness on the other side. The room fell motionless but for the lonely trail forged of one deserting tear, splashing cool and silent against thick skin now encasing hollow nothing—the very last drop of independent pride spent.

Evaporated.

.   .   .

The night was warmer than it had been in a while. The moon finally shed its bout of shyness and had turned out broad and bold, magnificent illumination and shadow, art and magic hung together without wire in a barren sky. A slow, gentle breeze beneath delivered the promise of a summer soon to be. (The anticipation has a taste like peaches in cream, drops of orange and lemon and light. A feeling like laughter on skin that breathes against the open air. It holds tears cried only of a misty rain beneath twin rainbows, lungs inhale deeply something simple and true, something from the far side of sadness…, the universe surrounds. And the sweet memory of river frogs, lazy dogs and time spent alone is not only but a dream…. An approaching summer…, one growing older never fails to welcome it, to expect it to bloom as carefree as the numbered days of youth taught it to be). While out amidst the air that floats across a night such as this, a soul could suddenly be found unbound, somehow freed from its clutter of guilt and confusion. While out amidst it, a spirit could become light and easily lifted. One could see clearly the horizon…, not so very far away after all. The smoothness of current flows readily onto the mind. Focus seems effortless. Intent, a natural ease. Confidence, on a night such as this, abounds. So tonight he would ask. He would ask her to come home with him. She could keep Mama company. She could do whatever she wanted…. He ached inside, hoping that she would say yes. That she would agree to be with him…, he could hardly wait.

"Well, if it ain't Legend Boy. Let me guess which whore you'll pick."

John Crenshaw was huddled toward the center of the crowded bar, obviously soaking up cheap gossip and bad booze for hours and, like a saturated sponge, he had to let some of it trickle back out. The entire group was liquored up heavily, oozing an electric hum of sinister laughter generated by the sarcastic lead of the richest and loudest man. The dark mood they had created harbored an atmosphere all its own. It warned tragedy, enveloping the edges of the room like a distant thunder. Lemn wanted to get her and leave. Immediately. He could sense the vapor rising off their thrashing tongues and he couldn't help but assume his mere presence the match. Why his good days had to run smack into everyone else's bad ones, he'd never know. Then just that quick, Jed peered out from behind Crenshaw's back. *Jed….* He had the audacity to wink at Lemn before downing a shot of whiskey. He wiped an escaping dribble from his lips with the back of his sleeve, mischievously sparkling eyes older, but glued with a sickening familiarly to Lemn's. Testing intimidation. Suddenly, Lemn's thoughts turned to Avi, how her eyes darted down from most whites' glances—hell of a prison, invisible like that.

"My good friend Jed here says you set a man up to die once. That so, Riley?"

A strange slash of fire instantaneously swept through Lemn's brain, cracking like horizontal lightning, heating up the connections—past to present. His head throbbed and his stomach pitched and lurched, threatening sickness. It was hard to swallow how civilized Crenshaw appeared, how well-mannered, while knowing it was only a carelessly flaunted charade, a loosely worn shroud veiling all the atrocities that lurked beneath. And no one had ever been able to disrobe his acts. Conscientious lungs seemed to squeeze inward at the thought, unwilling to take in the poisonous oxygen offered amidst an aura that loathsome. Crenshaw was a sore looser, like Slim, but encased a hundred times more evil. He made intellectual sport from obscured horrors, and, to Lemn's bewilderment, he had succeeded, unscathed, for decades. He was an old man who had developed a lifelong talent for concealing crudeness. He acted as though his age rendered him innocent, declared his sicknesses harmless…. And Lemn frequently wondered when Jed would present himself again, but so much time had passed since Slim died…he'd just relaxed a little. He'd allowed himself to relax a little too soon. The unfathomable union presented before him wired its electrical charge around every vertebrae along his spine, leaving a twinge of slanted pain to linger after it surged along that tender lumboaortic nerve. The very bones that were once so cruelly disjointed pressed a submerged memory up his spinal cord—his mind pictured the last blow that did it. He recalled, painfully, as *Jed's boot* kicked at the same dented spot, caving it deeper and deeper into *his young back*, mercilessly stomping, crushing the life out of him.

He hadn't received any preconceived notions, hadn't seen the second strike coming. They'd caught him completely off guard. What a wicked storm.

Crenshaw placed a knotty hand on Lemn's shoulder, grip more pungent than one would imagine possible. The force of evil adjured.

"I suggest you have a seat, boy."

Others shuffled down the full-length bar like minions, allowing room but not too much. They wanted to be in adequate earshot. Lemn's face flushed deeper with realization regarding the magnitude of the indiscreet attention surrounding him. The saloon was the stage and he was its star. The story had